BOMBERS AND NERDY GIRLS DO BRUNCH

by
Lisa Boero

ISBN: 0988990016
ISBN 13: 9780988990012
Library of Congress Control Number: 2013920150
Nerdy Girl Press
Marshfield, WI

Also by the author:
Murderers and Nerdy Girls Work Late

"Kept afloat by a plucky heroine, like a yuppie version of Stephanie Plum."
Kirkus Reviews

For Jaime, Lillie and Jaimito. Thanks for all of your continued support.

Bombers and Nerdy Girls Do Brunch

by Lisa Boero

CHAPTER 1

The smell was overwhelming. Charred metal and charred flesh. I gagged. This couldn't be happening. Not again. I put my head in my hands. The beginning of another mess.

"Liz!" I heard James calling from the floor below. "Come help me!"

James. I had to help James.

But it wasn't the beginning or even the end. Instead I'd landed smack dab in the middle of one of the most complicated cases of my ersatz career. Truth be told, the real beginning happened several months before, on a peaceful afternoon in the spring of 2006. I sat at my desk, trying to study for my last semester of law school. Unfortunately, it is virtually impossible to study when you start dating someone new.

I valiantly tried to finish my notes on the Administrative Procedures Act, but my thoughts kept shifting back in the direction of James Paperelli. James is a detective in the homicide division of the St. Louis Metropolitan Police Department. Unlike most detectives, however, he doesn't depend on his paycheck to live. His family owns the Paperelli pizza empire, which includes restaurants, franchises and frozen foods.

James and I are mismatched on just about every level. In fact, the only thing we have in common is that we are both the unlikeliest detectives. Our relationship began with my discovery of a body in the stairwell at the law firm where I was interning, which led to the discovery of an embezzlement scheme that almost brought down the firm, and culminated in a chase of a murder suspect across a golf course in heels. Well, I ditched the heels early on, but who's quibbling?

The top of this Jenga tower of startling improbabilities was the strangest occurrence of all – James' continued interest in me even after discovering my secret. I cannot recognize my own face in the mirror, let alone his. However, my appalling deficits don't seem to bother him. He says that he can recognize me, which is all that counts. James is sweet or crazy. It all depends on your perspective.

My deficits have a name – prosopagnosia. A tongue twister that tells you nothing. Doctors can be very creative. Most people just call it face blindness. What it really means is that I have to rely on a host of other details to have the "aha" moment everyone else has without thinking.

For instance, I knew it was James who had surprised me at my door that afternoon because of a myriad of small details: the way he stands tall and straight at the back; the little ring of gold flecks that outline the pupils in his intense sapphire blue eyes; his long dark lashes, which rival anything I could buy at the drugstore; the way his hair curls at his right temple; the little nick on the side of his left ear; and the way he rubs his index finger against the ridges of his thumbnail when he is lost in thought. I also knew him by less intimate details, like the cut of his expensive jacket and the fine leather of his designer shoes, both by-products of his family's business success.

Even in the dark, though, I would know him by the timber of his voice when he says my name and the heady smell of his skin when we are close. Fortunately, an excellent sense of smell is one of my compensatory talents. I took a deep breath as he leaned down to kiss me. The wonderful earthy sweetness of his skin filled my head, along with Eternity cologne, his favorite. Different soap recently. Not Ivory, maybe Dial. Hmm. I threw my notes on the floor. Administrative law could wait.

Later, after having entirely too much fun for a weeknight, I felt his arm come around me. He snuggled up close and whispered in my ear, "Can I ask you a huge favor?"

I sighed contentedly. "It depends on what you want." He kissed me behind the ear.

"You're off to a good start."

He did it again. "Well?" he said.

"Um. We're never getting up if you keep going."

He did it a third time. "Who needs dinner anyway?" he said.

He had a point, but I felt my stomach growling. "One can't live on love alone."

His arm tightened around me. "We can try."

I weighed my options.

"And you haven't answered," he said smoothly.

"About what?" All I could think about was the warmth of his arm around me.

"The favor. How 'bout it?"

"Whatever you want. I'm putty in your hands."

"That's why we get along so well." He started kissing my neck, working his way down to the collarbone.

My mind struggled. "So what is the favor?"

"Nothing too terrible. I just want you to come with me to a charity event."

"Charity – as in an afternoon at a soup kitchen?" Easy enough. I already did some of that at my church.

"Charity as in a society fundraiser."

I stiffened.

He pulled me closer still. "You'll be fine."

"You mean black tie-silent auction-big band-swing dance-type charity fundraiser?"

"I'm afraid so."

"But you know how – crowds of people I don't know – trying to keep them all straight —" I felt the panic rising in my chest.

"I understand, but I promise not to leave you for a moment the whole evening."

"But I'm not – I've never been to —" Although I had the good manners my practical Midwestern parents had drilled into me, I had no idea how to get on with the upper crust of St. Louis society. I certainly didn't come from money, unless you consider teachers and nurses to be extravagantly overpaid.

"Don't worry."

I pushed his arm so I could turn around and face him. He moved reluctantly and then pulled me so close that our noses touched across the pillow.

"I'll go with you, but not one moment of abandonment to speak with someone or to get a drink or anything."

He kissed me softly on the lips and then said, "I knew I could persuade you."

"Your persuasion is closer to blackmail."

He opened his eyes wide. "Me?"

"Yes you. I hardly call using your – er – talents as a weapon fair play."

"All's fair in love and —"

"I am aware of that. But what I don't understand is why you have to go to this event?"

"My mother."

"How old are you?" James was exactly a decade older than me. Something he liked to bring up whenever we disagreed.

He smiled sheepishly. "You don't know my mother." This was true. I had only met James' brother Mark, and that meeting had been entirely by chance. Given some of James' offhand comments about his parents and sister, this might be a good thing. Truth be told, I was afraid. Very afraid.

"Your mother wants you to go because?"

"Because the family is a big donor and my mom is being honored for her work."

"What exactly is the charity?"

"The Police Aid Society. It supports officers who are injured or killed in the line of duty and their families," he said.

"A worthy cause indeed. But let me see if I have this. I have agreed to go to a black tie event —"

"Dinner, dance and silent auction."

"And at this event I will meet your parents for the first time, who are also the guests of honor. I will also likely meet your superiors, including probably the mayor."

"Several mayors. The organization covers the city and county." The City of St. Louis was surrounded on three sides by St. Louis County, which was made up of a number of small municipalities, each with its own police force and mayor. The number of dignitaries who could possibly attend the affair was daunting.

"Okay, mayors. And I do all of this wearing my only formal attire – a red dress that I am trying desperately to salvage through my own sewing talent, but which will likely be fit only for sachets or pillows." Tackling a murder suspect had taken its toll on the fabric.

"Wait a minute, you sew your clothes?"

"Repair," I said. He looked so stunned, that I added, "Wisconsin women are very capable."

He laughed softly. "I should say so. Anyone who can singlehandedly solve a complex murder case and fix her own dress can certainly handle one night of inane chatter with politicians, businessmen and philanthropists."

"It's your family I'm worried about."

"Don't worry about them. I'll be there, remember? I've had some practice handling them over the years."

"I'll reserve judgment until I see you in action."

He ignored my skepticism. "I appreciate that the red dress may never be fit for duty again, so I have a plan. The dinner is next Saturday. I didn't mention that, did I?"

"No. I agreed to the favor without knowing any of the particulars."

He grinned. "Ah yes, my prodigious talents."

"I like a man who can use 'prodigious' in a sentence, but —"

"Part of my rigorous Jesuit education," he replied.

"And the plan?"

"I'm taking you shopping Thursday night."

"Really? You want to go shopping?" Man plus shopping? An entirely new concept. But I should have guessed. James clearly paid close attention to his wardrobe, although I had imagined that most of it was compiled in cyberspace and with free shipping.

"We'll go to Frontenac. I'm sure Neimans or Saks will have something."

Plaza Frontenac was an exclusive mall in St. Louis. It had everything a spendthrift St. Louisan could want. The prospect of a new dress was enticing. Even before its brush with crime, the red dress had been second-hand. Still. I sighed.

"You seem hesitant." He reached over and gently smoothed the furrow between my eyebrows. "Most women would jump at the chance."

"I'm not most women."

He planted a kiss where the finger had been. "I know. So what is the problem?"

"I have trouble allowing you to spend so freely on me for something so frivolous."

"I thought you were a poor law student? You didn't have a problem with free food."

"That's different. I had to have some excuse for wanting to go out with you when you were engaged to someone else. If I'd have told you the truth, I would have looked pathetic."

"The food was a pretext?"

"Now you know. I am pathetic."

"I'm clearly attracted to pathetic."

"You are a very strange man," I said.

"A man who wants to buy you a dress so you can go with him to what would have been a boring night, but now might be fun."

"You think I would make your evening fun? I'm more likely to horrify you with some outrageous *faux pas*."

"I'm willing to take the chance."

"So says a man who doesn't know what he is getting into."

"We'll see," he said enigmatically. Then he kissed me resolutely. "Now are we skipping dinner or what? Unfortunately, I have to go back to the office tonight."

I felt my stomach growl again. "Sorry, no. Should I get out the take-out menus?"

"If you must."

CHAPTER 2

We decided to meet at the Frontenac Cardwell's for an early dinner on Thursday evening. Cardwell's is on the first floor of the mall. From the mall side, you entered an area with little round tables and then the bar. As I walked to the hostess stand, I noticed that the bar was packed with well-dressed professional singles. The young professional class in St. Louis always had the same look. In spring of 2006, the women wore their hair straight – either short or long – cut in a modern choppy style. They wore natural makeup and lip gloss instead of lipstick. The men were clean-shaven, with short neat haircuts. Both sexes wore clothes that were expensive and trendy, but without edge. The men and women were always tan. They always had straight white teeth. In sum, they were uniformly attractive. They made me feel every inch the awkward small town girl.

A cheerful young woman looked up from the hostess stand. "Can I help you?"

"I'm meeting someone here – James Paperelli. My last name is Howe."

"Okay, one moment." She looked down at the computer screen. "Yes. Mr. Paperelli hasn't arrived yet. Would you like me to seat you, or would you like to wait at the bar?"

"Seat me, please." I preferred sitting alone to trying to pick him out in the dim light of the bar.

She motioned to a waitress who grabbed two menus and escorted me to our table. James had reserved a table in one of the alcoves. The alcoves were small rooms set into the wall, so that the table was surrounded on three sides. I took off my coat and folded it over the back of my chair. The weather had turned unexpectedly cold again. So much for spring. As I sat down, I noticed that the alcove not only screened me from view, but also reduced the ambient noise to a dull hum. The waitress reappeared and set out the water glasses. She asked if I wanted to start with a drink, but I told her I'd wait. She nodded and said she'd be back as soon as James arrived.

I stared at the striped walls a moment and then closed my eyes in relief. Just a minute to relax was all I needed. I'd spent the day in class and then over at Janice Harrington's new offices in Clayton, a ritzy suburb of St. Louis. Janice was my mentor and friend. She had left the old firm as soon as she could. Murder and embezzlement didn't sit well with her, nor with the firm's estate planning clients. They all flew the coop, giving Janice Harrington and Associates, LLC a giant flock of business. As a result, she'd talked me into starting part-time legal work for her. At the moment, the work involved unpacking boxes and trying to locate files.

"Don't tell me you're asleep already," James said.

My eyes snapped open.

He grinned at me from the entrance to the alcove. "You're twenty-five, not eighty-five." He ambled over and kissed me on the cheek. "And here I thought I was dating a younger woman." He sat down across from me.

"I'm not the trophy girlfriend type," I replied. "I don't have acrylic nails."

"Clearly a prerequisite. What was I thinking?"

"I wonder that myself."

"I don't." He gave me that intense look that made my knees go all wobbly. I blushed bright red and picked up a menu. I didn't know how to handle that look – at least not in public.

"So what is good here?" Having lived my entire time in St. Louis as a student, my knowledge of good restaurants was woefully inadequate.

James picked up his own menu. "Everything I've tried."

"Do you come here often?"

He paused and then made an odd face. "Yes, with Angie." The ex-fiancée. "Although we usually sat at one of those tables by the bar."

"Next to the bar?" I couldn't think of a worse location for an intimate dinner. Between the noise of the mall and the customers at the bar, you could barely hear yourself think.

He took a sip of water. "You seem surprised."

"It's just that I don't know how you could carry on a conversation at one of those tables."

"Angie liked to watch for people she knew. Then she'd get up and go into the mall to talk with them."

"You two didn't talk?"

"Not usually. We'd been together for a while. A little conversation went a long way."

"Hmm."

He looked at me indulgently. "Clearly you've never been with someone long enough to run out of things to say."

I thought about Nick Lee, my high school boyfriend and longest relationship to date. Talking had never been our problem – arguing yes – talking no. "I guess not."

He studied me a moment. "If I ask you a personal question, will you answer it?" I started to open my mouth. "And don't say 'it depends,'" he continued.

He knew me too well. "Sure."

"Who were you thinking of just now?"

"Nick Lee."

"And he was?"

"High school boyfriend. We dated off and on from sophomore year to the end of senior year."

"Off and on?"

"We fought a lot."

"And where is this Nick now? Or have you lost track?"

I'd told Nick about James, but Nick, being Nick, hadn't given up. He still wanted me back. I was sure I had at least one email from him sitting in my inbox, waiting for a reply. So far I'd been able to keep him from dropping in on me here in St. Louis.

"We're in contact." I made my voice as smooth and indifferent as possible. "I saw him over Christmas break."

"So I have another rival?" James knew about the interest of a friend and fellow law student, Vince Lopez, and Joe Henderson, the son of my downstairs neighbors. Vince had taken the news that I was dating James with good grace. Joe just glared at James whenever they happened to meet on the stairs. Really, it was annoying. I'd had no interest for years, and suddenly a pack of guys was nipping at my heels.

I looked James in the eye.

"No accusation. I just need to size up the competition."

"There's no competition."

"I'm not worried. I can take them out."

"That sounds very militant – and don't start with the 'all's fair' bit again. War is not required."

He chuckled. "How do you do that?"

"What?"

"Read my thoughts and finish my sentences."

I felt mortified. "It's a bad habit – I'll try to remember to be better."

The chuckle turned to a laugh.

"What's so funny?"

He got himself back under control. "You."

Now I felt mortified and offended. I hung my head. That just set him off again. "What?" I said with an exasperated sigh. "Tell me."

"Don't get angry. It's just that every time I try to say something nice you take it the wrong way. It's like you have a deflector shield against compliments."

"Most men don't want women to interrupt them."

"I agree, but that is not what I was saying."

I waited expectantly.

"I've never met anyone who seems to know me so well after such a short period of time."

"Oh."

"Yes. That's all. I can be myself around you. And that's a good thing – at least for me."

"It's a good thing," I said shyly. "I feel the same way."

He grinned and picked up the menu. "The waitress is coming over so we'd better come up with something to order."

I scanned the menu and then looked up at James. "Would you mind very much if I ordered the filet mignon?" What can I say? I like meat.

"No, why would I mind?"

"I don't always order the most expensive thing on the menu. Especially since you want to buy me a dress. Please don't think I'm pressing my luck."

He shook his head once. What did that mean? And he thought I could read his mind.

The waitress reappeared and promptly apologized. The restaurant was unexpectedly full for a Thursday night and they were short staffed. James ordered wine for us. I normally don't drink in public because alcohol addles my already limited brain, and we had serious shopping to do. I gave him a look. "I'll take care of you," he said.

We decided to go straight for the entrees – no mucking about with appetizers. I ordered the filet as rare as possible. You never get a bad cut of meat when it's rare. James ordered some sort of chicken with a cream sauce and gnocchi. As if to make up for the previous wait, the wine arrived in record time.

"Cheers," I said, lifting my glass.

"Cheers," he replied. We both took a sip and set our glasses down. The wine was delicious. A Pinot Noir. It tasted faintly of violets.

"By the way, you don't have to worry about money." He gave me a mischievous smile. "I'll tell you if something is out of my reach. Although you're so down to earth, you wouldn't ask for anything I couldn't easily give you."

"Is that what the head shake was about? You looked like you were thinking about some private joke."

He took another sip of wine. "I was just thinking how sweet you are to worry about overextending my credit. It's refreshing."

I looked at him questioningly.

"I can't imagine Angie ever knew what anything cost. She just wanted more."

"I don't have that much taste or imagination."

"You have something more to think about than shopping." He swirled the wine around in his glass. "Not that I'm against shopping, but Angie seemed obsessed with one-upping the girlfriends."

"Did she work?"

"Off and on. Mostly for her dad's company."

"Of course. She has a business degree, right? Your engagement announcement spelled it all out."

"Did you memorize that announcement?"

"Well —" I picked at the tablecloth. "I've read it a couple of times." A couple thousand times. "What does the company do?" I added.

"Import and export. Ceramics and crystal from Eastern Europe and I'm not sure what back. Mr. Zakarias was always vague about it."

"And work didn't help?"

"With the shopping addiction?" I nodded. "Not really. Don't get me wrong, Angie is a bright woman, but she doesn't have focus. Sometimes it's hard to know what to do when everything has been given to you."

"You don't seem to have any problem. And neither do your siblings – although I haven't met your sister yet."

"It took me a year of wandering around Europe before I knew what I wanted. My sister always wanted to run the business, so she doesn't really count. And Mark is too smart for the rest of us. He had to get a PhD in something."

I had a special place in my heart for Mark. He'd urged James to break off his engagement to Angelica because he could see that James was falling for me.

"Speaking of Mark, he would like to get together again sometime. He asked if you could invite Holly?" James said.

"Holly is living with someone right now."

"I'll let Mark take his chances. He can be very persuasive when he wants to be."

"Like his brother then."

Our food arrived. We sat in silence for several minutes drinking wine and eating. My filet had a savory sauce over it. White wine, wild mushroom and butter, with a bit of something different. Nutmeg perhaps? I took another bite. Yes nutmeg.

"Is the filet good?" James said.

"Delicious, and I'm picky about these things."

He nodded knowingly. "No need to remind me that you are from Wisconsin."

"Would you like a bite?"

"Don't be offended, but I like my steak just a little more done."

"You don't want it to 'moo' at you?"

"Definitely not. Would you like some chicken?"

"No thank you. But I'll try one of the gnocchi if you don't mind."

"Sure. They're good. Not as good as my grandmother's, of course."

"Of course." I thought he would fork one and put it on my plate. Instead he held it up on the fork and leaned across the table to feed it to me. I felt as if we were crossing some invisible barrier that separated casual dating from coupledom. I didn't hesitate as I took the fork between my teeth.

"You!" said a voice from the entrance to the alcove. James dropped the fork and it clattered to the table. I almost choked on the gnocchi – it blocked my airway for a second and then sat like a sticky ball in my throat. I looked over at James. A slow red burn crept up his cheeks. His jaw tightened. His lips pushed together so tightly, they formed a straight line.

I looked at the cause – a petite woman, slim and self-possessed. She was expensively dressed and tan, just like every other St. Louis single at the bar. She stared at James and then at me and then back at him. Her whole body shuddered with anger. She tossed her long hair back with one hand as if girding for battle. The mystery of her identity was solved. I'd seen that hand before. Small, with short slim fingers and a precise French manicure that squared the tips of her nails. The last time I saw it, it was resting on James' shoulder in the engagement photograph.

As if to confirm my wordless calculations, James said, "Angelica." A whisper between gritted teeth.

"Jamie." I saw her make a visible effort to control her fury. "I see you have company." She looked me up and down like a piece of meat – weighing each one of my defects. I took a deep breath and stared back defiantly. I wasn't cowed that easily.

"Yes," he spat out. "Liz." He turned to me with a speaking glance. "This is Angelica Zakarias." He turned back to her. "Angelica, this is my girlfriend Elizabeth Howe." He said the word "girlfriend" with such emphasis that Angie visibly flinched.

She recovered quickly. "I know who she is." She sent me a look even more venomous than the last.

"Angie," James said icily, "unless you want to cause a scene in front of everyone you know at the bar, leave now."

"You," she said again, this time with deadly softness. She turned on her heel and stomped off. A faint smell of strong perfume and something else hung in her wake. White Diamonds. Strange.

I grabbed my wine glass and took a giant gulp. The wine burned down my throat, dislodging the gnocchi. I glanced at James. The flush had left his cheeks, but his eyes had a distracted look. His forehead puckered with either pain or deep thought. I wasn't sure which.

"Are you all right?" I reached over and touched his hand. Despite everything, I couldn't be angry at Angie. I thought about how I'd feel if I saw him with another woman. But I'm the type that would have slunk away and cried myself to sleep. You have to be reckless to confront the Other Woman.

He clasped my wrist and looked at me strangely, then took my hand between both of his. A slow smile lit up his eyes. We studied each other for a long moment.

"Liz," he finally said. His voice was soft and tender. I felt my heart leap in my chest. "I love you."

"I love you too," I said calmly. My feelings were longstanding and sincere.

He used my hand to pull me to him. I found myself kissing him over the table. I wondered idly if my sweater now had filet sauce all over it. White wine and butter. That would never come out.

CHAPTER 3

While James paid the bill, I discovered several suspicious spots down the front of my sweater. One sat right on the shelf of my bosom. It was too hot to put my coat back on. I had to tough it out. He appeared spotless, of course. How did he do that?

We escaped the restaurant and strolled into Neiman Marcus. Ritzy stores like that made me feel even more inadequate than being surrounded by posh St. Louis singles. James, on the other hand, seemed like a king in his castle. He guided me up the escalator to women's evening dresses with a smile and a greeting for every salesperson we met. I saw the dawning of recognition in the eyes of the saleslady when we reached our destination. Clearly, this was not the first time he'd taken a girl to buy a formal dress. Hmm.

The saleslady was a chic woman in her mid-fifties with light brown bobbed hair. "May I help you?" She looked at James and then at me.

James smiled and said, "Yes. We are looking for a dress for a charity dinner."

I had a sudden moment of panic that the saleslady might think I was the charity.

"Black tie?" she said. "Dot" was printed on her name tag. She had a St. Louis accent that she was trying to overcome with precise diction.

"Yes," James said.

Dot turned to me. "What sort of dress did you have in mind?"

"I don't know. Maybe something in black?" Again, I don't have enough imagination to really spend money. Fortunately for my fashion-challenged brain, James had other ideas.

He looked at me. "Maybe a brighter color?" And to Dot, "I think close to the body – with a corset-type bodice." I stared at him wide-eyed. He shrugged his shoulders. "Between my mother and Angie, I know something about dresses."

I'm sure.

"Of course," Dot replied. "I have a couple of things that will look just lovely." She sized me up with her eyes and then walked over to the racks and started pulling dresses out. I'd been afraid when James suggested color because minty green and orange were very popular at the moment. Both made me look jaundiced.

I shouldn't have worried. I was dealing with a professional. Dot came back with five dresses: one in turquoise, one midnight blue, one red (that was almost the color of my dear departed formal) and one purple, somewhere between amethyst and aubergine. They were all fitted through the waist with long skirts – either A-line or straight.

I tried them on one by one. For the first time in my life, I didn't look at the price tags. Well, not immediately. It went without saying that the clothes cost a small fortune. I contemplated my rent and my loans, then banished the thought. I didn't want to embarrass James at this event – at least, not more than usual.

James wanted to see the dresses. As he was buying, I figured he did have some say in the matter. It turned out to be much less awkward than I anticipated. I knew when I'd found the one. He said,

"Wow." I felt my heart start to flutter. Maybe I should take him shopping more often. There was a reason he had so much experience.

It was the purple dress, sleeveless with a draped collar in front and a plunge in back. The A-line skirt brushed the floor. The bodice fit very tightly and held me up. Amazing. I wouldn't have to find some complicated and ultimately non-supportive undergarment to wear with it. I'd go bra-less. It was truly a miracle. I could have kissed James, or Dot for that matter, right there.

"Miss wears the dress beautifully," Dot said. "That skirt demands some height. Petite women can't carry it off."

James nodded. I couldn't help but think of petite Angie. One point in my favor. I went back to change. When I re-emerged, James and Dot were huddled together in conversation. They stopped. James took the purple dress from me and gave it to Dot. "We'll be right back," he said.

"I'll hang the dress here behind the counter. Just let them know," Dot said.

James nodded and took my hand. "Come along."

He dragged me out into shoes. I tried to protest. "I have the silver ones." The silver stilettos had not been injured in the pursuit of a murderer. Thank goodness. I had it on good authority that they did something fantastic for my legs.

James stopped. "I think you ought to have at least one other pair of good heels."

"Yes, sir," I said. How could I argue with such sound logic?

He caught the attention of the saleswoman. She was a straw blond so well preserved that she could have been anywhere from forty to sixty, depending on the amount of plastic surgery. Her name tag said "Corrie." James explained what I needed. She motioned for us to take a seat and then went off to find something appropriate.

"I don't think I've ever had someone actually find me a pair of shoes. I'm usually the one looking through the bargain racks." And trying unsuccessfully to get the other shoe.

"This is easier. They know their stock. If you have something specific in mind, they can find it faster than you can."

I nodded and then looked down at my hands, clasping and unclasping my fingers.

"What are you thinking?"

"We come from very different places."

He reached over, took my hand, and gave it a little squeeze. "Not incompatible ones."

Not entirely.

Corrie came back with five different pairs of pointy-toed black high heels, two pairs with the new more rounded toes and one pair that was the exact color of my dress. The purple ones even had a little platform in front so the heel didn't feel quite so high. I loved them on sight. Then the practical half of my brain took over. What was I going to do with a pair of purple shoes after Saturday night?

I dutifully walked around in every pair. Three I eliminated because the pain was so intense I could barely stand. Two were out of the running because I could tell from James' face that he didn't like them. He told me that they were okay, but he blinked as he said it, so I knew. That left one pair of black patent Ferragamos with a thin stiletto heel, another pair of Ferragamos with a rounded toe and a slightly thicker heel that made them surprisingly comfortable, and the purple pair I was so drawn to. I turned one of the purple shoes over. It had a bright pink sole with the name, "Farfalla" in a fanciful script. I'd never heard of that. Strange. I prided myself on my knowledge of labels even if I couldn't imagine wearing any of the clothes I saw in magazines.

"The Farfallas are very exclusive. One of our buyers got several hundred lots directly from the designer. It was sheer luck, because they are impossible to find. I don't know when we will get more. Just look at the workmanship, and that leather is to die for," Corrie said.

I felt the buttery smooth instep and nodded. I put them back down. The black shoes were the practical choice, but I looked longingly at the Farfallas. I tried each pair on again and walked around in them. I couldn't make up my mind. James watched me with a hint of a smile at the corners of his mouth.

"What do you think?" I finally said.

"I think – we should get all three." He turned to Corrie. "We'll need an evening bag to go with the purple ones."

I stared at him in shock.

"We have just the thing," Corrie said, and then scurried off down the escalator to confer with the doyen of handbags.

No one in my entire life had ever spent that much money on me in one sitting. Forget the sitting – ever. I couldn't get my mind around it.

"You don't have to look at me like that," James said. "You would notice if you didn't fit in."

I sat down beside him. My throat felt tight. I swallowed hard. He leaned over and said, "You're worth it."

"I'm not so sure."

"But I am."

Corrie returned with a small satin clutch. It was made of purple ribbon cunningly woven into fabric. She opened it so I could see the kid leather interior and the fine gold chain to carry it. I touched the leather. Soft as velvet.

"We'll take it," James said without asking the price. He turned to me. "Now about some jewelry?"

"I have amethyst earrings from my grandmother," I said quickly.

He thought a moment. "Yes, better to keep it simple. We're ready then." He stood up. "We have a dress hanging over by Dot."

"Of course, please wait right here." Corrie scurried a way to retrieve it. She came back five minutes later carrying the dress. James handed her his Neiman Marcus credit card.

"Shop here often?" I said.

He smiled at my naïveté. "They only take AmEx or their own card. But, yes. I like getting the catalog."

"Oh." I hoped I wouldn't make another slip. I watched Corrie scan and wrap each item, but tried not to look at the final total. When we were done, I gathered up the bags and the dress.

"Do you need help with that?" James said.

"I don't think so." I put my coat back on and picked up the bags. I threw the dress over my arm. I stumbled along for a couple of yards before James forcibly wrested two of the bags away from me.

"Where are you parked?" he said as we reached the mall.

"On the opposite side by Saks. I'm sorry. I haven't been here often so I don't know where anything is."

"No problem. We can window shop."

"Please just window shopping. I'll have an anxiety attack if you buy me one more thing."

I could finally understand the plaintive notes of the bird in the gilded cage. I'm not saying I wasn't a happy bird, but still. I didn't know how to play the Pretty Woman. My throat felt tight again. I reached up and pulled on the collar of my sweater. Some people would do anything to be that bird. Angie? But she had family money too. Another world.

He showed me his favorite stores. I remained wide-eyed at the selection and the prices. He seemed contented just to flip through racks of clothes. Something dawned on me.

"You like to shop, but are forced to do it alone," I said as we entered the Mont Blanc store. He appeared to be very interested in several of the new fountain pens.

"My friends don't shop unless it's for some tech gadget, and I can't even mention it at work."

"It's not the most macho thing to admit to."

"It was worse when I was on the beat. I had to wear the uniform all of the time, and I couldn't justify buying clothes just for my days off. Now I can browse without guilt."

"But no one to do it with? Not even Angie?"

"Angie wasn't interested in my shopping. Just her own."

I wondered who else he'd gone dress shopping with if it wasn't Angie, but didn't want to get into that. "I would have thought shopping was shopping."

He smiled. "You clearly don't do it enough."

We went down to the first floor and wandered some more. I was just beginning to wonder if we were turned around. Hadn't we passed Ylang Ylang before? Then a marquee caught my eye. Tiffany and Co. I'd seen *Breakfast at Tiffany's* a thousand times.

A second's hesitation was enough for James to say, "Do you want to go in?"

"I've never been in one." The prospect was alluring and nerve racking.

"No time like the present." He nodded to the guard in plain clothes as we walked through the entrance.

I'm not sure what I was expecting, but it seemed like any other jewelry store, except the jewelry was very very pretty. I noticed that the cases at the back held baby gifts. What baby would ever notice that the cup he bit down on was from Tiffany and Co.? Then again, the parents would know.

As we looked through the cases, James asked me casually about my likes and dislikes. No guy had done that in years. I thought about Nick. Outside of my family, I'd known him better than anyone. I looked over at James. Maybe one day.

"What do you think?" James said. We stood in front of a case of Elsa Peretti designs in gold and silver. Her work was simple with a tactile beauty. James pointed to a necklace made of fine gold mesh that hung around the throat like a diaphanous scarf.

"Spectacular," I said.

"You like chain mail? That has interesting implications."

The saleslady approached us just in time to prevent me from elbowing him in the ribs. "Can I show you anything?"

James spoke up. "Yes, we'd like to see that necklace." I gave him a doubtful look. "Go on, it doesn't hurt."

The saleslady made approving noises as she removed it from the case and set it on a black velvet pad. "This is really lovely on. Would miss like to try it?"

"I'm not really dressed —" I hesitated. My sweater had a mock turtleneck.

"Just roll the neck down a little," James said.

"You will see how beautifully it lays on the collarbone," the saleslady said.

I bowed to the pressure, rolling the sweater down as far as it would go. The saleslady came up and placed the necklace around my throat. She stepped back and turned a mirror so I could see my reflection. The necklace was absolutely beautiful, lumpy sweater and all. I caught James' eyes in the mirror. There was a hint of mirth in their expression. I must've looked pretty ridiculous standing there in my stained sweater.

I motioned for the saleslady to help me take it off. "Thank you for letting me try it on." I watched it return to its place under the counter.

"Now I can say I've been to Tiffany's," I said lightly as we walked out.

"If I'd known you were interested in jewelry, I would have introduced you to my mom before now."

"Why?"

"She could take you to a jewelry auction."

"There are jewelry auctions in St. Louis?" Farm auctions I'd heard of. Livestock auctions I'd heard of. Jewelry? News to me.

"Yes, at the Harville-Chouteau auctions. And furniture, paintings, silver, you name it. I've bought all sorts of things over the years."

I mentally scrolled through his house in Lafayette Square. Lafayette Square was a beautiful neighborhood of turn of the last century homes. James' house was one of the smaller ones, but it was impeccably restored by a prior owner and impeccably maintained by James. He had furnished it simply with an Edwardian sensibility. Lots of mahogany and dark leather. I had only been there twice. It always seemed easier to meet somewhere, and we ended up at my apartment more often than not, braving the dark looks of Joe Henderson. Despite my brief experience of the house, I'd paid close attention, hoarding examples of his taste for future use.

"Which pieces did you buy at auction?" I said.

"That pair of club chairs in the office and the dining room set. Also the rugs in the living room and my bedroom."

"Where did the dining room set come from?"

"Spain originally. Probably made during the late 1800's."

"And why did you pick that set? It's very beautiful, but the ornate carving is such a contrast to the simplicity of the rest of the furniture."

"It reminded me of the time I spent in Spain – I don't know. Every now and then you have to take a chance on something different."

I nodded.

We walked in silence for a moment and then he said, "Thank you for reacting so well to Angie's – well, to Angie."

"I just stared at her rudely. It didn't require any extra effort on my part."

"You didn't flinch. That took nerve. She's looked at me like that before. Like I'm the lowest of the low. It's intimidating."

"You stood firm," I said reassuringly.

"Only because the part of my brain that wasn't in shock knew I couldn't let you down. Otherwise, Angie's had years to wear down my defenses."

What to say to a statement like that? I had a million questions about their relationship, but none of them seemed appropriate, so I started on a completely different track. "You call her Angie and she called you Jamie. So I call you James, but I won't call you that if that's what your parents called you when you were in trouble – like my mother always called me Elizabeth Anne. I just started with James. I realize that this is probably a silly question after we've, well —"

"James is what I prefer, but thanks for asking even if we are way beyond 'hello.' My family and some old friends still call me Jamie or even Jimbo. Angie called me Jamie when she wanted to annoy me. But I want to be James, particularly to you."

We reached my very dented but functional 1994 Chevrolet Corsica. I'd parked under a light for safety. James was wearing off on me. I opened the door with a pull and threw my purse onto the passenger seat.

"And you?" he said, opening the back door and setting my bags carefully inside.

"Oh, Liz is fine. I would have told you before if it wasn't. I've got my share of strange nicknames, though. My sister used to call me Li when she was little, and my dad still calls me Pookie when he forgets that I'm not a kid."

"You look like you were a Pookie."

"What's that supposed to mean?"

"I can imagine you as a girl, all cute and sassy. I bet you were something at eleven or twelve."

"I was something all right, but not cute and sassy. Those were my lost years."

"Because?"

"I developed seizures when I was eleven. Not the kind where you black out and thrash around, but the kind where you look down at your test and can't read any of the words. I hid those for almost a year."

James didn't speak, so I continued on, the words coming out of me like a river through a dam break. "One day, my mom caught me mid-seizure and forced me to go see a doctor. She was furious that I hadn't told her, but at that age, you just hope things will go away. A single MRI informed the doctors that I had a brain tumor. The surgery was relatively easy, seven hours and a u-shaped scar, but the rest was not. I had to have radiation therapy so my hair fell out in big clumps."

I looked down and knotted my hands together. "It's hard to be that different at thirteen. Even your friends can be unintentionally cruel. As you have probably inferred, the surgery stopped the seizures but didn't fix the prosopagnosia. The doctors thought the tumor destroyed that functionality completely, so there was no getting it back."

"You poor kid. I'm sorry."

"It was a long time ago." I leaned in conspiratorially. Pity was not what I was after. "In any case, my prosopagnosia is what brought me to you, so I don't have any regrets."

"Regrets," James repeated. He took my face in his hands and studied it intently.

"Yes?" I said.

Then he was kissing me. And not a normal kiss. We were fused together so tightly and so completely that I didn't know where my skin ended and his began. I had to have this man. Come what may, I couldn't let him go.

I heard a noise in the background, a snatch of loud music from a car and footfalls running toward us. James pulled away abruptly.

"Get in," he said. "Now!"

I blindly followed his command, levering myself over the shift to the passenger side, and falling on top of my purse. He jumped in the driver's seat and quickly shut the door. I handed him the key I always had in my hand when I approached my car. He jammed it into the ignition and started the engine.

Two teenage boys ran by us on their way to their car. James watched keenly as they got in and drove off.

"What is it?" I asked. "Do you know them? Are they wanted by the police?"

I had a sudden image of us chasing down felons in my old Corsica.

"No, I don't think so. Something just struck me as odd."

"Teenagers shopping here?"

His mouth relaxed and his eyes lit up. "Yes, now that you mention it. But there are theaters and restaurants in the mall, so that could account for it. Sorry to hustle you like that. Are you okay?"

"The only thing bruised is my dignity."

"Again sorry. And I interrupted an excellent goodbye."

"Goodbye?" I looked at my watch. "The night is still young and my classes don't start till 10:00."

"But I have to be at work by 7:00."

"I keep forgetting you have a real job."

"Yes I do," he said dryly. He negotiated my car around the parking lot towards his car. He pulled up alongside and parked.

"So this is goodnight, then?" I tried not to sound disappointed. James did have a demanding job. I should let him sleep. Not that I was getting much these days, either. Then again, I couldn't be the bird. I probably needed the distance more than he did.

"No." He sounded surprised. "Not unless you want to go home?"

"But your sleep?"

"Sleep is greatly overrated." He hopped out of the car and came around to open my door. I marveled at his manners. His mother had cracked the whip. I got out and walked to the driver's side.

"See you soon." He clicked his car remote. "Oh and Liz?"

"Yes?"

"You need to get a new car."

"The rattle is normal," I replied. "You just don't recognize the purr of a seasoned engine."

He opened the door of his Infinity G-35. "I'll come pick you up when it gives up the ghost."

"Ha!" I jumped in my car and gunned the engine, feeling a sudden release from all of the strange tension of the evening. James. So much had been said and yet there were still so many unanswered questions. What was going on with those teenagers? Why had he bundled me into the car so fast? Then there was Angie. Talk about a piece of unfinished business. What was she up to confronting us like that? And what would she do next?

Unfortunately, these mysteries were only the tip of a very large and complicated iceberg.

CHAPTER 4

When my friend Holly found out where James was taking me, she invited herself over in the afternoon to help me dress. That was her excuse to hang around long enough to size him up. We weren't dating when she first met him, so she claimed she'd missed the opportunity to really assess his boyfriend potential. That, and his brother Mark had diverted her attention. I told her she could come, but not before 4:00. I absolutely positively had to get some work done on my outlines.

Outlines are the notes law students keep for each class. Law school classes are taught by Socratic Method, which means that you discuss seemingly random cases for an entire semester and then, right before the final exams, you scramble to impose order on the chaos. Enough order, at any rate, to be able to write a good essay about an even more random fact pattern. Every previous semester I'd been able to assemble my outlines as the course went along. This semester was the exception. Between chasing murderers and dating James, my outlines were a mess. I could feel the panic setting in.

My classes this semester were a mixture of courses I'd selected for fun and courses I hoped would help me on the bar exam. I also elected to do a practicum called a Clinic. Washington University had a number of Clinics, each focused on a different area of law. Students in the Clinic worked with practicing attorneys on real cases pro bono. It was good experience, and it allowed you to give back before the weight of debt and billable hours forced you to do as little pro bono work as the bar would allow.

I'd signed up for the Civil Justice Clinic. This Clinic offered law students to local judges as Guardian Ad Litems or GALs for children caught in the middle of nasty domestic situations. Under the auspices of an attorney, we were assigned to represent these vulnerable children and act as a judge's eyes and ears. The attorney in charge of the Clinic was Gwen Zenner, a gifted woman in her mid-forties with short dark hair and a great collection of dangle earrings, who had worked as a social worker before she went back to law school. She'd opened her own firm, specializing in family law, but the lure of a steady paycheck and more regular hours drew her to the position at Washington University. This was her fourth year as the director of the Civil Justice Clinic. She leveraged her private practice contacts to ensure that her students worked with some of the best judges in the city and all the surrounding counties.

I had three cases. They were a study in contrasts. One was a nasty divorce between two highly-paid accountants, George and Selena Bailey. The Baileys not only shared a very successful practice, but also a luxurious house in Clayton and three pampered children. I was assigned as a GAL for all three. The next couple, Casey Hamm and Kellie Richards, lived together but weren't married. They had one three-year-old son. They were such a joy to work with. I couldn't tell which one was more incompetent to raise a child. In the end, I recommended custody for the grandmother. At least she paid enough attention not to let the boy wander around in the street on his own.

The third couple, Andrew and Elsa Stimpkin, lived in Jefferson County, to the south of St. Louis. Elsa was from Kosovo, a blond beauty brought to the United States by her National Guard husband. Once home, the romance soured. Elsa suspected that Andrew was using methamphetamine. She feared for the safety of her two-year-old son and year-old daughter. At least, that was what I got from Elsa's broken English, hand signs and a harried court translator.

Andrew had quit his job with a local construction company. He claimed he couldn't find work, even though construction jobs in Jefferson County were plentiful. The area was booming with new developments. Given the volatility of the situation, I got assigned to the son and another law student, my friend Amelia, to the daughter. We worked the case up together.

So, aside from my other classes, law review and James, I drove all over St. Louis making site visits, interviewing parents and anyone else who would talk to me, preparing reports for the judges and going to court on my clients' behalf. Needless to say, I didn't tell James about most of my work for the Clinic. I spent significant time in some bad neighborhoods. He worried about me at the mall parking lot. He had no idea.

I did a good job with the concentration until about 3:30, when my constant musings about James and the anticipation of getting to talk with Holly got the better of me. I gave up and went to take a shower. As a slave to my hairdresser, I followed her instructions to the letter. The secret to turning my dull frizzy hair into something that looked like an advertisement was the generous application of product. Multiple products. Then I had to let my hair air dry. I hadn't really mastered the art of the blow dryer and the round brush.

Holly arrived punctually at 4:00. She and I had been friends since our undergraduate days. She was currently slogging through a PhD in Electrical Engineering. Granola with a twist is how you could describe Holly – vegetarian, with political views Dennis Kucinich would be proud of, but a whiz with hair and make-up. How she had managed to be born to ultraconservative parents in the heart of Amish country was beyond anyone's understanding. She certainly tried to put as much distance between herself and Lancaster, Pennsylvania as she could.

"Okay, so let me see this dress actually picked out and purchased by a guy," she said as she stepped in the door.

"I know. How strange is that?"

She shook her head. Her red hair swished back and forth. "It's a waste. You've never been interested in clothes."

"He also bought me shoes and a clutch."

Holly pushed past me and stalked to the bedroom. "This I really have to see."

She climbed up on the bed and sat cross-legged, waiting for the formal presentation. I took the dress out and laid it on the bed beside her. I slowly pushed up the plastic covering.

"Oh, that color is beautiful." She gently touched the silk of the bodice. "Sustainable fabric even – I'm impressed. James has good taste."

"He's dating me."

"I realize that, but I'm sure your other boyfriends couldn't be trusted to buy you something this fabulous."

"Boyfriend. But you're right."

"Where are the shoes? Those aren't green I assume."

"If by green you mean made of hemp or some non-animal product, then no."

"No Stella McCartney?"

"They're just butter soft Italian leather." I took them out and handed one to her. Despite the fact that she would never stoop to leather herself, Holly examined it closely.

"Hmm. Farfalla. I've never heard of that brand before. And why the pink sole?"

"I was told that they are very very exclusive. I think the pink sole is the trademark."

"Well." She handed the shoe back to me. "How much did James end up spending on you?" Holly didn't beat around the bush.

I hedged. "I don't know the exact figure, but it was several thousand dollars."

Her mouth dropped open and stayed there.

I nodded. "Unreal. I kept thinking I'd wake up."

"I don't even spend that kind of money in my dreams."

"Me neither. I'm not cut out to be Julia Roberts. This level of expenditure makes me nervous."

"Geez Liz, if a guy wants to buy you things, let him. Period. What other loot did you haul home?"

"Two more pairs of shoes and a purse to go with the purple ones." I pulled each shoe out of its box and then pulled the purse out of the cloth bag it came in. She examined each item, turning it over and over in her hands.

"What are you looking for?"

"Nothing. I'm just amazed at the attention to detail."

"James is all about quality over quantity."

She smiled. "For someone so politically opposite to me, we actually agree. We don't need any more disposable junk cluttering up this world."

"You think James is right wing?"

"You're pretty far to the right."

"I voted for Kerry."

"You know Howard Dean was robbed." This was an old discussion of ours. I knew she was only half serious.

"Don't talk to me," I said virtuously. "Talk to the people of Iowa. They nailed Dick Gephardt too, and he was the local boy."

Holly worked passionately for Howard Dean until the very end. She was still smarting from the defeat, especially since she felt Kerry's moderate stance on the war in Iraq had cost him the election.

"So you think James is in league with the devil?" I teased.

"He looks like a Bushie to me."

"I know they are one and the same to you."

"Goes without saying."

"Knowing him, I think he's probably more of an Independent."

She looked at me skeptically.

"Hey, he lives in the city, so he has to vote Democratic or he'd never have any voice." The real political contests were in the primary races. Missouri had open primaries, so anyone could cross over if they wanted to.

"Hmm."

"If I had to guess, I'd say he's probably a McCain in 2000 sort of voter." John McCain's rapprochement with George Bush made Holly lose any respect she might have had for his early moderate positions.

"But James has the family money and all —"

"He is never what you think he'll be," I said defensively. "I'll still love him even if he votes Socialist."

"Nothing wrong with Socialist. But wait, when did you progress to love?"

"I've been in love with him for months."

"Yes, but did he tell you he loves you?"

"He did. On Thursday."

"That's big!"

"He's said it in so many words before."

"But L-O-V-E is really something. Most men never let the word cross their lips in the first year – maybe two."

"He's not most men. He bought me half of Neiman Marcus, for goodness sake."

"How did it come up, or do I not want this information?"

"The context at that moment was G rated, I assure you. He said it while we ate dinner."

"He chewed a bite of food and said, 'Liz, I love you.'"

"There was more to it than that." I paused, wondering how to phrase the next part. "We'd just had a run in with Angelica."

"You mean the Angelica he broke the engagement with so he could date you?"

"She broke the engagement. He refused to take her back."

"Details. Details. Tell me what happened."

I gave her a short recitation of the events. "James was upset and I comforted him. That's when he told me he loved me."

"So he was under stress when he said it."

"Yes, I won't really believe it until he mentions it a couple more times."

"And not when you're —"

"Holly, I do understand that men don't usually mean what they say in that situation."

"I'm sure they think they mean it."

"They're not thinking with their brains."

"No. Just be careful, Liz. This Angelica is not going to give up."

"I am well aware. She gave me a look Medusa would envy."

"Did you turn to stone?"

"I stared back at her. I didn't happen to have a mirror on hand."

Holly smiled. "Why weren't you a classics major?"

"My Latin is rusty and my Greek is nonexistent."

"Aramaic?" Holly tried not to giggle.

"I apparently prefer dead bodies to dead languages."

"Especially if they come with hot detectives."

"Seriously, it's the only way to go."

That set Holly off. After the fit of giggles subsided she said, "Sorry, what were we talking about?"

I deftly steered her away from more dangerous subjects. "Politics. Didn't you tell me you were involved in some campaign?" Holly had recovered sufficiently from the 2004 debacle to gear herself up for the 2006 mid-term elections.

"There are clear frontrunners in most of the races I care about, so I'm helping a dark horse candidate in another Congressional district."

"Really? Who?"

"Kevin Mason."

"I repeat. Who?"

She gave me a look of disbelief. "You are clearly out of it. He's an adjunct professor here."

"At Washington University?"

Holly rolled her eyes. "Yes. In Political Science. He worked as a political consultant too, but now he's running against Sharon Timmons in the primaries. I think she's certifiable, so we have a real chance to make it to the general election."

"What district is this?"

"Chris Boggs' district."

Finally, a name that meant something to me. He was a two-term Republican Congressman from a district that included parts of Clayton and parts of Ladue, two of the wealthiest suburbs of St. Louis. I'd read that he came from a long line of Missouri politicians. This line included a Dixiecrat grandfather who'd served one term as governor, and a Congressman father who'd served three terms in the House of Representatives as part of the Reagan revolution of the 1980's.

"Kevin Mason sounds certifiable for taking on Chris Boggs. That district is conservative."

"No he's not," Holly said militantly. "Things are changing. This will be our year." Before I could argue, she added, "Boggs has had a huge number of scandals. Did you know that he had to pay back taxes? And I heard he was cheating on his wife with an aide."

"Uh oh." I recognized that sparkle in her eye. "It's Howard Dean all over again isn't it?"

"This is better. You have to see him. He's got something. I mean, I watched him give a speech, and I could just feel it. I promise you that Kevin Mason is going places."

"As a Democratic Congressional candidate from a Republican district in Missouri?"

"Stranger things have happened."

Now it was my turn to roll my eyes. "I'll take your word for it."

"You can come with me and volunteer. Then you'll see what I mean."

"With all my spare time?"

"Come on – it's only a couple of hours here or there."

"I'll think about it. Hey, weren't you going to help me get ready at some point?"

"Speaking of." She jumped off the bed and walked into the living room. She came back carrying her purse by the strap, digging through it with the other hand. "What jewelry are you wearing?"

"My grandmother's amethyst earrings."

"And this." Holly pulled a small black box from her purse and handed it to me.

"What's this?"

"My inheritance."

"Your what?"

"The only thing I got when my grandparents passed on."

I opened the box with anticipation. There, tucked in the black velvet was a giant amethyst ring.

"When you told me that your dress was purple, I figured you wouldn't have anything that spectacular to wear with it."

"I've never seen anything that spectacular before." The amethyst had to be at least twenty carats, faceted all around, and set high in a simple rose gold mounting. The band was large and thick, so the ring sat securely on the finger. I slipped it on my right ring finger. It fit me perfectly.

"Where did this come from?" I couldn't imagine her grandparents with such opulence.

"No one has any idea. I found it in the pocket of an old pair of Granddad's pants that I was going to throw away. He was in the army when he was young, so maybe he bought it when he was abroad. I wish I knew."

"You found it so you got to keep it?"

"Sort of. I had to renounce any claim to Grandma's Hummel figurines."

"A fair trade in my book."

"I thought so, but my aunts are still fighting over them."

I moved my hand this way and that, watching the ring sparkle in the light. "Why don't you ever wear it?"

"It's too big for me."

"You could have it sized," I said.

"I hardly live the life that ring deserves. I don't call black lights and garbage cans of jungle juice elegant."

"No. This ring implies martinis, not wood alcohol and Kool-Aid."

"So the ring will thank you if you wear it this evening. Where is this party, anyway?"

"Starlight Room at the Chase." This was the ballroom at the top floor of the Chase Park Plaza Hotel in the Central West End of St. Louis City. The Chase had been refurbished to its original Art Deco splendor.

"I've heard the views of the city are spectacular."

"It should be beautiful at night."

Holly jumped to attention. "Okay. So let's get you beautiful."

She helped me get into the dress, wrapped a towel around me to protect it, and worked her magic. The makeup was a subtle variation of the smoky-eye matte-lip look popular at the moment. The hairstyle she improvised – pulling some pieces back from my face and leaving other tendrils at my cheekbones. The back she left down, but she worked furiously with a round brush and a curling iron to get my waves just so. It looked amazing when she was done. I stared at it using a hand mirror and the full-length mirror on the back of my door. I was too dumbfounded to speak.

She smiled proudly. "You're going to knock 'em dead, Liz."

"You're absolutely wonderful!" I hugged her.

"Now don't go messing the hair and makeup," she said, pulling away. "That's for James to do." She wagged her finger. "But only at the end of the night. You tell him to behave himself till then."

"I think I'm the likely offender, but I will try to be good."

She gave me a stern look. "Make sure you are – no matter how much you're tempted."

"I'm tempted every moment I'm with him."

She opened her mouth to speak, but was interrupted by a knock at the door. "I'll get it!" she yelled as she ran out of the bedroom. "You'll kiss him hello and ruin my work."

"I think I can keep myself in check while you're here."

Holly flung open the door and stepped back. "James," she said, extending her arm. "Come in. Come in."

He blinked in surprise. "Holly."

"Liz is over there." Holly pointed to where I stood in the doorway of the bedroom. He looked incredibly dashing in his tuxedo. I wondered for the thousandth time how I'd ever managed to get him to give me a second look.

"You look very handsome, James," I said lamely.

"You look beautiful," he said, walking across the living room in long strides. "Holly helped you get ready?"

"You know me well enough to know that I couldn't pull this off by myself."

He reached me and put an arm around my shoulder.

"Don't mess with the hair or makeup, please!" Holly called.

"I wouldn't dream of it." He leaned down and kissed me quickly on the neck, right above the collarbone. I told myself to behave. Several times.

Holly could sense trouble, so she approached us and said, "James, it is good to see you again."

"And you. Mark says 'hi' by the way."

"How is the dissertation going?"

"He's told me, but to be honest, I can't really understand all of the details. You'll have to ask him yourself if you really want to know."

"Okay. Liz, I'll get my stuff and head home." She looked at James. "You take good care of her."

"Yes, ma'am."

She passed beside me into the bedroom and returned with her purse slung over her shoulder. "Have a good night you two."

I broke away from James and walked with her to the door. "I want details," she whispered to me as I closed the door behind her.

I turned to face James. He still leaned against the bedroom doorjamb. "She wants details, doesn't she?" he said.

"I'll be judicious, don't worry."

He stood up straight and walked over to me. "You can brag about me all you want." He put his hands on my bare arms. "I promised not to muss you, but I don't know if I can resist."

I smiled up at him. "We should go."

CHAPTER 5

The Starlight Room was as beautiful as the name implied. Only my growing anxiety about meeting scores of people in general, and James' family in particular, kept me from enjoying the atmosphere. Masses of candles and giant floral centerpieces adorned every table. The round tables seated eight comfortably. They were laid out so as to provide space to move, but retained a certain intimate ambiance. There was a dance floor at one end and a large podium with a rectangular VIP table at the other.

A banner hung from the ceiling directly over the podium. It read, "Shoot for the Stars." While appropriate for the location, this phrase seemed a poor choice for an organization dedicated to the aid of fallen officers. I opened my mouth and then closed it. Better not ask too many questions.

Given the theme, stars dominated the decoration – rising out of the floral centerpieces and twinkling from wires on the ceiling. There were even stars impressed into the pats of butter on the table. I eyed those with suspicion. Someone had clearly gone overboard.

James stuck close to my side as we made our way slowly through the room. The number and variety of his acquaintances astounded me. I tried desperately to keep up. He introduced me as his girlfriend. I caught a look from several people that let me know not everyone knew James' engagement was off. Most people appeared to be friends of the family, business associates, or the higher echelon of the city and county police forces.

At one point, after an extended conversation with an elderly gentleman who seemed to know James since birth, I turned to James and whispered, "I was lost thirty people ago. You know that, right?"

He whispered back, "No one expects you to remember all of the people I've introduced you to."

"I won't remember even one," I hissed.

"Calm down. I'm here." He pulled me closer to him with the arm that rested on my waist.

"That's the only thing keeping the hysteria in check."

He gave me a peck on the cheek. "Don't think I don't appreciate it. Just a little more and we'll get to our table."

We continued to move through the crowd, and a sudden horrifying thought grabbed hold of my brain. We weren't destined for the VIP table, were we? I prayed silently. Please. Please let us sit away from the limelight. We'd just arrived at the cluster of tables in front of the dais, when I heard someone call James. We both turned and looked back.

A portly gentleman came striding up to us. He had graying hair and a bushy mustache. He moved with a barely suppressed energy, and seemed like he might pop a stud on his shirt at any moment. He was a modern day Teddy Roosevelt – all vim and vigor. There was genuine warmth in the toothy smile that he flashed as soon as he got to us.

"Detective Fischer." James extended a hand that was promptly pumped up and down. James' voice sounded deferential. Detective

Fischer must be someone important. I studied him closely, committing as many details as I could to memory.

"Good to see you James," Detective Fischer said and then looked at me, anticipating a presentation.

"This is my girlfriend, Elizabeth Howe." James turned to me. "Detective Fischer is the head of the Homicide Division." Ah. The boss. That explained it.

Detective Fischer shook my hand, and I gave him my best smile, despite the fact that he was crushing my fingers. "Pleased to finally meet you, Liz. And what's with all the formality? Call me Bill."

"Pleased to meet you too, Bill," I said. Finally meet me? What?

"Well, James has said a lot about you, but he didn't tell me you were quite so lovely." He gave James a sly glance.

James looked sheepish. Clearly this conversation wasn't going as planned.

Bill Fischer turned back to me. "You and I should have a chat one of these days. I've got a lot of questions I'd like to ask you."

"Of course," I replied sweetly. And James had some serious explaining to do.

James jumped in. "I think I need to get Liz to our table." The waiters were plating the salad all around us. "Maybe we can talk later?" he added plaintively.

"Sure," Bill replied. "Wouldn't want to keep you from dinner. Liz, a pleasure. James, we'll talk."

James nodded and pulled me even closer to his side. "I'll explain everything. Just not now."

I nodded, secretly meaning to weasel it out of him by night's end. We took another two steps and were surrounded by a group of chattering people. I started to step back, but James' arm prevented me. I looked at him in surprise. "Family," he whispered.

Oh no. I plastered on a smile, but I thought I might be ill just the same.

A petite woman who was probably sixty – but didn't look a day over fifty – said, "Well? Aren't you going to introduce us?"

She had James' dark hair, but straight and cut in layers to her chin. She also had long dark lashes and James' blue blue eyes. His mother.

"Sure," James said testily. "If you all would stop talking for one second, you might actually hear me do it." Four faces turned and gave us their full attention. I blinked.

"Liz, this is my mother, Beverly, and this is my father Antonio." He indicated a tall stout older man who, when he extended his hand, I instantly recognized from the television commercials I'd seen for years. His hand was meaty with large rounded fingers.

"This is my sister, Marie." James gestured toward a long slim woman with chestnut colored hair and honey-brown eyes. She wore a sinuous blood red dress. James really should have mentioned that his sister looked like a runway model. I managed a weak smile in her direction. She returned it with a hard look. Her handshake was as brief as possible.

"And this is my brother-in-law Theo." Theo was the only one who seemed genuinely happy to meet me. He smiled and grabbed my hand. There was just a hint of mischief in his kind eyes.

"Everyone. This is Liz," James said.

I swallowed hard and then smiled as broadly as I could manage with the panic. "I'm delighted to finally meet the rest of the family."

James continued on, seemingly unaware of the chilly quality of my reception, "I think I forgot to tell you all, but Liz will be working at a law firm in Clayton when she graduates."

"Oh. What area of law will you practice?" Beverly said.

"Estate planning. At Janice Harrington and Associates."

"Very interesting." There was a certain calculation in her glance. I figured that I would quickly be tapped for free legal advice that she would then double and triple check with her own attorneys. At least the first thousand times.

"I'm hungry," Antonio said patting a stomach that seemed trapped behind a very tight cummerbund. "I say let's sit down."

I looked at James. "Not the VIP table," I silently plead.

He read my thoughts without much effort. "We're at the table over there." He pointed to a table off to the side of the podium. We said goodbye to his family and made our way over.

"How did Mark manage to get out of coming to this?" I said.

James grinned. "Luck. He caught my mom on a good day."

I felt like I could finally breathe. Our table consisted of members of the steering committee and their spouses. The committee members were housewives. The spouses seemed to be businessmen. However, one or two didn't explain themselves well enough to be that. I suspected some serious family money. I looked quickly at James, wondering what that must be like.

James knew everyone and everyone knew him. He introduced me around the table, and I went into work mode. I tried to fix each name to each person and to memorize the little details that could make my life easy if I got them right. Then I tested myself. The woman with the blonde hair and the slight tremor was Louise. The man who cleared his throat with the wheezy cough was George. The woman with the artificial fingernails and the obviously fake breasts was named Honey of all things. She had a strange accent too, like she was trying to cover a latent speech defect. She mentioned she worked in television, but I didn't catch exactly what that meant.

Fortunately for me, my work was unimpeded by the necessity of making conversation. Everyone spent so much time asking about people I didn't know and catching up that there was no need for me to say a word. I slowly ate my salad and watched. They'd served the pear and gorgonzola salad that had suddenly become so popular. I wondered just how much brown sugar was in the balsamic vinegar dressing. The walnuts seemed to have been toasted with it as well. Not as diet friendly as I'd hoped.

The waiters came by and filled our wine glasses. I resisted the urge to imbibe. I needed every available neuron if I was to get out of this evening with my dignity intact. I sipped my water and wondered when the bread would arrive. The salad wasn't that filling. If bread didn't come soon, I might be forced to attack the pats of butter. What would my fellow diners say to that? I smiled to myself.

James leaned over and whispered in my ear, "Are you doing okay?"

"I'm fine – just hungry."

James squeezed my hand under the table. "I know." I felt his finger touch Holly's ring. "Is this also grandmother's?"

"Holly's grandmother."

"Part of the assistance."

"It takes a village."

He chuckled and then turned back to the conversation.

Mercifully, the bread came. This was followed soon after by the dinner itself. A chicken marsala or vegetarian paella. I took the chicken and eagerly chewed a forkful. Hmm. Well executed, but without the panache of individually prepared dishes. James once told me that the secret to good food was an excessive amount of butter. I took another bite. Maybe they had scrimped. I thought about how hard I'd have to workout tomorrow. Scrimping could be a good thing.

A waiter approached to refill my water glass. As he poured, he looked at me with a puzzled expression. "I'm sorry," he finally said, "but do I know you?"

I wanted to tell him that I was the least likely person to answer that question, but then I saw his hand as he held the water pitcher. A memory floated to the surface. I leaned a little closer to him. A faint whiff of linseed oil and a chip of green paint on his thumbnail. I had it.

"You worked at that Indian-Mexican restaurant in Clayton," I said. I remembered the afternoon well. Janice Harrington, my boss, had invited me to lunch. She was smart enough to guess that something was very odd about me, and I'd finally confessed my limitations. At that lunch, I found a friend and mentor. And in between, I had made nice with a surly waiter who turned out to be a very talented painter.

"I knew it," he said sloshing the water in the pitcher with excitement. "Liz Howe."

"Matt Crandall," I said, suddenly remembering his name.

"It's good to see you again. I wanted to tell you – I submitted my work for the art fair in Clayton."

The Saint Louis Art Fair was held every September. The streets in the center of Clayton were closed to all but pedestrian traffic. Artists of every type set up booths to sell their works in a carnival atmosphere of food and live music. The show was juried and very prestigious. It could also be very profitable if an artist struck a popular chord.

"Good for you! I think your work will show very well."

"I'm keeping my fingers crossed. I just wanted to tell you and to thank you."

"Thank me?"

"I – well – I was at sort of a low point and your interest in my work inspired me."

"Really?"

"Yeah. I was thinking of giving it up completely."

"I had no idea."

He grinned. "I know. But I thought I'd tell you if I ever got the chance."

"I'm so glad. And I meant what I said. I think your painting will take off."

Another waiter signaled to him. "I guess I should get back to work." Then he was off to a different table.

I looked down at my plate. What an evening.

"Is that another of my rivals?" James' voice was even, but with a flint edge. He had been immersed in a conversation with the couple to his right, so I wasn't sure how much he'd heard. He couldn't be jealous, could he? It was ludicrous. I could guarantee that Matt would never take an interest in me.

"No." I looked James squarely in the face. "Just a waiter I met once." James seemed skeptical. "I guessed he was a painter and so I asked about his work." I summarized our conversation. "He wanted to thank me. That's it. Just thanks."

"You do make an impression," James said dryly.

I opened my mouth to reply, but a commotion over at a corner table caught my eye. Someone had arrived late. Someone important. The people at the table stood up and clustered around him, shaking hands.

"Who is that?" I whispered to James.

He looked over and then smiled at me indulgently. "The great white hope of the Democratic Party, Kevin Mason."

"Oh-h. Holly was just talking about him. She wants me to volunteer for his campaign."

"You're interested in politics?"

I shrugged my shoulders. "Holly thinks I should get more involved."

"Holly must have a lot of time on her hands."

"She makes time for the things she cares about."

"And figures you can spend time with her while she does it?"

He was probably right about that. She did have a habit of dragging me into things. "Some people go shopping," I replied.

He laughed. "Touché." Then he started to stand. "I'll introduce you."

I stood up. "You know him personally?"

"Sure. I know practically everyone at this organization. Kevin has always supported our work. In fact, he volunteered for the celebrity car wash my mom organized last month."

"He washed cars?"

"My mom can be very persuasive. She even got Mayor Slay to roll up his sleeves. Fortunately, we had that spell of warm weather."

I looked at James, duly impressed. Francis Slay was the Mayor of St. Louis City.

We extricated ourselves from our table and wove in and out between the other tables. James stopped to say hello to someone at almost every one. He introduced me, but I didn't really have time to keep track. My brain was full up with haircuts and facial tics. James slowed to a stop as we reached the outer ring of Kevin Mason's admirers. How long would it take us to get through? Poor Kevin wouldn't get a meal at this rate. James' height saved us from missing ours.

"James!" Kevin said. Heads swiveled around and the crowd parted so that Kevin could shake James' hand. Friendship? Or the fact that James could be a potential donor? I decided to give Kevin the benefit of the doubt.

Kevin was a slight, fresh-faced man in his mid-thirties. He had full, dark hair that waved softly back from a youthful forehead, intelligent brown eyes, and expressive eyebrows. His movements were bird-like and abrupt, as if he couldn't contain his natural energy. Attractive enough, but how could this be the same man Holly had described? A veritable god on earth?

"Kevin. Let me introduce you to my girlfriend, Liz Howe. She's a third year law student at Wash U."

Kevin turned and shook my hand. "Pleased to meet you. I think I might have seen you around campus."

I stood there transfixed by the intensity and power of his gaze. Like a mouse confronted by a snake, I was unable to move. I swallowed hard and blinked. My mind went blank. I recovered the power of speech by force of will alone. "Yes, pleased to finally meet you."

His handshake was gentle but too long. I couldn't pull away. I felt my cheeks burning. I tried to look down, but couldn't do that either. So this was what Holly meant. Kevin Mason's charisma was like an aura that radiated out in every direction. He now seemed larger than life.

James came to my rescue by putting an arm around my shoulder and saying, "I just wanted to thank you again for your help with the car wash. We should get back to our table. Good luck with the campaign."

Kevin turned to him, releasing me. I stepped farther into James' arm.

"Good seeing you again. And please tell your mom I congratulate her on her award tonight. No one deserves it more."

"Will do." Then the crowd closed in and we were done. We got back to the table in time for dessert. Good. A waiter set what appeared to be a double chocolate cheesecake in front of me. Without alcohol, I needed some chocolate to calm my nerves. I took the first delicious bite and instantly felt better. It had cinnamon too, which amplified the bite of the cocoa.

The program and awards ceremony was more touching than my cynical mind expected. They played a video montage of all of the families that the organization had helped that year. I looked at James. What would it be like to hear that he had been killed in the line of duty? Just the thought made my heart race with fear. I made a mental note to talk to Janice. We could offer pro bono legal advice. It wasn't much, but maybe it would help.

James' mother was gracious and brief in her acceptance speech of the Merit Award for Service. She was immediately followed by the conclusion of the silent auction. A mad scramble ensued as everyone tried to place one final bid. I remained seated.

I had gone to a gala auction once with Nick and his parents. His father had extra tickets and thought Nick might like to take me somewhere nice. How he got Nick to agree, I'll never know. We were easily the youngest couple by twenty years. Having nothing else to do, we spent the night talking to Nick's parents and watching the other attendees.

There is something about small town events that brings out the competitive spirit. Every woman eyed every other woman, trying to figure out where she had purchased her dress. Likely the Twin Cities. Every man looked around for someone important to talk to. From where I sat, St. Louis society wasn't much different. Of course this auction didn't involve pounds and pounds of beef, or any livestock that I could see. I smiled to myself. If only James had been there. At the time I didn't know purchasing a hundred pounds of frozen steak at a charity auction wasn't the most normal thing in the world. You live in one place long enough, and even the bizarre becomes commonplace.

I looked up to see James watching me over his cup of coffee. "Nothing you want to bid on?"

I shook my head. My disposable income didn't extend that far. "I was just thinking of home."

"We might be able to escape."

"I meant Marshfield. We don't have to leave."

Marshfield is a small town in the center of Wisconsin. It's home to the Marshfield Clinic, a giant health care system that brings state of the art medicine to the middle of nowhere. The town itself is filled with so many medical professionals that a call of "Is there a doctor in the house?" routinely produces a dozen physicians of every stripe. Having that many physicians in one place does create some strange situations. The father of my high school boyfriend was also my neurologist. I was treated in the Oncology department where my mother is a nurse. Secrets can't stay hidden for long in a place like that.

"Marshfield?" James said.

"Just remembering, that's all." No need to mention meat. You had to be there.

"I'd like to go with you sometime."

"Really?" Most people didn't see the appeal.

"Sure. See where you grew up, meet the family, that sort of thing. I think it might be the key to how that brain of yours works."

"You know how it works."

"Not that part," he said referring to my prosopagnosia. "I'm talking about something more subtle."

"You must have me confused with someone else. I've never been accused of subtlety."

"That's exactly what I'm talking about," he said with a smile. "That weird humility you have. I tell you that you're wonderful and you list ten things wrong with you."

"There are way more than ten."

James gave me a look. "I'd like to go with you next time." He paused. "If you don't mind."

"Mind? Of course not." I'd show him off to the whole town if I could. I could see the headline in the *News-Herald* – Local Girl Dates Model-like Pizza Heir. It was just – I tried to visualize James walking down Central Avenue, but couldn't. I would need to take him to Fleet Farm to get proper clothes, for a start. I bet he didn't own an ounce of flannel or a feather of down. And real boots. That would be the first thing. Plus a shearling cap with ear flaps. James would brave frostbite before he'd be seen in that.

"We should go in the summer," I said.

"Okay."

"It's better weather."

"Won't you be studying for the bar?"

"Right after the bar exam. In August, when it's 100 degrees and 99 percent humidity here."

"Done." He extended his hand and we shook on the deal.

Then he leaned over and gave me a quick peck on the lips. Or it would have been quick if I hadn't taken a deep breath at that moment. He always smelled so sweet. So right. I took control. It's hard to explain to someone who does not have my hyperactive nose, but I use my sense of smell to guide me in ways that my other senses can't. And not just for recognition, although I can tell people apart if I get close enough. Smell also acts as a warning signal. Things smell right or they don't. And if they don't, I want to know why.

I knew James was right for me even when he wasn't free to be mine. And now, dating him, I only had to stand close enough to send my senses spinning out of control. Desire. I'd never felt anything like it.

"We should go," he said softly, pulling away. "Especially if you are going to kiss me like that again."

"Sorry. I forget where I am."

"Don't be sorry."

I heard a shuffling sound and an "Ahem" behind me. I turned around in my seat, only to cringe back again. Marie was standing there, her arms folded across her chest. Theo hovered behind. Great. Of all the people to catch me misbehaving, it had to be James' disapproving sister. James smiled serenely, unperturbed. I guess he was used to dating loose women.

"What?" he said.

"Mom wants you." Marie pointed her finger at the opposite side of the ballroom. "She's got Mayor Slay cornered and thinks you should make an appearance instead of sitting here kissing your girlfriend."

"I've met him a thousand times already," James grumbled, but he got up anyway. I looked at Marie. She had an authority that only the oldest child in a family really understands. I sized her up and knew instinctively that I was in deep, deep trouble.

"I'll be right back," James said to me.

Marie grabbed his arm and literally hauled him off with her. I could still hear the familiar sibling bickering several tables away. I looked down at my lap, wondering what I should do with myself while James was gone. I turned Holly's ring over and over on my finger. It was really amazing how many facets it had. And so clear for an amethyst. Then I felt someone staring at me, so I looked up. Marie's husband Theo regarded me, a rueful look in his kind eyes.

"Have a seat," I said, indicating the place beside me.

He smiled as he sat down, slouching into the chair. "You're a brave woman."

"Or not very bright."

He chuckled.

"Are they always like this?" I said.

"Pretty much. The key is to stay back. Let them do their own thing. They're like a cyclone. You'll get pulverized if you get in the middle."

"There's no calm eye at the center?"

"Not with the Paperellis. Trust me."

"Okay. Stay back. I can follow those instructions." I looked over at Theo and decided to take a chance on him. "So what if the storm is me?"

"What do you mean?" He shifted in the chair uncomfortably.

"Don't take this the wrong way, because I'd like to think that I am totally off, but I get the distinct impression that I'm not everyone's favorite person."

He looked down and didn't say anything. I could tell he was trying to choose his words carefully. "It's not that you aren't a great person. It's just that you're not Angie."

"Angie is still very close to the family?"

"She's been Marie's best friend for a long time. She was with James for years and Beverly and Antonio sort of adopted her. She was like another daughter."

"And now she's not."

"I don't know if they've accepted that. She's still Marie's best friend. That's not changing." He sounded as if he wasn't totally happy about the situation.

I smiled at him. "Thank you. It's good to know where you stand, even if it's in the line of fire."

"Just remember I'm not the one with the gun."

"Duly noted."

"And don't worry too much. They'll come around eventually."

"I won't go away as long as James still wants me here."

Theo smiled with genuine warmth. "I don't think he'll change his mind. I've known him a number of years, and I've never seen him this way before."

"Even with Angie? Before things went south?"

"Maybe at first, I guess, but not any time lately. He can't stop talking about you."

That was a positive sign, assuming the comments were appropriate. We sat for a couple of minutes in silence and then I said, "You're a good man, Theo. Thanks."

"I try to be. Ah, I see the cyclone heading our direction."

I looked where Theo was looking. It was hard to miss the two tall figures. The family resemblance was uncanny in the way they moved in long confident strides, and the way they spoke with their hands gesturing in every direction. They were engaged in a serious discussion, and then James said something that made Marie laugh uproariously. They stopped a moment, her hand leaning on his shoulder as she nearly doubled over with laughter. I knew in that instant what a long hard road I had in front of me. His family was his family. There was nothing I could do about it.

James and Marie finally arrived at the table, relaxed and smiling in the afterglow of their private joke. James grabbed my hand and pulled me up. "Let's dance. The music is about to start."

"Big band swing?"

"What else?" He put his arm around my waist. "See you later," he said to Marie. "We'll talk some other time."

"Okay," she said flatly.

I caught Theo's eye.

We reached the dance floor just as the band started. A slow number. Thank goodness. I didn't know about my ability to swing anything, particularly in those shoes. The heel was high enough and the dress was long enough that I just might do myself a mischief. James proved to be a strong lead, which, given my dancing deficits, was a good thing. Even a slow song required serious work. I had new respect for my grandparents' generation. They must have been fit. James pulled me back from a smooth twirl and said, "You survived a conversation with Theo?"

I had to watch my feet for a moment before I could reply. "Theo is delightful. But you should be ashamed of yourself for breaking your promise."

"My promise?"

"Leaving me alone. Or have you forgotten so easily?"

His face fell. "No. Yes. I'm sorry."

I laughed. He looked so dejected. "Relax. I'm just giving you a hard time."

"I wasn't thinking."

"You are completely forgiven. Besides, Theo gave me some sage advice. Stay back. Way back."

"From me?"

"From your family fights."

"How my sister managed to catch such a good guy is beyond me."

"Aside from her brilliant intellect, I'm sure the fact that she looks like a model helped some."

"She'll be happy you think so. But in case you haven't noticed, my sister is just a little bit high maintenance."

"I had noticed."

"I love her, but I don't know how Theo does it."

"The price of beauty?"

"It usually is," he said.

Angie perhaps? I didn't have that kind of beauty, but I also didn't have that kind of temper – most of the time. Maybe it was my allure for a man like James. Who knew a lack of tantrums could be an asset?

"What are you thinking?" James said.

I snapped back to attention. "Nothing. My mind just wanders around. It's a bad habit."

"No negatives, remember?" After a slight pause he said, "You really look beautiful tonight."

"Shocking, isn't it?" and then before he could reply, I added, "But you should take the credit as the originator of the outfit."

"The outfit is secondary. Although it does bring out your – um —," he looked quickly down at my rather abundant cleavage, cinched in and pushed up by the bodice of the dress, "assets."

I felt my cheeks getting pink. "You want to go because of a simple kiss and yet —"

"I make inappropriate remarks?"

"And while I'm trying to dance in heels. I don't want to embarrass you."

"No problem." He stopped and held me close. The song wound down. "I think I've had enough for one evening."

"Your place or mine?" I said.

"Now who's making inappropriate remarks?"

"It was just a suggestion. I won't be offended if you've had enough of me this week."

"On one of the few nights I won't have to leave you at the crack of dawn to go in to work?"

"Well —"

"I'm not absolutely insane and —"

"And?"

He leaned over and whispered something in my ear that made my pink cheeks flush a deep dark crimson.

"Talk about inappropriate remarks!" I said, putting my hands to my face.

James just laughed as he guided me off the dance floor.

CHAPTER 6

It turned out that my patience was sorely tested. I didn't get an opportunity to ask James about Detective Fischer until the following Wednesday at lunch. It wasn't that I didn't try. But James had a way of distracting me whenever I thought to mention it. He clearly did not want to discuss the matter. And he didn't repeat the L-word. Not even when I wouldn't have believed him anyway. It made me uneasy.

I drove over to the MetroLink station on Delmar Boulevard, parked my car and then took the train into downtown. The new line that would bring the trains into Clayton and close to Janice's office was set to open at the end of the summer. Still, I knew from hard experience how difficult it would be to find a parking space in the city, so I didn't mind the extra detour.

I met James at a sandwich shop several blocks from the police headquarters. It was more of a brunch date. My watch just said 11:00 when I walked out of the station. But I didn't complain. It was the only time he could escape and I was hungry. We ordered our sandwiches, and then I got to the heart of the matter. He couldn't try his distractions in public.

"What did Detective Fischer mean when he said he'd heard of me?" I said.

James took a long sip of water from his glass before he replied, "I knew this was coming."

"You promised me answers if I played along. You've been stalling."

"I had other things on my mind." He tried the sly smile, but I wasn't having any of it. He sighed. "Just promise you'll hear me out before you go ballistic."

"Have I ever gone ballistic on you?" I thought the lack of ballistics was what he liked about me.

"Only once and I totally deserved it." I could tell he was thinking about the night he'd forced me to tell him about my prosopagnosia. I didn't want to think about that night. Although, I suppose that we wouldn't be together without it. James fought with Angelica when he got home, and she stormed out, breaking the engagement.

"You did. Now tell me what I want to know," I said.

"Let me take you back a little. Remember when I was taken off the Harding case?"

"Yes. That was right before I went home for Christmas."

"And you told me that you were going to investigate on your own."

"Of course."

"That was the strangest conversation." He took another sip of water and then the man behind the counter called out our order. James got up to get it.

He came back in a minute with our plates. I pulled the frilly toothpick out of one half of my sandwich and took a bite. Grilled portabella mushrooms. Crispy on the edges and soft in the middle. Delicious. I looked at him and waited. He took a bite of his BLT and chewed slowly. Then he swallowed and said, "You knew I was trying to ask you out, didn't you?"

I dropped the sandwich on the plate. "What?" A piece of portabella went down the wrong way and I coughed.

"I can see by your reaction that you didn't. I'm an idiot."

I recovered enough to speak. "I'm clearly the idiot. You were asking me out?"

"I thought you were dating Vince, but I didn't know how serious that was, so I hinted around to see. But you obviously didn't get the hint. I should have just asked."

"That question about plans for Saturday?" It was all coming back to me. The pieces fitted neatly into place.

He nodded. "My lame attempt. And you still thought I was engaged. Maybe it's good you didn't know what I was talking about."

I nodded dumbly. I should have banged my head on the table. Talk about dense. To think that I could have been with him that much longer. But wait.

"So, knowing I was trying to ask you out, you may be wondering —" he said.

"Why didn't you do it when I got back from Marshfield?"

"Because I couldn't. I was back on the case."

Of course. "I was your informant."

"You were more than that. You found John Harding's body and you overheard that conversation between the killers, so you had valuable eye-witness information. If we were together, our relationship would taint your testimony."

"But we're dating now and they haven't yet taken the case to grand jury."

"That's where Bill Fischer comes in. After you practically solved the case for me and I kissed you – which I obviously wanted to do again – I went to talk to Bill. Really, I begged him to help me. I didn't want to ruin everything we'd worked so hard on, but I also wasn't going to give you up. Bill was impressed with all you'd done. He's fascinated by your attention to detail. That's why he wants to speak to you."

"Did you tell him why I notice so much detail?"

"No."

I sighed with relief.

"I figured you could tell him yourself."

I looked at him, horrified.

James reached over the table and took my hand. "There is nothing to be ashamed of. You are a brilliant woman. You could tell everyone about your diagnosis and it wouldn't matter. I'm proud of you. I don't know why you don't understand that."

I felt tears welling up and couldn't think of a thing to say. My heart was too full.

He squeezed my hand. "I'm sorry I had to ask his permission, but I didn't know what else to do."

"Bill Fischer gave you permission," I finally got out.

"It took a couple of weeks. That's when I called you to go to dinner. We had to verify your theories. Bill told me that if we could corroborate everything, we wouldn't have to depend solely on your testimony."

"And when I didn't see you, it wasn't because you were too busy —"

"I couldn't see you until we were in the clear. By the way, your theories checked out perfectly."

"But what about your emails?" There had been enough in those to keep me hanging on.

"I pride myself on being a master of subtlety. And I didn't tell Bill about those. I couldn't just ignore you for weeks on end."

"I'll go back and look. I must have read a lot more into them."

"I hoped you would. And I figured that when I finally saw you, I could be more explicit." He smiled smugly.

I felt myself blushing. Obviously, we remembered the same things about that first date. "So you lied to me when you said you needed time to extricate Angelica from your life?" I didn't like the lying part.

"Half-truth," he said apologetically. "That was only part of the reason."

"Why didn't you tell me this before?"

"I thought you'd be angry with me for telling the department about you. I'd promised you a low profile, remember?"

"True, but not if it meant I couldn't be with you."

He smiled. "My thoughts exact–" He would have said "exactly," but at that moment we heard a popping sound and then a resonant rumble. It seemed close, but it was impossible to tell in what direction.

"Stay where you are," James said in a deadly calm voice. He jumped up out of his chair and ran out of the restaurant, reaching for the gun he usually wore concealed under his jacket. I sat for a moment, half in shock, half meekly obeying his instructions. Then

I caught a whiff of something. I grabbed my purse and dashed out the door.

I nearly collided with James on the sidewalk. He stood still, looking around him. The street seemed supernaturally quiet. He moved his hand down, away from the gun holster. The smell was stronger outside. Sulfur and cement. Not good. I scanned the buildings around us, looking for a sign. Across the street a multistory office building rose into the skyline. I recognized it as the building that housed Hart and Klein, Vince's future employer. But what was that? A thin wisp of smoke swirled up seemingly out of nowhere. And then another, perhaps coming from the ground floor?

"James, over there." I pulled on his sleeve and pointed at the smoke. He dashed across the street. I ran close behind him. Then, as if someone flipped a switch, all hell broke loose.

Crowds of people poured out of the building. A few brave souls tried to impose order on the chaos, but it was hopeless. James and I fought against the tide of bodies pushing outwards until we finally reached the lobby. James stopped, unsure of where to go. The people continued to stream around us, but in the babble of voices no one could tell us what had happened.

But the smell kept getting stronger. I tried to locate the source by opening one door after another. Finally, I pulled on a door and the stench made me feel lightheaded and sick. I'd found the underground parking garage.

"James!" I yelled above the din, "Here!" I started down the steps before James could prevent me. The horrible smell got worse and worse with each step. My head finally put a name to it. Burning flesh.

I stopped. "Someone is seriously hurt," I said. James pushed past me, gun in hand.

"You stay back, you understand?" he yelled up. I nodded and put my hand over my mouth so I couldn't scream. I felt my whole body shake with a fear so deep and buried that I'd thought it was gone forever. The nightmares would be back. I sat down on the steps, willing my mind not to replay the image of John Harding covered in blood, lying in the stairwell, but it wouldn't listen. I thought I really would be sick this time.

"Liz!" I heard James calling from the floor below. "Come help me!"

I shook my head twice, trying to clear it.

"Come!" he said.

James needed me. I got up and hurried down the stairs.

I followed his voice until I found him squatting down beside a mangled silver Mercedes that was parked two rows away from the stairwell, next to a wall. One look was enough to tell me that something had exploded next to the car. The car, the ceiling above and the floor below were all a sooty black. The driver's side door had been blown off its hinges. It hung limply to the side, still attached to the chassis by a thin mangled strip of metal. There was broken glass and bits of debris everywhere. Some pieces still smoldered where they lay. The interior of the car was unrecognizable. I figured it had sustained most of the blast. Smoke continued to billow about. I coughed.

James crouched on the floor a couple of feet away, bent over a body that appeared as blackened as the Mercedes. "Help me with this tourniquet," he said.

I stepped around the head, my boots crunching as I walked. I squatted down and then wobbled a little and fell back into a sitting position. I heard another crunch. Bad idea. Maybe my jeans would be thick enough to protect me from the glass and who knew what else I was sitting on. I had to breathe through my mouth, and even then I could taste the horrible stench at the back of my throat. Be strong. Be strong. I forced myself to look down and focus on what James wanted me to do.

The arm of the body, or I should say person, because up close I could tell he was softly moaning, had been completely mangled, the hand vaporized, leaving a jagged blackened stump. Blood continued to flow from the parts that hadn't been cauterized by the heat of the blast.

James had taken the cashmere scarf he was wearing at lunch and used it to tie up the wound. He had a long piece of metal in his fingers, which I saw in an instant he meant to use as a turnkey. But he needed another pair of hands. I knotted the scarf as he held the metal and then we twisted it around and around trying to stem the bleeding. Finally, he held it in place with both hands.

"Okay. Reach into the inside pocket of my jacket and get my BlackBerry."

I reached around his arms and found the BlackBerry. My hands were slick and sticky with blood and charcoal dust. It took a couple of tries before I could get it out.

"Good," he said calmly. "Now press '1' and hit dial." I obeyed, but my hands shook so much, that I could barely do it. It was the speed dial for the department. "Put it up to my ear."

I heard it ring several times. In the distance I caught the sound of sirens. "I think the police are already coming."

He ignored me, waiting till he finally got someone on the line. He explained the situation to whoever had picked up. Then he said, "Yes, we need the bomb squad, but this guy needs help." He paused, listening. "Yes, I know. I'll get her out as soon as we can move him." Another pause. "Yes, but she's holding the phone right now." He looked ruefully at me and then smiled.

Another pause. Only this time the person must have hung up because he said, "All done. Why don't you put the phone back in my pocket, so I'll know where to find it."

I did as he asked. Then he said, "Any moment now, don't worry. You're doing just fine. Thank you."

I nodded, but it was a struggle to swallow back the bile in my throat. I looked down at the victim, wondering who he was. He certainly wasn't in a condition to identify himself.

He looked like he was wearing a navy suit with cordovan shoes. At least that is what I got from the small parts of him that were not blackened. The shoes seemed well worn, but obviously expensive. Allen Edmonds by the narrow shape. The suit was a fine wool, with a little bit of shine on the fabric at the end of the cuffed pant leg. Again, expensive but not new.

"Do you think he'll be okay?" I said.

"I hope so – if the paramedics get here soon. I think we stopped most of the bleeding. That's the important part." He gave me his best reassuring smile. "You're great under fire, but we really should stop meeting like this."

I tried to smile, but accidentally inhaled through my nose. I felt the acrid taste at the back of my throat. It took all my willpower to keep my stomach under control. If only my sense of smell weren't quite so good. James seemed completely unaffected. I finally heard footsteps behind us.

"Over here," James called. Two burly and very capable men appeared. They took over. And then two more appeared with a stretcher. James pulled me up beside him and we got out of the way. He hurried me out of the area and up the stairs as quickly as possible. We met some people coming the other way. The bomb squad.

When we finally made it outside, past the police cordon, James said, "Are you okay? Really?"

I inhaled deeply. The air smelled incredibly sweet. "I think so." I took a step and felt a telltale twinge. "But I might have a piece or two of glass imbedded in me." I twisted around trying to see.

James started to laugh. "Only you would —" And then he caught himself. "Sorry. You should get that looked at." He motioned over one of the medical personnel who were swarming just outside the police barrier. By this time, the main victim was being carried to another waiting ambulance, so the paramedic took my arm and told me to come with him.

"I need to talk to a few people but I'll be over to check on you in a moment." James patted my arm and let me go.

"Let me take a look at that wound," the paramedic said as he helped me up into the back of the ambulance. He seemed to be my age or only a little older and relatively attractive. I thanked my lucky stars that I was now attached. As a single, date-hungry woman, this would have been so much more awkward. Still, I felt a certain reluctance to part with my jeans. However, when I held them up, I could see that the whole backside was encrusted with glass and other debris. It glinted in the light. "I'll put those in a bag," he said, "or its going to rain glass in here." He pulled out a plastic bag and stuffed them in.

"Now let me see what we have." I pulled down my now tattered and stained underwear and bent over so he could get a better look. "Hmm," he said, "It looks like you do have some glass in there." It turned out to be three pieces, but the cuts were not deep. The paramedic removed the shards and swabbed the wounds. Mercifully, I did not need stitches, just some heavy cotton bandages.

"We could take you to the emergency room if you want a second opinion. I wouldn't want you to have any scarring."

"No thanks. I'd like to go home. You wouldn't happen to have any pants in here, would you?"

The paramedic wasn't really sure how to deal with the problem. Finally, he dug out a thin sheet. "You can wrap this around you for now, but you should probably give me your underwear too. There might be glass still stuck to them. That would be bad if you sit down again." I wrapped the sheet around my legs and then pulled my underwear off and handed them over. He stuffed them in the bag with the jeans, and ran a bit of tape around the top to seal it. "Wouldn't want them to escape," he said smiling. "I'll go out and see what we can do about the pants, okay?"

I nodded and then sat down very gingerly.

I watched through the ambulance windows as the paramedic wandered over to where James stood talking to the other officers. James probably wouldn't have time to go home and get me another pair of pants. He looked pretty beat up himself. His clothes were stained with blood and dust and his hair looked wild, with pieces going in every direction. Yet he still managed to look good, like some punk model on a photo shoot. Insane.

I wiped my hands on a bit of gauze until I got most of the rest of the blood off before I grabbed my purse from the floor and fished around for my cell phone. My purse had a black stain on the bottom from where I'd thrown it down. At this rate, I'd have to buy a whole new wardrobe.

"Come on Holly," I said as I dialed. "Please pick up."

She did. My luck was starting to change.

"Holly, I have a huge favor to ask – could you come get me and bring a pair of pants? And maybe some underwear, if you have any big pairs that might fit me." I could go commando if I had to.

"What on God's earth are you up to?"

"It's a long story. I'll tell you when you get here. Just please hurry. I'm trapped in an ambulance." I gave her my location.

"This is crazy – even for you," she said as she hung up. I shifted on the seat. Ouch. I hoped the cuts healed soon. I looked back out the window. James and the paramedic were laughing. Of all the nerve. I felt my blood start to boil.

James walked back towards the ambulance with a leisurely stroll. He was still smiling as he pulled open the back and climbed up in. He seemed strangely ebullient – in his element with carnage and mayhem.

"You," I said before he could open his mouth, "better not be laughing at me."

"I'm laughing with you."

I gave him a steely look. He returned it with that boyish smile I found so hard to resist. "You have to admit that being trapped in the ambulance because you don't have any clothes is just a little funny."

"You want me to walk around in a sheet?"

"That I would object to."

He sat down and put an arm around me. I noticed that he too had tried to clean his hands, but there were smears of dried blood on his wrists. He smelled like blood and sour smoke, but I wasn't going to complain. His jacket would probably have to be bagged up like my clothes. There was no way dry cleaning could get that out.

Despite the fact that I fizzed with resentment, the weight of his arm on my shoulder made me feel infinitely better. "I called Holly and told her to bring me pants," I said.

"Good. Are you okay?"

"Just a few small cuts."

"I'll wait with you till Holly comes."

"I don't look that bad, do I?"

"You don't want me to stay? I'm sorry I —"

"Of course I want you to stay." I could feel the anger oozing away. "Just don't laugh at my distress, okay?"

"Done. Although it is funny —"

"Don't start."

He smiled. "I owe you a pair of jeans."

"You don't owe me anything. I'm the one who decided to sit on the floor. The jeans are now studded with all sorts of trash."

"You Bedazzled them?"

I started to laugh in spite of myself. "No machine required."

When he finally recovered from a fit of laughter much longer than the joke really merited, he said. "Hey, where are they?"

I pointed to the plastic bag. "The paramedic didn't want me to shed glass."

"Right. I'll get him to tag that properly. Forensics just might want them for something. Now back to the question of new jeans. I'll buy them if you don't mind."

"Sure, but —"

"Trust me. Every pair you own is way too big." Then he got a wicked look in his eye. "There is one exception. We'll keep those, but the rest have to go." He pointed to the bag. "You've done a great service by destroying that pair."

"You want me to put myself in your hands?"

He looked at the bag. "You've already done worse."

"I'm not sure I'm cut out to be your personal Barbie doll."

"Okay, not Barbie."

"Although she is from Wisconsin."

"You're kidding."

"That was the back story. But we have nothing else in common."

"You're not plastic, which has its advantages."

"You'll find I'm harder to dress."

"Take a chance. Let me see what I can do."

"Fair enough. One pair of jeans. It will be a true test of your skills. I'll worry about the underwear myself."

"Underwear?"

"Why do you think I'm wearing a sheet? They're in the bag too."

He gave me a look.

"Don't get any ideas. I'll show you my scars at some future date, and in private."

"Can't wait." He glanced out the window. "I think Holly's here. That was quick."

"You'll take care of yourself, won't you?" I said.

"I always do. You're the one who seems to get in trouble lately."

"And it may be some time."

"What?" he said.

"Till you see my scars. I have a feeling that this case is going to take over your life."

"The case may be assigned to someone else."

"After today, you won't let it go. I know you better than you think."

He gave my shoulder a squeeze. "I'll try to break away as often as I can."

"I'm so behind on my school work that I'm going to have to shut myself up in my apartment anyway."

"That's what I want to hear. No parties. No boyfriends. No nothing."

"I can promise the no boyfriends. You are the only one for me."

The doors swung open as I spoke. "How touching," Holly said, closing them behind her.

"Holly!" I jumped up, hitting my head on the roof of the ambulance. Ouch. I sat back down and rubbed my skull.

"I assume that you are responsible for the loss of Liz's pants," Holly said to James.

"It wasn't me this time, I swear."

"I sat on some glass. My jeans are a mess so I can't put them back on," I said.

"And what happened to the two of you? You look awful. And you smell worse. No one would tell me anything out there."

"A bomb went off in that building." James pointed out the window. "We were just having lunch across the street and heard it. We went to help the victim. It was a little messy."

"I'd say."

"Thanks so much for bringing me something to wear, Holly." I reached over and grabbed a plastic bag from her hand. I pulled out a pair of black sweat pants and some serviceable but clearly stretched panties. The sweat pants would be too short and the underwear might not fit, but I wasn't going to complain.

"Now I wish I'd stopped at your apartment and gotten your clothes instead. I don't think I'll want those back," Holly said.

"Make it up to you." I tried to get the underwear on without dropping the sheet.

"You can lose the sheet Liz, we've both seen this before," Holly said.

I glared at her, but finally managed to get the underwear up over my injuries. Only then did I let the sheet go. "Okay, now pass me the pants." I saw James smile but he refrained from laughing this time. Good man. He even let me lean on his shoulder for support. The sweatpants were at least two sizes too small, but I didn't care. A pant was a pant.

"Well ladies," James said, "I'm going to leave you now. I need to find the paramedic to tag this bag." He got up and edged past Holly to the back.

"Eew," Holly said as he passed. "You should go home and shower. You smell even worse than Liz."

"Thanks for stating the obvious. Liz," he turned back to me, "I'll call you when I can. Okay? I'd kiss you goodbye, but I don't think it would be fun for either of us."

"Thank goodness," Holly said. "You two are sickening enough together as it is."

"She's just jealous," I said to James.

"She should be." Then he pushed open the back doors and got down more gracefully than I could have imagined.

"Let's get out of here," Holly said.

It took some effort to get me out of the ambulance. James came back with the paramedic just as I'd finally managed to put both feet on the ground. He hugged me, and then Holly and I started the long trek back through the emergency vehicles to where the police had let her park her car. People crawled over the building like ants on a mound. When we'd finally gotten through that mess, there were throngs of curious onlookers beyond. I even saw television crews. There were local newscasters I'd never actually seen in person before, and then, overhead, the buzz of at least two helicopters.

"What a zoo!" Holly said as I climbed into her Geo Metro. I had to tuck my knees under my chin. Holly was petite so the obvious lack of legroom didn't seem to bother her. In any case, my knees made a good resting spot for my head, which was starting to spin again, now that the excitement and anxiety of the afternoon were at an end. I calmly waited out the aftershocks of panic and revulsion. I'd been through this once before.

"You look green," Holly said as she carefully made her way out of the cordoned off zone and into the mass of gawkers beyond. I didn't respond and she didn't press me. Several police officers helped her navigate through the crowd and even shooed away some reporters who figured she must have a story to tell if she'd gotten through the police barricade. We finally made it out. The city streets bustled with the tail end of the lunchtime traffic.

"So, where is your car?"

"The Delmar MetroLink station. Just drop me off and I'll be fine."

"I'm not going to just drop you off," Holly said scornfully. "I'll get someone to go get your car. Right now I'm taking you home."

"You don't need to stay with me." I tried to lift my head, but thought better of it. The spinning hadn't stopped yet.

"Yes, I do."

"Okay, Mom."

"Good, the sarcasm's back. You had me worried there for a moment. And Liz?"

"Umm?"

"As much as you love James, you need to stop showing up at his crime scenes."

I laughed weakly. "I promise I'll try."

CHAPTER 7

As soon as I'd sufficiently recovered, and Holly finally left me in peace, I called Vince. I didn't think that his work at Hart and Klein started until after he passed the bar, but I wanted to be sure. He called me back the next day, missing me, but leaving a message that he was fine and hadn't been in the building. Then we played phone tag. It's amazing how unreachable law students can get.

I met Vince when we were both summer associates at Ghebish and Long. We were now friends, although we'd almost been more. Vince just couldn't compete with James for that rush of adrenaline-infused attraction. That was the main problem – my hormones. He did me the favor of remaining my friend. We kept in touch through email and occasional coffees. I didn't mention the coffees to James, who seemed surprisingly touchy about Vince for someone who's ex fiancée wandered around accosting him at dinner.

So, for the next two weeks, I managed to keep my promise to Holly about the crime scenes and left Vince messages. One day, I was finally home when he called.

"Hello?" he said.

"Thank goodness. I was thinking you were a figment of my imagination."

"Nope. I'm real – just insanely busy. And why can't you ever pick up?"

"Maybe it's the fact that I've crammed too many classes in this semester, the Clinic that has me driving all over to interview people who don't want to talk to me, or that I can't seem to fall asleep at night so I'm catatonic throughout the day. The usual."

"The first part sounds like your normal life. Why can't you sleep?"

"The bombing has me a little unsettled."

My nightmares seemed to repeat themselves with only slight variation. I was in the parking garage again. I heard James call my name. I ran down the stairs. There I found James, lying in a pool of blood, his wavy hair sticky and matted, his long thin fingers curled into fists, and one of his Ferragamo loafers half off his foot.

I always woke up screaming at the top of my lungs. The last time, I had Joe Henderson, the landlord's son, banging on my door afterward. He insisted on coming in and would only leave once I persuaded him that I would positively be able to sleep without him standing guard in the living room.

"Is James on the investigation?"

"Yes, but that's not the part I'm having trouble with. We were there when it happened. It was pretty horrific. That's why I was so worried when I called you."

"You were there?"

"James and I were eating lunch across the street when the bomb went off."

"No —"

"We got to the victim ahead of the paramedics. I had to help James staunch the bleeding."

"The paper said that Arthur was seriously hurt." The *St. Louis Post-Dispatch* named the victim as Arthur Thornton, an unmarried accountant, age fifty-four, who lived in a neat house on a cul-de-sac in Olivette.

"You knew him?" I had a momentary vision of his blackened stump of an arm.

"Yeah. I forgot to tell you that Hart and Klein offered me a part-time position till I take the bar, so I've been over there a lot. Art's firm has offices on the other side of the building, but I ran into him all the time. He's quiet but friendly with everyone." Vince let out a low whistle. "I just can't imagine anyone wanting to hurt him. I really hope he pulls through."

"So do I. But if he does, he's not going to be the same."

"It's so ironic. My parents came to the US from Colombia to get away from stuff like this, and here I am in the middle of a murder and a bombing within a year. What's wrong with this picture?"

"I'm afraid I'm the problem," I said. "I have a knack for stumbling into crime scenes. Is your family worried?"

"I've had calls from cousins in Bogota inviting me back home for my own safety."

"No need to move. Just stay away from me."

"I couldn't do that," he said quickly.

I held my breath, hoping he wasn't going to say something I didn't want to hear.

"Who would listen to me complain all the time?"

I breathed out. "I'm glad you don't feel the need to abandon me just because I'm cursed."

"That would be rude."

"Always the gentleman."

"Speaking of – I think I owe you a coffee. Haven't you bought the last two times?"

"I thought you'd never remember. I've been wondering how to suggest coffee without having to pay for it."

"I swear I won't forget my wallet this time."

"A likely story."

"No, really, I might even throw in a muffin," he said.

"How can I resist such temptation?"

"It's hard."

"How about next Tuesday?"

"Sure. Where?"

"I've got to do some research at SLU, so I could meet you at that coffee shop on Lindell," I said.

"Done."

"What are you researching?" he said.

"Islam in Kosovo, for my own information."

"Huh?"

"I'll explain over coffee. It's convoluted," I replied.

"Isn't it always with you?"

I always marveled at how Saint Louis University continued to expand. As I drove around the block, looking for a parking space, I noticed yet another new building on Spring Avenue. The sign said "Aquinas Institute." I seemed to remember that it was originally located on the main campus, near the library. Maybe Vince would know more.

I parked and walked to the library. I didn't know much about Kosovo, except that it required peacekeepers. My history degree hadn't included coursework beyond the fall of the Hapsburg Empire. An intimate knowledge of Emperor Franz Joseph didn't help me understand Elsa Stimpkin. The Saint Louis University library had a fantastic collection of books on ethno-religious topics, so I figured it must have something I could use. We had to give our reports to the judge soon, and I didn't really have a handle on the situation.

I scanned the catalog at a computer terminal and came up with several likely sources. My best discoveries usually happened when I wandered the stacks alone. I went down to level two and dug around in the DR's. I found a couple of promising books, so I jotted down the numbers and titles. I would get them through interlibrary loan. I had connections. My friend Katarina Steines was a Government Documents Librarian at the law school. Kat had helped me solve a murder. Interlibrary loan she could do in her sleep.

Browsing in the stacks is one of my secret pleasures. I still had time until I was to meet Vince, so I moved from shelf to shelf, reading random titles and letting my mind drift. If something caught my eye, I'd pull it out and read a bit. I was at the end of an aisle when I saw a plaque on the wall. I smiled. Saint Louis University wasn't immune to the plaque proliferation. At my law school, they sprouted like weeds on just about every surface. I guess it took more than the Busch family to maintain Anheuser-Busch Hall.

The plaque stated that this floor of the library was dedicated to the memory of Eunice Smith Wayman. The money came from one William A. Wayman. Wayman. I turned the name over in my mind. I knew someone with that name, but couldn't place it at the moment. The plaque looked original to the building, which seemed to have been built in the 1980's.

Did these Waymans still have money, or had the intervening years been unkind to them? If they had money, I bet they knew the Paperellis. Probably the Paperellis had plaques all over Saint Louis University as well. It was James' alma mater. I would have to look when I walked around campus. His family was likely terrified that one day my name might appear on one of those – the Mrs. behind the Mr. James Paperelli.

I froze at the direction my thoughts had taken. When did I get thinking about marriage? We'd only been dating a short time. The L-word was still hanging there uncomfortably, spoken once but not repeated. Yet I had a vision of myself in white, walking on my father's arm. James stood at an altar in his tuxedo, smiling at me. The image was so intense, I started to hyperventilate right there in the stacks. I shook my head back and forth trying to shake some sense into my addled brain.

James didn't exactly have the best track record with engagements. He certainly wouldn't jump into another after he'd just escaped the last. And I wasn't really in the market for a husband at twenty-five. I'd barely even dated. But the picture was so seductive that I couldn't entirely talk it away. It hovered like a ghost in the back of my mind and reappeared no matter how many times I tried to banish it. In my heart of hearts, I knew what answer I'd give him if he asked me tomorrow. Pathetic. That's exactly what I was.

I pulled myself together enough to make my appointment with Vince. I spent the dreaded moment in the doorway of the coffee shop trying to fix on some identifying detail, but then I recognized his thick dark hair. He'd grown it out a little, so I could see the wave. He looked up as I approached the table, giving me the smile that confirmed his identity. "Liz!" he said, obviously happy to see me.

"Where's my muffin?" I said.

"You're just here for food?"

"Why else?"

"To listen to me complain."

I shook my head. "I'm going away if I get much more of that."

"I promise. Nothing but sweetness."

I sat down. "The coffee and muffin you're buying me right now?"

"Sweet enough. What do you want?"

I squinted up at the board, which was covered with chalk scrawl.

"A latte would be fine. And," I scanned the list of food items, "could I go out on a limb and ask for a scone?"

"That might be pressing your luck."

"You're terribly cheap – you know that?"

"Cut me some slack. I'm putting myself through law school."

"Don't give me the poor law student routine. I invented it," I replied.

"Okay. One latte and one scone. But that's it. Cinnamon or lemon poppy seed?"

"Surprise me."

"A risk taker?"

"That's me – living life on the edge."

He walked over to the counter and put in our order. He was dressed casually and it suited him. He wasn't bad looking. Shorter and stockier than James, but really, who wasn't? He had that thick hair, dense as a fine Turkish carpet, and warm eyes the color of rich chocolate. Although he claimed to be pasty from all of the studying, his skin was a lovely shade of caramel, a color my pale skin could never hope to achieve. I hoped Vince would find someone who would be good to him. He deserved it.

He sat down again. "What's new with you?"

"Aside from the bombing?"

"I guess so, but that seems to be the elephant in the room."

"Do you know how Mr. Thornton is doing? The newspapers haven't been very specific."

"Word around the office is that they had to amputate part of his arm."

I nodded, and he looked at me questioningly. "I'm not surprised that they had to amputate," I said.

"Got it. Rumor has it that he's going to be in the hospital a long time – that he might have a serious head injury as well as a bunch of broken bones. No one I know has seen him, though."

"I assume that the firm is still pretty nervous about it."

"One attorney actually resigned. I think he was planning to go anyway, but just moved up the date up. Still, the office is tense."

"It just seems unreal. Arthur Thornton was such an unlikely target," I said.

"That's what has everyone so spooked. I mean, you have a guy who's so ordinary and methodical that he parked in the same space every day. Ate the same lunch every day. Lived in the same house for twenty years and all of a sudden someone wants to blow him up? Who's next?"

"Maybe he had a secret life? A life that brought him into contact with dangerous people?" I said.

"I can't imagine that. He didn't seem the type."

I heard them calling out my order, so I started up. Vince held up his hand. "No. I'll get it." He came back with two café lattes and two cinnamon scones.

"Copycat," I said, taking one of each.

"It sounded good." He sat down. "Let's get off the bombing – it's too depressing. What else have you been up to?"

"I'm working at a Clinic this semester. It's like a practicum. This one focuses on women and children in crisis. We get assigned as GALs for contested cases."

"Sounds interesting." He took a sip of coffee.

"It turns you off marriage and children, that's for sure." Okay. Not strictly true in my case, but I wasn't going to mention that to Vince.

"Bad situations?"

I nodded. "I'm working a case with my friend Amelia where the mother doesn't speak English and the father seems to be addicted to meth. I'm not sure what to tell the judge about the kids."

"Where is the mom from?"

"Kosovo. She met the husband over there. He was in the Guard until two or three years ago. She's frightened, and he seems alternately controlling or out of it. I haven't had much luck getting information from her, and something tells me that it's not just the language problem. That's why I'm here, searching for books that might help me understand her better."

Vince looked thoughtful a moment, then he said, "Does she have a green card yet, or is it still somewhere in process?"

"I never thought to ask. Do you think she's here illegally?"

"Maybe. Maybe not. But he could be holding that over her. She can do a VAWA petition if there is abuse."

"A VAWA petition?"

"The Violence Against Women Act. There are ways to get a green card if the citizen spouse is abusive and won't file the paperwork."

"How do you know these things?"

"I help with an immigration project through Catholic Charities."

"Do you know someone I could talk to?"

"Sister Rita would be a good start. Here." He grabbed a napkin and jotted down a phone number. "She'll be able to tell you if they can help or not."

"Thanks Vince. You always surprise me."

"Catholic Charities helped my family a lot when we first got to the US, so I do what I can."

"You're a good person."

He shook his head, not wanting to discuss his finer points. The conversation lulled. We drank our coffee, while I searched for another topic. I wasn't coming up with much, so I said, "I saw that new building on Spring for the Aquinas Institute. When did that open? I could have sworn that wasn't there the last time I came to SLU."

"In January. It's very nice – much better than their old space."

"It provides theological training, right?"

"For seminarians and lay people. I'm taking a class there. I did some work with the Spiritual Exercises in college and decided I should probably get back into faith coursework."

"Exercises?"

"The Father Ignatius Exercises."

"You're speaking to a Methodist here."

"Right. I forget that not everyone in this town is Catholic."

"Or Jewish. You can't forget that. Protestants seem to be the minority."

"Okay. Let me back up. The founder of the Jesuit Order was Father Ignatius of Loyola. He developed a series of spiritual exercises. I worked through most of them in a modified form when I was an undergrad here. It was really good for me – got me to reconnect with my faith, to take it seriously and live the way I'm supposed to live." He looked at me intently and started to say something, but stopped.

"Anyway," he continued. "So, now that I'm seeing the light at the end of the tunnel with law school, I thought it might be good to start taking some classes again."

I wasn't sure how to respond to a profession of such sincere devotion, so I said, "I'd forgotten that you went to SLU as an undergrad."

"Yeah, I'm really going to have to donate as a double alum."

"Me too. Wash U will have me on speed dial for the rest of my days."

We sat for a moment, eating our scones. I have to say that I was very impressed. The scone had a smooth buttery consistency. I took another bite, analyzing the taste to see if I could approximate it at home. Real vanilla and real butter.

Then I realized that we had been silent for too long again. I said, "So what else am I missing in not being Catholic in St. Louis?" I extended my fingers one by one, counting them off. "You have Catholic Charities that does all sorts of work I knew nothing about. You have the Aquinas Institute that helps people, even a lowly law student, lead a more spiritually fulfilled life. What else?"

"There's a hidden world, Liz."

"No, I'm serious —"

"So am I. There are a huge number of service organizations and Catholic-oriented legal societies. If I wanted to do nothing but pro bono legal work, I would have a full time job. Of course, I couldn't pay my loans."

"There goes your halo."

"Most lawyers don't qualify for halos anyway."

"I've met some good ones."

"Janice?" he said.

"Of course. And a couple of divorce attorneys I've worked with lately. Brian Kepple comes to mind. He's with your firm, isn't he?"

Vince nodded. "Brian's a nice guy. That's why he does so well with women in messy divorces."

"He's representing the wife in another case I'm involved with. Two accountants in Clayton. Joint practice, kids, everything. Husband was stepping out with a friend of the wife. It's incredibly nasty, but Brian has been wonderful to work with."

"He's very calm."

"A consummate professional. Even when the husband's attorney is grandstanding in front of the judge."

"Who is he?"

"Reginald Butler."

"Oh."

"That was my reaction too."

Reginald Butler was probably the most noticeable and flamboyant of Washington University's alumni. He'd donated so much money to the law school over the years that you couldn't turn around without seeing his name on a plaque. In person, he was a large man with a big booming voice and a flair for the dramatic. He was always immaculately and elegantly dressed, but in a way that was sure to demonstrate how much his suit cost. In court, he wore highly starched shirts with stiff collar points and French cuffs. His cufflinks were amazing. My favorite pair was a set of gold disks, with a "B" picked out in diamonds on the face.

Reginald Butler's law practice consisted almost entirely of representing St. Louis' elite husbands in their marital disputes. I heard that if there was a mistress on the side and assets to hide, he was your man. I found out later that he'd been John Harding's attorney. Surprise. Surprise.

Vince smiled. "Butler is an alum of Aquinas too. Did you know that?"

"I'm a little skeptical of his spiritual growth. And, no, I didn't know it. I'm a heretic. You must keep that in mind."

"Not a bad heretic."

"You've caught me on a good day."

"The halo isn't lost yet?"

"I don't have one to lose."

"We can't all be perfect."

"Like you?"

"My mom thinks so," he said ruefully.

"She would. How's the graduation party planning going?" We only had another month and a half to go. Vince still lived at home – in part to save money and in part because his mother couldn't let him go.

"It will be the party to end all parties. You should be getting an invite in a couple of weeks. It's going to be Colombian-style."

"What does that mean?"

"It starts at night and goes until the next day."

"Wow. Drinking?"

"And eating and dancing. You're kind of tired afterwards."

"Dancing?"

"It wouldn't be a party without dancing."

"I didn't know you knew how to dance." Not being the best dancer myself, I'd never actually considered the point before.

"Of course I can dance. I'm Colombian." He said this like it was too obvious to discuss.

"Sorry. I'm a heretic and a gringa. I thought I made that clear."

"I won't hold it against you. You have to come, even if you are the worst dancer ever." He paused. "You and James."

"I anxiously await the invitation. I might even see what I can do about the dancing since it sounds like it's an integral part of the ritual."

"I can teach you," he said eagerly. Then, after a moment's hesitation, "Unless James has a problem with that."

I thought about the sexy Latin dancing I'd watched on television. But this wasn't like that at all. Vince was my friend. "He won't have a problem."

Vince smiled. "I would if I were him."

I wasn't sure how to take that so I gathered up my things. "I should be going. Send me an email about the next coffee, okay?"

He gave me a very proper friend-like hug and followed me to my car to make sure I got off safely. He was a true gentleman.

CHAPTER 8

I left a couple of voicemail messages for Sister Rita before she finally called me back. I explained the situation and told her that Vince had recommended I contact her. At the mere mention of his name, she suddenly became warm and effusive. He was like a beloved son. After we mutually sang his praises – I wasn't going to argue – she asked me precise and detailed questions about Elsa Stimpkin. Then she gave me a list of questions to ask to determine what Elsa's current immigration status might be. Finally, she told me to call her if it looked like she might be able to do anything with the case. I thanked her profusely.

"Anything for a friend of Vince's," she replied.

So, it was with a spring in my step that I met up with Amelia in the Clinic offices. Amelia Carson and I met in Contracts – my very first class of my first day of law school. Every lawyer I've met believes that they were taught by the model for the tyrannical law professor in the movie, *The Paper Chase*. My nominee for that honor was my professor for Contracts. He fired seemingly random questions like missiles into our midst, enjoying the terror that gripped every one of us.

I got there early that first day and took the open seat next to Amelia. We introduced ourselves. In the few minutes before class, I found out that she was from Charleston, South Carolina, which

I had already guessed because of the soft lilt of her voice and the impeccable application of her makeup. She told me that her father was in business, selling boats and other watercraft, and her mother taught kindergarten. Amelia had an older brother in the Air Force and two younger sisters in college and high school, respectively.

Then the professor cleared his throat and we hushed. What happened next continues to be a topic of conversation between us. It sealed our friendship from that point forward. The professor, seeing a likely victim, called on Amelia to state the issue of the first case. Amelia read what she thought was the issue directly from the case brief she had dutifully prepared. The professor frowned, clearly not satisfied. He asked her to state it again. She scrambled, unsure of what he wanted, and came up with a slight variation on her first answer.

The professor continued to frown. I could feel the other students getting restless – shifting in their seats with nervous energy. Amelia scrolled frantically through the notes on her laptop and tried a third time. Still no luck. By this point, no amount of makeup could conceal the red flush that spread across her face. She was so flustered that she couldn't think straight. Every eye was on her, watching the train wreck in process. I'd figured out what the professor wanted by the second frown, and feeling her desperation, scribbled my answer on a slip of paper torn from my legal pad. I passed it to her ever so carefully. She glanced down, saw what I wrote, and seeming to read from her notes, recited my statement of the issue.

The professor's face lit up. "Very good Miss Carson. Read that again so everyone can hear." Then, with a twinkle in his eye, he was on to his next victim. The cycle of hemming and hawing started up again. Amelia turned to me with a look of gratitude that I will never forget.

After that trial by fire, we sat together whenever we could and met after class as well. Although, given our overload of work, anything beyond study group seemed impossible most days. Amelia was also reserved in a way I wasn't used to with Holly. Despite Amelia's Southern poise and the vivaciousness that she exhibited under certain circumstances, she was fundamentally shy, and our friendship deepened slowly over the three years of law school. I now counted her as one of my best friends even though our hectic schedules still limited our ability to hang out in non-law settings.

I never told her my secret, however, because face blindness did not pose a problem when I had to pick her out of a crowd. Her Southern attention to grooming – she always wore tasteful makeup, brushed her chestnut hair in the same neat style and polished her squared nails shell pink – made her stand out.

She also dressed up more than most law students. While the rest of us spent our days in saggy jeans and tee shirts, Amelia favored dress slacks and a twinset, or in a pinch, a nice blouse with dark jeans. For special occasions, she had a variety of suits and tailored dresses. When I asked her why she took such trouble when we were only going to class, she smiled and said, "Why would I leave the house looking bad?" I guess she had a point.

Consequently, she was the only one of my fellow law students who did not have to buy a whole new wardrobe when she landed the summer associate position at a big firm. She worked for two summers with Baxter, Edison and Ripley. Unlike me, a dead body had not dissuaded her from a big firm career. She was set to join them after graduation.

Despite all of this poise and organization, Amelia suffered from a fatal affliction. She had the stamp of spinsterhood on her forehead. As unlikely as it sounded, she had never had a real boyfriend. She dated, she said, but nothing stuck. Could every man she met be blind to the lovely, intelligent woman he was face to face with? Her shyness couldn't be the only factor, I thought. I had seen her switch on the charm with men she knew from school. She could be fun and flirtatious. Still, none of those men asked her out. She was always sunny and positive, though, and let me bend her ear about James without any obvious resentment.

Amelia was in her usual good mood when we sat down to compare notes and talk about what to do with the Stimpkins. I showed her the notes I had taken while talking to Sister Rita.

"Sister Rita said we needed to find out if he ever filed an I-130 or an I-485 and then find out what status she had when she entered the country. Apparently, there is a 'K' visa for fiancées. They got married here, correct?"

"Yes." Amelia puzzled over the notes. "So many letters and numbers. Why don't they just call it a fiancée visa if that's what it is?"

I shrugged my shoulders. I tried to diagram the process out for her, but ended up confusing myself even more. Finally, I said, "I think we need to talk to Sister Rita again."

"Good idea."

I called, but got voicemail, so I left a message with Amelia's and my cell phone numbers. My cell phone rang almost as soon as I hit the end button. Could that be Rita so soon? Or maybe James. He'd promised to call way more often than he actually had. I didn't want to feel irritated. He was so into the bombing case that he barely slept these days. But still, how hard was a phone call now and then?

It wasn't Rita or James. It was Vince.

"Hey, I was just talking to my sister and she wants to help me teach you to dance. Do you have time tonight to come to the house for dinner?" Mayte, or May as Vince called her, also lived at home. Like my sister Ashley, she was a freshman in college. She went to Fontbonne, which was a small liberal arts college located near the Washington University campus.

"I'd love to," I said, looking over at Amelia, "but I promised to go out with my friend Amelia."

"Bring her along. There'll be more than enough food. My mom has started cooking already."

I'd never been to Vince's house, so the prospect was too tempting. "Hold on a minute and I'll ask her." I put my hand over the end of the phone. "How about Latin dance lessons and dinner at my friend Vince's house?"

Amelia whispered. "Is he single?"

I nodded. She gave me the thumbs up.

"You're on," I said into the phone. "What time? What can I bring?"

"7:00. Don't bring anything."

Sister Rita still had not gotten back to me by the time we left for Vince's house, so we tabled that discussion. Instead, I told Amelia everything I knew about Vince and his family as we drove over in my car. The Lopez family lived in a ranch-style house in Creve Coeur on a winding road off of Lindbergh Boulevard. Creve Coeur is a sprawling suburb in St. Louis County. Vince told me that his parents had scrimped and saved to buy it in the mid 1990's after years of living in a very small apartment. For Vince and his sisters, the house meant that they could finally invite friends over without embarrassment. Vince moved off of a sofa bed into his own bedroom. The one thing that the move did not change was school. Vince's parents selected that apartment because it was located in one of the best school districts in the area, Ladue. They refused to buy a house until they could afford one in the same district.

I thought about this as we pulled into the neighborhood. I'd lived in St. Louis long enough to know that where you went to high school was very important. And Ladue schools meant money. Lots of it. James told me that his parents owned a house in the heart of Ladue. That undoubtedly meant their house cost multiple millions of dollars. Minimum. As I looked at the nice but not extravagant ranch homes around me, I chuckled. The Lopez family had sneaked into the exclusive enclave inhabited by people like the Paperellis. Good for them.

Vince's house sat on a corner lot on the top of a gentle hill. The lot sloped down in front and on one side so that part of the basement level was above ground. It was a long lean house with very large windows – a more elegant version of my own home in Marshfield. I liked it immediately.

We pulled up the driveway and parked next to the garage door. As we got out of the car, I saw Vince open the front door. The hair was unmistakable. "Come in," he called.

Amelia turned to me and said in a whisper, "You should have told me he was that cute. I'm not dressed for this."

I looked at her – all perfectly groomed and presentable in a tailored black dress and heels. How much more effort did she need to put into it?

Vince reached us and I made the introduction. There was a woman behind him with long black hair. She elbowed Vince playfully out of the way. "Let me meet the famous Liz. I'm May." I put my hand out, but she grabbed my arm and pulled me into a hug instead. "I've heard so much about you."

I pulled back and introduced her to Amelia.

"Vince wants me to teach you two how to dance, but we can't do anything until we eat. Come on. *Pasa. Pasa.*" May dragged Amelia away.

"Sorry. She's a force of nature," Vince said to me in a low voice.

"She's delightful."

"Not if you live with her."

"She just has you wrapped around her little finger," I said.

"More than one finger. We need to hurry or she will completely overwhelm your friend."

"Amelia can handle herself."

"She seems capable."

"Amelia is more than that. You'll like her when you get to know her. I promise."

"No doubt." He opened the door for me to enter.

"The rice!" I said. The house was redolent with the aroma of delicious food, but underneath the various scents, I recognized the smell of savory cooked rice that impregnated Vince's clothes.

Vince laughed. "Now you know the source. Actually it's rice with chopped noodles mixed in. My mom calls it Arab rice."

I gave him a questioning look.

"My mom's from Barranquilla – on the coast of Colombia – but that side of the family came from Palestine."

"It smells wonderful. Is that plantain?"

He nodded. "*Patacones.* Just a bit of home cooking. My mom does most of it, but my sister and I help out when we can."

"And this evening?"

"My dad grilled the steaks. May and I weren't much help."

"Your mom has her hands full."

"It's just so much better when she does it."

"An honest answer. How about another? Am I going to be able to handle the spice level? I'm not sure I'm in the mood for a chemical burn."

"My mom's food isn't spicy."

"But I thought you mainlined Tabasco sauce?" Vince had admitted his addiction to the stuff on our one and only date.

"That's just me. I told you – I'm not normal."

"Oh good."

Vince smiled and opened the door to the kitchen. "Mama, this is Liz."

I have often noted that some of the best cooks prepare food in the worst kitchens. Mrs. Lopez was certainly one of those. She stood busily frying the plantains on a stove that likely predated my birth. The kitchen was dark in that brick and black oak way that only people in the 1970's thought was attractive. The hood of the stove, which hovered over the cave-like enclosure, would have smacked anyone of normal height in the eye. Who had the builders designed this house for? Gnomes?

Fortunately, Mrs. Lopez was tiny. She gave the plantains another expert flip with the spatula and then turned around, wiping her hands on her apron. She had short dark hair and Vince's large brown eyes. I extended my hand and she took it in both of hers. Mine was easily twice the size. "So glad you could come," she said.

"Thank you so much for inviting us." I took a quick look around. Amelia had disappeared completely. May must have carried her off. "Everything smells delicious," I said.

"Vince said you would want to try some Colombian food. Do you cook?"

"Yes," I said. She seemed pleased with that answer. "But nothing fancy. I do more baking now – when I get the chance. That reminds me. I left the rhubarb bars in the car."

My mom, as usual, had sent me enough rhubarb in the fall to last me to the end of my days. I'd whipped up some bars to bring with me because I never took the "don't bring anything" instructions very seriously. I excused myself and walked back out.

I got the Tupperware container from the car and tucked it awkwardly under my arm. Then I heard the muffled ring of my cell phone as I slammed the car door shut. I managed to dig the phone out of my pocket without dropping the bars, but forgot to see who it was before I answered.

"Hello?"

"I'm sorry I haven't called —"

"James!" I almost dropped the bars again. "It's good to hear your voice."

"Don't make it sound like an eternity. I feel bad enough."

"I miss you."

"So what are you up to this evening?" His voice was seductively tender.

"Well, I'm over at Vince's house. His sister said she'd teach Amelia and me to dance *salsa* and then Vince's mom made Colombian food so we're eating and —" This wasn't coming out smoothly. I started to feel uneasy.

"Why the sudden interest in Latin dance?"

"The graduation party." When I'd told James about the party, he had seemed indifferent. Was he now going to claim that he couldn't remember? "I don't want to look like an idiot."

"You won't look like an idiot," he said dismissively.

I didn't respond. What did he know about social awkwardness? He'd certainly never been a wallflower.

"Well," he said after a moment, "I guess I'll postpone my plans since your social calendar filled up so fast."

The sarcastic tone was not appreciated. I responded as evenly as I could. "You can't not call me for days and then expect me to drop everything when you do. It's not fair."

I heard the front door open behind me, and footsteps. I could tell by the walk that it was Vince. "Liz? Are you okay?" he said.

I turned around and showed him that I was on the cell phone. I handed him the rhubarb bars.

"I'll take these in," he said quietly and then turned to go back in the house.

"Is that Vince?" James said. His voice had a steely edge to it.

"Yes. I just gave him the bars I made for dessert."

James stayed quiet on the other end of the line. I waited. Finally I said, "I'm going to have to go back in. I'm missing dinner."

"Fine. I'll call you later." He hung up.

I sighed and walked slowly to the door.

The dinner was as delicious as it smelled, and the family's easy banter reminded me of my own. I quizzed Vince's mom as politely as I could about the preparation of each and every dish. That seemed to go over well. One cook can always talk to another. I found Amelia looking at Vince when she thought he wasn't looking and wondered what he thought of her. He did look back once or twice.

The rhubarb bars emerged at the end of the meal along with a delicious flan and the strongest coffee I had ever had. Fortunately for my reputation, the bars came out perfectly. No one present had ever had one before, but I saw Vince reach for his fourth just as May announced that she was ready to start the lessons.

She led the way to the basement, which was basically one long room with a smooth tile floor. Despite the gnome kitchen, the architect had managed to build this basement without a single pole or pillar anywhere. With the furniture pushed to the side, it was the perfect dance floor. May went to the stereo sitting on a table on one end and started to pull out CDs. She popped one in and the lesson began.

Salsa, mergengue, and *cumbia* depend heavily on weight shifts from the ball of the foot to the heel and from side to side. They also require a stiff torso and loose hips. Finally, you have to count the on and off beats of the syncopation and move your body in time. Even with the dedicated assistance of May and Vince, these key points took me all night. Amelia seemed to have it down in fifteen minutes.

"Where did you learn to dance?" I asked her. Vince had wandered over to help May pick out more music on the other side of the room.

"I had to do Cotillion. You never forget that."

"What?"

"Cotillion. You know, debutante stuff."

"You danced *salsa* as a debutante?"

She gave me an exasperated look. "No silly, but they make you take ballroom. This really isn't any different."

"You took ballroom dancing lessons?" Was Charleston trapped in a time warp?

She rolled her eyes. "Trust me. We all do it. Of course my mom would be horrified to know what I'm doing with my Cotillion training."

"This is hardly sinful."

"It will be if I can work it." She looked over at Vince.

Well. Well.

Vince and May finally decided on a CD, an up-tempo rock-infused number. They came towards us. Vince said, "Liz, do you want to dance this one with me?"

"Sure."

He put his arm around my waist and clasped my other hand. He was trying to move slowly enough for me to follow. I concentrated on not grinding his toe into the ground with my foot. After a minute he said, "Not bad."

"I'm not Amelia, but I guess I'm okay for a Wisconsin girl."

"Excellent for a Wisconsin girl. See, you can even talk while you dance."

We danced some more and he felt confident enough in my abilities to give me a spin out and back.

"I like this song," I said as we came back together.

"It was a big hit worldwide."

"Who does it?"

"Juanes. He's one of our own."

"Colombian?"

"Yes. It's called '*A Dios le Pido*.'"

"I Ask God?" My high school Spanish was coming back to me.

"Very good." He swung me out and brought me back.

"That's an odd title."

"It's about asking God for all of the good things in life, for another minute to enjoy love and family."

"Songs in Spanish are so much more – sweet."

"You can say things in Spanish that you can't in English."

"They sound better too. Everything rhymes. English is such a mish mash of things that songwriters struggle."

"You should try learning to spell English after learning Spanish."

"Nothing is spelled as it sounds," I agreed.

The song wound down. "See," Vince said, still holding my hand. "That wasn't too hard."

I detached my fingers from his. "Just keep me talking and I'm fine."

May went over to the stereo to change the music. She pulled the CD out of the machine and put it back in its jewel box. I took it from her and studied the cover. The album was called *Un Día Normal*. I would have liked to listen to the rest of it.

I heard Vince approach me from behind. "I'll make you a copy if you want," he said.

"Thanks. You've read my mind."

"It's not hard."

"Now what does that imply?"

"I know you pretty well," he said softly.

I felt myself starting to blush. Time for evasive measures. I turned to May. "Would you mind showing me the *cumbia* again? I don't know if I really have it. And what was that other, *vallenato*?"

"Sure. I was actually looking for something by Carlos Vives – I'm tired of Juanes. That song's been played to death." She paused, looking through the stack of CDs on the table. "Here it is!" She slid another disc in the machine.

May walked me through the dance one more time. Out of the corner of my eye, I saw Vince dancing with Amelia. She was considerably closer to him than I had been. They moved well together. She had that look I had seen before. The switch was definitely on.

CHAPTER 9

We'd hit midnight by the time we got to my car. I checked my cell phone. No calls. Had I driven James away? Yet how could he expect me to have no life without him? Okay, it was not much of one before him, but still. I wouldn't jump every time he said jump, although part of me wanted to. I couldn't escape pathetic.

We were half way home when Amelia got a call on her cell phone.

"Hello? Oh, Elsa. Thanks for calling back." She paused and then said, "Wait. Wait. I don't understand." Another long pause. "Where are you? Okay. Okay. Stay where you are. We're coming." She held the phone down. "Can I have your cell?" Her voice shook.

"What happened?"

"Elsa. She's in trouble. I've got her on the other line, but I need to call 911. Pull over where you can."

I pulled into an empty parking lot, hoping I hadn't hit one of the cell phone dead zones that Ladue seemed to have. I got the cell out and looked at it. Service. Thank goodness. "Here." I handed it to Amelia and took hers in exchange. "What's going on?"

"I'll explain in a moment." She took my phone and dialed. When someone picked up, she said, "Hello, I need someone to call the police. I just got a call from Elsa Stimpkin, and from what I can gather, her husband has been holding her at gunpoint for the last two days. She just got out of the house, but her kids are still there."

She gave the dispatcher the address. "Yes. I've got her on my other phone. She's at the neighbor's house. Yes. I'm not sure who they've called, but I wanted to make sure someone got out there. So you'll coordinate? Yes. Thank you." We traded phones again and she told Elsa we'd be right there.

"Step on it," she said.

We got to Elsa's house in record time. Fortunately, the police had already arrived. Elsa clung to us and sobbed uncontrollably. In fact, I could barely peel her off long enough to call Gwen. Gwen told me to stay put. She would get there as soon as she could.

I hesitated a moment before I called James. I was still unsettled about the whole Vince issue, and I knew that he couldn't do anything. But he was the only person who would really understand.

His phone rang and rang. I almost hung up when it went to voicemail, but then I heard a beep and a groggy voice said, "Hello?"

"James," I said, relieved and nervous. "I'm sorry to wake you up but you're never going to believe what's happening —"

"Liz." Did he sound relieved? Angry? I couldn't tell.

"I'm at a house in Jefferson County." Out the window I saw a new group arrive. "They've just sent the SWAT team."

"What?" He sounded panicked now. I summarized the evening's activities. "Just stay where you are. I'm coming," he said.

The next hour was a blur. The SWAT team brought along a hostage negotiator to try and reason with Andrew Stimpkin. I heard from one of the police officers that they thought Andrew was high on something. His irrational ranting didn't lend itself to meaningful negotiation. With the children inside, the situation was extremely delicate. The police cleared several houses on either side, and we stood beyond the cordon in the street waiting for Gwen.

Gwen finally arrived, all nervous energy and jangling earrings, and took control of the situation. Elsa sat like a pale rag doll on the curb. Nothing we could do or say was going to really help her. Nonetheless, we went into action, lining up a place to stay and any other arrangements we thought might be useful. Assuming, of course, that the children got out of this alive. That was a big if.

Gwen and I were in the middle of discussing what I'd gleaned from Sister Rita – Gwen understood it better than I did – when I heard some familiar footsteps. I stopped talking and spun around. "James!" I was so happy to see him that I literally ran and threw my arms around his neck.

He released me quickly. "Let me find out what's going on." He walked off towards a group of officers who were on the lawn of the neighbor's house. Talking with them, he assumed that indefinable mantle of police authority. You could tell it from the way he stood. After twenty minutes, he came back, stopping to speak briefly with Gwen. Then he said to me, "We have to leave. The SWAT team will go in if the negotiations keep heading in the same direction. And they're worried he might have explosives. No one is safe out here. I'm going to follow you and Amelia home and Gwen will take Elsa to the hotel."

It took Gwen, Amelia, James and me twenty minutes of talking and cajoling to get Elsa to leave. Finally, we loaded her in Gwen's car and Gwen drove away. James followed me out. I dropped Amelia off at her apartment and headed for home. I pulled up in front of my apartment and James pulled in behind me. We got out and stood on the sidewalk facing each other.

"Are you coming in?" I finally asked.

"I'm not leaving you alone tonight."

"Thank goodness for that." I shivered.

He put his arms around me. "I – I overreacted and – sorry."

I nodded and hugged him back. When we got inside, I was still so agitated that I couldn't do more than pace back and forth. James stopped me on the seventh pass across the living room and forced me to sit down on the sofa. "I'll make you a cup of tea."

"It's just that I can't stop thinking about the kids. God, what if he hurts them?"

"I know," James said from the kitchen. I heard him fill the kettle with water and then put it on the burner. "But there is nothing you can do right now. They have one of the best hostage negotiators on the scene. If he can't do it, no one can. We just have to be patient."

I drummed my fingers on the arm of the sofa. I couldn't stand it. I got up and walked to the kitchen. James put his arm around my shoulder. I felt a little better. We stood side-by-side, watching the kettle heat up in silence. When it whistled, he turned off the burner and filled two mugs with steaming water. He handed one to me. I moved the tea bag up and down, watching the brown liquid disperse.

"You know what's funny?" James said.

"What?" Nothing seemed very amusing at the moment.

"I could have taught you to dance if I'd known you wanted to learn."

He'd caught me totally off guard. "What? *Salsa?*"

"Yes. Well, I'm sure I'm not as good as Vince – he's Colombian. But I could have managed."

"Where did you learn? Don't tell me you had to do Cotillion, too?"

"Cotillion? No. My high school girlfriend was from Peru."

"How did you meet her?"

"She was an exchange student at Mary Institute." He saw my questioning look. "That merged with Country Day. It's now MICDS."

"Oh." Another high-end private high school in this town. My family in Marshfield would be was amazed at how the other half lived.

"She taught me everything I needed to know."

"I'm sure she did," I said dryly. "What happened to her?"

"She went back to Peru. We still keep in touch every now and then. She married a businessman in Lima. They have two kids. She seems to be doing well."

"What's her name?" I couldn't resist indulging my overwhelming curiosity.

"Lourdes." Then he looked at me speculatively. "You don't have to worry about the other women I've dated. I hope you know that."

I nodded. "You don't have to fear my past, either." Not that there was much to fear.

"I don't know why Vince gets under my skin."

"He's a good friend. He's moved on."

"I'm not sure how he can move on so easily." James smiled at me with that sweet tender smile that made my knees give out.

I set my mug down, wrapped my arms around his waist, and laid my head against his chest. I could hear the low thump, thump of his heart. I closed my eyes and took a deep breath. His warmth. The delicious smell of his skin. I felt my pulse start to race. I could have stayed like that forever.

"We should sit down," he said after a moment. "It's going to be a long night."

"Hmm," I replied, not moving.

I felt him rub my back, and I opened my eyes. He had the two mugs by the handle in his other hand. "Come on. Let's sit on the couch." He sat down and tucked me in beside him. Then he handed me my tea. "Drink this. You'll feel better, I promise."

I obediently took a sip. The warm liquid slid down my throat.

"Better?"

I nodded. "I'm sorry to be so much trouble."

"No trouble. I'm amazed at what you can handle."

"Not as well as you."

"Unfortunately, you get used to it." His eyes had a distant look to them. Some far-off memory. I had my suspicions.

"Why did you become a police officer? I know what you've told me is not the whole story."

"It's a long story." He sounded incredibly tired.

"We have time. Unless it's too painful to talk about."

He took a sip of tea and when he spoke, he kept his voice even. "A friend of mine was murdered in front of my eyes and I've never really gotten over it."

"Oh, dear!" I waited for him to say more, but he didn't for several minutes. I drank my tea and wondered if I should change the subject.

"I met Alex in college," he said at last. "We just clicked, you know? He was my best friend. It was senior year, right before graduation.

May 5th to be exact. We were going to meet some friends and go drinking for Cinco de Mayo. Someone suggested a hole in the wall place in the city. I don't even remember the name now or where it was supposed to be."

He stopped for a moment and pressed his fingers into the bridge of his nose. I could see that this was hard. Very hard. I waited patiently while he took a deep breath and settled himself.

"Anyway, Alex had just gotten a new Range Rover from his parents as a graduation present. He wanted to drive it around. In hindsight, that was not a smart idea, but we weren't thinking. I rode with him. I remember that we rolled the windows down because it was hot and Alex thought it looked better. Cooler. The music was on full blast. Alex loved Pink Floyd and that song, 'Money, Money' was playing. So ironic." He took another gulp of tea.

"We got lost trying to find the place, and Alex drove onto a side street to turn around. We pulled up to a stop sign, and I heard running footsteps and then a crackling – like an engine sputtering."

"Alex slumped into my side. He was making a terrible rattling sound. I didn't know what was happening. I leaned my head down to check him and felt a searing burn on my ear. Then I knew. Those were bullets. I fumbled with my seat belt and managed to push the passenger door open. I fell onto the road as the car rolled slowly away from me. I scrambled up and ran away as fast as I could. I think they tried to shoot after me, but I didn't look back. It was that damn car. They killed Alex for a stupid car."

"What did you do?"

"I ran until I found someone and got them to call the police. By the time the police got to the intersection, Alex's body was thrown down in the road. The car was gone. They told me later that the bullet killed him within thirty seconds, but that was long enough. I know he suffered. And I left him. I left him! I ran away like a fucking coward."

"You would be dead otherwise." I reached up and touched the nick on his left ear.

"That doesn't ease my conscience."

"Did they ever catch the carjackers?"

"Yes. One was fourteen, the other eighteen. Stolen gun, of course. It was senseless. Completely senseless. They are both still in prison. The fourteen-year-old was tried as an adult, or he would have been out long ago."

I looked down. The teenagers running toward the car must have been what spooked him at the mall. "And so you went to Europe to get away?"

He nodded. "I'd been planning to work as a tech in one of the labs on campus. I thought I might do a PhD the following year, so I'd looked into a couple of programs. But after Alex died – it was all too —"

"I understand."

He smiled. "You always do."

"You're pretty predictable."

"I take it that's a good thing?"

"It is."

"You know the rest. I wandered around Europe for a year – running away again, just like that night. I thought I was on some spiritual journey, but looking back, I just had classic survivor's guilt. Alex was a better person than I'll ever be. It didn't seem fair."

"When did you decide to join the police?"

"One day I was walking along La Rambla in Barcelona, and for some reason I stopped at a flower stall. I noticed they had the most beautiful blood red roses and the smell was amazing. Heavenly. Then it hit me. The old saying about stopping to smell the roses. That's all I'd done for a year. Alex would never be able to achieve something with his life, but I could do something with mine. And what better way to atone than to stop the criminals who kill innocent people like Alex? I came back and enrolled in the Police Academy. It was one of the hardest things I've ever done."

"The other recruits didn't take to you?"

"In a word – no. I had to prove myself over and over again. Even after graduation. I got assigned to a beat, and my own partner, Kyle, tried to get me reassigned. He said I stood out so much that I made him a target. He was right, I guess, but I wouldn't acknowledge that. After I'd gotten him out of some tight situations, he trusted me and we did some good work." James grinned suddenly. "We had a great 'good cop, bad cop' routine."

"Which one were you?"

"The bad cop, of course."

"You don't seem that scary."

"In certain parts of St. Louis, I'm the devil incarnate. Kyle played the reasonable one, and I pretended to be the out of control Italian guy. You work with people's stereotypes. We'd switch roles if the situation called for it."

Like with women? I'd seen him in action with female witnesses. Namely me. He was good. Very good.

"But your heart was in homicide?" I said.

"Yes. I applied for the transfer as soon as I could. It took time and hard work, but I'm finally doing what I was meant to do." He took a sip of tea. "I see Alex in every crime scene."

"How do you do it? I was fine with John Harding, but now, I don't know. The nightmares don't seem to go away this time." Except when I was with James. Then I slept better.

"I'm not myself when I'm working. I have to turn everything off. But you should see someone if it gets bad."

"Student Health? Did you ever actually go to them? They have trouble with routine angst. How am I going to explain this?"

He pulled me a little closer. "I know people that you could see. I went to a friend of mine informally for a while after I joined the force. I still had issues."

"I'll think about it."

"Don't suffer."

We sat quietly for a minute or two. Then I said, "Have they made any headway in the investigation?"

"Not as much as we would like. Arthur Thornton seems to have led a very quiet life. There doesn't appear to be anyone who might have wanted to hurt him."

"That was Vince's impression, too."

"Vince knows him?"

"Vince's firm is in the same building. According to Vince, everyone in the building knew Arthur."

"Did Vince know he was a serious art collector?"

"He didn't mention it."

"The house is filled with paintings – floor to ceiling. He was also supposed to judge submissions for the art fair in Clayton. That's not going to happen now."

"Does Arthur have any idea who might have done this to him?"

James shook his head. "He's not in a condition to remember anything."

"I wondered about that. The blast would have thrown his head against the concrete pretty hard."

"I've been told it's also caused blindness. They don't know if it's temporary or permanent. But you didn't hear that from me."

"No." I sighed. I knew a little something about neurological damage. It wasn't pretty.

James looked at me. "On a completely different and I hope not depressing subject, when are we going to buy those jeans?"

I shrugged my shoulders. "Whenever you have a free evening."

"They let us roam out of our pen every so often. How about tomorrow night?"

"I don't know if I'll be in a mood to shop tomorrow."

Then my cell phone rang. I jumped off the couch and grabbed it from the table.

"Liz!" It was Amelia. "They got the kids out!"

"Oh, thank goodness!" The relief was so intense that I started to cry. "Did Andrew surrender?"

"Not yet. They're still trying to talk him out. But Gwen is taking Elsa to pick them up. She wants to meet with us tomorrow to figure out what to do next."

"Okay. Call me if anything else happens. I hope he surrenders without anyone getting hurt."

James was right beside me. I wiped my tears with the back of my hand.

"Let's hope Andrew Stimpkin has some sense left. Why don't you try to sleep? You'll wake up with the phone," he said.

"I'm okay. Really."

"Then I'm going to bed. I have an early morning tomorrow."

"You're leaving?"

He put an arm around my shoulder. "Not unless you want me to."

"Sleep doesn't sound so bad after all."

CHAPTER 10

Andrew Stimpkin was not smart. The standoff dragged on. I slept fitfully, expecting a call at any moment. I finally got it around 5:00 a.m. Amelia said that he had surrendered and was in police custody. Of course he'd escaped any harm. Only the good die young.

James was already up. I called to him through the bathroom door. He opened it and gave me a thumbs up as he brushed his teeth. I couldn't go back to bed if he was up, so I hauled myself to the kitchen to make some coffee. He joined me there, crisply dressed even in yesterday's clothes. I ran a hand through my rumpled hair, trying to push down a few stubborn cowlicks.

"Don't," he said smiling. "I like your hair when it curls up."

I gave him a look. "You are really strange – it never ceases to amaze me."

"I don't get to see you like this enough."

"You could spend more time with me." I tried not to sound petulant, but did not succeed, so I said, "But don't think I'm the jealous type, even if the mistress is your work. I do understand why I can't see you as much as I'd like."

"That's one of the great things about you. You don't call me ten times a day to find out when I'm getting home."

"Angie did that?"

"Among other things."

"That would have driven me crazy."

"I think I've mentioned that we fought a lot."

"But you can call me, you know, every now and then. A happy medium."

"I can do more than that." He looked me in the eye. "I've been thinking how nice it would be to see you like this every morning."

"What are you saying?"

"You could give up this apartment and move in with me."

I stared blankly at him. This was too soon, way too soon. And convenient. Despite my marriage fantasies, I was not the sort of girl who would sit at home waiting for her man. Too Tammy Wynette in a gilded cage. I felt the bars close in.

"I've caught you off guard."

"Yes," I said baldly.

He leaned down and kissed me lightly on the lips. "Just think about it."

"Wouldn't that be a little sudden? I mean, with Angie and your family?"

"I don't care whether they think it's sudden or not. It's what I want. The only question is whether it's what you want or not."

I didn't know how to answer. I wanted to believe in his sincerity. But move in? Really? And what if we weren't happy living together? I had a bunch of single girl habits that would be hard to break. I would eventually get on his nerves. Breaking up with him and moving out at the same time would be really traumatic. I didn't know if I was up to so much drama. And where would I go then?

He touched my arm and I looked at him. "When is your lease up?"

"October 1st," I said.

"You have months and months. I'm not going anywhere."

I nodded, but my head continued to spin.

Later that morning, Gwen, Amelia and I met in the Clinic offices. I'd already talked to Sister Rita. When I told her what happened, she got fired up. "I'm coming by to help y'all," she said.

She arrived just as we'd plotted out our GAL strategy and outlined the motions we would need to prepare for the judge to have the children placed in Elsa's sole custody. Sister Rita managed to look just as I pictured her in my head. A little woman with a Texas-sized personality, she had salt and pepper hair, cut short, and small round glasses that magnified her dark, intelligent eyes. She was casually dressed in jeans and a fitted shirt, with the only sign of her calling a simple gold band that she twisted around and around her finger as she spoke.

I made the introductions, and we walked her through the discussion so far. At the end of it, she said, "Well chickies, I think we have it down, right and tight. I'm going to get the green card bit together as fast as I can. I need to meet Miss Elsa as soon as possible."

Gwen offered to make all of the arrangements, and she and Sister Rita exchanged contact information. The meeting broke up. I walked with Sister Rita out to her car, a beat-up gray Camry.

"Thank you again for all of your help," I said.

"It's nothing. If this case doesn't fly, you can slap me upside the head. I probably wouldn't have to file anything, just send the USCIS the police report, and we'd be good to go."

"Thank goodness no one was hurt."

"Makes me glad I'm a nun." She opened the car door and got behind the wheel. "Say hi to Señor Vicente for me, will you? Tell him not to be a stranger."

"I will."

"Now if every guy were Vince —" She didn't finish the thought, but instead turned the key and shut the door.

The judge in Jefferson County ordered an emergency hearing in light of the new developments. He sustained our motions for the assignment of custody. There was no argument. Andrew did not have a lawyer and wasn't in a position to protest. Gwen took Elsa back to the hotel. Amelia and I decided to grab lunch before heading back into the city. There was a sandwich place near the courthouse.

We sat down and stared at each other, too tired for once to even talk.

"What a day," I finally said.

"And it started out so well."

I raised my eyebrows.

"Vince," she said. "But that was technically yesterday, so maybe it doesn't count."

"You've already impressed him with your moves. It shouldn't be too hard."

"He's still interested in you."

"We're just friends."

"That means I have a window of opportunity. It doesn't mean he'll respond."

"I've watched you in action. You can charm the pants off anyone."

She looked at me with a twinkle in her eye. "I haven't been able to do that so far."

"Poor choice of words."

"Right words. That's the problem."

I wrinkled my nose. "I understand completely. Before James, I had years and years of no one." I thought a moment about college. "Well, a couple of very bad ideas, and then no one."

She sighed. "Men."

"Men," I said. Then my cell phone rang. I looked at the number, hoping it might be James. It was Holly.

"Holly, what's up?" I heard sniffing and then a sob. "Holly?" More sobs. "What's wrong? Are you okay?"

"Ben," she said, and then sniffles.

"What happened with Ben?"

"He's breaking up with me." More sobbing.

"What are you talking about?" Ben worshiped the ground Holly walked on.

"Either he moves out or I do."

"Wait, I'm coming to get you. Where are you now?"

"At the apartment."

"I'll get there as soon as I can." I snapped the phone shut. "I think this day just got longer."

"A man?" Amelia said, taking a bite of sandwich.

"Yes, and my friend Holly. Can I drop you off at campus? I'm not going to be able to do anything until I deal with this."

She agreed. We finished our sandwiches in silence. I drove like a maniac back to St. Louis and, after the briefest of good-byes, I was at

Holly's apartment, pounding on the door. She opened it, puffy-eyed, but coherent.

I gave her a hug. "Oh, Holly."

"Just get me out. I can't be in this apartment when he comes back."

"Let's go to my place." Holly grabbed her purse and followed me to my car.

She was quiet on the drive over. I looked at her surreptitiously. Her face was bright red and her eyes were so enflamed that her eyelashes had disappeared. That must have been some fight. When we got to my apartment, I sat her on the couch while I made her a cup of strong tea. It had worked for me.

I handed her the mug saying, "Now start from the beginning."

What finally came out, after many twists and turns, could be summarized as follows: Holly became more involved with the Kevin Mason campaign. Ben accused her of ignoring him. They began to fight. Then, Kevin Mason won the Democratic primary. The other candidate was crazy to take him on. Kevin won by a landslide. He took a bunch of his staffers out to celebrate after the party and Holly went along. Holly thought she kissed Kevin rather than the other way around, but she swore to me that nothing else happened. At least she didn't think anything happened. She'd had a lot to drink. She got home at 4:00 a.m. and went to bed.

Ben woke up furious. He suspected the worst. She promised to spend more time with him, but she couldn't give up on the campaign now that Kevin had the nomination. So she sneaked around. That morning Ben came to a decision. He told Holly that it was him or the campaign. She refused to make a choice. He told her that meant that she had chosen the campaign. He was done.

"I told Ben it was blackmail, plain and simple. How can I give up the campaign when I've put so much into it? I didn't ask him to give up Halo 2 when he started playing twenty-four seven, did I?"

"No." I patted her arm. "I think you both need to calm down and ask yourselves if you want this relationship to end. I mean, are you interested in Kevin Mason? It sounds more like you had too much to drink."

"He's amazing."

"Amazing as in admiration, or desire? There is a big difference."

"I don't know," she said quietly.

"Hmm."

"I feel so alive when I'm with him. It's strange."

"Then you should take time away from Ben."

She nodded forlornly.

I looked at her and shook my head. "I know that I'm going to regret this, but you can stay here until you and Ben work things out – one way or the other."

She threw her arms around my neck, dribbling tea down my back. "You are the best, Liz. You really are."

I patted her back. "Just repeat that when my habits make you want to pull your hair out. And no commentary on the hamburger I have in my freezer."

"I wouldn't dream of it."

James called me later that afternoon. He caught me as I was just trying to stuff a small selection of Holly's clothes into the living room closet. The door wouldn't close, no matter what I did. Uff. I pushed it again.

"You called," I said.

"I'm trying to do better."

"It's not that hard, is it?"

"No, surprisingly easy. I'm a reformed man. So how about dinner and shopping?" The jeans. I'd completely forgotten.

"I'd love to, but I'm not sure if I can leave Holly alone tonight."

"Holly?"

"My new roommate." I briefly explained the situation.

"Should I come by with take out?"

"I like the reformed James. I've only got meat products in my fridge and that doesn't work for Holly."

"One order of Buddhist Delight coming up. I'm going to have to behave myself, aren't I?"

"At least for tonight."

"You could have warned me you were getting a chaperone."

"I'll see what I can do to escape curfew."

"I should have taken better advantage of last night."

"The reformed James is a gentleman," I said.

"See you at 6:00."

He was true to his word. I flung the door open. He held a couple of steaming bags in his hands. I greeted him with a hug and a kiss. Holly stayed back in my room, trying to deal with the puffy eyes. She did have her pride.

"What's this?" he said. "I thought I was supposed to behave."

I took a bag from him. "You've brought food."

"More than that. I thought you might want your birthday present early."

"I'd completely forgotten." My birthday was the following day.

My mom always said I was the only good thing that ever happened on April 15th. Otherwise it was all death and taxes. Between the Titanic sinking, Lincoln dying, and having to sign your life away to the federal government, it wasn't a particularly celebratory occasion. Of course, later I would even get to add the Boston Marathon bombing to the grisly tally.

James smiled at my reaction. "I expected this since you never mentioned plans. I don't know how to deal with you. You defy all the stereotypes."

I shrugged my shoulders. "I've never been very into birthdays. It seems like such a fuss."

"I've made reservations for Pomme tomorrow at 7:00."

"For you, I'll put up with fuss."

He leaned in so Holly wouldn't hear. "I thought we could reminisce about our first date."

"Now we come to the ulterior motive," I replied.

He and I set out the food and then called Holly to come and join us. She emerged, still puffy and beaten down. I knew she was in a bad place because she did not say much and only picked at her food. James and I stuck to G rated subjects, like my classes. I managed to work it out so I only had one real exam. I had long form essays for the other classes and nothing for the Clinic. After all we'd done for Elsa, Amelia and I were pretty certain to get a high pass.

James' obsession with work had freed up most of my available time to write and to study, so I had the essay work done and felt fairly good about my exam. A positive development, since the exam was next week, and James now meant to distract me this weekend.

Holly excused herself early to go for a run. She wanted to get out while it was still light.

"She's in bad shape," James said when she left.

"I've never seen her this down. Not even when her grandparents died and she had to go home."

"Mark asked my mom to send her an invitation to his graduation party. Do you think that's a bad idea right now?"

"Probably not. At least it will get her out of the campaign offices for the afternoon."

"Has your invitation arrived?"

"Yes. Two days ago. Please thank your mother for including my family. It was very thoughtful, and they are happy to come." My parents and Ashley planned to descend on me for graduation. This was one less evening I would have to entertain them.

"And you'll be okay with the crowds?"

"My family will be with me."

"I'll be with you."

"They know not to abandon me," I said.

"I'm sorry."

"Don't be. It's going to happen again, and you can't always be apologizing."

"That's not very nice."

"I just mean that this is a family party. Your mother will want you to act like a host."

He sighed. "At least I get to meet your family. I'm excited about that."

"Talk to me after you've spent some time in their presence."

"We all feel that way about our relatives."

"Yours don't sound like extras from the movie *Fargo*."

James laughed. "You're exaggerating."

"You laugh now, but you'll see."

"I'm sure they will be very, very nice."

I rolled my eyes. "No comment."

I got up from the table to make some coffee. He followed me into the kitchen with the dirty plates. Then, after a few minor squabbles about what went where, we loaded the dishwasher. The coffee started to drip.

"Thank you," I said as he wiped the counter with a towel.

"See how homey this is. We could be working together every night." He smiled at me in the way that made my pulse jump.

"I thought you weren't going to pressure me?"

"Just an observation. I'll give you your gift while we wait for the coffee."

He took my hand and led me back to the living room. We sat down on the couch and he reached over to his jacket, which he'd left folded over the arm of the sofa. He pulled a small box out of an inner pocket and handed it to me. It was tied with a bright red ribbon.

"Happy 26th."

"Thank you," I replied. I held the box in my hands, enjoying the moment of anticipation.

"Don't thank me till you've opened it."

It took a little while to get the ribbon off and then the paper. As I had suspected from the shape and size, it was a jewelry box. I opened the lid slowly. Gold glittered on the black velvet. I gasped. I pulled out an earring like a cascading waterfall of gold mesh.

"They're absolutely gorgeous." I pulled the other one out and held them up to the light. I wasn't wearing any earrings, so I couldn't resist slipping them on.

James smiled. "They suit you." He reached over and smoothed my hair behind one ear.

"They're the most beautiful jewelry anyone has ever given me." I felt my throat tighten with emotion. Joy or panic? I think it was joy.

"It's nothing really. I can do more."

"I wouldn't trade them for the world."

"But maybe that necklace?"

I shook my head. The fine mesh brushed my neck as I moved, like the wings of a butterfly. "You couldn't have picked anything better." Joy. Yes, definitely joy. On impulse, I grabbed the collar of his shirt and pulled him to me. He didn't try to move away for several minutes.

"That will not induce me to behave," he said, catching his breath.

"Holly's not back yet."

"Just hold on. You can thank me properly tomorrow night."

"I'll tell Holly not to wait up."

"That's how to handle a chaperone."

I took one earring off to look at it again. The workmanship was exquisite. "I've never seen anything like it. Where did you buy them?"

"Would you believe a jewelry auction? I saw them in the Harville-Chouteau catalog and knew I had to get them for you."

"Is this the same auction you told me about?"

"Yes."

"Someday I'd like to go with you," I said, fingering the delicate gold.

The door opened suddenly. Holly had arrived, sweaty and exhausted, but certainly less gray.

I quickly put the earring back on. "Holly, look what James gave me for my birthday." I pulled my hair back with my hands.

"Your birthday?" And then a worried look. "Your birthday."

I chuckled. "I forgot it myself, but James didn't. He's taking me to dinner tomorrow night. Don't expect me back."

She nodded her head in understanding.

"Coffee?" James said, getting up.

"No thanks," Holly replied. "I think I'm going to shower and then sleep."

I stood up. "Just let me know when you're ready, and I'll pull out the sofa bed."

"Will do. Night James." She walked into the bathroom and resolutely shut the door. After a minute, I heard the shower.

James ambled to the kitchen and poured a coffee. He handed it to me and poured another for himself.

"Holly will be out of the shower soon. I should go."

"Sorry about this."

"How long do you think it will take her to sort her life out?"

"Look on the bright side. I'll be spending a lot more time at your house."

"You're moving in?"

"Not so fast. Has it ever crossed your mind that I might be terrible to live with?"

"I've lived with Angie. Nothing can be worse than that."

"Thanks for the vote of confidence."

"All I'm saying is that I can put up with major mood swings, tantrums, and a serious passive aggressive attitude. I wouldn't be surprised by anything you'd do," he said.

"If things were so bad, how were you together so long?"

"Stupidity? A high tolerance for pain? The fact that I was never home? Who knows?"

"It can't always have been like that. You proposed, after all."

"I thank God every day that I'm out of that engagement."

I shook my head. "Not that I want to defend her, but you must have been happy once."

"At the beginning. I was on the beat with Kyle then, and she seemed so normal. Headstrong, but so am I, so we fit. Unfortunately, the relationship changed. After a while, she was either laughing or screaming, and not much in between. She pouted if she didn't get her way. I wouldn't give in to her all the time, so we fought. I hated the drama – I got enough of that at my job – but I figured that we would eventually work it out. Then I met you and saw there might be another way."

"If it weren't for me, you'd be married to her now?"

"I'd have gotten out just the same. Angie changed, or maybe I changed. You were just a very good excuse to do what needed to be done."

"Glad to be of assistance."

He laughed and then leaned down to kiss me. The sound of the shower stopped abruptly. "Bad timing. I'll see you tomorrow night," he said.

CHAPTER 11

Holly made up for forgetting my birthday by helping me clean the apartment. From my perspective, this was gift enough. She continued to feel guilty, however, so she went to buy food and came back with more vegetables than my refrigerator could hold. We had to put the rutabaga and the kale on top of the fridge, next to my emergency stash of potato chips. She also got me a black satin clutch for my special birthday dinner.

When James knocked at the door at 6:30, I was properly attired for an elegant dinner out. From my new earrings, to my little black dress, to the clutch, to the Ferragamos on my feet, I actually looked like I might aspire to be James' date for the evening. He seemed pleased at the transformation. "You should retain Holly as your stylist on a permanent basis."

"I did the hair and makeup myself this time. I'm not a completely lost cause."

"From Wisconsin farm girl to this – amazing."

"I'm from town."

"From town or from Fargo?"

"Both."

"I would never have known. Your accent is so civilized."

"I might say the same for you, except you say Missoura, which is just plain wrong."

"You look beautiful as always. Is that the same dress you wore —"

"I thought you might like the homage."

"The best first date I've ever been on."

"Cards," I said. It was an old joke between us.

"Let's go. Dessert awaits."

The restaurant was lit with candlelight and the soft glow of amber glass chandeliers. Our waiter escorted us to an intimate table against the wall and towards the back. I reviewed the menu while James looked at the wine list.

"Red or white?" he said.

"Surprise me." Wine was not my area of expertise. James' brow creased as his eyes scanned the page. Maybe I should study it. Wine selection could be yet another detail in my arsenal, but that knowledge might crowd out some vital information needed for the bar exam. Better not. Wine snobbery could wait.

"Are you okay with an Alsatian?"

"Is that white?"

"Yes." He seemed amused at my ignorance.

"Sounds lovely." Let him feel superior. I'd have plenty of time to learn my wines after the bar exam.

The waiter came and James ordered the wine. I still hadn't decided on an entrée or anything else, so I put him off. I looked at the menu again. Filet or trout? The standby or the wild card? Hard to decide. Maybe some soup to start. They had a soup with mussels that sounded divine. I'd just opted for the trout when I heard a commotion behind me.

The door of the restaurant clanged shut, and then there was boisterous laughter. Clearly a group. Maybe tipsy. I turned my head slightly so I could see without being obvious. Three beefy men of indeterminate middle age and three women in their twenties who were dressed suggestively and expensively. The blondes showed a lot of skin, but the brunette had a silk tunic that was much more modest. She was very striking, with her caramel skin and long dark hair. She moved well, too, sliding her hair off her shoulder with an elegant gesture.

One man seemed to be the leader of the group. He had a booming voice that carried to the back of the restaurant. He looked like an older, darker version of Marlon Brando. Brando in a *Street Car Named Desire*. This man had that dangerous animal magnetism. I looked again. Yes. He must have been something in his twenties. He carried himself like he still was something. The hostess tried to hustle them to a table without more commotion. That was impossible.

I looked at the man again and this time he caught me staring. Oops. I turned away quickly, but not before a Cheshire Cat smile spread across his face.

"Jamie!" he said. His voice echoed across the room. I saw James flinch and then struggle to control his expression. He managed an impassive look – neither hostile nor friendly. The man got up and strode over to our table. He was even more imposing up close, carrying himself with an easy confidence. His suit was precisely tailored to his broad shoulders. I noticed a gold Rolex and a large man's ring on his right hand. It was in the shape of a two-headed eagle with outstretched wings forming the band. I felt the urge to hold my nose.

His cologne was overpoweringly strong. Boucheron, one I normally liked. But instead of sweet and spicy, it smelled sharp and acidic on him.

"Good to see you again." He stuck out a meaty hand and gave James' a vigorous shake. "It's been a while." He turned slightly and gave me a once over, waiting for the introduction.

"Liz, this is Sean Thomas. Sean, Elizabeth Howe, my girlfriend."

Sean gave me another up and down that seemed to stop at my cleavage. Then he smiled. I could feel James tense from the other side of the table. I extended my hand.

"Pleased to meet you." He had a powerful grip. Thank goodness I didn't have any rings to dig into my bones.

With one eye still on my bosom, he said, "Liz. Charmed." He looked back at James without releasing my hand. "Doing well, I see."

James nodded curtly.

"I should let you two get back to your dinner."

"Good seeing you." James' tone said that the conversation was over.

Sean finally let my fingers go. I put my hand in my lap. As I did so, I noticed that it now had that acidic smell. Maybe chemical was a better word. It was the smell of something out in the sun too long. I watched him stride back to his table. He sat down next to the woman with dark hair.

"He's got a connection with Angie, doesn't he?" I said. James raised an eyebrow. "He called you Jamie."

"Yes. A friend of Angie's family. He worked with Angie's dad for a while. I've met him at her dad's house over the years. My mom knows his ex-wife."

Another round of raucous laughter exploded from the table and ricocheted around the room. "He was more restrained before," James added.

"Before?"

"Before the affair and the baby. I don't think that the divorce is final, but that doesn't seem to matter."

"Who was he married to?" Something about this story seemed too familiar.

"Elaine Wayman. She's part of the family that owns the trucking company. They're big in St. Louis politics, too. I'm sure you've heard of them."

The pieces fell into place. Of course I had heard of them. I had been mooning over their plaque at the SLU library, and even eating meals with one of the clan. "She has a sister Susan, doesn't she?"

"I think so. She's a lawyer?"

I nodded. "I've had lunch with her a bunch of times, but forgot her last name. She's a friend of Janice's. She told us about the divorce."

"Then you know it's gotten really nasty. My mom fills me in when I eat at home. She can't stand Sean."

"Do you know which attorneys are involved?"

"Why do you ask?"

"Curiosity. The divorce bar is a strange lot. One half can't stand the other half. It's so not helpful when their clients are already at each other's throats."

"I don't know about him. Elaine's got Brian Kepple."

"He's representing the wife in a case I was assigned for Clinic."

I last saw Brian at a mediation for the Clayton accountants. Brian impressed me again with his calmness and professionalism.

In contrast, Reginald Butler blustered through the whole thing. For laughs, I played the dewy-eyed blond and got Butler going at the break. He told one outlandish story after another – name dropping a bunch of local politicos I didn't even know.

The *pièce de r*ésistance was a story about what he allegedly said to Bill Clinton at a golf outing. I doubted Butler had gotten close enough to shake Clinton's hand from the crowd, but held my tongue. Playing dumb got me joint custody with a rational visitation schedule that would not have the kids shuttling back and forth like a bunch of ping pong balls. The financial settlement was still in negotiations, but my part was done.

I wasn't sure how my exercise in flattering the oversized male ego would go over with James, so I merely added, "And Kepple works at Vince's firm."

"Ah." James took a sip of water. I waited for him to make some comment about Vince, but he wisely refrained. Instead he said, "I keep forgetting to mention – Bill Fischer came to see me yesterday, looking for a favor. They pulled surveillance tape of the parking garage and a suspicious guy shows up on a couple of sections. He's wandering around the garage with a package in one hand and a bunch of balloons in the other. Later, he seems to exit the garage with just the balloons."

"Definitely odd. What is the favor?"

"They can't identify him so Bill wants you to look at the tape."

"But surely the department has tech people who could analyze the images enough to make an identification?"

"No. The balloons cover his face completely."

"I see."

"I know it's a long shot, but I promised I'd ask. Bill thinks you might notice some detail his people have missed."

"I'm willing to try."

"Thank you. I'll let you know when I have the tape. Bill said that there would be some paperwork before he could release it to me to show you."

The waiter arrived just at that moment. We ordered. Trout for me and short ribs for James.

As the waiter walked away, I said, "I'm going to wash my hands before I touch anything. My hand smells like I stuck it in a vat of chemicals."

"What?"

"You didn't notice?"

"No."

"Sean Thomas has been handling something. The smell rubbed off on me when I shook his hand."

"If I didn't know you, I'd say you're crazy. I don't smell a thing." He lifted his hand to his nose. "No. Absolutely nothing."

"Trust me." I stood up and stepped away from the table.

"I'll wash mine when you get back." He put a hand on my arm. "Anything else I should know about?"

"Our waiter is an actor. Shakespearean, probably." He looked at me expectantly. "That combination of flair and diction is unmistakable." I heard his chuckle as I walked away.

I had to wash my hand three times to get the smell off. Whatever it was had seeped into my skin.

"Wash carefully," I said when I got back to the table.

"Will do." He stood up.

I took a sip of the wine that had arrived in my absence. It was fantastic. I took another.

"Don't drink the whole bottle before I get back," James said.

"I can't drink you under the table. I'm a cheap date."

"You've never been cheap."

"You know what I mean."

"Although the thought of drinking you under the table does have possibilities."

"Not with those hands."

"Understood." He walked back to the washroom.

I spent most of the next day relaxing. Well, maybe not relaxing, but James and I got up around noon. The jeans errand could wait. For a Wisconsin girl, nothing is more decadent than spending half of a Sunday in bed. I tried to banish the nagging guilt. God would just have to understand.

We made a lazy breakfast turned lunch in James' kitchen. I leaned against the island watching him whisk an omelet in a metal bowl. And then it hit me. We'd never prepared a meal together before. For two people who claimed to enjoy cooking, this seemed like a travesty.

James' birthday fell at the end of May. I was at a loss as to a gift. I did not have the required budget, but perhaps cooking was my answer. I surreptitiously scanned the shelves at the end of the room – good. It would take determined searching and maybe the Internet, but I knew where to start.

"What are you thinking?" James said.

"Just happy to spend time with you."

"You had that look you get when you're up to something."

"I'm not up to anything bad —"

"I didn't say bad, I said something."

"You're getting paranoid. Can I help you with that?"

"I've got it, thanks. And I'm not paranoid. I just know you too well."

"That's not very flattering."

"You don't like compliments, so I thought I'd try another tactic."

"Very romantic."

"Romance is overrated." He poured the omelet mixture into the pan and poked at the edges with a wooden spoon.

"Speak for yourself."

He watched the omelet thoughtfully for a moment and then looked at me. His expression was sweet and a little wistful. "So you would be okay with a big romantic gesture? Something completely over the top?"

"Of course. What did you have in mind?"

"Secrets are essential for romantic gestures. Surely you know that."

"I have to wait?"

He nodded.

"I'm not very patient," I said.

He laughed and then expertly flipped the omelet to one side, patting it lightly with the spoon. "Breakfast is served."

Amelia and I met at 7:30 Tuesday morning in the parking lot of the courthouse in Jefferson County. The judge, who was an activist in the best sense of the word, had set a hearing on our motions for permanent assignment of custody as soon as he possibly could.

Gwen Zenner hugged us when we walked in and sat down at the table in front of the courtroom. She had chosen large, but relatively conservative, silver hoops for court. "Elsa's changing Tasha's diaper. She'll be here in a moment. How are you girls holding up?"

"Nervous," Amelia said.

"Don't be. We're prepared and Judge Chambers doesn't take kindly to men who hold their families hostage."

Judge Chambers had a reputation as a maverick. He was a defender of women and children, and seemed to think as little of men as Sister Rita. He threw deadbeat fathers in jail for contempt of court faster than their attorneys could object. Especially around the holidays. He said there was nothing like Christmas in the slammer to bring some men around to a sense of their obligations. His relationship with Gwen Zenner went way back, and he'd asked her to send her students to his courtroom as soon as she got the Clinic program up and running.

I heard the door open at the back and Elsa came in, the baby on one arm and her little boy by the hand. He clung to her leg so tightly that she could only take mincing steps. We got up and went over to help. After disentangling her pudgy fist from Elsa's long hair, I took Tasha in my arms.

Clarice, one of Judge Chambers' clerks emerged from the back room and came over to us. She crouched down and, eye to eye with little Timothy, tried to convince him to come with her to her office. Letting him see his father again, in handcuffs, and after such an ordeal, didn't seem like a good idea to anyone. Clarice promised a puzzle and a coloring book, but only the lure of a cookie finally got him to break the hold on his mother.

I gave Tasha back, but not after a quick kiss on the head. I have never met a baby who did not smell deliciously kissable. There is something about their smooth sweet skin. Elsa hugged Tasha to her chest and looked forlornly around the courtroom. I wanted to comfort her, but didn't know how. Amelia and I sat down to go through our motions for the thousandth time.

"What a sad bunch of bananas!" a voice said behind me. The sound echoed in the stillness of the courtroom.

I jumped up and turned around. "Sister Rita!"

She approached the table with that brisk walk of hers. "Y'all didn't think I'd miss this? When pigs fly."

"I'm just so glad you're here," I said.

"I didn't come for y'all," she replied matter-of-factly. She put an arm around Elsa. "How's my little chickie this fine morning?" I'm not sure how much her little chickie actually understood, but she gave Sister Rita a mournful look. Rita squeezed Elsa's shoulder. "Buck up. We'll get you through this."

Rita turned to Gwen. "Where's Timmy?" Gwen explained that he was off with Clarice. "Very sensible." Rita turned to Amelia. "Scoot over, and I'll sit with you folks. I'm thinking I might be needed." Amelia made room and Sister Rita sat down.

We waited another five minutes and then the bailiff who'd been hanging around our table chatting with Gwen, stood at attention. "All rise," he said.

We stood just as Judge Chambers entered. His robe hung open showing his habitual judicial uniform – a pair of jeans and a blue button down shirt. No tie.

He sat down and we followed. "Are we waiting on Mr. Stimpkin?" he said to the bailiff.

The bailiff nodded. "They're bringing him over now."

"Good enough," Judge Chambers said. He looked at us. "Well, ladies, I guess we have to wait." His gaze fixed on Sister Rita. "I'm afraid I don't know everyone."

Sister Rita stood up. "I'm Sister Margarita, your honor. I'm with Catholic Charities, helping Ms. Stimpkin with her immigration paperwork."

"Good to meet you, Sister. I've been worried about that. Welcome aboard."

She smiled. "Glad to help."

Just then the door closest to me opened with a bang. Andrew Stimpkin stood in the doorway, his hands handcuffed in front of him and a guard on either arm. His rounded shoulders slumped noticeably. His arms seemed too long for his body. His skin was ashen. And he blinked compulsively – like he'd come from a darkened room into the light. The guard moved him forward, shuffling.

A smell wafted through the courtroom, and I cringed. It was hard to describe – sweat, adrenaline, with a heavy note of ammonia and something else. Suddenly, the hairs on the back of my neck stood up. That could not be right. I looked quickly at Amelia, but she didn't react. Maybe I was the only one who noticed the smell. I took a shallow breath through my mouth, but I could not stay like a guppy all through the proceeding. I closed my mouth and took a deep breath when the guards moved Andrew to the center of the courtroom. Distance helped.

Judge Chambers granted custody of the children to Elsa. I learned that Andrew's bail hearing was set for the next day, but there was no expectation that he would receive an amount low enough to post. His extended family was not willing to risk it, in any case. I could understand why. Andrew was a twitchy mess, unable to concentrate even when the Judge asked him a question. After it was over, the guards walked him out through the door he came in. He did not even look up.

CHAPTER 12

A couple of days later, I took a break from class to meet Vince for a late lunch. His car was in the shop. He'd taken a taxi into work, trying to get a few more billable hours under his belt before buckling down for final exams. Despite my natural aversion to the scene of the bombing, as a favor to Vince I agreed to meet him in the lobby of the building at 1:00. There was a restaurant called Rooster six or seven blocks away that served crepes. We'd both been interested in trying it out. Besides, it was a surprisingly nice day, cool but sunny, and a walk would do us good.

However, there was no way I was parking in that garage. I found a metered parking space on a side street next to the building, but it was tight and my parallel parking skills are poor at best. I could have easily pulverized the silver Mercedes in front of me with one swipe of my Corsica's bumper. After at least ten attempts, I finally pulled it straight. As I got out of the car, I heard someone call my name. I turned. A man waved at me from down the street. I recognized the voice and the hair – both smooth. Brian Kepple.

"How are you?" I said.

"Good. What are you doing in these parts?"

"Meeting a friend. Vince Lopez."

"Oh, Vince." He clicked the silver Mercedes open with a remote. "I'm off to another meeting. Some days I wish I didn't have to get up."

"The clients won't leave you alone?"

He smiled. "With the bombing, I've had to rearrange everything. I'm up to my ears in continuances and postponements. It's a mess, but there is no way to fix it now – except by having more meetings."

"Short term parking?" I gestured at the meter.

"The bombing has a lot of us rattled. I don't park in the garage unless I have to."

"It's unnerving."

He nodded. "Hey, I was going to ask you at the mediation, but never got the chance – rumor has it that you were here when it happened."

"Who told you that?"

"I don't remember, maybe Janice Harrington? You're working for her, aren't you?"

"Yes. I didn't know you knew Janice."

"We went to high school together. Although she's held up better than I have."

"I'll tell her you said that. Which high school?" This was the question St. Louisans asked each other.

"Kirkwood." Kirkwood was as close to a small town as you could get in the St. Louis suburbs. It had grown up around the train station and still boasted a charming main street, turn of the last century houses and white picket fences.

"We had some good times," Brian added. He wore a wedding ring, but looking at his expression, I wondered if Janice was the one who got away. Then he seemed to snap out of it, and said, "I've got to go. Good to see you, Liz."

"You too. Take care." I stepped aside so he could get into his car. He pulled out of the space much more gracefully than I could have, and with a little wave was gone.

Vince waited for me in the lobby. He had a small square CD envelope in his hand. "The album you liked," he said.

"Thank you! I can't wait to play it when I get home." We started on our hike.

After a couple of minutes he said, "So you feel prepared for the party?"

"As much as a gringa can be. Amelia puts me to shame. Who knew a Southern belle could move like that?"

"She's certainly a surprise." There was a note of speculation in his voice.

I decided to press her case. "Amelia is amazing. You wouldn't believe what happened after we left your house."

I recounted the whole story of the hostage siege. It took practically the entire walk. "Amelia was calm and in control. I was shaking like a leaf the whole time and she acted like this was the most normal thing – she knew just what to do."

We stopped in front of Rooster. The smell of seared butter and egg was enveloping. It was almost better than the taste. Then again, crepes are about the world's most perfect food. Delicious themselves, and a vehicle for any number of other fantastic flavors.

Vince opened the door for me. "You're the amazing one."

Hmm. Not the response I was hoping for.

Then he said, "Now you have poor Amelia ensnared in your curse."

Much better. "You should stay away from me. My bad karma is obviously infectious."

"I can't do that," he said.

I didn't reply.

The restaurant had small tables inside and on the sidewalk, with the kitchen and line for ordering at the back. Like a lot of St. Louis City establishments, it was housed in an old building that had been refurbished. We ordered and then sat to wait inside. I looked down. Someone had done an amazing tile mosaic on the floor. Our table had one short leg and any movement tipped it. Vince and I played table tag, shifting it back and forth as we talked. He was telling me about one of his classmates when I couldn't take it another second.

I got up, grabbed a wad of napkins from the dispenser, and stuffed them under the errant leg. Then I pushed down. Success.

"That couldn't wait till I'd finished my story?" Vince was either amused or annoyed.

"I couldn't concentrate with the table moving around."

"You haven't given me your undivided attention?"

It was amusement. Good. "Go ahead."

"What was I saying?"

"An outline that's missing and —"

"Never mind. If it can't compete with the table leg, it's not worth telling."

"Sorry."

"I wanted to ask about something else anyway, but wasn't sure if you'd think it was too personal."

"Ask away," I said cautiously.

"Are you okay? I mean, I've been worried about the nightmares and all. You've got some dark circles going under your eyes."

"I forgot the foundation today."

"It's not getting any better?"

"It was, but since the whole hostage situation thing, they've come back. Or I should say, it's come back. The same bad dream *ad infinitum*."

"Does James have an opinion, or hasn't he noticed?"

"He's noticed," I replied defensively. "He thinks I should see someone about it."

"And you don't want to?"

"Who would I see?"

"Doesn't your church have a pastor?"

"I'm considering my options."

"Okay." We heard our order being called. "I'll get it," he said.

When Vince came back with the coffee and our crepes, I realized that I had not told him about Holly.

"I have a new roommate," I said as he took a bite of a crepe covered in berries and whipped cream.

He looked startled and swallowed hard. "James?"

"No, of course not." I tried not to notice his obvious relief. "My friend Holly. She's sleeping on my couch for an indefinite period of time." I gave him a sanitized version of events, not including what I thought happened on the night Holly could not remember.

"I have a funny story about Kevin Mason," he said when I finished. "I almost tackled him to the ground once."

"What?"

"I didn't know who he was. This was several months ago, before his name got everywhere."

Kevin Mason had become something of a media darling. It did not hurt that Chris Boggs continued to suffer from an intense rumor mill. The latest was that he did drugs and solicited prostitutes. Holly updated me daily. It was as if Chris Boggs could do no right.

"I saw this guy wandering around the parking garage at work. He was dressed in jeans and a sweatshirt, so he didn't look like someone who'd come for an appointment. He kept ducking in and around the cars. I got suspicious. Really, it seemed like he was looking for a car to break into. I followed him for a while, until I thought I had him cornered. I shouted, 'You! What are you doing?' I was all ready to lunge, when he turned around like nothing had happened, stuck out his hand and said, 'Hi. I'm Kevin Mason. Could you help me? I've lost my car. All the levels look the same.' Turns out, he was meeting a friend for lunch." Vince smiled. "I'm so glad I didn't try to take him down. Imagine what the partners at the firm would've said?"

I smiled at the image of Vince wrestling the slight Kevin Mason to the ground. "I assume you helped him find his car?"

"Yeah. It was on another level."

"I have trouble with things like that."

"You wouldn't now. That garage is practically empty. Everyone's on the street."

"Do they give your building a break on the parking tickets? A victim of crime discount or something?"

"I wish. There's a contest at work to see who's got the most tickets in a single week. Brian Kepple is in the running almost every time."

I took another bite of my crepe. I had gone out on a limb and ordered a savory crepe with mushrooms. It was fantastic. If only I knew how to get the batter so thin and light. Perhaps I didn't use enough butter.

"Oh, I saw Grant the other day," Vince said. "He says 'hi.'" Grant was the devilishly handsome and extravagantly tattooed Casanova we worked with as summer associates. At one point he got himself tangled up in our ex-firm's embezzlement scheme, but the police were only able to prove that he worked for crooks, not that he was one.

"Where did you see him? I thought he went to Mizzou." University of Missouri in Columbia. Go Tigers.

"I ran into him at lunch one day. He has some crazy class schedule that allows him to come to St. Louis a couple of days a week, so he got a head start on his new job. You'll never guess who he's working for."

"Who?"

"Reginald Butler."

"That actually doesn't surprise me. Grant never thought much of women, and I'm sure Butler's clients think he's cool."

"Because?"

"I'll start with the last part. Butler's clients are men who are looking for a man's lawyer. Tattoos say tough. It's like the old men with potbellies you see on Harley-Davidsons all over Wisconsin. You can buy tough if you have money. And with the women, you have to have noticed how he played one woman against another. Kelsey, Becca and Samantha were in a tizzy all summer."

"I wasn't paying attention to the other summer associates."

I took a sip of my soda. If Vince was interested, why hadn't he asked me out sooner? I certainly could have used a date that summer. Maybe it was me. What I took for friendship could have been something else. A very timid something else. But if we had really dated, I would have broken it off for James. That much was sure. And that would have been worse than any awkwardness now. I sighed. Never mind.

I asked Vince about his finals, and we talked about that and other law-related subjects as we walked back to his office. He came with me to check that I had not gotten a parking ticket. I wished him luck on his exams and promised to practice my moves for the party. He gave me a brief hug, and we parted ways on the sidewalk.

That night, Holly woke me up at 2:30 a.m. "You're screaming again," she said, giving my shoulder yet another shake. "You will go to Student Health as soon as they open if I have to drag you by the hair."

"I'm fine," I mumbled into my pillow.

"You may be, but I'm not getting up in the middle of the night one more time."

"I'll try not to scream, I promise."

"Student Health," she insisted.

"Okay. Okay. Just stop shaking me."

So at 9:00 in the morning, I sat with Holly in the cramped waiting room. "This is silly," I said to her.

"I don't care. The worst that can happen is they do nothing."

When my name was called, I got up very reluctantly and followed the surly physician's assistant to a back room. I sat down on an uncomfortable vinyl-covered chair and waited. And waited. Finally, a harried woman in a white coat came in.

"Hello, I'm Dr. Ward." She extended her hand. She looked down at a clipboard. "You're Liz Howe?"

"Yes."

"What can I do for you?"

"I'm having nightmares."

"About?"

"Murder mostly. Sometimes explosions."

She gave me a critical look. "Are these things you're thinking about when you're awake? Or just nightmares?"

"Both."

"Hmm. Have you always had these fantasies?"

"No."

"How long have you had them?"

"Since the first body. It comes and goes."

I saw her blanch. "Okay." She backed up towards the door. "So, when did you kill your first victim?"

I burst out laughing. "I haven't killed anyone! I keep getting involved with other people's crimes."

Her shoulders relaxed. I explained everything that had happened since the night I found the body in the stairwell. I told her about James and the dream that haunted me. Dr. Ward started to take notes, but after a while she gave up and listened intently. Finally, I stopped and looked at her.

"Very interesting," she said with a smile. "I think your nightmares are perfectly understandable, and probably an after-effect of the stress you've been under. I would recommend counseling. Weekly at first and then tapering off. Unfortunately, there is no quick fix."

"You can't just give me a pill or something?"

"You didn't think it would be that easy, did you? I could give you a drug for anxiety, but it doesn't sound like you have any other symptoms."

"Normally I'm pretty together."

"Are there any circumstances that seem to favor the nightmares or to make them go away?"

"I don't have them when I'm with James."

"The policeman boyfriend?"

"Yes. I – um – don't seem to wake up when he's – ur – with me."

"That makes sense. He's the focus of your anxiety. If you don't want to do counseling, maybe you should just spend more time with him."

"Are you giving me a prescription for —"

She smiled. "Not necessarily, but it sounds like it helps. Assuming you're practicing safe —"

"Yes," I said quickly.

"Look, Liz, you are a healthy young woman who's gotten involved with some pretty scary things. The nightmares are the result. I can suggest counseling, but I can't make you do it. If you don't, you'll just have to figure out how to deal with them on your own. And if that involves spending more time with the boyfriend, so much the better. We're not islands. We all need the support of other people. The human connection is as important as anything I could give you."

I looked at her, stunned. Connections. What if?

CHAPTER 13

The next couple of weeks went by so quickly that I didn't have time to think about Dr. Ward's prescription. The nightmares did seem to be getting better. Before I knew it, the doorbell rang and there stood my family, waiting for me to invite them in. My overloaded apartment couldn't handle more, so I got my parents a room at the Red Roof Inn in Westport. I would have gotten one for Ashley, too, but she preferred to sleep on the floor.

They came into the apartment in a babble of crossed conversations. There'd been a fight over the shortest route to my apartment and they had hit traffic crossing over from Illinois. A general condemnation of big city driving and misleading signage ensued. I listened with as much patience as I could, while I helped Ashley haul her duffle bag and a cooler of frozen food in from the hall.

Fortunately, I'd been forewarned and had already cleaned out my freezer. I flipped the lid of the cooler open. The usual steaks, and what looked like frozen zucchini and summer squash. I found the package of cheese carefully wrapped to prevent freezing.

"No rhubarb?" I said to my mom when the driving argument finally ran out of steam.

"It's under the corn." I shifted a few of the freezer bags. Indeed, more chopped rhubarb lay under some ears of frozen sweet corn. My mom must have emptied the freezer of all of last summer's bounty.

"There is another bag of stuff in the car," she added. "Beer. You know your dad. I just sent him out to get it."

"Bud not good enough now?" I said.

My mother made a face. My parents might be humble, but they were snobs about beer. Living in the land of Belgian-style microbrews did that to you.

"Don't say anything while you're in St. Louis, okay? Anheuser-Busch is a religion in this town."

"My lips are sealed." She drew her fingers across her lips like a zipper.

I pulled the cooler into the kitchen.

"I'll help you with that," Mom said.

I opened the freezer and stuffed packages in as Mom handed them to me. I looked down and realized that I had a package of meat in my hand. "You remembered," I said as I put it in the back of the freezer for safekeeping.

"Of course." Mom handed me the corn.

I stuffed the last package in and closed the door. "I'm making spaghetti for dinner tonight. Holly's going to be here, so I'm baking the meatballs separately." I wiped my damp hands on my jeans.

"So that's what smells so good." Mom walked over to the Crock Pot where my sauce was bubbling away. As a true Crock Pot cook, she looked through the glass, but did not lift the lid.

"And James?" Her tone was innocently casual. Ashley, who had avoided any of the putting away, now sidled over to listen.

"He's got a family dinner to go to. Aunts, uncles and some cousins, I think. He'll come over after that."

"His brother's party is Friday night?"

"Yes. It starts at 5:00."

"What are you wearing?" Ashley said.

"I've got a new dress. James helped me pick it out."

"There's some hope then."

I gave her a look, but she merely shrugged her shoulders. "For someone who can pick out a Gucci purse at a hundred yards, you don't seem to be able to put yourself together."

"I'm not that bad."

"By Marshfield standards, you're okay."

"Thanks."

"I'm just saying. There's a whole world out there, sis."

"And UW is a center of fashion now? Besides, I was making improvements pre-James," I said.

"Your hair was better. I'll give you that. But those jeans. Don't tell me that's the best you can do."

"What's wrong with the jeans?" I looked down. They did hang funny on me since I'd lost weight. I didn't think it was that noticeable. "They're comfortable. And I don't have to dress up for family. I have a better pair to change into."

"James?" my mother said from inside the refrigerator.

"What are you doing in there?" I said.

"Just organizing your fridge. What's this?" She held up a plastic container of indeterminate origin.

"Not sure."

"So, James?" Ashley said.

"What?" I turned back to her.

Ashley rolled her eyes. "Pay attention. Did James pick out the better pair of jeans?"

"Yes. I think they may be too tight."

"Does James think they're too tight?"

"Obviously not. He bought them," I said.

"Then they look good."

"You haven't even met him. How can you be so confident of his taste?"

Ashley looked at me.

"I was really that bad before?" I said.

"Don't make me answer."

"Why don't you do something useful?" I pulled a bowl of risen bread dough towards me. "Help me shape this into loaves." I moved to the sink to wash my hands.

"Oh sure. Invite me here and then make me work." Ashley wandered off to the bathroom to wash hers and probably to stall.

I heard the front door open. My dad appeared with a paper grocery bag. Numerous bottles clinked together.

"How much did you bring?" I said.

"Enough for a couple of days. Is there room in the fridge?"

"I don't know. Mom?"

"Give me a minute." She continued to dig around. "You have a bunch of things that need to go."

"At least I cleaned the freezer."

"If you get ptomaine poisoning, you'll only have yourself to blame," Mom said.

"Is ptomaine poisoning even possible?"

"Very good Liz," my dad said with a chuckle. "As I'm sure your mother is well aware, it's not the alkaloids but the bacteria that cause the problems with decayed food." Once a science teacher, always a science teacher.

"I do not keep decayed food in my fridge. And with modern standards of refrigeration, I'm sure a day or two won't poison anyone," I replied.

"You can never be too careful," Mom said. She pulled out eight separate containers and dumped their contents in the trash.

My dad started loading the refrigerator with beer, and Ashley came back to help me with the bread. "What did I miss?" she said.

"A treatise on foodborne pathogens."

"Oh good. I'm glad I re-did my makeup."

I looked carefully. Yes, she had actually added another layer of silver-blue on her eyelids. The mascara edged toward Tammy Faye.

"One of these days I'll sign you up for kabuki theater," I said.

"I think you have to be a man for that."

"A little more eye shadow and you could pass for one."

"Some of them are gorgeous."

"You're no Ru Paul."

"This from the woman in mom jeans?" Ashley said.

"Hey, I heard that." My mom looked up from her garbage duty. "And just for the record, I wouldn't be caught dead in those jeans."

It felt good to be with family again. I persuaded Dad to hand over some of the beer. We stood chatting and drinking while I finished up the bread and stuck it in the oven. Holly appeared just as the bread toasted golden brown on the top. My dad had a soft spot for Holly, so he parted with another beer. She settled in like a member of the Howe clan. I hadn't seen her in such a good mood in a long time. She even kept silent about the meatballs sitting in a pan on the counter.

At dinner we laughed and ate way too much. Especially since Ashley had made me change into the tight jeans. I was just considering undoing the button, when I heard a knock at the door. I jumped up and sucked in my stomach. Only one person knocked like that. I looked at my mom, who sat up and pulled down her shirt.

As I opened the door, I stepped into the hall, so that they couldn't see me. "Good evening," I said, standing on my toes to give him a quick kiss on the lips.

"Is that to inspire me with courage?" James said, kissing me back. "I'm so glad I got you these jeans." His hand went down, skimming the back pocket.

I pulled away. This had gone far enough. "The lion's den awaits."

He followed me into the room. My parents stood up. My mom tugged at her shirt once more for good measure.

"Mom and Dad, this is James. James, my mom, Shirley, and my dad, Don."

"Mr. and Mrs. Howe, it's so good to finally meet you." He took a long step, his hand extended. My mom gave me a look I knew well. She was impressed. Dad seemed more wary.

"Hello," Ashley said, pushing her way to the front. "I'm Ashley. The sister."

James shook her hand. "Hello, Ashley the sister. I've heard about you, too."

"All good," she said.

"Of course," he replied.

James turned back to my parents and asked about their trip down. He was doing his best to be charming, but I could see my dad held back. Finally, the pleasantries were done, and there was the dreaded moment of silence.

"Should we have a seat?" I gestured to the table and the circle of mismatched chairs around it. "Are you still hungry, James? We're not quite to dessert yet."

He looked at me and smiled. "You know I can't miss dessert." I felt the blush creep up my cheek. Then something caught his attention at the table. "New Glarus. You have New Glarus."

My dad perked up. "Want some?"

James was already examining the bottle. It was large, like a wine bottle with a red wax seal at the top. My dad's absolute favorite beer. And made in Wisconsin, so easily purchased in Marshfield. I hadn't had a meal at home without at least one bottle being consumed, usually at the end, when a pie made its appearance.

"I've never actually tasted it before, but Michael Jackson raves about it," James said.

"Michael Jackson?" Ashley said.

"The beer guy, not the singer," Dad replied. I could feel the first crack in my dad's armor. Anyone who liked beer was a friend of his.

They sat down and poured the beer. I served my dad a fourth helping of meatballs and then went to the kitchen to start the coffee. My mom came over to help – or in this case, to grill me.

"You didn't tell me he was like a model," she said in a soft voice. I looked around the low hanging cabinets that divided the kitchen from the dining area. James and Dad seemed engrossed in conversation.

"I think I mentioned something about it."

"I'm still blinded by those teeth." She shook her head. "Are you sure he's a cop? It seems a waste."

"I'm sure and it's not a waste. He's very sharp – behind the teeth."

"He seems nice." This was high praise from my mother. "As long as he treats you well, I don't have a problem with him."

"Thanks. I think." I hit the button and the first drop sizzled in the carafe.

"Is it serious?"

"In what sense?"

"Are you?" She gave me a significant look.

"I can't believe you're asking me this. I'm 26. What do you think?"

"Well, I would." She looked over at him speculatively.

"I'm going to pretend you didn't just say that. In fact, I'm going to forget we ever had this conversation."

"Don't think your generation invented everything."

"We are now in the too much information zone."

"Coward."

"Holly and Ash seem to have a lot to say to each other." They were carrying on a non-beer conversation on the other side of the table.

"Holly is a sweet girl. Too bad that boyfriend sounds like a jerk."

"Ex-boyfriend. And she's not telling the whole story – it's complicated. They're trying to sublet the apartment, but until then, she's on my couch."

"How does James feel about that?"

"You're not going to quit, are you?"

"Just a concerned mom."

"Right. Go live vicariously through Ash. My life is off limits."

"Ash won't even tell me if she is dating anyone."

"Smart girl," I said a little too loudly.

"What are you saying about me?" Ash got up from the table and came into the kitchen. Holly followed.

"Just that you tell me everything," Mom said sweetly.

"Go on thinking that," Ashley replied.

Holly laughed. "That's right. Keep them in the dark."

"We're not as in the dark as you think," Mom said.

"Don't get her started," I said to Holly. "Soon she'll have you confessing everything."

"My life isn't very exciting. I can confess to pretty much anything right now."

"Guys are useless," Ashley agreed. I gave her a questioning look. "We'll talk later when someone's mother isn't standing right here," she said.

"I'm here for you when you're ready to talk." Mom reached over and patted her shoulder. Ashley glared at her, but I could tell Mom was trying not to laugh.

"You're terrible," I said. Mom opened her mouth to say something that was sure to be sarcastic, but then my phone rang.

"You're never going to believe this." It was Amelia.

"What?" I said.

"He escaped!"

"Andrew Stimpkin?" He was the only one I knew who had any reason to escape anything.

"Yes. Out of the county jail."

"Incredible. Does Elsa know?"

"Gwen got a hold of her and Sister Rita before she called me."

"Did he break out of his cell?"

"Gwen said they were transporting him to a hearing. He overpowered the guards and got away."

"How could the man we saw do that?"

"I don't know. Just lock your door tonight."

"And Elsa and the kids?"

"Sister Rita went to get them. She's taking them somewhere safe."

"Thank goodness for Sister Rita."

"I know. Hey –" I heard noise in the background, "turn on your TV. They're covering the story."

"What channel?"

"Every channel. It's leading the ten o'clock news."

"Call you later, okay?" I hung up the phone and walked over to flip on my old television. It hummed and buzzed and then slowly brought up a picture. Sure enough, there was a bad photo of Andrew Stimpkin.

James came over and stood behind me. "What's going on?"

"Andrew Stimpkin has escaped. Can you believe it?"

"How?" We listened to the news anchor. It was pretty much what Amelia told me.

I shook my head. "That still doesn't make sense. The man I saw in the courtroom wasn't strong enough to overpower anyone. And how did he get away? Did no one notice the man in the orange jumpsuit running down the road? Wasn't he in handcuffs? How did he get those off?"

"Maybe the guards were sloppy with procedures. Maybe he smuggled a knife on him."

"Or bolt cutters to cut the handcuffs off his own hands?"

James grinned. "I agree with you. There is a lot more to this story."

"No offense, but it sounds like an inside job."

"Not all correctional officers are saints, but —"

"But?"

"It would take a lot of persuasion to let someone like Andrew Stimpkin escape. Think how it looks."

"What's going to happen now?" I turned off the TV and looked back at the family group. They'd gotten the ice cream out and were cutting the apple pie I'd pulled together that morning. None of them seemed to have noticed the TV, or they pretended not to.

James put an arm around me. "Do you want me to stay?"

"For my protection or for the pie?"

"Your protection. But I'll take the pie, too."

"It's tempting, but you'd have to face both Ashley and Holly in the morning. I won't put you through that gauntlet."

"I'm not afraid."

"You should be. And anyway, I don't think Andrew Stimpkin knows who I am. Elsa's in more danger. He didn't seem with it enough to figure out where she is and who she's with." I briefly explained the Sister Rita connection.

"They'll get to him before he can put two and two together. As you've pointed out, escapees have trouble blending in. My guess is that he'll be killed or captured in the next couple of days."

CHAPTER 14

Despite James' assurances and my own rational analysis of the situation, I couldn't help but look behind me when I went to the Order of the Coif ceremony the next afternoon. Order of the Coif is the designation you receive if you're in the top ten percent of your class. I was number four. Numbers one through three were just a bit obsessive, if you ask me. We had about 200 students in our class, so there were nineteen of us at the ceremony. Amelia was number eleven. She'd come a long way from that first day.

I didn't have a chance to talk to her before the ceremony, but I noticed her parents, and what looked to be a sister, in the audience. You cannot mistake a Southern family. That kind of polish does not come from anywhere else.

I wondered what they thought of the Andrew Stimpkin situation. My mother, who had been paying attention after all, interrogated me over breakfast. I had finally convinced her not to forcibly move me back to Marshfield. I am sure Amelia's family was very happy with her big firm job. As far away from family law as possible.

James, who managed a couple of hours off, and Holly augmented my group. Then Janice arrived, which was a complete surprise. I made all of the introductions that needed to be made and then had to go up front because the ceremony was about to start.

It was mercifully short and to the point. We received our good wishes from the Dean, a firm handshake, our ridiculously oversized certificates, and a round of applause from the audience. Afterwards, both James and my father insisted on taking pictures. James had the smallest and thinnest digital camera I had ever seen. I saw my dad's eyes light up when James pulled it out of his pocket. My dad asked a few questions and they were off on another interminable conversation, this one about pixels and other digital esoterica.

Then James insisted that my dad take a couple of pictures of the two of us. I wondered how they would turn out – the model and the nerdy girl. Maybe like the fashion dos and don'ts. I would be the one with the black line through my eyes. But when James showed them to me in a postage stamp sized viewer, I did not look that bad. Really, with a little photoshopping, it might actually appear that I belonged with James. Not in his league, but on the farm team.

Janice gave me a big hug. "You did good, kid."

"I try to live up to the Harrington and Associates standard."

"I'm really proud of you. You know that."

Holly gave me a hug. "What's a coif anyway?"

"Good question. It's a judicial headdress of some sort. Janice, do you know?"

"No. I was Order of the Woolsack – and don't ask me what that is, either."

I heard Ashley laugh and looked over. She and James were ribbing each other about something. James had completely conquered the field. If only it were that easy for me. I thought about Mark's party the next day and my stomach knotted up. So many variables and so many ways to fall flat on my face.

Amelia introduced me to her parents and her sister Charlotte. We chatted in a friendly way for a couple of minutes. They had the drawl particular to the Low Country, but their easy manners masked a sharp intelligence. It did not take me long to see that the apple had not fallen far from the tree. Mrs. Carson mentioned that they would be flying back on Saturday.

"So soon?" I said.

"We've got a boat show next week. I need to be there on Sunday to make sure everything is on track," Mr. Carson explained.

"We're coming back for a week at the end of June, right after my niece's wedding," Mrs. Carson said.

"Of course. St. Louis is lovely in June," I said with a smile. "Nice and hot."

"It's nothing compared to Charleston. And I'm not looking forward to that wedding."

"Historic church," Charlotte chimed in. "No AC."

"Father Benedict is probably going to collapse. It's hot under that cassock," Amelia said.

"What about the bride?" I said. "Did she at least pick something light and strapless?"

"No. It's *Gone with the Wind* from start to finish. I just barely escaped being a bridesmaid. Can you imagine? The dresses have hoops!"

"Is *Gone with the Wind* normal for Charleston?" I said.

Charlotte shook her head. "She's just weird."

"We can always sit in the car if it gets too bad," Mr. Carson said.

"Can't we just skip it?" Charlotte said.

"No." Mrs. Carson glared at her. "Although I would have liked to come back here sooner."

"At least you all will give me time to study for the bar," Amelia said.

Amelia and every other law student who planned to stay in St. Louis had signed up for bar review classes. It was going to be like one big reunion – all of us crammed like sardines, or maybe lemmings, in a giant auditorium.

"Please don't say the B-word," I replied.

"Sorry." Amelia closed her mouth with a smile.

The law school graduation ceremony was simple and relatively short. The university graduation ceremony was not simple and not short. We sat on hard metal chairs while the parade of speakers droned on. The keynote speaker was John Major. Even though I am a sucker for an English accent, and have an unusually high tolerance for dry historical ramblings, I caught myself checking my watch multiple times.

Then I had a moment of unadulterated panic as the function broke up. My family had not really coordinated our post ceremony plans, including a location where we would all meet. I spent a good ten minutes fruitlessly searching the crowds, trying to remember what everyone had been wearing that morning. I even approached several groups of people only to realize that the wrinkled sport coat and khaki pants did not belong to my father and the woman with the short spiky hair was not my mother. I finally gave up and sat down on some stone steps off of the quadrangle. I pulled out my cell phone. Had my parents remembered to charge their phone that morning? Doubtful. I tried Ashley instead. The phone rang and rang.

I felt a tap on my shoulder and looked up.

"You could have called me," James said, sitting down on the steps.

"I didn't want to take you away from your family. You're here for Mark." Despite this statement, I couldn't contain the relief I felt.

He put a hand on my knee. "Mark doesn't care. He's just happy to have the dissertation over with."

"Your mother?"

"My mother can wait."

My cell phone rang. Ashley had found my parents on the other side of the quadrangle. James sat with me until I finally saw them emerge from the crowd. He leaned over and planted a kiss right behind my ear. "See you tonight."

"I wouldn't miss it." I smiled bravely, but a spasm of fear shot through my heart.

We pulled up to the Paperelli house at 5:30. The extra half an hour was required to fix me up to Ashley's standards. My family lives in a town full of physicians. We had seen our fair share of large houses, but nothing prepared us for the Paperelli spread. The house was set back from the road on acres of prime Ladue real estate. It had a neo-gothic feel – all nubby stone and crenellated roofing. If you looked at it from a distance, you might have thought it was a small castle.

We stood in front of the house like a bunch of hayseeds as the valet drove my Corsica away. Some Cinderella I turned out to be. I did not even have the heart to ring the doorbell. Ashley was the only one who took it in stride.

"Good going," she said. "See if you can get James to propose."

I shot her a look.

She laughed. "Come on, it's only money."

"You're right." I straightened up and pressed the doorbell. A pleasant young man with black pants and a crisp white shirt opened the door. He had a clipboard in his hand.

"I'm Liz Howe and this is my family."

"Welcome Ms. Howe – and family." He nodded in my parents' direction. "You can follow the other guests around back." He pointed to a sign staked in the yard that we had obviously missed. "Or come in through the house."

"The house," Ashley said, stepping forward.

"Very well." He held the door open for us to pass through. I saw him surreptitiously check our names off on his clipboard.

The hall was the size of my living room, maybe two of them. The young man said, "If you walk straight back all the way down, the party is out the French doors on the terrace.

"Thank you," I said, hurrying my family as they stopped to gawk. I could not blame them. We walked past room after room – a living room, a hall bathroom, a library, a study, another living room which seemed to lead into a kitchen bigger than my whole apartment, some bedrooms, another bathroom and beyond where I couldn't see, an indoor pool. I could smell the chlorine.

We finally rounded a bend and came to an enormous tile-floored sunroom with a glass wall of windows. The windows looked out on a series of terraces and beyond to an immaculate green lawn. People milled about in and around several long white tents. Somewhere, in the distance, I heard a string quartet. In the center of the glass wall was a set of oversized French doors. There was another white-shirted black-panted attendant on the other side of the doors. She looked up and opened one side for us to pass.

"Welcome," she said. "The bar is over there." She gestured to her left. "And the buffet is laid out in the tents below." She pointed. "If there is anything you need, please just let me know."

I thanked her and then scanned the lawn for James or anyone else I could identify.

"I'm hungry. Let's go check out the food," Ashley said.

I gave her an exasperated look.

"What? I don't know anyone here. I might as well eat," she replied.

"Go ahead," a voice behind us said.

"James." I turned around.

He reached out and took my hand in his. Then he said, "Mr. and Mrs. Howe, I'm so glad you could make it. Let me take you to meet my parents."

"Sure," my mom replied confidently. I saw her pull her blouse down just the same. "Ash —"

"She can go eat. My parents won't be offended."

"Thank God for that." Ashley turned and scurried down the stone steps. I envied her like I have never envied anyone in my life.

We started the death march. James leaned down and said in my ear, "It's going to be fine. You don't have to cut off my circulation."

I looked at our intertwined fingers. My knuckles were white. "Sorry." I forced my fingers to let go.

"You look very nice – that's always been a good color on you."

"It should be. You picked it out." The dress was a dark rose, sleeveless and cut just above the knee. It had a sweetheart neckline that, with the proper foundation, did show off my assets. I wore the silver heels that had always brought me luck. One could only hope I wouldn't be called on to put them to the test yet again. I thought of my red dress, now adorning the sofa as pillows. As long as I didn't have to tackle a suspect, this one might survive long enough for a second wearing.

"Oh no," James said under his breath. Maybe I spoke too soon. He slowed our pace. I followed his gaze. There was a group in front of us, standing around talking. I went into analysis mode. One was James' dad – the stomach tucked behind a tight but clearly expensive suit vest was a dead giveaway. One was James' mom. I recognized the hair, and those eyes were hard to miss, even at a distance. The third person had to be Marie. No one else could look that fabulous in broad daylight. Then Theo. He had a distinctive sweet smile and those warm eyes.

Another woman stood with Marie and James' mother. Her back was to us. She was petite with long, smooth brown hair. She wore a sapphire blue dress that managed to be both short and backless. She also wore very, very high heels. I could see how her calves tensed with the effort at maintaining her balance. The stance was familiar, but when she flicked her hair back with her hand, I knew. Angelica.

I stood still. James said, "Just follow my lead, okay?"

I nodded.

He possessively put his arm around my shoulder, and we continued to walk at a stately pace. I heard my parents behind me, but couldn't turn around to see if they noticed.

James' father was the first to welcome us. He greeted me with a jolly smile. "Good to see you again, Liz."

James pivoted to include my parents in the conversation. "Dad, I want you to meet Don and Shirley Howe. Mr. and Mrs. Howe, my father Antonio."

"Pleased to meet you folks. Here, let me introduce you to my Bev." He interrupted her conversation.

She looked up and a superior, and not all together genuine, smile spread across her lips. "Oh, how do you do?" She extended an elegant hand. "You must be Liz's parents. I can see the resemblance." Again the forced smile. "Let me introduce you to my daughter Marie, my son-in-law Theo and Angelica." She paused. "A dear friend of the family."

My mom raised her eyebrows but said nothing. I was not sure if she remembered the name. I hoped not. They all shook hands.

"Liz," Beverly said, "have you and Angelica met?" I could feel James tense beside me.

I virtuously took the high road. "Good to see you again, Angelica." I extended my hand. Hers was clammy to the touch.

I was close enough now to get a good look at her. Despite being sewn into the dress, she seemed thinner. Certainly paler. I could easily see where her foundation ended in a line along her jaw. There was also a strange hard sparkle in her eye. That was new. The smell was the same. White Diamonds. On her it had a musky undertone that was not very pleasant, at least to me. I edged away from her and closer to James. The others did not seem to notice.

"Our son Mark is the proud graduate," Beverly was saying. I'd missed part of the conversation. "He just left to go meet Congressman Boggs at the door. Chris was kind enough to drop by to wish him well. We're hoping Mark can persuade him to join us for some refreshment. He'll be back at any moment."

I looked quickly around for Holly. This should be good.

Antonio asked my parents about Marshfield and the trip down. They chatted for several minutes while Beverly, Marie, James and Angelica continued to eye each other uneasily.

Finally, Beverly turned to me and said, "So Liz, James tells me you have graduated at the top of your class. I'm sure that's quite an achievement." She managed to sound less than sure.

"Thank you."

"I don't know how you do it," Angelica said with a sneer, "I'd be bored to death."

"Good thing they wouldn't have let you in," James said in a low voice.

Marie jumped to her friend's defense. "Angie could do anything she wanted to."

"Aha. Here's Mark." Beverly looked beyond me.

I turned and waved at the approaching figure. He smiled and waved back. Mark and James were clearly brothers, although Mark seemed to favor his father. He was shorter and stockier than James, with brown eyes and dark hair.

He gave me a hug when he reached us. "Good to see you." And then quietly so the others couldn't hear. "Holly?"

"Coming."

He grinned. "Good."

"Chris?" Beverly said.

"Couldn't stay. The campaign and everything. Told me to tell you to count him in for the car wash again next year." I breathed a sigh of relief.

James made the introduction to my parents. We were just finishing when Ashley materialized. We did it all over again. Ashley seemed very impressed with Mark. I caught her looking him over when he was talking to my dad. The introduction to Angelica elicited a hard look in my direction. Unlike my parents, Ashley knew exactly who she was. There was sure to be some commentary when we got home.

We mercifully finished, and Beverly turned to James. "I want you to meet the Oswalds." She took his arm possessively and then looked at my parents. "Please excuse us. And make yourselves at home – our house is your house."

James looked at me, but I smiled and motioned for him to go. My instincts had not failed me.

I walked with my family in the direction of the food. Mark walked with us for a bit and then stopped to talk to a classmate.

"You didn't tell me James had a hot brother," Ashley hissed in my ear as soon as Mark left.

"I told you about Mark."

"You forgot the hot part."

"I guess I didn't notice," I said with a smile.

"You're impossible."

"Don't get your hopes up. He's interested in Holly."

"She should snap him up."

"Tell her that – she didn't seem in the mood to snap anything up the last time I talked to her about it."

"If she doesn't, I will. Some people don't know how good they have it."

Ashley had poured out yet another tale of woe to me the day before. Another boyfriend had dated and dumped her. I tried, in my sisterly way, to tell her that she was looking for the wrong things in a man. I mean, hot is good. I clearly had nothing against it. But it was not going to be enough without common interests. At least not beyond a couple of months. My little sermon was not well received.

When we got to the tents, Ashley abandoned us in search of further prey. I followed my parents but soon felt ready to collapse from exhaustion. My parents went from one tent to the other sampling this thing and that, like bees in a field of flowers. Chatty bees. There was a steady flow of commentary, continuously punctuated with "Would you look at that!" and "I wonder what that could be?" or "Isn't that the darnedest thing!"

I grabbed a glass of lemonade but was too anxious to be hungry. I then went in search of Ashley and stood with her at the dessert table. Even with Ashley by my side, I remained on high alert. At any moment someone I knew might come along and surprise me. Ashley got talking to a friend of Mark's from school, and I hung on as an awkward third for as long as I could. Ashley's flirting reached a painful crescendo, and I just couldn't stand more. I had to go to the ladies room anyway.

I pictured the house in my mind and started the long walk back. The closest bathroom was off the hall before that giant living room with the fireplace. There was certain to be someone to direct me, even if I could not find James. I scanned the crowd but did not see him. Maybe the Oswalds were a fascinating couple.

The attendant still stood beside the French doors.

"Bathroom?" I said.

"Down the hall, fourth door on your left." She opened the door for me to pass through.

I walked along the quiet hall. The house was ten times bigger than I had imagined. The Paperellis confused me. Why would you want the sort of home that a person could get lost in? I found the bathroom on the second try. The sink had the most amazing granite counter – green with chunks of blue iridescence. I had seen expensive jewelry that was not as pretty as that counter. When I was done, I double-checked that the humidity had not run my makeup or frizzed my hair. So far so good.

I stepped out into the hall again and surveyed my surroundings. The living room with the giant fireplace was off to the left. I noticed some photographs lined up on the mantle. Were any of them James? Would I even know? I have a terrible time with photographs. The images are fixed, so I cannot use my normal bag of tricks. Sometimes I recognized clothing, but that was it. Still, my curiosity got the better of me.

I walked over and examined each photograph. I found one that had to be him. The police uniform was a dead giveaway. It had been taken a while ago. James' face seemed rounder, less chiseled. I leaned in closer, studying his younger self. The age difference between us had never been a problem, but I often wondered what a younger James would have thought of me. I looked at the photograph. That devilish grin. Those blue eyes. "You wouldn't have given me a second look." I said to the image.

And then I caught a whiff of something and knew I wasn't alone. I turned around slowly, trying to look calm and indifferent.

She stood in the doorway, her arms crossed, her legs apart. She shifted her weight back and forth in constant movement. I thought she might pop out of that blue dress at any minute, but everything stayed where it should. Maybe she used double-sided tape.

"He wouldn't have. You don't belong here."

Whether she meant in this room or in general, I could not tell. I said nothing.

She looked smug. "He's been using you."

"I don't know what you're talking about." She was not going to fluster me. I reminded my lungs to breathe.

"You know. He was smart to pick you, but the game's over."

I did not dignify that with a response.

"He tried to make me jealous and it worked, but he doesn't need you anymore. I'm back."

"Maybe he doesn't want you back," I said softly.

She laughed. "I can see he's a good liar. But we've talked."

"Not likely," I said with more bravado than I felt.

She laughed again. "You think he wants you? With all of your fancy degrees, you're as stupid as they come."

I stood very, very still, exercising extreme self-control not to speak. She entered the room and then paced back and forth like a caged animal. Finally, she stopped and looked at me with that piercing hatred I had seen before. It took all of my effort to stare back.

"He doesn't want you. I can't believe you thought he did. You're a fucking idiot – and – and he told me what you are. You're a freak!"

My heart leapt into my throat, but I continued to stare. Somehow she knew she had found a foothold. She dug in.

"You're a real live freak. You can't tell one person from another. Do you even know who I am?" She laughed. "Maybe you don't. Well, let me give you a clue. I'm Angelica, James' fiancée."

I took a step back involuntarily and gulped down the bile that swelled in my throat. How could he have told her? I felt my strength beginning to fade. Come on, I chided myself. You've tackled a murderer, you can stand up to her.

She grinned so wide, I could see her gums. They looked almost white. I forced my mind back. She was walking towards me, with a slow sashay of her hips.

"Yes. Poor little Liz. But how could you think? Why would anyone like James want you? You're fucked up, you know?"

She was close, so close. The haze of her perfume made me lightheaded. Do not do it. But my hand itched.

Then she said, "James would have told you himself, but now we've worked it out. He couldn't take another second with y—"

Slap. The sound rang through the empty room. She staggered back, her hand to her cheek.

"I don't care who you are or what you think you know, but don't ever speak to me like that again." My voice was as menacing as I could manage with the hysteria.

I looked down on her with all of the hatred and disgust I felt. It was not her look, but it did the trick. I saw her start to wither. She took a step back. I took one forward. One back. One forward. I backed her out of the room and down the hall. When she did not move fast enough, I raised my hand as if to strike her again. She turned and ran from me, her heels clicking away into the distance.

As soon as she was out of sight, the tears came. Blinded with them, I stumbled into the first room I came to and closed the door. It was the library. The books stared down from their shelves. I collapsed into a leather chair, completely and utterly lost. How could he tell her? Surely she was lying about the rest – he took so much trouble. He said so many things. He seemed happy. But why? Why? And even if he had an answer, it was betrayal, plain and simple. I put my head in my hands.

I sat for a good ten minutes sobbing my heart out, until my head took over and forced my body to pull itself together. A distraction. I needed something to read until I could stop crying and escape. Get out of this giant monstrosity of a house and go home. Books had always been my friends. They'd never let me down.

I looked at the nearest shelf. There, just at eye level, was a row of thin white books. I read the spines. The Harville-Chouteau auction catalogs. I pulled one out towards the end of the group. January 2005. I flipped through it. Paintings, paintings, and more paintings. One caught my eye. The lot description said it was from the collection of Arthur Thornton. I scanned down the page. The following one, too. I went back and counted. There were six paintings in total.

I pulled out the prior catalog. Jewelry. Not good. I put it back. The next one had some paintings. Sure enough, there were three from his collection. I looked at the frontispiece. September 2004. What would make an avid collector sell part of his collection? I heard a knock. I hastily shoved the catalog back on the shelf and looked frantically around. There was no place to hide. I went over to the high windows at the back of the room and turned away.

The window looked out over a beautiful expanse of lawn and manicured plantings. There was a willow tree to the right, bent over and twisted like an old man. The sun hung low in the sky, gilding the leaves of the drooping branches. A gentle breeze wafted through, shifting it like a golden sea anemone. I furiously wiped my eyes with the back of my hand and took deep breaths. I heard the knob turn slowly. I hoped whoever it was would not notice I had been crying. Fat chance.

The door opened with a creak and then James' voice, "Liz, are you in here?"

My throat felt dry. I could not speak. I heard the door swing open, but I did not turn around.

"There you are," he said. I heard a step. And then another. "Are you okay?"

"No! How could you?" I screamed inside my head.

"Liz?"

"Don't." My voice was barely above a whisper.

"What?"

"I'm going," I said quietly. "Please thank your mother for her hospitality." I felt disconnected from my body as I slowly, very slowly, turned and started toward the door. I was in a movie. That was it. A movie of my life. Silent and in slow motion. A comedy? A tragedy? I did not want to know.

"What's going on? Do you feel okay? I'll take you home." He reached for my arm as I passed.

"Don't touch me."

He moved his hand back as if I had burned him. I left him standing in the middle of the room and slammed the door behind me.

I found Ashley and told her I felt sick. She did not believe me, but did not ask questions. We rounded up my parents, briefly said goodbye to the Paperellis and made a clean getaway. We dropped my parents off. I stopped my mother from grilling me with one anguished look. She could not withstand that look. When Ashley and I got home, I banged around the apartment until Ashley had had enough.

"I'm going to the gym," I said.

"Good. Do some work with a punching bag. Whatever James did, you'll forgive him in the morning."

James called me three times while I ran on the treadmill and two more times as I did the strength training circuit. And then another time as I rode on the stationary bike because I could not think of anything else to do, but did not want to go home. Each time I thought about answering, I felt the rage suffocate me. How could he? I kept on going. I did not listen to the voicemail.

I got home and crawled into bed without changing out of my clothes. Holly had arrived by then. She and Ashley watched me walk into my room without a word. Just as well. I would not have known what to say anyway. The next morning, I felt as if someone had taken my head and banged it against the wall over and over again. There was a pain at my temple that throbbed with a heartbeat all its own. My thoughts swam to the surface through molasses. I was at the point of nonplus anyway. No matter how I approached the problem, the only conclusion was betrayal.

At breakfast, I asked Holly about the party. She looked at me strangely, but answered my questions. She arrived after us and Mark pounced on her. He rolled out the charm. Unfortunately, as much as

Holly liked charm, she still was not in the mood. Ashley got annoyed and told her she was crazy. Holly only laughed, which did not bode well for Mark's chances.

After picking at my cereal, I threw most of the soggy mess away. Holly suggested some Tylenol, and I took too many. Then I headed to the shower. The warm water was comforting, but did nothing to clear my head. I crawled back in bed. My phone was on the nightstand. It held several text messages. The latest read, "Call me. Please." Only my inherent frugality stopped me from destroying a perfectly good phone by hurling it against the wall.

I waited in suspended animation with my head under the covers. Surely the Tylenol would do something. I heard a phone ring off in the distance. Or maybe it was muffled by the blanket. I couldn't move. Then I heard voices. It sounded like Ashley had picked up. I eventually fell asleep and woke up suffocated. I wriggled around in the sheet until I got my head free. I took a deep breath. The cold air hit my lungs with a shock. I sat up. Someone tapped softly on my door. "Come in," I said weakly. My mom stuck her head around the door.

"Time to get up," she said in just the tone of voice she used with me as a girl.

"What time is it?"

"One o'clock. Time for you to leave that bed and stop feeling sorry for yourself." I could tell from her expression that she wanted to ask questions.

"I don't want to talk."

"Now, honey."

"Please. I'm still too angry to discuss it."

"Okay." She really meant it was my loss.

The day passed with excruciating slowness and warp speed. Ten minutes would take an eternity and two hours would be gone in a blink. Ashley wanted to see the St. Louis Science Center, so we went out. The Science Center has two sides that are joined by a long bridge over the highway that divides them. There are radar guns that you can point at the cars. Ashley loved that. She played *Charlie's Angels* while I listlessly watched the traffic. I would have to face James at some point. Not today. And maybe not tomorrow. I couldn't think. The cars flowed under me. My mind wandered. Blue ones. Red ones. I had a sudden flash of insight.

Vince's party was a blessing and a curse. At least it got me out of the house. My parents decided to call it a night. Nine o'clock was late to them. Holly declined the invitation since she did not know Vince and wasn't very confident in her salsa skills. Ashley had no such scruples. She and I set out together. When we pulled up to the house, the cars already lined the street. We parked way down the road. I noticed Amelia's car towards the front. She worked fast.

As we walked up the steep driveway, the music flowed out into the night. I looked at Ashley and knew she felt the same sense of déjà vu. "Who's supposed to give who the 'buck up little camper' speech?" she asked.

I smiled for the first time all day. "I think it's you. Haul me home if I do something crazy, okay?"

"That's supposed to be my line."

"Not anymore."

Ashley patted my shoulder, and I started to feel better. Plus, Latin music doesn't allow for much ennui. The beat was infectious.

The front door of the house stood wide open. People spilled out onto the lawn. I wondered how long it would take for the police to show up. Then again, maybe Vince's parents had invited the neighbors. There were enough people to fill a small town.

We muscled our way in through several loud Spanish conversations. I smelled food. Someone appeared to be cooking in the kitchen. Rice certainly. I saw a person who I was pretty sure was Vince's dad in the middle of the living room. He had a host-like demeanor. He saw me and waved me over. When I reached him, he gave me a hug and a kiss on the cheek. It took me a second to remember that this was normal behavior. I handed him the bottle of wine I brought and Vince's gift, a lawyer-like pen set. He thanked me profusely and set them down on a table at his elbow. I presented Ashley. She did not flinch at so much affection.

"The kids are downstairs," he said above the din. I could feel the beat from the music through the floor. I took Ashley's arm and we moved toward the stairs. We wended our way past people of every age and description. There were even little kids racing in and out amongst the adults in some endless game of tag. It was glorious pandemonium. I had never seen a party like it.

The basement was dimly lit with a red light. What I could see had a pink tint to it. The furniture was at the ends of the room, with the middle one long expanse of dance floor. There were people everywhere. Couples swirling around. Women dancing in groups. Men standing, beers in hand. I turned to Ashley, who stood transfixed. The dancing couples moved together as if they were one body. In and out. How they managed to miss each other in the crowd was beyond me.

Now, how to proceed? If I couldn't find Vince, it was a night of standing against the wall. Then I noticed a hand above the crowd. I squinted. Maybe. It waved at me, and I knew.

"Vince," I said loudly into Ashley's ear.

"Let's go." She pulled us into the maelstrom. I was clumsier than the average partygoer and bumped into three different couples before I got to Vince. He pulled away from his partner, who turned out to be Amelia. I recognized the perfect little black dress. She was flushed and smiling from the dancing. That boded well.

"Welcome," Vince shouted as he gave me a quick hug and a kiss on the cheek. Apparently a party brought out the Colombian in him.

"Great party," I shouted back, and then pointing in her direction, "My sister, Ashley."

"Vince." He gave her a hug and a kiss as well. "Do you dance?"

"Not well," she replied. Vince gestured to someone behind him. A man emerged from the mass of dancers. He seemed younger than Vince, but there was something familiar about the way he stood. Vince slapped him on the back. "My cousin, Juan. From Texas."

Vince gestured to Ashley and then leaned over and said something into Juan's ear. Juan hugged and kissed us both. Then he spoke to Vince in Spanish. I couldn't catch it. Vince nodded and Juan smiled. He seemed to size Ashley up with his eyes and, grinning, extended a hand to her. She grasped it and he pulled her in. After a moment I could not see her at all.

Vince turned to Amelia and gestured at me. "Do you mind?"

She gave way gracefully. "No, I'm tired."

Vince grabbed my hand before I could react. We disappeared into the mass of dancers. Vince pulled me closer than in any of our practice runs. The song was a fast *merengue*, and I had to concentrate really hard. I avoided Vince's toes more times than not. He laughed gallantly whenever I crushed his foot, but did not let me go. We danced a while in silence, but when I looked at his face, his eyes questioned me. "James?" he finally said.

"Not good."

His eyes got very big for a moment, and then I felt his arm tighten around my waist and his hand flex against my back. He pulled me closer still, chest to chest. We moved together in time. It felt strange to be in his arms, but not bad. No, not bad at all. There was something about dancing that made Vince seem – well – I could see why Amelia had arrived early. He was wearing a different cologne than I remembered. Gucci maybe. His skin smelled dark and musky. A sensual smell. I thought about our one and only date. And that kiss. His eyes met mine. His look was intense. Focused. If I just let go a second I might give in to it. Forget about James. Forget about everything.

I felt his breath on my cheek. One inch more and our mouths would touch. Skin on skin. My throat felt dry. I touched my lip with my tongue. He tilted his head slightly. I felt my own head tilting. And then he flinched. I'd stepped on him again. I pulled back and shook my head, trying to knock some sense into my brain. I could not use him to solve my problems. He did not deserve that.

He spun me out and I crashed into another dancer. Then he tried it again, and I got it right. When he pulled me back this time, he crossed his arms in front of me like an embrace. He held me there a few seconds. I waited, part of me still half wanting him to try something, but then I was out again into a lopsided pinwheel. Finally, I faced him once more, laughing at my profound inadequacy.

He laughed with me. I knew then that he knew the game was up. For the present, there would be nothing but friendship between us. Oddly, he seemed more relieved than disappointed.

Despite the potential for injury, he indicated we should keep going into the next song. It was another fast number. A *salsa*. I tried very hard to pull this one off. In fact, I was concentrating so hard on my footwork and avoiding death to myself or Vince that I did not see the figure making his way through the crowd until he was next to me. I looked up. James.

Vince stopped, but held my arm protectively. James had a look on his face I recognized instantly. Fury. I felt my own white hot anger blaze up. I stared back.

"Outside," he shouted over the din. Vince tightened his grip on my arm.

I glanced at Vince. "I'll take care of this," I said. He let go reluctantly.

I turned and started towards the stairs. I did not look back as I marched up to the front door and then out onto the lawn. People were milling about on the front stoop and clustered around the house, smoking, drinking, and generally carrying on. I walked down the grass slope until I reached the street. I moved beyond the line of parked cars and then turned, crossing my arms in front of me. This ought to be good.

He stopped and glared at me. "You have some nerve. Stalking off like that. Putting me through hell and then coming here to Vince – like nothing – like you can just move on." His voice was low and bitter hard.

I couldn't believe my ears. "Me? You have no excuse for what you've done!"

"What have I done, Elizabeth? See, that's the whole problem."

I wanted to wipe that patronizing smirk off his face with my fist, but I held it together. "You don't even know what you've done?" My voice went up an octave. "It was that insignificant you don't even know?"

"How could I, when you won't tell me what the hell is going on?"

"Going on?" Now I was really wound up. "Don't play innocent with me. You damn well know what's going on. You started it!"

"What? What did I start? Tell me."

I lost it. "Go talk to your precious Angie. Your fucking friend of the family!" I screamed so loud that I saw heads turn from the lawn. The sound of my voice echoed back to me from around the bend in the road. Even the guys with the cigarettes and beer on the porch looked over to see what was going on.

I put my hands to my face and turned away. James grabbed my arm and forced me to look at him. "What the hell does Angie have to do with all of this?"

"You told her! That's what she has to do with this!"

He let go of me and raked his hand through his hair. "For the love of God, what did I tell her? What could I possibly have told her?"

"About me!" The echo sounded hysterical. I took a deep breath. "You told her about me. It wasn't your secret to tell. God damn it! How could you?" I wiped my wet face with the back of my hand.

"What?" He seemed confused.

"Don't lie to me. It only makes it worse. Even you must see that."

"Okay." He raked his hand through his hair again. "Let's start from the beginning. What did Angie say to you?"

"Oh, I don't know. Only that you told her I couldn't recognize anyone. And maybe that I was a freak. Oh yes and I forgot, that you were just using me to get her back."

"You believed her?"

"Gee, I don't know, it sounds pretty convincing coming from someone who shouldn't know anything about me. How could you? It was hard enough to confess to you – let alone the Angies of this world." My hands were wet, but the tears kept coming. If only I had thought to grab a tissue.

James stared at the ground. "I didn't tell Angie."

"She didn't guess, James. Please, I'm not that stupid."

"She knew, but I didn't tell her."

"Okay, then who did you tell? Just how many people around here know what kind of freak I am?"

"You're not a freak. Stop saying that." He hung his head. "I told my family. Well, my mom and Marie. They must have told Angie."

"Your whole family knows?" This was even worse. "You had no right. No right at all!"

"Look, I'm sorry. I shouldn't have told them. I wouldn't have told them, but I couldn't help it. They were running you down and I – I love you."

There was the L-word again. Convenient. I was not in the mood. "Telling them how disabled I am was your solution? I can see how that would be very, very helpful."

"No! Can you stop for a minute and let me explain?"

I crossed my arms and looked at him.

"I was trying to tell them how great you are and —"

I continued to stare.

"Oh, you're impossible!"

"I'm impossible? Thanks so much."

He took my shoulders and forced me to look at him. "You are not defective. You are not damaged. You are – are the most wonderful person I've ever met, and I don't care. Do you understand? I don't care who knows it."

"But I do. Damn it. It's my secret."

"But why is it a secret?"

"You haven't lived my life. Hell! You don't know what it's like. And you've just given more ammunition to the one person who could do the most damage."

"It's only ammunition if you let it be."

"No." I saw someone approaching us out of the corner of my eye. I turned. James looked over. I could tell from the walk that it was Vince.

"Damn," James said under his breath, and then, "let's go back in."

I wiped my face with my hand again. "I'm not —"

"You're not making this any easier. Please. Be an adult. We can talk about this later."

"Don't pull rank on me." I turned on my heel and marched back up the hill. As I passed Vince, I smiled at him. I hoped that the light was too dim to see the tear streaks on my face and that the waterproof mascara lived up to the promises on the package. I heard him say something to James, but kept walking. I looked back only as I reached the door. They were standing together on the lawn, so I made my getaway.

Once inside the house, I found the hall bathroom. I shut the door and turned the lock. I ran some water in the sink and washed my face. That made me feel better. I looked at myself critically. My foundation was almost gone, and I had smeared my eye shadow, but the mascara held. My hair was a mess. I ran more water and tried to tamp it down. So-so results. What I really needed was some good product.

I took a deep breath. So maybe James had not betrayed me. Well, he had, but for good reasons. At least that was the story. He seemed sincere, and I could see how he could have blurted it out. He'd promised to deal with his family on my behalf. Up till now, I had not imagined what that entailed. Yelling. Screaming. Fights over me. Isn't that what every girl dreams of? A knight in shining armor to champion her. Except, my heart still felt broken.

I'm not sure how long I stayed in the bathroom. Long enough for a line to form. I smiled a weak apology as I opened the door. I decided to go back downstairs. If I could find Ashley, this night might finally end. I did not want to talk to James. I was pretty sure I couldn't do it without sobbing. And I did not feel like giving him the satisfaction. I stood a little inside the basement doorway, trying to get my bearing in the dim light. No luck. All I could see was a mass of pulsing bodies. A new song started up. Another *merengue*. I felt an arm come around my waist from behind, but before I could protest, James turned me in his arms and held me fast.

Then he was moving me into the crowd. He held me so tightly that I could not break away. It was as if we were soldered together.

Whenever I moved, he moved. He could not have designed a better trap for me. I was dealing with a chess master.

I looked at him resentfully. His eyes bored into mine with a look that was fierce and tender. I looked away. My body felt raw. Like someone had chewed me up and spit me out. I wanted to make it all go away. He was so close to me now that the sweet smell of his skin filled my head. My heart sped up like it always did. I felt the first stirrings of desire. Traitor.

"I'm lost," he said into my ear. "Tell me what to do."

"I don't know." I leaned my head against him and let him carry me through the rest of the dance. My anger had slipped away somehow, only to be replaced by something worse – sadness. The next song was a slow number, old by the sound of the recording. And known. I saw James silently mouthing the words.

"Lourdes liked these old songs," he said into my ear. Lourdes. Great. Another thing I did not want to think about.

"I meant what I said before."

"Which part?" I said.

"The part about – I didn't mean to hurt you. I never want to hurt you. You have to believe me."

"I'm trying to remember that."

"But?"

"This is a brave new world you've pushed me into. I always trusted the people who knew."

"I'll deal with my family. I just want a chance to make things right. Please?"

I hesitated a moment, but I could not resist him. That was my fatal flaw. I nodded.

"Thank you." He hugged me as the music stopped.

"Liz!" Ashley called from behind me. I saw a head and then she emerged from the crowd, dragging someone. "James!" she said, then looking at me, "Good to see you." The look said she would force the details out of me later. She turned to the guy at her side. "Carlos. Meet my sister. Liz, this is Carlos. He's at UW, can you believe it?" Carlos was thin, a little shorter than Ashley in heels, but handsome in a boyish way.

I pulled away from James. "Nice to meet you Carlos." I leaned in, expecting the kiss on the cheek, but he shook my hand. One didn't know which way to go with this crowd.

James stepped forward. "James. Liz's boyfriend." Check. They shook hands. James turned away from me and focused on Ashley. He pulled out the winning smile. "Ash, you don't want to go home yet, do you?" Check.

"No." Ashley looked shyly at Carlos.

"Then I'll take Liz home. She's pretty tired." Another smile at Ashley. I could see her melting where she stood. Check. I opened my mouth to speak but he cut me off.

"Come on Liz." An arm casually but firmly around my shoulders. "Let's say goodbye to Vince." Checkmate.

"I need to get the keys from you," Ashley said. She followed us up the stairs. Despite the narrow space, James managed to keep a tight hold on me. I finally gave up trying to get away. I didn't have the energy left to fight. I found my purse and handed the keys to her. She stuck them in her pocket. "Good night, you two – don't worry James, you'll get out of the doghouse sometime this century."

I found Vince and thanked him for a lovely party. He thanked us both for coming, but as I leaned in for the kiss on the cheek, he said, "If you don't want to leave, I'll throw him out."

"I'm okay, but thanks," I whispered back.

Then we found Vince's parents and repeated the procedure. Amelia was just coming up the stairs to claim Vince for a dance as we finished, so we waved to her as we walked out the door.

I closed my eyes and sat back in the seat as James started the car. When I opened them, I knew from the street that he was taking me back to his house. So much the better, I guess. At least we would be alone. The raw feeling felt more like fatigue now, my body weighted with cement. A mob victim floating down to the bottom of the sea. I looked at James out of the corner of my eye. He was Italian, after all.

He helped me out of the car and all but carried me into the house. I flopped like a rag doll on the couch. James sat down beside me. "I'm only going to ask you to do this once, but could you please tell me exactly what happened with Angie? I want to have all of my facts straight when I take my sister on."

"You're sure it was Marie?"

"No doubt. She'd tell Angie anything. Just ask Theo."

"That man is a saint."

"You don't know the half of it. So tell me."

I recounted the dialog word for word. James' expression turned hard.

"Oh, and I kind of did something I shouldn't have."

"What?"

"Do you really want to know? I tried to resist, but she made me so angry —" I hoped they would still let me sit for the bar exam. Assault convictions do not look good on your record.

"Now I have to know." There was a twinkle in his eye.

"I slapped her as hard as I could."

He burst out laughing.

"It's not funny." But I could not stop the smile that sprang to my lips.

"I'm sorry." He wiped his eyes. "I would have given anything to see that. She did look red in the face when I saw her later."

"You, of all people, shouldn't condone violence."

"She deserved it."

"Something's wrong with her."

He shook his head. "Unfortunately, she's been like that for years."

His arm came around me. "I've put you through hell. Are you ever going to forgive me?"

"I told you I'm working on it."

"I just wish you'd see that there's no deep dark secret. Angie can't hurt you."

"She's done a fine job so far."

"What I mean is that there's no reason to be ashamed of anything. It's who you are. It's why I love you."

Love. He'd said it again. Could I trust that he meant it? I had to ask. "You wouldn't love me if I were normal?"

"No. I mean, yes. This isn't coming out right. I love you for you."

Hmm. Three times in one night. "Oh."

"I don't like the sound of that."

"I'm just having trouble with the concept – you love me because I'm defective?"

"You're not defective. It's just you." He paused and then said, "Do you love me for my defects?"

"Until a day ago, I didn't know you had any. Wait. I take that back. You hum off key."

"And for some unknown reason you still love me?"

The hesitation moved me in a way that no amount of persuasion ever could. He was unsure. Could it be that the L-word hung over him, too? I'd never thought – it seemed impossible. His eyes were unusually blue in the soft light.

"I tried not to love you," I said. "Remember?"

He ran a finger down my cheek, tracing the outline of my face. "And I tried. Remember?" Our lips met. Sweet and seductive. I seemed powerless to resist.

Love. That is what it meant. I wanted to forgive him. I wanted to give him my whole heart no matter what it cost me. I disengaged and took a deep breath. I was still sad. I was still resentful. But I loved him, and so I would forgive him.

"Liz?" The anxiety in his voice struck me to the bone.

"I forgive you."

"I'll try to fix this, I promise."

"There's no way to fix it, but that doesn't matter anymore."

He smiled that lazy smile that started at the back of his eyes. "Then let me make it up to you."

I guess I would have to be satisfied with that.

CHAPTER 15

On Sunday, I told James I could not handle his family birthday celebration the following Saturday. He said it wouldn't be the same without me. "I'm sure," was all I said in return. He did try the pleading expression I found so hard to resist, but I stood firm. Let them talk about me behind my back. It was better than dealing with them in my present state of mind. Forgiveness is difficult. I had forgiven James, although it might have helped if he truly understood what he had done. He'd fed me to the wolves. Now how was I supposed to forgive the wolves?

This did not mean I had no plans for his birthday, which was actually Monday the 29th. I refused to tell him anything except that he should not stay too late at work. My first task was locating the gift. I set out for the antique mall on Thursday morning right after seeing my parents and Ashley out the door. If that didn't work, I would still have time to locate an alternate gift somewhere else.

Antique malls are strange places. There usually isn't much antique about them. Most are like giant garage sales with a few valuable items thrown in. And so much depends on the booth. Each booth is rented by a different person with different ideas about what will sell. I love them. They are like walking through a time machine. And you can touch everything.

The one I went to had a couple of booths dedicated to 1950's kitchen implements and cookbooks. James was a devotee of Julia Child, but he lacked a few important volumes. One was *Secrets of the Great French Restaurants* by Louisette Bertholle, Julia Child's collaborator. Another was the *Larousse Gastronomique,* the golden bible of French cuisine. I remembered seeing both, along with a number of out of print titles, at the antique mall. I only hoped that they were still there.

As I walked through the front door, a familiar voice hailed me from the cash register. "Liz Howe!"

"Matt Crandall. I didn't know you worked here. Do you ever sleep?"

He grinned. "I pitch in every now and then. My boyfriend's parents own this place. Hey, let me introduce you." He picked up the microphone for the sound system. "Would Blair please report to the front desk? Customer needs assistance."

"I don't want to bother him."

"No bother," a voice said. I turned around. There stood a very slight blond man. He had such even features he could have been called beautiful. He was dressed in dark-wash jeans and a dark purple jacket, cut like a motorcycle jacket, with rivets at the hem. The jacket was covered with the most amazing collection of brooches I'd ever seen. They glittered under the fluorescent light.

I extended my hand. "Liz. Your pins are amazing."

"Blair." He gave my hand a shake. "Glad I can finally meet you. And thanks – I've been collecting a long time."

I turned back to Matt. "I'm sorry I haven't been able to come see your work yet. I still have your business card."

"Maybe you can come to this." Matt handed me a glossy brochure across the counter. "We're all doing a show to benefit Arthur Thornton. You know, the guy injured by that bombing downtown."

"Yes. How is he doing?" Vince told me he was back home, but struggling with all of his injuries. These still included blindness brought on by the head trauma.

"Not good," Blair answered. "He's done so much for the local art scene, that we just couldn't sit by and do nothing. We decided a show might raise some money to help him with expenses. We've all pledged a portion of the proceeds."

"Are you an artist as well?"

"Jewelry." Matt and Blair said at the same time.

"I'll certainly come." I looked down at the flyer. The show was in two weeks.

A middle-aged woman approached the counter with a large and very ugly piece of pottery. She set it down and got out her wallet to pay. Blair and I gave each other a look. I knew then that we were kindred spirits. Matt began to ring the purchase up.

"So what are you looking for today?" Blair asked.

"Cookbooks. French cuisine. It's a birthday present."

"For?"

"My boyfriend."

"Ah. Matt mentioned him." Blair smiled at me. "So he cooks, too?"

"When he has time."

"Lucky girl. Let me show you a few things."

After picking out James' gifts, which included the two books I wanted and a third written by the chef of the Kennedy White House,

Blair and I wandered around. The sarcasm flowed freely. Pottery was just the start of the bizarre items up for sale. Who would not love troll canisters, a bright orange recliner, lamps made out of beer cans and a giant plastic Smurf head? Then there were the sublimely beautiful items, like the crystal chandelier with the teardrop pendants. It showered the space below with a thousand fragments of rainbow. Or a Victorian carved coral locket depicting the three muses. And a set of Italian demitasse cups from the mod 1960's that were so delicate, you could see your hand through them.

We stopped at one case. "I think you'll like this." Blair pointed to a ceramic bowl decorated with an intricate pattern of multi-colored glazes. The colors were saturated and intense.

"I do like it." And then I had a brilliant idea. It was just the right size and shape. "Could you get it out for me?"

I turned the bowl over in my hands. I could read "Tira" incised on the bottom, but nothing more. "What do you think this would look like with some roses and floating candles?"

Blair's eyes lit up. "Gorgeous, but the roses have to be dark red."

"You've read my mind." I looked at the tag. "I think I can handle twenty-five dollars."

"A steal. And since it's over twenty I can give you a ten percent discount. I'm not supposed to tell you that."

"I knew I liked you."

We walked back to the counter, where I had left the books. Matt was gone.

"Tell your boyfriend he's a lucky guy," Blair said as he rang me up.

"Tell yours the same."

Blair laughed. "Oh I do. Don't worry. I'll see you at the show, right?"

"I wouldn't miss it."

On Monday afternoon, I let myself into James' house with my key. I had never used the key before. It felt strange to wander his rooms by myself. I curbed my curiosity. I muscled the cooler in from the car and then hauled in the other bags. I wasn't sure where James stored everything, so it took me a little while to assemble what I needed. Then I got to work.

At precisely 7:05, I heard James' keys in the lock. I lit the final floating candle and blew out the match.

"What smells so good?" I heard him say.

"Dinner," I replied, reaching the kitchen. He caught me around the waist.

"What have you been up to?" He planted a kiss on my lips. He might have gone farther, but I stepped back.

"That can wait. I'm just ready to do the filets."

He shrugged out of his jacket and went to hang the jacket and store the holster in the hall closet. When he returned, he said, "Wow. This is a lot of food."

"A Wisconsin feast. I had my parents bring a few things when they came. The rest of the tenderloin is in the freezer for later. I figured we couldn't eat more than a couple filets."

"They brought a whole tenderloin?"

"It's nice to be able to cut the filets a little thicker, don't you think?"

"I suppose so."

"And it's local beef. No hormones or anything like that."

He leaned over the stove and lifted a lid. "Um – squash?"

"Zucchini and yellow squash from my parents' garden. Sautéed with onion and herbs."

He lifted another. "And this?"

"Wax beans with bacon. Also from the garden. They're my favorite."

He lifted the lid on a small saucepan. "That smells fantastic."

"Morel mushrooms in wine sauce – for the filets."

"And?" He gestured at a platter of nibbles set out on the island.

"Cheese. You have to have cheese. Try the blue. It is out of this world."

He popped a piece in his mouth. "Amazing."

"We do know something about cheese where I come from. Should I start the steaks?"

"Please. I'm starving. And I see wine. Can I pour you a glass?"

"Sure." I turned on the burner and the butter started to sizzle. When it was really hot, I placed two filets in the pan. The key is to give them a good searing on the outside.

"Where did you find the wine? It's very good." He sounded suspicious.

"The salesperson at the Wine Merchant suggested it."

He set a glass down beside me on the counter. "Cheers."

We clinked glasses and I took a sip. The wine was really good.

He put a hand on my shoulder. "So how do you know when they are done? I don't have much practice cooking them in a pan like that."

"Smell mostly. I suppose I could time it." I felt his hand move up until it rested on my neck. His fingers slid up and down, brushing my skin lightly. I shivered, remembering another time and place. I wondered if he had any clue what an accidental touch could do.

I moved one filet to the plate. It was very rare. "Medium or well done?"

"Medium. May I?"

I turned. "May you what?"

He put his arms around me. "Distract the chef." He leaned in.

"You have no idea what you do to me," I said.

"I have some idea."

"Don't get any ideas until after dinner." But he kissed me before I could say more.

We sat together at one end of the dining room table. I turned the lights down low. The candles flickered, throwing shadows on the walls. James' steak was only a little overdone, but he didn't complain.

"I like what you've done with the table," he said, taking another bite of filet.

"It helps when you have beautiful things to work with. Just how do you happen to have proper table linens?"

"I'm not a savage." He took a sip of wine. "I don't recognize the bowl. Is that new?"

"Not new, but not one of yours. I bought it."

"Seems familiar. I think Angie must have had something like it."

"Don't tell me we have the same taste."

"Except in me."

"Very funny."

"I found out what happened," he said.

"Do I want to know?"

"You already do. It was my sister." He bit down on a mushroom. "This is delicious. If I'd known you could cook, I'd have asked you out sooner."

"Thanks." I chewed on a yellow bean. The bacon-infused taste of home.

"You're sure you're not Italian?"

"English, Swedish, Russian and maybe Native American – yes. Italian – no."

"You've mastered the food is love concept."

"That's universal."

"Works for me."

"This digression is your idea of distracting me?" I said.

He nodded.

"It's not going to work. Why did Marie tell Angie? Does she hate me that much?"

He sipped his wine. "I think it was partly misplaced loyalty to Angie and partly because I didn't tell her not to."

"Wouldn't she have known to keep it to herself?"

"This comes back to our fundamental difference of opinion. I might have indicated that you were open about your issues."

"Still not there yet."

"I know. I'm just explaining what happened," he said.

"What did happen? I mean, what did your mother and sister say that made you want to blurt my secret out?"

"I had my reasons."

"I'd like to know what I'm dealing with."

"And what am I dealing with?" he said.

"Umm?"

"Your family. They must have something to say about me."

"Nothing but good things. My parents think you treat me well – despite the graduation party fiasco – so they're fine with you."

"And Ashley?"

"She lets you call her Ash. I don't think you'll have problems there." I took another sip of wine. "Besides, she thinks you're hot."

He threw back his head and laughed. "She didn't actually say that?"

"She did. Don't get too excited. You haven't met some of her other boyfriends."

"Low standards?"

"Let's say unusual taste," I replied.

"And you?"

"You know my taste."

"You've never said much about your past."

"There isn't much to tell. And weren't we speaking of yours, namely Angie?"

"I'm dealing with my family and I'll deal with Angie. They will come around."

I had my doubts. "So your sister originally set you up with Angie?" I said.

"I'll answer yours if you answer mine."

"Fair enough, but you go first."

"More like she invited Angie over so much that I got the hint."

"I doubt you were forced into it."

"Angie can be very charming and —"

"She's beautiful," I added.

"It's more than that. She's like a force of nature. She'd moved in before I even knew what happened."

"You were helpless to resist?"

"In some ways." He paused, considering his words. "I was ready for a relationship no matter how bad it got. You have no idea the pressure I felt."

"You don't seem the type to buckle under pressure."

"I thought I was in love with Angie. Everyone told me I was. You'll believe a lie if it's repeated often enough."

"I'm sure you were in love."

He shook his head. "I can talk to you. I could never do that with her."

"Why not? It seems like it would be a prerequisite for spending your life together."

"I never knew whether she'd hug me or bite my head off. I was in a constant state of suspense."

"Hmm." I ate a piece of zucchini. Buttery with the smooth savory sweetness of sautéed onion. My mom had outdone herself with the produce.

"You sound like you know what I'm talking about."

"Maybe. But it's still your turn."

"What else do you want to know?"

"Didn't your sister see how miserable you were?"

"I tried to hide it and Angie looks up to Marie. She'd never show Marie her dark side."

"Just to you."

"And you." He got that mischievous look in his eye. "I would have loved to see you take her on."

"It wasn't my finest hour. I was just trying to avoid excessive sobbing."

"I'm sorry."

I reached for my wine glass and realized it was empty. James refilled it without a word.

"Don't do that to me ever again, okay?" he said.

"What?"

"Give me the silent treatment. Whatever it is – whatever I've done – yell at me, I don't care. Not knowing was worse than anything."

"I didn't know what to say or what to think," I said quietly.

He reached across the table and took my hand. "Just talk to me – even if all you do is scream. I need the chance to make it right."

"I promise."

"And so do I."

I smiled. "I'm sure I'm going to do something at some point that will make you mad enough to regret that promise."

"Doubt it."

"Give me time." I started in on the second glass of wine.

"Don't take it like a personal challenge."

"I won't need to. But I'm not looking for a fight right now."

"And I'm not picking one either, unless you plan to renege on our deal."

"Deal?"

"It's my turn to ask questions."

"Ask away. The answers will disappoint you."

"Hardly. Let's start with Nick Lee."

"You remembered his name."

"It's the only name you gave me."

"It's the only one that counts for much of anything," I said.

"First love?"

"So to speak."

"You sound unsure."

"I do understand volatile relationships."

"Did he hurt you?" James' voice was low and serious.

"Not like that."

He seemed relieved.

"We hurt each other, fighting over silly things. It was good when we weren't fighting."

"Why did it end?"

"A fight over calculus. Look, this is silly. I was in high school."

"I still get to ask the questions."

"But why do you care about the answers? I had one serious boyfriend before I met you, and I met him when I was fifteen."

"You didn't meet anyone in college?"

"A couple of errors in judgment that were quickly rectified and had no lasting consequences. I'm now careful about who I drink with."

"Law school?"

"You've met the one person who asked me out," I said.

"It's a mystery."

"Not really. I'm not the sort of woman men my age fall for. I can't pull off cute and perky. Perky is very popular."

"Perky is annoying," he said.

"That explains that."

"Not entirely. Joe Henderson and Vince Lopez were clearly interested. And, if you're so unattractive, how did you get Nick in the first place?" James took a sip of wine.

"I seduced him."

James choked and then swallowed hard. "At fifteen?"

"He was fifteen too. It didn't take much."

"It doesn't at that age. How did this happen?"

"At the movies."

"In the theater?" The look of shock on his face was priceless.

I laughed. "No. I attacked him at the theater, but the movie wasn't that long. We had to sneak around before we could consummate the relationship."

"Such lawyerly precision. It was your first?"

"For both of us. And you? I'm guessing Lourdes?"

"No actually."

I almost dropped my glass. "Don't tell me it was middle school?"

"After. Lourdes was a good Catholic girl. Not that I didn't try."

"So?"

"I had a lot of fun in college."

"I can imagine. But you must have studied at some point. You graduated *summa cum laude* if I remember correctly."

"The engagement announcement?"

I nodded.

"My life's an open book."

"For the readers of the *Ladue News*. How did you accommodate so much fun in your schedule?"

"I slept with smart girls."

"That gives new meaning to study group."

"I was a biology major. I'm sure you remember that."

"Of course. I just never put that spin on it before."

"Extracurricular studies." He drank the last of his wine, poured himself a third glass and then filled my glass with the rest of the bottle.

"Are you trying to drink me under the table again?"

"You found me out."

"There's no need."

"I understand that now. I'll have to watch out when I take you to the movies."

"Nick didn't have it so bad."

"I envy him. I assume he's never gotten over you?"

"Why do you say that?"

"You wouldn't be easy to forget."

"He says he wants to get back together," I admitted, "but he's on the rebound from his college girlfriend."

"And you're not available."

"I've made that clear."

"You're still in contact," he said.

"He sends me email now and then. He's in New York, working on Wall Street."

"Smart then."

I gave him a wry look. "I slept with smart boys. Have we hashed out my pathetic love life enough or should I continue to hold dessert?"

"We can hash and serve dessert." He stood up and started to clear the table. "It smells like you baked me something."

"Something you don't deserve after this conversation." I picked up a plate.

"What?"

"Angel food cake."

We started walking to the kitchen. "From scratch?" He seemed impressed.

"I have two pound cakes in your freezer to prove it."

He looked at me questioningly.

"You have to do something with twelve yolks. Besides, pound cake freezes well."

"Ever practical, Liz." We set the dishes on the counter, and then retrieved the rest.

I pulled the angel food pan towards me and flipped it over onto a plate. "Wait. You don't own a cake stand do you?"

"No. Is that a problem?"

"Not at all. I was shocked at the table linens. The plate will be fine." I jiggled the cake form until the angel food wriggled out. "Voila. And now the glaze." I pulled another bowl towards me. It was still comfortably warm. "Do you want the glaze on the cake now, or do you want it on the pieces individually?"

"What is it?"

"A Concord grape and brown sugar glaze." I showed him the bowl.

"Where did you get Concord grapes?"

"The oncologist my mom works for has an arbor in his yard."

"That must be some yard."

"It is. So what would you like?"

"If you put it on the pieces, does that mean I can have more on mine?"

"Sure." I picked up the cake. He took the bowl. "You're the birthday boy. Interested in candles?"

We set the things down on the dining room table. "Do I get the song too?" he said.

"A la Marilyn Monroe if you want."

"JFK would envy me."

"Not likely. But I bet she couldn't cook."

"Whereas you have the full package – the body and the food," he said.

"You're a good liar, you know that?"

"Most women wouldn't object if their boyfriends told them they looked like Marilyn Monroe."

"Even if it's ridiculous?"

"They'd blush and say thank you."

"I can't manage the blush, but thank you," I replied.

"We'll work on the blush later."

"It may be hard." I put the candles on the cake as I gave him a low and breathy Happy Birthday. "The blue are tens, the green are ones and this red is one to grow on." I struck a match and lit each candle. James watched me in silence.

"Why hard?" he finally said.

"I seduced a boy at fifteen. Apparently, I'm capable of anything. Did you make a wish?"

"Yes. And you've given me a challenge I can't resist." He inhaled and then blew out all of the candles.

I clapped. "Very good."

"Every year it gets harder. I'm winded."

"You're lucky I thought of the decade candles."

"Otherwise it'd be a sea of wax."

"That would ruin the cake." I cut him a large slice and then doused it liberally with the purple-black glaze. I handed it to him and waited for the verdict.

He took a bite and chewed slowly. "This is a slice of heaven. And the sauce," he took the spoon and ladled more sauce on his piece, "is phenomenal. How did you make it?"

"It doesn't taste like the grape jelly you get in the store, does it?"

"Not even close."

I served myself a piece and spread some of the sauce over the top. James had almost finished his. I took a bite. There is nothing like homemade angel food. And the grape sauce was tart and sweet in one glorious mouthful.

"You pop the grapes first," I said.

"Pop them?"

"Press them between your fingers and they pop open. You separate the pulp from the peel."

"Each grape?"

"I'm sure you could probably cook them all together, but it's my grandmother's recipe, so I do it the way she did it. You heat the pulp until the pulp pulls away from the seed. The idea is to strain the seeds out. Then you add the peel back in and cook the mixture some more."

"How long?"

"I've never timed it – I do it by smell, like everything else. The strange thing about Concord grapes is that the pulp and the peel have completely different colors. The pulp is a pale brownish green. The peel is blackish purple. They also smell different. The pulp smells earthy and the peel smells like citrus. It's only when you put them together again that you get the chemical reaction. It's the boom that produces this smell, this color and this taste. You can see it happen before your eyes. The whole mixture turns purple at once." I stopped. Some things became blindingly clear. Of course. Chemistry.

"What are you thinking about?" James said.

"Nothing. Then you strain the peels and cook the liquid with the brown sugar. It's simple." I still didn't have all of the answers.

"May I?" he said, indicating the cake.

"Of course." I cut him another slice and covered it liberally with sauce. "This is completely off topic, but you haven't heard anything about Andrew Stimpkin, have you?"

"No. It's very odd. He must be much smarter than the average criminal. Are you worried about him?"

"Just about Elsa and the kids, although Sister Rita has the situation in hand. I doubt he'd ever find them. I'm sorry. I don't mean to ruin dinner with depressing topics. What shall we talk about next? We've covered exes and cooking."

"We could talk about us."

"I thought that subject was included with the exes."

"Have you given any more thought to coming here permanently?"

"It's the food, isn't it? Now be honest," I said.

"The meal only added to your other charms."

"Such a polite way to put it."

"It's not just that, either. How about it?"

"Honestly?" I said.

"Yes."

"I think it's too soon – your family – Angie. We need to give it time or we'll have a riot on our hands."

"I don't care what they think."

I put my hand on his. "I'm not going to force you to fight your family. And I'm not going to make myself more of a target. Let's lay low."

"But —"

I cut him off. "You know I'm right about this."

"So your objections have to do with my family – and not —"

"Not you. Plus this gives you time to think twice. Remember, I'm capable of anything."

"I wish I'd been in Nick Lee's shoes."

"I'll see what I can do." I got up. "But first your gift."

James held my arm. "I thought you were the gift."

"I wanted to give you something you wouldn't have to explain when your family asks."

"I think I can explain it," James said seriously.

"What?" I said, my hand on my crimson cheek.

He burst out laughing. "I knew I could."

CHAPTER 16

Although I'm terrible with crowds, I had no trouble recognizing Blair. You could not miss the brooches. This time they were pinned to a nipped in sports jacket made of a shimmery fabric that went from pale green to gold as he moved. He was standing in a corner talking to a thin woman with long dark hair and tight black jeans. They both spoke with expressive extravagant hand gestures. Her back was to me, and as she stood, she shifted her weight from foot to foot. I caught a flash of bright pink sole. Farfalla. Expensive taste for a starving artist.

I took a second look at her hair. It seemed familiar. Then she moved, swishing it off her shoulders. Yes. Sean Thomas' lady friend. Blair saw me out of the corner of his eye and waved me over.

"Liz. Come meet Marisol." Marisol turned as I approached. She had a beautiful and completely symmetrical face, like a Latina Barbie.

We greeted each other with a handshake. Her touch was very light.

Blair cut in. "Marisol, this is Liz Howe, my new BFF."

"I'm honored," I said.

"Don't let that pretty face fool you," Marisol said. "He says that to everyone."

"Jealous?" Blair said.

"Honey, I have more friends then I know what to do with." Her voice seemed strangely sad.

Blair didn't notice. "Just because your friends are so important – you've forgotten all about me. Ignore her Liz. I shouldn't have introduced you." He put a protective hand on my arm.

"Some friend. See how he abandons me?" Marisol said.

"I'm not getting in the middle – 'Kumbaya' anyone?"

"I can't sing," she said with a smile, "but I'm sure Blair can help you out."

Blair turned to me. "See how she treats me? She knows I've got stage fright. It's like a dagger to my heart." He made a stabbing motion at his chest.

Marisol laughed. "Drama queen."

"Tsk. Tsk. Don't say anything you'll regret."

"I don't regret anything I say to you."

"One day you'll pay for so much abuse. Liz." He started to pull me away by the arm. "Let's leave Marisol to her real friends."

"Lovely to meet you, Marisol," I said over my shoulder as Blair continued to drag me away.

"Good to meet you. Bye Blair. Don't let the door hit you on the way out."

Blair laughed. "Witch. And the word that rhymes with it!"

When we were out of earshot, I said, "What kind of work does she do?" The show took up most of the room in the converted warehouse space. There were art pieces of every description. I had not realized what an impact Arthur Thornton had had on the art scene in St. Louis before I walked in the door.

"Multimedia work and some film. Documentaries mostly. She has an installation over there." Blair pointed to a corner. There stood what appeared to be a giant fabric collage, except that some parts moved. I dragged him closer. Interesting. She'd mounted televisions behind semi-transparent cloth. The televisions played loops of images and then cut off at intervals. The effect was like a theater scrim. One minute an image, and then the design on the cloth itself.

"Beautiful," I said.

"I know. She's very talented."

"Successful?"

"A couple of small shows locally, but nothing has taken off. Fortunately, she doesn't need art to live."

"Sean Thomas?"

"You know him?"

"I met him once. Marisol was with him. I knew she looked familiar," I said.

"Yes. Well. I've known her for years, but I've never met him. No one knew she was even dating him until she got pregnant. And then, surprise!"

"I heard about that part, too."

"No need to tell you anything, is there?"

I shrugged my shoulders. "I actually know the sister of the ex-wife. She's a lawyer."

"Small town."

"St. Louis is a megalopolis compared to where I'm from."

"Which is?"

"Marshfield, Wisconsin."

"Never heard of it."

"It's about two hours from Madison. In the center of the state."

"Madison I've heard of, but I don't remember why," he said.

"State capitol. I'm sure someone made you memorize those in school."

"I tried to forget everything I learned in school."

"Smart. So where are you taking me?"

"To see the crown jewel of the show – my work." He guided me through the crowd until we reached a long glass case over on one side.

"Nice presentation."

Blair introduced me to the young woman who had been manning the case for him, a teen-aged cousin named Brittany with pimples and very thick glasses. I could see the reflection of Blair's brooches in their coke bottle depths.

I leaned over the case and gasped. "Blair!" He had taken copper wire and twisted it into the most fantastic shapes. I recognized his work instantly.

"Don't sound so surprised."

"Sorry. I didn't know what to expect."

"Blair's a great artist. He's in stores," Brittany said reverently.

"I sell some pieces to Lane's – thanks to Auntie Cindy. I'm hoping to get a couple of other places interested. If not in these pieces, then at least in my designs."

Lane Jewelers in Ladue. Incredible. He was the artist who did the designs I'd so admired: John Harding's mistress' pendants and maybe even Angie's engagement ring.

Blair gave me a wry smile. "You could get that boyfriend of yours to buy you something nice."

"I'll mention it, but if your pieces aren't too exorbitant, I can buy something from you now."

"I'll give you a deal."

"You better. What would that bracelet set me back?" I pointed at an amazingly delicate twist of copper wire.

Brittany took it out and slipped it on my wrist. It fit me perfectly.

"Oh, that's nice," Blair said.

I looked at the tag. It said $50.00.

"For you, I'll do $40.00."

"If you make it $35.00, you have a deal," I replied.

"Hard bargainer."

"Did you expect something else?" I handed the money to Brittany.

"You lawyers are all the same."

"Hey, Liz." I turned at the sound of Matt's voice. "Is Blair causing trouble again?"

"Love you too, sweetie." Blair blew him a kiss.

"Just selling me one of his fabulous creations." I extended my wrist.

"Showoff," Matt said.

"Can I help it if you're intimidated by the presence of true genius?" Blair said.

Matt smiled. "I'm not intimidated by myself."

"Now boys. You're both geniuses in my book, no need to fight," I said.

Matt laughed. "What do you think keeps our relationship going?"

"You said it, not me," Blair replied.

"I've never seen a couple so meant for each other," I said.

"We've been together a long time," Matt admitted.

"How long?"

"Four years," they both said at once.

"Long enough to finish each other's sentences, I see."

Matt rolled his eyes. "If I can ever get a word in edgewise."

"You're just tongue-tied," Blair said.

"Matt seems perfectly able to communicate with me."

"Liz." Blair did the dagger to the heart again. "I thought you were my BFF?"

Matt turned to me. "Not you, too. He says that to everyone."

"I heard."

"Take her away." Blair shooed me with his hand. "A BFF wouldn't take your side in an argument. Liz, I'm done with you."

Matt took my arm. "Good. Let me show you my stuff."

"Blair, it's been a pleasure," I said.

"Fickle woman."

Matt guided me through the crowd. The attendance at the show was truly impressive.

"He's a keeper," I said to Matt.

"You don't have to live with him." But it was all in fun. The connection between Matt and Blair was so strong that I could feel it in the air, like a strange magnetic force. Would James and I ever be like that? I had a sudden vision of us as an old married couple – you couldn't tell where one ended and the other began. I blinked and the vision was gone.

Matt's work hung like a wall of beautiful decay, each image a pristine rendition of rusting iron and crumbling concrete.

"What are you going to paint when St. Louis is completely gentrified?"

"Yeah, right. There will always be something to paint in this town."

"Your work makes it a tragedy to do repairs. Destruction won't seem the same after this."

"You know just what to say to a guy."

I leaned in to get a closer look. His paintings were photorealistic in their precision. One painting in particular attracted me. It was of a dilapidated clapboard house with a black roof and a red brick chimney. The house had originally been painted white, but the weather was slowly removing the paint, leaving sections of exposed wood. It was unusual for Matt's work, which tended to focus on small details. And the house seemed to sit in a rural landscape. There was nothing urban about it.

"You like that one?" Matt said.

"Love it. The siding looks like snakeskin."

"That's exactly what I thought."

"Like houses you see in Wisconsin. There is something so beautiful and desolate in rural landscapes."

"I've been thinking about a rural building series. This was the test painting."

"Where is the house?"

"I don't know. Friends give me photos of stuff they think I'll like. Most times I don't think anything more about it." He paused a moment. "This one may have been part of that bunch Marisol gave me. She has an eye."

"Her work is impressive."

"Yeah. No wonder Arthur took such an interest in her."

"They were friends?" I said.

"She helped organize this show. Maybe they were more than friends. I just know that he funded some of her work – and her stuff is not cheap."

"But I thought Sean Thomas was well off?"

"Blair told you about him?"

"I knew about it before."

"Word travels fast," he said.

"Scandal does."

"Arthur knew her before the scandal – or at least before anyone knew she was pregnant," Matt said.

"When did she have the baby?"

"Six months ago."

"Wow." I thought about her figure in tight jeans.

Matt read my mind. "She looks like she always did."

"Arthur helped her out?"

"She lived with him at one point. She was between jobs and needed a place to crash."

"What does she do normally? I mean, her non-art job."

"She's a videographer. Weddings, Bar Mitzvahs, that kind of thing. She hasn't had to do that since she met Sean."

"A kept woman."

"Yeah. She has a sweet apartment. One of those buildings with a doorman."

"The ladder of success," I said.

"On her back."

I smiled. "Jealous?"

"I wouldn't trade Blair."

"But it would be nice not to have three jobs?"

He nodded. "I need to sell something and soon."

"Have you heard anything about the St. Louis Art Fair?"

"The whole thing with Arthur set the judging back this year. I should hear something by the end of July."

"I think you'll get in. Your work is better than everything I saw last year."

"I'm so glad I met you."

"That's what they all say."

"No. I mean it. I want you to have this." He reached over and unhooked the painting of the dilapidated house from the scaffold.

"I can't take a painting. Not when you should be selling them." But if I put off one of my all too necessary but expensive haircuts for a couple of extra weeks and cut a few other things out, I could swing something. "I can come up with three hundred dollars. I'm sure you could get more for it, but that's all I can manage right now."

"I couldn't take money from you —"

"What do you mean? Blair already has." I held up my wrist.

"He's terrible."

I dug in my purse and produced a checkbook. "We'll call this a small down payment on your brilliant future. You won't forget me when you're rich and famous, will you?"

"I couldn't forget you. And I'll paint something else – something special just for you."

"Another building?"

"Or maybe a new concept."

"I know I'll love it."

Blair wandered back over to us. "What are you doing?"

"She's buying a painting," Matt said.

"What? Don't waste your money, Liz."

"We need money to live. You are very expensive."

"But so worth it. Here." Blair pulled out a small camera. "I'll take a picture to commemorate the joyous event." He organized us on either side of the painting, moving us around until he was completely satisfied with the composition. "Now say 'Blair is a genius.'" He snapped the photograph.

I hung the painting in my living room as soon as I got home. Holly hated it.

"Why would you want to look at a run-down building all day?"

"It reminds me of home."

"Doesn't Wisconsin have building codes?"

I gave her a hard look.

"Okay, suit yourself. I'm going over to campaign headquarters. Want to come?"

Holly asked me this every day, and every day I found an excuse to get out of it. Unfortunately, I was running out of ideas.

I started my usual, "I have to," but then stopped. I did not have anything to do at that moment. Bar review started next week and there wasn't much on my plate until then. I could clean my apartment.

"You don't have to clean the apartment," Holly said. She was too good.

"Okay. Okay. As long as you don't make me canvass." I could think of nothing worse than walking in the heat and talking to strangers.

"Scouts honor," she said, entirely too pleased with herself.

Thirty minutes later we were dolefully trudging from house to house.

"What kind of scout were you?" I said.

"This isn't so bad," Holly replied cheerfully.

"Speak for yourself."

As we walked, Holly gave me a blow-by-blow account of the state of the campaign. As usual, Boggs was plagued with scandals. Word leaked that he once used a racial slur. Boggs denied everything. There were rumors of a gay lover hidden away somewhere. Boggs' wife denied everything. There was talk of serious financial improprieties. His accountant and the treasurer for the campaign denied everything. But flyers with those rumors continued to paper the Wash U campus and the surrounding neighborhoods. Mason was gaining on Boggs with the number of yard signs. It appeared that the tide had turned.

"Boggs' campaign is full of leaks," Holly explained as we walked up to yet another house. So far we had three doors slammed in our face, one polite "no thank you" and seven no one homes. Even if people planned to vote for Mason, they still did not want to talk to us.

"We always know when Boggs is going to have a rally or something." Holly rang the doorbell. We waited patiently. I heard the faint sound of footsteps. Maybe we would finally be able to unload some literature. My backpack was heavy. The footsteps stopped and nothing happened. We rang the doorbell again, but got only silence.

"Their loss," Holly said, hopping back down the steps. I lumbered after her.

"So you disrupt Boggs' rallies?" I said.

"What?"

"When you know he is going to have a rally."

We reached the street. "We think of them as counter demonstrations. I even got to heckle Dick Chaney once." She grinned.

"Isn't that dangerous? I mean, don't they have security to keep people like you away?"

"Of course. But I told you. The campaign is leaky. We always know what the tickets look like."

"You make fake tickets?" This seemed extreme.

"All's fair in politics."

"I thought it was only love or war."

"This is war. A battle between good and evil."

I hoped she was kidding, but her expression was hard to read. "Just be careful you know which is which."

"Kevin is the real thing," she scoffed. "He has a stump speech called 'A Normal Day in America.' You should hear it, Liz. He's so right on all of the important issues. Poverty. Personal freedom. Peace."

"The three P's?"

"You think it's a joke, but once you see him give that speech, you're never the same again."

"I'll take your word for it."

We walked a little farther, and then she stopped. "I'll get you a copy. Marisol must have gotten him on tape at least a couple of hundred times."

"Marisol?"

"Ramirez. She's making a documentary of the campaign."

"Is she thin, with long dark hair? About so tall?" I indicated her height with my hand.

"Do you know her?"

"She's a friend of the artist friends of mine. I just met her at the benefit this morning. She had a multimedia piece in the show."

"Small world. She's been a big help on the campaign. She and Sean Thomas both."

"He's with the campaign, too?"

"Sure. He donated the office space," she said.

"That explains that." The Kevin Mason for Congress offices were hardly the shoestring outfit I expected. Located in a swank Clayton office building and taking up most of a floor, the offices looked much more like a law firm than a political organization.

"How do you know Sean?" Holly said.

"I met him once. He is a friend of Angie's family."

"So you heard about the divorce."

"One of Janice's friends is the sister of his ex-wife. She told me last year, but I didn't know any of the people involved until now."

"Marisol is really very sweet. She brought her daughter in one day. What a love."

"I thought you didn't like children?"

"I'm okay if they are other people's."

"I will live to see the day when you have six."

"Don't bet on it. I have to have a man first."

"Mark seems interested."

"He's nice enough. I just don't feel up to it, you know? Plus, we'd fight. He votes Republican, of all things." She wrinkled her nose.

"There are some good Republicans."

"I'm sure."

One entire afternoon of canvassing yielded one very pleasant young woman who was already planning to vote for Kevin Mason. I was drenched in sweat when we finally pulled up in front of the apartment.

"I'm never doing that again," I told Holly as I jammed the key in the lock of the outside door.

"Come on. Some days are better than others."

I could tell by her voice that she was in the mood to argue with me. Like the coward I am, I decided to sue for peace. "Tell you what. I will continue to volunteer as long as you swear by all that you hold dear, that I will never have to canvass again."

She hesitated. I could almost hear the gears turning in her head, justifying my anti-canvassing position to the higher ups. She would probably give me some disabling injury. "Great!" she finally said. "You won't regret getting involved with the Mason campaign. I promise."

CHAPTER 17

I regretted my surrender immediately. I didn't have to canvass, but Holly dragged me along to do just about everything else. And I had to explain how I managed to walk so well on a fractured leg. I began to wish that bar review had already started. At least then I would get a rest.

James couldn't understand it. "Can't you just say no?"

"It's easier to stuff envelopes than to argue."

"So you'll do anything if someone hounds you long enough?"

"Probably."

"I'll file that information away for future use." He gave me another of his sly smiles.

I volunteered so often that I began to recognize my fellow volunteers, at least as much as I could recognize anyone. Most were young and passionate like Holly, swept up in the excitement of the political battle. Others were from the old guard. Liberals with a capital "L" who regaled each other with stories of draft card burnings, nuclear weapons protests, and Earth Day celebrations. The Kevin Mason campaign was tame in comparison to the tall tales of arrests, police beatings, and tear gas. I guess those were the days.

On the morning before bar review, I walked into the offices and saw a woman hunched over a computer screen, pounding the keys in frustration. I recognized the muttered insults almost immediately.

"Sister Rita!"

She spun around in her chair. "Liz Howe. Why chickie, what have you been up to?"

I hugged her. "I didn't know you were working on the campaign."

"Of course."

"But I thought the Archbishop —" The Archbishop of St. Louis had taken such a strong stand against pro-choice candidates that there was talk of refusing communion to them and to anyone who had the temerity to support them.

"What the boys in Rome don't know won't hurt," she said tartly. "I gave up sex, not my opinions."

I laughed and then thought maybe I shouldn't have. She saw my confusion and smiled. "I've known Kevin for so many years I couldn't say no when he asked for help. He's been very involved in the Hispanic community."

"I didn't know that."

"Lived in Colombia as a kid, so he understands where people are coming from."

"His Spanish must be good."

"*Sì lo es.*" She nodded. "He's the only politician in this town who gets immigrant issues."

"I can't think he'll be able to do much good in this district. Clayton's not a hotbed of immigration that I can see."

"Ha! The restaurants? Who do you think works in those kitchens?"

She had a point. In most local restaurants, you could hear Latin music every time the kitchen door swung open.

"Besides, we all know this seat is just a step – Kevin's climbing to the moon," she added.

"Or maybe Pennsylvania Avenue. I'm glad we'll be working together for a while," I said.

"As long as it takes, chickie. Oh, and I've been meaning to tell you. Elsa's fine. I made sure those cops in Jeff County got someone to patrol – to make sure she and the kids are safe."

"They weren't doing that already?"

"They claimed they didn't have the manpower." She shook her head. "After they caused all the trouble. How'd they let him escape?"

"It seems very odd to me."

"Stupid is what it is. They still don't know where he got to."

"Strange."

"Well, I filed Elsa's paperwork, so we'll see where that goes. That Gwen Zenner is a doll, by the way. And she's sharp, which you don't see much of nowadays."

"I think you do," I said, indicating Sister Rita herself.

"Thanks, but if I'm so damn smart, why can't I get this blasted machine to do what I want?"

"What do you need it to do?" I sat down beside her.

"It's these donor lists. I've got cells going every which way on this spreadsheet and it's driving me nuts."

"Let me do the driving," I said, grabbing the mouse.

We worked efficiently for the next hour, entering names and donation amounts into a massive spreadsheet. All donations had to be recorded properly for tracking purposes. She had agreed to handle all of the donor lists. The work was tedious, but so much better than pounding the pavement. I offered to help her any time.

"I'm not great with numbers and this machine and I haven't seen eye to eye since I got here, but Kevin wants someone he can trust," she said.

"And you trust me?"

"You're hired. Unless you have some test you need to be studying for."

"Only an exam that will decide my entire fate, but I'll make time."

"Nothing to worry about."

"Do you have an in with the bar examiners?"

She laughed and pointed to the ceiling. "Higher up."

We made a tentative schedule. She gave me a key so that I could come in and work in one of the back offices even if she wasn't there. Another item on my "to do" list. After I left Sister Rita, Janice called with a couple of small things. The office was finally unpacked and officially open for business. Just in time. It seemed everyone had money these days and wanted a fancy trust instrument to sock it away. Janice even hired two paralegals to help us out.

I got up early on the first day of bar review and went to the gym. Exercise seemed to calm my nerves. I'd had another bad night. Maybe I should have taken James up on his offer to move in. Then I thought about his family's reaction. Maybe not. There were nightmares and then there were Nightmares.

As I walked into the auditorium, I tried to guess how long it would be before I would recognize one of the law students I knew. Two minutes and thirty-five seconds exactly, and that was only because Amelia waved at me. She even saved two extra seats.

"Vince?" I said.

"I wanted to give him a chance," she replied. Due to my fight with James, it was two days before I could get the minute-by-minute account of Amelia's experience at Vince's party. She had danced with him exactly six times and had tried to kiss him once during a slow number. He'd not taken the bait. I felt a twinge of guilt, but pushed it aside. Whatever might have happened between us was over. I now had to help Vince move on. I suggested we orchestrate a bunch of friendly meetings at bar review, a bit of chatter and a latte as often as she could get him to come, and then maybe more.

"I'll assist you any way I can," I added.

"Please do. My strike out rate is getting embarrassing."

"No worries. But you should also probably come up with a plan B." I scanned the room. "How about that guy over there?"

"The one with the tattoos?"

Tattoos? Wait. I looked again. He had all the parts – the hair, the smile, and yes, the tattoos showed with the short sleeve shirt. It had to be Grant.

"No thanks. I'm sorry Liz, but he's just gross."

I laughed. "You'd be surprised at the number of intelligent women who'd argue with you." I looked around. "I'm sure at least one of his admirers is here somewhere." Becca, Samantha, and Kelsey had all been nuts about him. As if on cue, a blond woman sat down beside Grant. It was one of the three, but I couldn't tell which from across the room. Then the strangest thing happened. Grant looked up and our eyes met. I could tell from his expression that he did not recognize me right away. But when he did, he smiled and got up.

"I think he's coming over here," I said in surprise.

Amelia looked over. "To talk?"

"I have no idea."

"Liz," Grant said, sitting down beside Amelia in the chair she saved for Vince, and leaning over her, "How's it going?"

"Um fine. Amelia, this is Grant. We were both associates at Ghebish and Long last summer."

Grant finally seemed to notice Amelia, "Oh, hey, sorry. Good to meet you." He leaned back over her, "So Liz —"

"Why don't I move over so you two can chat?" Amelia said.

"Yeah, good idea." Grant stood up and they switched seats.

"So anyway, how's it going? I heard you went with Janice Harrington."

"Yes. And you're with Reginald Butler? Do you like working for him?" With Grant it was always better to let him talk about himself. He was going to do it anyway, and it saved you the trouble of conversation.

"Reggie's the best there is. You'd be amazed at what he can do."

I would have told him that nothing Butler did would surprise me, but at that moment, the lights dimmed and the speaker started in on a review of corporate law.

The bar exam for Missouri, like most states, consists of two parts – the essays and the multiple choice questions. The essays test your knowledge of Missouri law and the multiple choice questions test your knowledge of general principles that apply to many states, so that part is known as the "multi-state." I had separate review classes lined up for that portion of the exam a little later in the summer.

I listened and took notes, but still found room within my skull to let my mind wander. I looked to see if I could find Vince. Finally, I did.

I could not mistake that hair. He sat on the opposite side of the room, a little to my right. After a minute or two, I caught his eye. He smiled.

Grant leaned in and whispered in my ear, "Could this get any more boring?" While I had to agree that it wasn't the most scintillating lecture I ever sat through, I did not respond.

Grant tried again, "Reggie's got crazy clients. I could tell you some stories."

I debated whether or not to give in to the inevitable, but there was no stopping Grant, so I said, "Really?" in the most non-committal whisper I could muster.

It was enough to give me an abundance of war stories about bitchy women and gold diggers and how Butler had outfoxed them and their conniving lawyers time and time again. I listened with half an ear, all the while keeping up an unspoken conversation with Vince. My eye rolls were obvious even in the darkened room.

Grant did not stop, even at the break when Samantha came over to investigate what Grant could possibly be talking to me about. She stalked away unenlightened, her verbena-scented body spray wafting behind her like a tail. I nodded when strictly necessary and made all of the approving noises required. That was enough to keep Grant firmly by my side.

The lights dimmed again, and I settled in for another hour of boredom, but before the robotic lecturer could even start, Grant said something that made me prick up my ears.

"So then I told him he was nuts. I mean, I didn't sign up for criminal defense."

"What did he want you to do again?" I had apparently missed the first part of a good story. I gave him my best dumb-blonde smile.

He leaned in even closer. If this had been James, I would have been in a haze of hormone-induced distraction. But Grant's overuse of Drakkar Noir was starting to give me a headache. I tried not to notice the dull pain between my eyes.

"He sent me to visit this guy in jail out in Jeff County."

"A client?" Butler's clients were usually too rich to end up in jail, at least immediately.

"Some friend of a friend. The guy barely talked."

"Why did Butler want you to go?"

"Something about checking on him."

I nodded in encouragement. "What was this guy's name?"

"I don't even remember. He was fucked up. Big time."

"Aren't visits regulated? How did you get to see this person?"

"I just told them I worked for Reggie. The head guy knew Reggie from way back." Grant paused and then smiled. "It's great talking to you, Liz. You're such a good listener."

"Um. Thanks."

"You know, after everything that happened, I started thinking about you – and me – and —"

The light dawned with blinding intensity. I blinked, half expecting the intervention of a deity. The *deus ex machina* of a Greek play. Instead, I felt time slow down as my world flipped over. Grant continued to talk while I stared, so I only heard the last part.

"How about it?"

"Hmm?" Another dumb-blonde smile.

"We should go out sometime."

"Oh."

"Well?" he said.

I cleared my throat. "Thanks, but I can't." He looked like he might argue, so I added. "I'm dating someone right now."

"Who?" It was clear from his expression that he suspected I had made it up.

I should have told him it was none of his business, but my thought process was disordered. I blurted out, "James Paperelli."

"The police detective?"

"Yes."

Grant seemed to chew on this information. Then he said, "Suit yourself, I guess. Hey, I've been wondering, is he related to that pizza guy on those TV commercials?"

"That's his father."

I was sure that some part of Grant's brain still did not believe me. The other part was trying to calculate the Paperellis' net worth. "Wow," he said, and then was silent for the rest of the lecture.

Afterwards, I left him for Samantha to deal with. Vince caught up with Amelia and me in the hall.

Amelia seemed tongue-tied, so I said, "We're going to Bread Co. for a late lunch. Want to come?" St. Louis Bread Company, or Panera, as it is known to the rest of the country, was one of Amelia's favorite places to eat.

"Sure," Vince said. "Should we meet there?"

"Yes. The one on Clayton Road," I replied.

Vince walked in as Amelia and I were standing at the back looking up at the menu selection. Although it wasn't on the diet plan, part of me was dying to order the broccoli cheese soup in the giant sourdough bread bowl. You can't buy comfort like that every day. After a thorough discussion of the meal options, including an analysis of the merits of each one of the panini sandwiches, we finally decided on our orders. I went for the bread bowl after all.

We stood in line. Vince tapped me on the shoulder. "So what was the deal with Grant? He never stopped talking."

"Yes." Amelia turned back to me. "Why was he so talkative?"

"No idea." I shook my head. "I guess I'm the only one who could fake interest through two hours of monologue."

"You certainly let a lot of people sit in your office and complain last summer," Vince said.

"Maybe that's why he decided to ask me out – so he wouldn't have to stop talking just because the lecture ended," I replied.

"He asked you out?" Amelia said.

"I'm pretty sure it was an afterthought. Grant wanted to horn in on my projects with the senior partners, but that was his only interest last summer."

"You've changed," Vince said.

I looked at him. "Not that much."

Amelia studied at me critically. "You look like a different person with that haircut."

"Really?"

She nodded. "And I want the name of your hairdresser. That woman is a miracle worker."

"Annie Sullivan," I said.

"Funny. No, the real name. You can't keep her to yourself forever."

I gave her Marcela's particulars, and she typed them into the contacts on her phone. Then we had to order. The crowd thinned by the time our food came, so we easily found a table. I took the opportunity to slip off to the restroom. That would give my soup time to cool and Amelia a break from further Liz Howe-related discussions.

As I washed my hands, I stared at my reflection in the mirror. I did look thinner and more polished. Anything else was impossible to gauge. I wouldn't have recognized myself before, and I couldn't do it now. But polish could not account for my sudden attractiveness, could it? Had Vince indeed waited until I was attractive enough to ask out? That didn't seem like him at all. But then what about James?

He'd told me he was interested in me from early on, although he couldn't admit it to himself. Perhaps that was the present coloring the past. Or maybe there really was something to the notion of chemistry, that haze of electrons that hovered around us. I certainly could not match Angie for beauty. Not now. Not ever. By contrast, my attraction to James was easy to explain. Chemistry or no, he was uniformly attractive. Even Matt would tell me that. I studied my face again and sighed.

I walked back to the table. Vince and Amelia were laughing. It sounded like she was giving him a rundown of the *Gone with the Wind* wedding. They looked so right sitting there together. There was attraction on her side, and there had to be on his. Who would not find Amelia attractive? Okay, a lot of guys, judging by her dry spell. But Vince wasn't like most guys. So we had attraction. Now we just needed chemistry. Maybe chemistry could be helped along. I decided to make the post review lunch a regular thing. I would find as many reasons as I could to slip away.

I said "hi" to Grant the next day and every day after that. His response was friendly, but he never tried to sit next to me again. Instead, Vince assumed his rightful place. This was good for a number of reasons, not the least of which was that Vince actually paid attention to the lectures. No more Chatty Cathy in my ear.

When things got too dull, I had the luxury of my own thoughts. Certain pieces of the puzzle were falling into place. I debated whether to tell James about my suspicions, but there were so many moving parts that I could easily be wrong about some of them. And if I were, he would never take me seriously again.

I decided to tell him nothing.

CHAPTER 18

As I got further into bar review, I began to look forward to campaign work or Janice's projects. Even running on the treadmill was preferable. Only absolute unadulterated terror kept me focused on the task at hand. I used every study skill I had ever learned – and some I made up on the one in a million chance they would actually work – to cram everything into my overflowing head. I made outlines. I made flash cards. I made a condensed set of flash cards. I made a smaller outline from the flash cards. I went to the multi-state review class and listened with rapt attention to the man who had taken the bar exam in all fifty states. And then I followed his advice and did 1500 multiple-choice questions. Eventually, I found myself wandering the apartment talking out loud to no one in particular.

Holly laughed. "If I didn't know you better, I'd send you back to the psychiatrist." I ignored her. I had to do whatever it took and then some.

James insisted on dragging me out to eat at least twice a week. I am not sure how he could stand it. I could not think about anything but bar review. Holly's computer science friends had nothing on me now. I had become the most boring date ever.

Janice called one morning about two weeks before the exam. "How's it going?"

"Okay." I didn't sound convincing. "If it's about another project, I'm not sure I can handle —"

"I just wanted to take you out to lunch one more time."

"Before I'm certifiably crazy?"

"Yes. I won't want to know you for the next two weeks."

"I should probably give James a heads up. I didn't think I could get any more incoherent."

"You will. But don't warn him, a man may be the only thing that'll keep you sane."

"Janice!"

She laughed. "I've wandered into the too much information category, haven't I?"

"Definitely."

"Just keep it in mind."

"Duly noted. Can we move on?"

"So about lunch. I'm meeting Susan and Maddie. They've been asking about you." Susan Wayman and Maddie Harding were two of Janice's closest friends.

"And you warned them I'm over the edge?"

"Pretty much."

"Then, I accept."

They were meeting at a restaurant in Ladue that I had never been to before. Janice gave me directions, but I was too distracted to read them closely. I cursed as I took the wrong turn and headed into a neighborhood. If I just kept going, maybe I could find a good spot to turn around. I passed a blue Corolla parked on the street. It sported a Kevin Mason for Congress bumper sticker.

The young man who was just getting out had a campaign tee shirt on. He also had the regulation clipboard and a backpack. A canvasser. My heart filled with pity. The St. Louis summer had hit us full force with all of its molasses humidity. I slowed down so I wouldn't hit him. He was just walking up to the house as I drove past.

I got to the end of a cul-de-sac and turned around. I expected to see the canvasser trudging along the sidewalk on my way back, but he was nowhere to be found. Had someone actually invited him inside? Amazing.

I was only ten minutes late to the restaurant. Janice, Susan and Maddie were their usual irrepressible selves. And Susan still had great shoes – dark green alligator pumps. I hoped that this would be me one day: a smart woman who was sure of her own identity and comfortable in her own skin. Okay. Their love lives left something to be desired. Janice was divorced. Maddie was divorced and a widow and Susan was single. Could I possibly have the wisdom and the man? Surely they were not mutually exclusive.

The subject of men inevitably came up. Susan had signed on with a dating service that pairs singles for lunch. After a number of duds, she finally met someone of interest, a divorced doctor with two children in college. They were trying to arrange a second date between very busy schedules.

"I'm always nervous when it's someone I might like," Susan said.

"Where are you meeting him?" I said.

"Pomme. You know that place in Clayton —"

"It's perfect for a date," I said. That first date with James had started with good and ended with amazing.

"Sounds like experience talking," Susan said.

"She's thinking about James," Janice said. "She always looks like that when she talks about him."

"Who's James?" Maddie asked.

"How did you meet him?" Susan chimed in.

"We met during the investigation." I looked at Maddie, whose ex-husband was the victim and subject of the investigation, trying to gauge her reaction.

"Into John's death?" she said evenly.

"Yes."

She seemed to be processing the information. I wondered if the get-together was over right then. I wouldn't have blamed her. Who wants to bring up philandering, dead ex-husbands at lunch?

A sudden brightness lit her eyes. "You don't mean James Paperelli, do you?"

"That James? Maddie, you didn't tell me he was on the investigation," Susan said.

"Sorry. He only interviewed me once."

"Lucky you," Susan said.

Janice laughed. "You're like a couple of school girls."

Susan widened her eyes. "What? He's gorgeous. So Liz, do tell."

I put my hands on my red cheeks. "What do you want to know? I'm not saying I'll give you any answers —"

"Just let them use their imagination," Janice said.

"That's not better," I replied.

"When did you two start dating?" Maddie said.

"In February. He asked me to dinner. We went to Pomme. The food was delicious and it was quiet enough that we could actually carry on a conversation."

"That must have been some conversation," Susan said.

"What?" I said.

"You've got that look again," Janice explained.

"Fallen hard?" Susan asked.

"Hardest fall of my life."

"Let's hope he deserves you," Maddie said.

Susan nodded. "And if he doesn't, at least enjoy it while it's good."

Maddie smiled. "Who wouldn't?"

They tried for more information, but I held firm. As I drove away, I realized that I had not thought about the bar exam in over an hour. A minor miracle. Those women were something else.

I got home and checked my messages. Sister Rita wanted me to make one last stop at the campaign headquarters. She was struggling with the spreadsheet again and needed my help. She promised that this was the last favor she would need before the bar exam. I called her back and left a message that I would see what I could do. But now my anxiety returned full force. I sat down and put in a marathon session on Commercial Paper. I focused on my work with laser-like concentration. When I finally looked up, the sun was setting. At least I had the Holder in Due Course rule nailed down. I tried to stand, but my legs wouldn't move. I felt one knee pop.

My mind insisted on study, but my body cried out for exercise. A quick trip to the gym would do me good. I longed for the oblivion of the thump, thump of my feet on the treadmill and my head filled with the music from my headphones. I got back in a little over two hours. I would have to hurry to deal with Sister Rita's spreadsheet fiasco before my mind cried uncle for the day.

I showered, dressed, and then gulped down a granola bar with a glass of water and several ibuprofen. The up side of the stress was that I had gone down another two pounds. Not that I would recommend the bar exam as a diet regimen. It gave me a blinding headache.

The headquarters seemed deserted when I arrived. The door was locked, but I used the key Rita had given me. The lights were on, though, so maybe I wasn't alone. It was hard to tell in the warren of offices. I sat down and booted up a computer. I got into the network using Sister Rita's password. No one had ever bothered to issue me one.

Sure enough, she had done something. The columns and rows did not line up properly. For such a capable woman, she was a digital disaster. I tried to copy and paste them back, but that triggered an error in the calculations. When I'd straightened the sums out, I noticed that some of the cells had a strange format. I worked with the formatting for a couple of minutes and realized that Rita must have triggered automatic formatting of some kind. It would not go away no matter what I did. Now our spreadsheet had mutant cells. Great.

I thought about creating a new spreadsheet, but when I scrolled back through it, I realized that it was way too big. I was just about to move down to my wacky cells again, when I noticed a familiar name. Arthur Thornton. I scrolled back up and found six different entries over the space of six months. I did some quick math in my head. Two thousand one hundred dollars in total. Exactly the then-current legal limit for an individual donation to a candidate. The last entry was in February.

Interesting. But I still had to fix the spreadsheet, so I went into the document properties. Maybe the answer was there. Hmm. I stared at the screen. Arthur Thornton was the creator of the spreadsheet as well. Very interesting. I stared at the screen a couple of minutes, lost in my own thoughts. Then I noticed the time on the monitor. It was late and I needed some sleep.

I tried one last gambit on those pesky cells. It worked! It actually worked! I gave a little shout of joy. My voice echoed back to me from the empty offices. I felt goose bumps on my arms. Time to go. Right after the ladies room. I shut the computer down and grabbed my purse.

I was walking out of the bathroom when I heard something like a quiet moan. I moved in the direction of the sound. Yes. It definitely came from one of the inside offices down the long hall. I walked very slowly and deliberately, the plush carpet muffling my footsteps. The door to the office at the end of the hall was slightly open. The office was dark, but I could see just inside the door from the light of the hall.

I stepped closer and all of a sudden the situation became abundantly clear. I recognized those noises. I had certainly heard them often enough from behind the closed doors of the firm. A couple *in flagrante delicto*. But who? I could not help myself. I crept up to the door and stood very still. I heard an indistinct, murmured conversation and then laughter. A man's voice. It seemed vaguely familiar. I listened harder. Yes. It was definitely him. Kevin Mason.

Holly's story replayed itself in my head. Who now? I listened for another minute, but still could not make out the individual words. Probably it was better not to hear. Retreat was my only option. I didn't want anyone to find me listening at the door. I saw a flash of color through the opening, and then heard an object hit the door jamb with a thunk. I leapt back. Spurts of giggled laughter erupted from the office.

And then I saw why. A high-heeled shoe with a bright pink sole lay in the doorway.

CHAPTER 19

The next two weeks went by in a haze of study-induced stupor. I felt completely disconnected from anything and everyone that belonged to my old life. That was BB – Before the Bar. God only knew what After the Bar would look like. Assuming I made it out alive.

Everything good in my life quietly slipped away. Holly came and went, but I barely looked up. James stopped coming to the apartment. Why bother? When he called, I did not respond with more than monosyllabic grunts to anything he said. Even food deserted me. My favorite comfort only made the knots in my stomach worse. Like a frightened rodent, I nibbled on cereal and fruit. Anything else was torture to force down. The only relief came at the end of the day in the numbing rumble of the treadmill. I lost another three pounds, but couldn't scavenge up the energy to rejoice.

Amelia and I set out for Jefferson City the morning before the exam. And if I had not known with whom I was driving, I might not have gotten in the car. Her new hairdo threw my radar way off. It was a short, layered bob that framed her face in a flattering way. Marcela had highlighted it with a coppery red that made Amelia's skin look like porcelain. Unfortunately, I was so focused on the bar that I didn't even think to ask her what Vince thought of the transformation.

We had booked a room at the hotel where the bar exam was to be given. I'd been told it was the better of the two bar exam hotels, but at that point, I did not care. The plan was to do a final round of study and then go to bed with four different alarm clocks set five minutes apart. You had to be prepared for every eventuality.

We pulled into the hotel around 2:00. Our room was not ready yet so we went to the hotel restaurant to eat. I called and left messages for my mother and for James as I picked at the fruit that came on the plate with my BLT. Then I set my phone down on the table and rummaged in my purse for the bottle of antacids. I was up to six that day. What was a couple more at a time like this? I chewed two and washed them down with Diet Coke. Amelia ate like there was no tomorrow. She devoured all of her sandwich and then the fruit. When she picked up the lettuce garnish, I offered her the unbitten half of my sandwich. She took it gratefully, saying, "I'm glad I brought a pair of my fat pants. I might not fit into anything else."

When our room was ready, we hauled our heavy suitcases up to the elevator. If only they were filled with clothes instead of books. Still, the plan had to be followed. We got to work. About two hours later my cell phone rang. It seemed incredibly loud in the silence of my room. I looked at it, wondering which of the messagees it could be.

I walked into the bathroom so I wouldn't disturb Amelia. "Hello James," I said.

"How are you holding up? I've been worried about you."

"Okay," I said listlessly.

"It's going to be fine. Trust me." His voice was amazingly tender for someone I had ignored completely for the last two weeks.

I felt a lump in my throat. "It's just —"

"Look. You are the smartest woman I know. If you can't pass the bar, no one can."

"I think you're a little biased."

"I am, but not about this. It's what made me fall in love with you." The lump turned into tears forming at the back of my eyes. I blinked and tried to think of a snappy comeback. I had been all out of snap lately.

"Not my Marilyn Monroe figure?"

"That too." He chuckled. "And your culinary gifts. That goes without saying."

I felt the haze lifting for the first time in days. It was so good to talk to him like this, like we were once again connected. I sat down on the edge of the tub.

"What about canning?" I said.

"As in jelly?"

"Jelly, jam, preserves, pickles and whatever else you care to boil and seal."

"Is there anything you Wisconsin girls can't do?"

"I'd have to think about it."

"Car repair?"

"You've finally reached my limits."

"I guess this is goodbye."

"Car repair is the deal breaker? The perfect woman doesn't exist, my friend." I could not keep a straight face any more. The urge to smile was too great.

"I think she does."

"Flattery will get you everywhere," I replied.

"That's an old line. I've used it for years."

"The flattery or the line?"

"Both," he said.

"You do it so smoothly."

"It's never been so difficult."

"I'm not putty in your hands?" I said.

"You are surprisingly resistant – to some things."

"For someone with your vast collegial experience, this should be old hat."

"Nothing is old hat with you."

"I never had a hat to begin with, so there isn't much room for comparison."

"From my perspective, hatless is best," he said.

"Amend that. I wouldn't say hatless. An eighth of a hat maybe."

"But no more hats from here on out. Unless we're talking my hat. *Après moi, le déluge.*"

"I love it when you talk history to me. Anyway, they'd have to pry your hat out of my cold dead hands," I said.

"I'm not sure I like where this metaphor is going."

"Macabre, isn't it? Sorry. I got carried away in the excitement."

"I like the 'carried away' part," he said.

"And the excitement?"

"That's good. Let's keep it."

"It never goes away."

"I was afraid it had the last two weeks."

"That was zombie Liz talking, not me."

"I'm glad you're back from the living dead, but I still love you even if you want to eat my brain."

"And you objected to the cold dead hands? That's the most macabre declaration I've ever heard. The only brain I need now is the one in my own head." I paused, and then said, "I love you, too. And thanks. It's so good to talk to you."

"Now go get some real food and a good night's sleep. That's an order."

"Yes sir. I'll call you tomorrow night."

"You better. Good night."

"Don't let the bed bugs bite." I heard his laughter as he hung up the phone.

I turned and saw Amelia in the doorway.

"Do you two talk in code? What was all that hat business?"

"Merely a metaphor. You wouldn't understand."

She gave me a mischievous look. "You'll have to get another code. Now I want to hear the macabre declaration of love."

I repeated the tail end of the conversation.

"That's devotion. Are you ready for dinner?" she said.

"Depends on what you mean," I replied.

She laughed.

CHAPTER 20

I took James' advice and woke up ready to seize the day. Amelia and I had an early breakfast and did one more run through my flash cards. Then we were off with our driver's licenses, our room keys, and at least ten sharpened #2 pencils in clear sandwich bags. The bar exam is like prison without the orange jumpsuits. They surely would have frisked us going in if they had not thought some smart law student would sue for emotional distress.

The exam room consisted of four large ballrooms connected to create a cavern with row after row of plastic folding tables. Every person had an assigned seat. The chairs were spaced far enough apart that you could not see the work of the person next to you. Hell cannot be more depressing than the bar exam. Coop too many law students up in one place and they start to go crazy. You could smell the fear – that funk that comes from sweat and nerves.

I sat down and tried to ignore the fidgeting of the other exam takers. I needed focus, but the woman next to me clucked her tongue against the roof of her mouth. Thank goodness we were allowed one set of foam earplugs. I'd brave injury to stuff mine in as far as they would go. A wizened woman got up in front of the microphone and read the instructions to us in a raspy, smoke-infused monotone. It was like Orwell's 1984. We would be told when to open our sealed exam booklets and when to close them. There was no talking allowed.

We had to keep our eyes focused on our booklets at all times. She would tell us when we had five minutes to go. There were no breaks, even for the bathroom, until the time was officially up. If we left, there was no coming back.

I took a deep breath and said a prayer. Somehow I had become a paragon of religious virtue in the last twenty-four hours. Not that I asked for a miracle. No. Just to finish the exam with a shred of dignity intact. And please, please, please let me pass. I picked up a pencil and fought the urge to bite down on it. I had a sudden flashback to second grade, gnawing on my pencil while I pondered subtraction with double-digit numbers. There was comfort in the taste of pine and graphite.

I realized with a start that the proctor had stopped talking. She shuffled her papers, looked at the clock, and then said, "Go!"

Like runners at the gate, we were off, ripping open our exam packets. I scanned the first essay. It was a complicated fact pattern involving the creation of a limited liability corporation. Hadn't the bar review assured us that we would not get a question on this? They said that there had been one on last year's exam and claimed that the bar never repeated itself. Good thing Amelia and I were obsessive enough to ignore bar review advice. I started to write.

The woman next to me clicked her tongue once. Then she did it again. Earplugs. Okay. Now it was just me and my essay. I caught the flip of a pencil out of the corner of my eye. The guy on the other side was nervously staring at his essay packet, spinning his pencil. For the love of God. Never mind. Now was not the time to blaspheme. I turned my whole body so I couldn't see him. Back to the essays.

The trick with the bar exam is not to write an essay. Instead, you jot down as many points as you can. Any issue you can think of will do because the reviewers have to read so many that they just skim for keywords. Get enough keywords, and you have the points to pass. Maximum points. Minimum time.

Time is another important factor. You have a limited amount of time and some essays are harder than others. If you waste too much time on one, you will miss the easy points you could have gotten on another. I looked at my watch. So far so good. I had just finished the second essay when the first student got up and left the room.

He was followed by two more. I looked back at my essay booklet. Did he walk out because he couldn't handle the stress? Or was he so brilliant that he didn't need more time? Better not to waste a moment wondering. Apparently, bar exam success required the ability to ignore your fellow human beings.

At the break for lunch, I practically ran back to the room. I wanted to avoid the clumps of students comparing notes. I did not need any more anxiety than I already had. Amelia arrived soon after. We ate the sandwiches we had ordered ahead of time to avoid the lunch rush and checked our phones for messages. Neither of us had much energy for chatting.

James had left me a message of encouragement. I had one from Ashley too. She wanted to remind me that her birthday was in two weeks, and could I please buy her something in St. Louis? She had some ideas she'd tell me about after I finished the exam. And she wished me well. I sighed. Her message reminded me that James and I were going to Wisconsin after the exam and before I started work.

The worst of it was that he seemed genuinely interested in seeing where I grew up. I did not have the heart to tell him that he would be bored after a day. There is not much to do in a small town other than spend time with family. That was the problem.

My parents' house is a three-bedroom ranch. My sister was home for the summer. This left only my minuscule bedroom unoccupied. I tactfully suggested staying with James at a hotel, but my normally compliant father would not hear of it. On to plan B. I reluctantly offered to stay with James in my old bedroom. James couldn't object to a few teen fan posters and a lumpy bed, could he? But my dad put his foot down. James could not stay with me. I was furious. How old did my dad think I was? Mom certainly didn't have any illusions.

James laughed when I told him about the dilemma. "What did you think he'd say? You're still his little girl."

My mom called me back when Dad wasn't in the house. We worked out a deal. I would nominally stay with them, and Mom would look the other way if I slipped out. But I needed to fix the terms. "Do I have to make an appearance at the breakfast table?"

"Don't worry. Your dad won't know you're not there. I'll get Ash to help." Oh great. But it was the best deal I was going to get, so I took it.

"You better not do this to me when I'm married. I'm not into the Lucy Ricardo twin bed thing."

"Liz, is there something you want to tell me? Should I be getting my wedding dress out?"

My mother's wedding dress was a Little House on the Prairie monstrosity. Just the thing in 1977. It gave Ashley and me nightmares.

We were sure that Mom would make one of us wear it. I was too tall and too fat. Or at least that was my excuse. Ashley was thin enough, but even taller than me. Mom liked to threaten us with alterations. There was enough fabric for anything.

"No!" I said.

"Just let me know. I agree with Ash."

"About what?"

"Get James to propose. I like that boy."

"He's not a boy."

"Anyone younger than me is a boy. And you're avoiding the question. Are you getting him to propose?"

"You liked Nick too, remember?"

"You could still have Nick if you'd just give him a chance."

"I'm ending this conversation right now."

"See you soon honey. Can't wait!"

"Neither can I."

Amelia and I got to the testing area early. My mind went blank. This did not bode well. The clicking tongue woman sat down beside me. She was already doing it, faster and faster. I could not wait for the earplugs. I looked around for the pencil twirler. Another minute and the doors would shut. I heard the smoky-voiced proctor. Where was he? They shut the doors. His exam was over. The proctor read the same instructions again. I noticed a number of empty seats. Stress or bad timing? I did not have the energy to worry.

"Go!" The race was on again.

It was the torts question. Torts are civil wrongs. Like all good bar essays, the fact pattern was complicated and arcane. A delivery truck ran into a pedestrian, causing a chain reaction of crashed cars, resulting in the fall of a light pole into a nearby office building. The deliveryman then got into a fistfight with the other drivers and some passersby as the moribund pedestrian was run over again by a stampede of frightened office workers, exiting the building. We were asked to analyze all of the torts involved.

I was just to the fistfight when the room went black and the whir of the air conditioners ceased. There was dead silence for two seconds and then screams. I heard the rasp of the proctor. "Don't panic. It's just a power outage. Sit where you are and don't move."

Move? It was so dark, I couldn't see my hands in front of my face. I put my head down. My thoughts ran a mile a minute. I could already feel the room getting sticky without the circulating air. It was at least a hundred degrees outside. How long would it be before the heat invaded?

I forced my mind to think about the torts question. I walked through each action in the story. Every person had committed a tort or was the victim of one. I analyzed the situations in turn, ending back at the deliveryman. How many minutes had I been sitting there? No one dared to talk in case they would be disqualified. I was alone in the silent darkness with my thoughts.

They went unbidden to another problem. The deliveryman. Of course. The tangled knot started to unwind. Could I be right? Maybe a little snooping would nail it down. I would have to do it casually. I could not attract attention. When I got back from Marshfield, I would have a couple of days before Janice demanded all of my time.

Then, as suddenly as it had died, the electricity sprang back to life. I sat up and blinked. My watch showed half an hour had slipped by. The proctor told us to start again. I opened my book and wrote the most compete essay of my entire legal career. My *magnum opus*. I even had time to spare.

CHAPTER 21

On the drive back, Amelia and I talked like we hadn't in weeks. She and Vince were going to see a movie. It wasn't really a date, she thought. They just happened to want to see the same thing.

"This could be the start. The hair, the movie —"

"I still have 'friend' written across my forehead. He's just asked me a bunch of stuff about my family, and he hasn't said anything about the hair."

"That doesn't mean he hasn't noticed. Anything can happen when the lights go off."

"That sounds like a story you are going to tell me whether you want to or not."

I told her about Nick and the infamous movie date. Amelia was impressed, but she frowned and said, "I'm not really seductress material."

"You can turn it on when you want to."

"Vince is completely immune."

"Defeat is not an option. I've watched him. He's interested. We've been going about this the wrong way."

"How could there be a wrong way?"

"Well, Vince took a long time to ask me out. Even then I wasn't sure it was a date. I've concluded that Vince is binary, like a light switch. You're friends so he's in off mode and then something happens and he puts you in the girlfriend category."

"And how am I supposed to turn him on?"

"That's the question, isn't it? I think you need a surprise attack."

"As in?" she said.

"Use my Nick strategy. Don't give Vince time to react."

"Can't I try something more subtle?"

"Subtle doesn't seem to be working for you."

"What if he pushes me away?"

"Simple. You get up and walk out. Take your own car so you won't be stranded."

"Just leave him there?" she said.

"Let him stew in his own juices."

"Like a roast?"

"Someone needs to stick a fork in him."

In two days I was back on the road, this time in James' little BMW sports car. He gleefully wove in and out of traffic. I closed my eyes so I wouldn't grip the dash. The car did have one benefit, however. Satellite radio. I usually listened to National Public Radio as far as I could into Illinois and then gave myself up to the mercy of country music stations. I studied the channel guide he'd stashed in his glove compartment.

"What do you want to listen to?" I asked. James' CD collection was eclectic, so I was at a loss to guess his present mood.

"No country unless it's bluegrass."

"Thank goodness."

"Didn't you grow up in rural Wisconsin?"

"I'm from town, but I heard enough of it as a girl."

"Your parents?"

"Friends. My parents listened to bad 70's stuff."

"Don't malign the 70's. You're talking to a kid who actually watched *Soul Train* when his parents weren't looking."

"You can't tell me disco was good," I said.

"It had its moments."

"My dad will get out some eight-tracks for you."

"He still has eight-tracks?"

"And a player. We even had one in the car. That's what we used on long car trips."

"What did he make you listen to?" James said.

"America. I know all the lyrics to 'Muskrat Love.'"

"Poor girl."

"Thank goodness the car died when I was seven. Otherwise, my entire childhood might have been warped."

"And after that?"

"No mandatory music. My dad didn't transition well into the cassette tape era," I said.

"Ah, yes. You missed out on the whole mixtape phenomenon."

"What was the big deal about recording a bunch of music on a cassette?"

"It's a lost art. Picking the perfect music for the girl you're trying to impress."

"This was another college activity?"

"The one led to the other. But you had to do it right," James said.

"And if you did it wrong?"

"Disaster. You couldn't live down a bad mixtape."

"Everyone I knew had more free music than they could listen to in a lifetime."

"There's no fun in that." He sighed.

"I'll humor your nostalgia," I said, turning to the 1980's channel. A Duran Duran song filled the car. James sang along, his voice noticeably off key. I smiled to myself.

"You know all of the words?" I said.

"I've heard this song a thousand times."

"I'm sorry."

"My Duran Duran is your Nirvana."

"That's the difference between us. No one can sing along with Nirvana. Past the chorus, the songs are unintelligible."

"You really like all that feedback?" he said.

"I was eleven when *Nevermind* came out, so thought it was cool. And the flannel shirts. All the older kids had cool flannel shirts."

"Why would you want to intentionally look homeless?"

"You're saying you never had a jacket with shoulder pads or acid washed jeans? And what about the punk look? Or neon? Besides, by the time I could buy my own clothes, everything was long skirts and chunky shoes."

He grinned and then started to sing again.

"No offense, but you can't sing," I said.

"I know."

"And yet you play the piano so beautifully."

"I can hear the pitch. I just can't match it," he said.

"Jack Sprat and his wife."

"What?"

"I can't play an instrument. The flute was a disaster. But I can sing on key. You're looking at the lead in the high school musical."

"What was it?"

"*Sound of Music.*"

"I'm having trouble seeing you as a nun."

"I've been told I was very convincing." I turned the music down and sang a few bars of "My Favorite Things."

"Go on. You have a lovely voice."

"You don't want to hear my entire *Sound of Music* repertoire. That music sticks in your head."

"You can sing to me any time you like."

"Just break out in song like a Disney cartoon?" I said.

"Sure. My own private Snow White."

I gave him a few notes of "Whistle While You Work." Then I said, "Too bad I don't get the birds as well. That was my secret childhood dream – to call animals with my voice."

"Ever try it?"

"The other kids thought I was crazy, wandering the woods singing."

"Nothing?" he said.

"The odd squirrel now and then."

"Not really the same."

"Yes, who ever heard of a princess who calls squirrels?" I sang another line, giving it plenty of vibrato. "See, even digging down deep in the throat, *nada.*"

"Are we talking *Deep Throat* or princess? Maybe that's the problem."

I gave him a look. "How quickly you move off the G rating. Anyway, I couldn't be a princess, so I became a lawyer."

"Definitely a come down."

"Adulthood is tough."

James leaned over and put a hand on my knee. "You're doing a good job of it."

"I still feel drained."

"You looked gray when you came back."

"I felt gray. Gray is not my color."

"You are as un-gray as they come," he said.

"Not bored with me yet?"

"You fascinate me."

"You've said that before. I was never sure if fascination meant attraction or horror."

"Attraction. How can you ask?"

"It's a fine line. You're compelled to watch, but all the time you're looking through the holes in your sweater." I smiled. "Maybe I've been spending too much time living the *Night of the Living Dead*."

"I guarantee that zombie Liz will be gone by the time we drive back to St. Louis. It's my mission on this trip."

We sat in silence for a minute, and then he looked at me seriously. "I've thought a lot about it."

"What?"

"Attraction. That night I met you. I told myself I wanted to see you because you were a puzzle. I should have recognized the signs when I called you later."

"You sounded distracted on the phone."

"I was nervous."

"What did you think I'd do? Refuse to meet you?"

"I don't know, but my heart was racing."

"Yet you seemed so smooth. You even tested me. Do you know how annoying that was?"

"Call it a defense mechanism. And I wanted to discover how your mind worked."

"Now you know."

"I'll never really understand."

"That means you're normal. Normal is good."

"Debatable. Speaking of which, I finally have that clip from the surveillance camera at the garage. The paperwork took a lot more time than Bill thought."

"I wondered if he'd thought better of the idea. I'll give it my best shot."

"That's all I ask. Thank you."

A Michael Jackson song, the real Michael Jackson, came on the radio and I turned up the music. We drove through the long flat stretches of Illinois, singing. We stopped to stretch and eat once, but did not linger. Home. Once across the border, I told him to turn the navigation system off. It would take us on I-39 and I knew a faster route. He hesitated.

"Don't you trust me? You won't see the real Wisconsin on 39."

"The real Wisconsin awaits." We drove on, passing the sign for the Wisconsin Dells. "What are the Dells?" he said.

"Only the biggest tourist destination in the state. Think Lake of the Ozarks but better."

"It can't be better than Lake of the Ozarks," he said with a smile.

"How about giant indoor and outdoor water parks in addition to the outlet shopping and the restaurants."

"Sounds like fun."

"It is. Just be prepared for the usual Northwoods kitsch."

"What?"

"Furniture made of roughhewn logs. Bears. Pine trees. Canoes."

"I have to see that."

"You will. The family room in my parents' house. My dad says it makes him feel like he's at a cottage on a lake."

"Okay," James said doubtfully.

"Owning a cottage up north is a Marshfield dream."

"They want to go farther north?"

"I know it sounds odd to a St. Louisan," I said.

"And you go to a cottage because —"

"To boat on the lake or fish, or hunt in season. Maybe cross country ski or snowmobile in winter. It's peaceful."

"And Marshfield isn't?"

"You have to be raised with it to understand."

"I think I'd prefer a vacation house somewhere."

"When I say cottage, it's a loose term. Some of the cottages are beautiful vacation homes."

"I'm warming up to the idea."

"You're not the cottage type."

"Does it show?"

I laughed. "But you must have roughed it when you traveled in Europe. How did you survive with all of your worldly possessions in a backpack?"

"It didn't matter where I went or what I did."

"I know something about that."

"It's why I can talk to you."

"It would be nice to travel, though. I've never been out of the country."

"You haven't?"

"Not even Canada. International travel was never in the budget."

"We should go."

"Where?"

"Italy, France, Spain. Where do you want?"

"Everywhere." I caught sight of the overhead signage. "We want to stay in the middle." The joined interstates were about to diverge. I guided him through several more bifurcations up through the center of the state. The traffic thinned to nothing. It was just us and the road. He sped up and joyfully took the turns.

"Aren't you supposed to obey the speed limit as a police officer?"

"Where else am I going to get to do this?" He accelerated into another turn.

"This isn't St. Louis. You can't plead your ticket down to a noise violation in Wisconsin."

"Spoil sport." He slowed down a little. "You're right of course."

"That's what I want to hear."

"Don't get used to it."

"I'm not going to dignify that with a response."

"Smart girl."

"That's your type, isn't it?" I said.

"You're my type."

"I'll take that as a compliment."

"You're getting used to the compliment thing."

"You've broken me in."

"Don't make it sound like you're an old pair of shoes," he said.

"That analogy is more my speed."

"I give you Marilyn Monroe and you give me old shoes."

"I'm a trial for a romantic like you."

"Sweeping you off your feet is a lot harder than I thought."

"You did it the night I met you. While you asked me questions, I wondered if you were single," I said.

He flung his head back and laughed.

"What's so funny?" Maybe I'd admitted too much.

He rubbed his eyes. "I wondered the same thing."

"But you were engaged to Angie —"

"I figured you might have had something to do with the murder, so I watched you."

"You thought I killed John Harding?"

"I had to examine every possibility. But you didn't do anything odd, other than cozy up to Vince."

"When did you decide I wasn't a suspect?"

"Almost immediately. Your honesty was charming."

"You're used to liars?"

"Honesty is unusual. Somewhere in the middle of the interview, I found myself wondering just where Vince fit in the picture. At the time, I thought it was the natural curiosity of a good detective."

We continued on through the woods and hills of Wisconsin. James was impressed with the beauty and the stillness. I turned the radio back on. The 80's had gotten old. We settled on the Latin music channel. It felt unreal, driving through the little towns of my childhood with a *salsa* soundtrack. As we passed Pittsville, my stomach contracted with anticipation and anxiety. Every time I had tried to imagine James in my hometown, I had given up. It was like matter and antimatter. The two worlds couldn't meet. It wasn't that he would criticize Marshfield. He wouldn't say a thing. But I would see it in his eyes and feel angry and ashamed. I did not want to regret where I came from.

"Are you okay?" James looked over at me. "You were honest with me about your family, right? They don't hate me —"

"No. No. They like you. Please keep in mind that I'm from a small town, okay?"

"What does that mean?"

"Things aren't the way they are in St. Louis."

James seemed to catch my meaning. "That can be good."

"When you grow up, everything is normal. Then, when you leave, you find out everything that seemed normal is really odd." I took a deep breath.

"If I wanted someone raised like me, I'd still be with Angie."

"You say that now, but we'll see after a week in a town with one main street. You're going to be bored, incredibly bored."

"The point of this trip is to spend time with you. You don't bore me."

"I hope my mental processes won't lose their fascination."

"Not likely." He smiled with such warmth that I felt a tear drip down my cheek. I brushed it away with a finger.

"Now what have I done to make you cry?"

"A good tear. Happiness only."

"I'm not sure I understand the tears of happiness concept."

I brushed another away. "I love you. That's all."

"If that's all, then sob away."

I continued to wipe them as we drove past Lake Dexter and the very picturesque conglomeration of industrial buildings on the outer limits of town. And then we were on Central Avenue, sitting at the train tracks that ran straight through town. The striped bars came down, blocking our path. The train sped past.

"I assume most of the shipments are from Canada?" James said.

"Yes. Or China via Canada." Cars with Chinese characters seemed to alternate with the Canadian National ones.

"No one knows where anything comes from in St. Louis. Things just magically appear on store shelves."

"Not here, at least with food. Even if we didn't see the trains, everyone knows someone who farms and most people have at least a small vegetable garden."

He chuckled. "I'm just trying to picture my mother or sister on their knees in a garden."

"And you?"

"It sounds sort of fun."

"It's relaxing. And you get to eat what you grow."

"Always a plus. I don't mind getting my hands dirty."

"Despite the aversion to cottages, you are surprisingly down to earth."

"A compliment?"

"Yes, although it didn't come out as it should," I said.

"I have to take what I can."

"I don't compliment you enough? You'd blush if I told you half the things that run through my head."

The train ended and the bars started to rise. "Feel free to tell me how wonderful I am at any time," he replied.

"I can show you tonight."

"I like your style."

I hoped Mom and Ashley were up for *Mission Impossible*.

CHAPTER 22

Ashley was sitting on the front stoop when we pulled into the driveway. She jumped up and ran over to the car before James could even turn the engine off. I got out and gave her a hug. She looked genuinely happy to see me.

"We've got a plan," she said into my ear. "Just send James to the hotel after dinner. I'll take care of the rest."

"This is stupid."

"Get James to propose and you'll be fine." She winked at me.

I rolled my eyes.

"James!" She hugged him like a long lost relative.

We walked together into the house. My parents' house seemed incredibly claustrophobic after the Paperelli mansion. And I couldn't help but notice how shabby the furniture had gotten after so many years of use. My mom had cleaned, but twenty years of accumulated knick-knacks attracted dust. I followed James warily.

"Where are Mom and Dad?" I said.

"Out back. Dad's grilling brats."

Bratwurst sausage. Great. I should have just presented James with a Cheesehead hat at the door. Maybe I could distract him with some of the photographs my mother had placed on every conceivable surface. Give him time to adjust to Wisconsindom.

"We'll be out in a couple minutes, okay?" I said. Ashley recognized my pleading look and followed instructions. This was a first. I trailed James into the living room.

Sure enough, the photographs on the mantel attracted him. I hovered behind as he examined one. Ashley and me in the backyard. I knew the outfits, the matching dresses my Aunt Elaine had sent us, and the sad rosebush that my dad maintained at all costs. It must have been one of Ashley's birthdays. She had a party hat on. I looked at it more closely. It had to be taken right before they diagnosed my tumor. I still had all of my hair.

"You don't have any photos of your family in your apartment," James said quietly.

"They remind me of what I'm missing."

"But surely you know that this is you." He pointed to the older girl. "And this is Ash."

"I know it's us because my mom wouldn't put pictures of other people's children on her mantle, and because I hated having to wear that dress. Who wants to match a sister half your age? But without those clues, they could be anyone."

I picked it up and ran my finger along the top of the frame. A little plume of dust flew into the air. I looked at it again. Yes, definitely pre-tumor. "You told me you would love to have seen me as a sassy twelve year old. Here you go. That was before my diagnosis, so it's as sassy as I got." I handed him back the photograph.

He looked at it with a strange expression on his face. Horror or attraction? I didn't know. Then he put it back on the mantle. "You're amazing. Have I told you that today?"

"It's getting to be a habit with you."

He leaned down and kissed me lightly on the lips. "What's the plan for this evening?"

"First you are going to be subjected to brats on the grill, sure to be accompanied by Jell-O salad and then a marshmallow fluff of some sort. There will also be an actual salad with vegetables from the garden. I'd eat that and skip the rest."

"Fluff?"

"I'll explain later."

"As long as there is beer, you have no need to worry," he said.

"And you'll be going to the hotel alone."

"Just as I feared."

"Ash has a plan. If that fails, I'll come over early tomorrow morning."

"You'll be welcome whenever you come." He leaned down as if to kiss me again, and I would have responded suitably, except that I heard voices. I pulled away just in time.

"Liz! James!" My parents descended.

The meal contained all of the predicted cuisine, except that my mother fixed yellow wax beans just for me. I had three helpings. James held up beautifully. He made small talk with my father about the beer and barbecue technique. He complimented my mother on the food and asked about the garden. He even had two servings of green pistachio fluff.

"What is this?" he said, licking the spoon.

"Marshmallow crème and food coloring mostly."

"Pure sugar and fat?"

"Yes."

He smiled. "I feel like a true Wisconsinite."

"You've obviously adopted the lifestyle." He'd stretched out on the lawn chair, a beer in one hand, his eyes closed.

"How could you leave this?" he said.

"You mean the weather?" It was 75 degrees and clear.

He sighed contentedly. "There aren't even bugs. Face it, this is paradise."

"We'll come back in January and then you can tell me why I left."

"It gets cold in St. Louis."

"You have no idea." I thought of James bundled up like a sausage in layers of down and smiled.

"Anyone for coffee?" my mom said. She bustled around the patio collecting paper plates. I started to help. James opened his eyes and sat up. "Anything I can do?"

"No. Of course not." Mom waved a hand at him.

"In other words, you're a guest. I'm still staff," I said.

James sat back in his chair and took another sip of beer. "As I was saying, this is the life."

I helped mom with the garbage and then went inside to make coffee. If I let my parents near the machine, it would be weak as water. I had come to depend on a good jolt of caffeine in the evening. Ashley came up as I ladled coffee into the filter.

"Anything embarrassing yet?" she said.

"Nothing I couldn't handle. But keep an eye on Mom. She's sure to suggest the videos."

"Ouch. I'd forgotten about them." My father had videotaped practically every aspect of our childhoods. Most videos were merely boring. Some could not see the light of day.

"James handles Dad pretty well," Ashley said.

"He was a biology major in college, so maybe Dad's ramblings aren't so boring to him. Then again, he could be faking it."

"Dad won't stop if he has an audience."

"I'll step in if I need to."

"I can help," Ashley said.

"Since when are you so helpful?"

"Since I might need you to return the favor sometime."

"Wait. You've been holding out. Who is he?"

"You met him. And don't look so surprised. At Vince's party. Carlos. The guy I was dancing with."

"The one at UW?"

"Duh."

"And it's serious? Why didn't you tell me?"

"It's not serious – yet. Like I would tell anyone in this family until I'm practically engaged."

"But I'm your sister."

"That's why I'm telling you now. Don't say anything to anyone."

"Got it."

"What?" Mom walked into the kitchen. Ashley gave me a look that said we would talk later. I concentrated on filling the coffee machine.

"Nothing, Mom. I was just showing Ash how much to put in for a good cup." I pushed the "on" switch.

"Don't make it too strong," Mom said.

"I'll heat milk for yours." I opened the refrigerator, looking for the pitcher. My mom always bought the local milk. It came in a plastic bag. I cut the corner of the still unopened bag and shoved it back into the pitcher. I poured some in a saucepan. The coffee sizzled into the carafe. The smell of warm milk and coffee filled the kitchen. I took a deep breath. Home.

I didn't feel quite so contented staring at the faded glow of the stars. I'd stuck them to my bedroom ceiling at age ten. My dad helped me to lay them out in real constellations. I stared at the Little Dipper as I had so many nights before. My bed felt lumpy. I shifted my weight and stretched my leg out. I put my arms behind my head. I was tired of waiting. I was just plain tired. If something didn't happen soon, I would be asleep. I thought about James at the hotel. This was ridiculous.

Finally, I heard a faint tapping at my door, followed by a crack of light from the hallway. Ashley's head appeared and then a hand. The hand beckoned me. The mattress creaked as I got off the bed. Ashley made a face. She grabbed my arm and dragged me down the hall. She closed the front door slowly and turned the lock. I started to say something, but she hissed at me. We walked to her car, parked down the lane.

"I can tell you didn't sneak out much – you almost gave us away. Parents sleep with the window open."

"I sneaked out, but obviously not as much as you. What were you doing in high school?" Living in St. Louis, I had not kept tabs on her.

"Same thing you were." She gave me a knowing look.

"Oh. I'm out of practice. I didn't think I'd still have to do this."

"Remember, you owe me." She pulled out and started towards the hotel.

"I won't forget. You're being careful, right Ash?"

"You sound just like Mom. I'm not a complete idiot."

"I didn't mean that. I remember college. Mistakes can happen," I said.

"There's a story —"

"I'll tell you some other time. Just watch what you do. Some men seem more attractive after a couple of drinks."

"I was sober when I met Carlos, thank you."

We pulled into the hotel lot.

"Here you go. Don't do anything I wouldn't do."

"That's not much of a limitation."

She grinned. "Remember —"

"I owe you. And I'm sure you'll ask for the favor at the worst possible moment."

"What are sisters for?"

"Thanks!" I shut the door before she could respond.

The front desk called up to James' room to find out if he was expecting a lone female late at night. He was. The lady looked at me strangely. I wondered if she knew me. There was nothing about her that seemed familiar, but I could never tell. It was one of the perils of a small town. My dad was sure to find out what I'd been up to. Let's hope it was after I was safely back in St. Louis.

James opened the door wearing a towel. I stepped back in surprise. He smiled and pulled me in. The soft fragrance of soap hung in the air. I forced myself to look at his face. "You got the honeymoon suite?"

"It's our first vacation together, so I thought we should enjoy it."

"I didn't expect much enjoyment visiting my parents."

"Given your misspent youth, I figured you'd get out of the house."

"I relied on Ash's expertise this time. I'll do better now that I know what is waiting for me."

"Then come on." I loved his wicked smile.

CHAPTER 23

The next morning I slept in. I'm not sure what Ashley or my mom did, but nothing was said when I showed up at the house well after noon and in the same clothes I'd worn the day before. I changed and helped Mom prepare lunch.

"Do you and James have plans for Friday night?" Mom said as she cut tomatoes for sandwiches.

"Not that I know of. Why?"

"Dr. Bergstrom is hosting the department party this year. He told me to bring you."

"Oh no." I shook my head. "Don't make us go. Please." My mother's department had known me way too many years. The number of embarrassing stories was limitless.

"You don't have to stay long." Her tone brooked no argument.

"You already told him we'd go, didn't you?"

"I didn't think you'd have such a problem with it."

I sighed. "And Ash?"

"She went last year."

"You mean no one wants to see her again."

Mom laughed. "She didn't do anything too outrageous."

"But you're taking preventative measures."

"What?" Ashley walked into the kitchen. "I heard my name."

"Nothing. You don't have to go to the department party," I said.

"Ha. Ha." Ashley opened the refrigerator and stuck her head in. "What's for lunch?"

"Sandwiches," Mom said. "There may be a brat or two." She turned around. "Hey, if you're going to waste electricity, you can at least help. Get out some of that cheese I bought yesterday and some pickles. James likes pickles, doesn't he?" James was puttering around in the yard with my dad.

"You know, that's one thing I've never asked," I said.

"Then get them out."

"Liz. A little help, maybe?" Ashley was trying to balance a giant jar of pickles and half a wheel of cheese. It was amazing how much food my mom could cram into one small refrigerator. I took the jar of pickles from Ashley and set it on the counter. At Mom's direction, Ashley and I ferried food until the counter groaned under the weight of the buffet.

Ashley saw me eye the spread. "I know," she said. "And we're going to have to put it all back in there."

"I'm not even hungry," I said in a low voice.

Ashley whispered, "Don't say that around here. It's a capital offense." Mom had her back to us, digging something out of a low cupboard.

"How was last night?" Ashley said.

"No comment."

"Come on. I got you out of the house. Just one detail or I won't help you tonight," she said.

"I can sneak out on my own."

"Your stories are all I've got right now."

"No local boy worth breaking curfew for?"

"Please. As if. One detail or I won't be your friend."

"Were you ever my friend?"

"I'm your very own sister."

"Fine. Fine. He got the honeymoon suite."

"With the big Jacu—"

I nodded.

"And you —"

"I'll leave it to your imagination," I said. "Now stop asking questions."

"Why can't I meet someone like that?"

"You're not discovering bodies in stairwells."

"I could if I wanted to."

"Too late. He's taken."

"I guess I'm stuck with Carlos."

"He doesn't sound so bad."

"No. I'll keep him if I can," she said.

"'If I can' being the operative phrase."

Mom stood up and turned around. "What are you girls chattering about over there?"

Ashley got a devilish look in her eye. "Just Liz's sex life. Nothing you'd be interested in."

I stared at her, my cheeks burning. Two could play at that game. "Ash's too. You know she's dating a new guy, Carlos. I think it's serious, so you might want to give her 'the talk' again."

Ashley went white. I'm not sure which was worse, the Carlos disclosure or the threat of "the talk." When your mom is a nurse, you get way too much detail way too soon.

Mom looked at us indulgently. "Now girls, there's no need to be embarrassed. I'm not going to pry. Unless you have some questions?"

Ashley and I looked at each other in horror. "No!" we said in unison.

"Okay. I'm going to the basement to get some things from the freezer for dinner tonight." She paused at the basement steps. "And Ash, I know all about Carlos. You really shouldn't leave your cell phone lying around. Anyone can read the text messages."

"Busted," I said, laughing so hard my eyes watered. Ashley ran from the room.

I told James about the exchange as we walked along Central Avenue later that afternoon.

"I'm glad I went to college before my every move was recorded."

"There aren't drunken frat party photos of you floating around on the Internet?"

"I hope not."

"Anyone can scan those old Polaroids in."

"Fortunately, most of my sins were committed in private."

"I can imagine. I didn't drink much, so there shouldn't be anything on me either."

"So prudent. So young."

I looked at him.

He laughed. "I'm just kidding. I know your explanation by heart."

A police car pulled up beside us and stopped. What had we done? The officer leaned out of the window. He had dark sunglasses and a short buzz cut.

"Liz Howe! I didn't know you were back in town!" My mind did a frantic assessment. The voice was really familiar. He had a long, slightly crooked nose.

"Jake Owens! When did you join the force?" I hadn't had an email from Jake in a long time.

"Last year. You're surprised, eh?" He grinned.

"I thought you didn't believe in authority?"

"If you can't fight the man, join him. Want to introduce us?" He looked at James, who had a wary expression.

I took James' hand and pulled him over. "Jake, this is my boyfriend, James Paperelli. He's a homicide detective with the St. Louis City police. James, this is Jake. A friend of mine from high school."

Jake put the car in park and got out. He and James shook hands, testing each other's grip. Then Jake leaned against the car, crossing his arms. He'd filled out with muscle since I'd last seen him. James put his arm around my shoulder.

"So, how long has it been?" Jake said.

"You were still an anarchist with goth makeup, so it's been several years. I almost didn't recognize you without the black lipstick and the chains."

"I don't need to wear those anymore." He put his hand on his gun holster. "Now they have to listen to me."

"Revenge is sweet."

Jake looked at James. "Liz was one of the few kids who was ever nice to me."

"She's like that," James said.

Jake nodded. "What do I hear about you becoming a lawyer?"

"I just took the bar exam last week, so we'll see."

"Are you going to practice around here?"

"No. St. Louis."

"Ah." He looked over at James. "What kind of law?"

"Estate planning, not criminal defense."

He smiled. "I don't take sides when it comes to lawyers. How long are you in town?"

"Just a week. Is anyone else in town I should make a point of seeing? I've lost touch with so many people."

"No. The people in town aren't ones you'd want to hang out with. And Nick's not here."

"I know. He's in New York. We email every once in a while," I said.

"Oh good. I'll get his email from you." Jake paused and then smiled. "Those were the days weren't they? You and Nick and me."

"Yes, I still can't believe we did half the stuff we did."

Jake shook his head. "We were stupid but – remember when we – oh hey, I should warn you. Lori's still here."

"Lori made our lives miserable. She has to be one of the meanest people I've ever met," I said to James. Then I looked back at Jake hopefully. "She's not in jail, is she?"

"I wish. She sells insurance. Her face is on a billboard down towards McMillan."

"Now that's something I don't want to see blown up."

Jake laughed so hard, he had to hold on to the car. "She still looks like a troll," he finally managed to get out.

"Age is not going to help with that."

"No." Jake wiped his eyes. "I'm just waiting to catch her with a moving violation or something."

"Note to all high school bullies – don't tick off the future cop."

"Yeah. You never know who might be writing you a ticket." He stood away from the car. "I've got to get going. It's great seeing you, Liz." He pulled out his cell phone and we exchanged numbers and emails. I gave him Nick's email as well. "Good to meet you James," he said, shaking hands once again. "Nice to know Liz is with a fellow officer. You take good care of her. She's the best."

"Will do," James replied.

Jake got in the car and drove away down the street.

"That's amazing. Jake a police officer! Last time I saw him, he had more piercings than I could count." We started walking.

"How did you know it was him?"

"His voice. And his crooked nose. Even pancake makeup can't hide that."

"He's right. You are the best." His tone was strangely flat.

I decided to ignore it. "I'm glad you think so. And now that my secret is out of the bag, I feel so much better."

"Which secret?"

"The one I've hidden so successfully up to now."

He stopped and looked at me.

"The fact that I was completely unpopular in high school," I said.

He smiled for the first time. "If that's all."

"I'm scarred for life and you say 'that's all.'"

He took my hand and started walking again. "It doesn't surprise me that high school kids couldn't understand your worth."

"That's the nicest explanation for a painful adolescence I've ever heard." I stopped, forcing him to stop with me. "So what's eating you?"

"Were all of your friends guys? I have yet to hear you talk about a single girlfriend."

"I had girlfriends, but they aren't here in Marshfield. Please don't tell me you're jealous of Jake. We were always just friends."

"And Nick?"

"Look, I'm not sure you can comprehend this, but misfits don't have many friends. You have to hold on to the only people who were ever good to you. That includes Nick. And Jake, now that he wants to stay in touch."

James stood for a moment lost in thought and then he said, "I wasn't popular either."

"How was such a thing possible?" I said.

"Easy. I was shy, awkward, and interested in science and math. What more did I need at a boys school?"

"But Lourdes?"

"We met at the Math Olympics."

"Wow."

"So I do understand."

"And what do your classmates say now? I assume a lot of them are still in St. Louis."

"Guys aren't going to apologize for giving you a hard time."

We wandered into the Railroad Antique Mall on Central. It was a familiar jumble of odds and ends. James' anger seemed to have dissipated, but I couldn't be sure. A little distraction might be a good thing. I picked up an indeterminate object. "What do you think this is?"

"No idea." He wandered over to a glass case. I lost sight of him. Was he still angry? Then I heard laughter. "Come look at this," he said.

"Where are you?"

"Over here." I followed the voice. He pointed to something on the third shelf. "It's my lunchbox."

A battered Peanuts lunchbox stared back at me. "You took a Snoopy lunchbox to school?"

"I was five. Snoopy was cool back then."

"I'm too young to know."

"Just you wait. Another five or ten years and your entire childhood will be considered an antique."

"Do you want to buy Snoopy? As a memento of the trip?" I said.

"I don't think I could carry it off the way I did then."

"You can do anything when you're five. There are some photos of me —"

"Now I have to see them."

"Good luck. I'm not going to tell you where they are, and in case you haven't noticed, my parents have a lot of stuff in that house."

"I'm sure your mom will be happy to get the albums out if I ask," he said.

"You wouldn't dare."

"What's so bad about the photos anyway?"

"I was creative with my clothing. There are photos of me with things, not hats, on my head."

"Everything you say just adds fuel to the fire."

"You want to embarrass me?"

"I want to know you." He paused. "And I'm sorry. I overreacted with Jake."

"Then I'll show you every shameful thing I have. Speaking of which, you will have to pick me up tonight. Ash is going out with a friend to lick her wounds from the Carlos text affair."

"Poor Ash."

"She gets what's coming to her most of the time."

That night at exactly 10:47, I escaped. My moves were rusty, but I shut the door without waking anyone. The old anticipation welled up within me as I walked down the road towards James' waiting car. Nick and me. What a long time ago that seemed. I could have done this when I saw Nick at Christmas. I am sure he was hoping I would. But I'd only have been thinking about James. I did let Nick kiss me in his car, but that was more curiosity than anything else. Just to see if the old spark was still there. It was, but everything else had changed. Then the sudden image of a pink-soled shoe filled my head. Sneaking around. Not just then, but before. That had to be it, but why?

I reached James' car and opened the passenger door. James grinned at me. "I like this whole sneaking out business. It makes me feel like I'm fifteen again."

"Don't say that. If you're fifteen, I'm five and you are a sick, sick boy." I sat down and buckled the seat belt. He started the car.

"Okay. Then you're fifteen and I'm twenty-five."

"Still a crime. What kind of police officer are you?"

"Eighteen and twenty-eight?"

"That's better. The advantage of age is that our accommodations are nicer than they were in high school."

"Because?"

I looked at him incredulously. "Tell me you never made a move on Lourdes in your car – but wait, you didn't, did you? I keep forgetting."

"I said we never did it, not that I didn't make a move. You're right, though. Not the most comfortable spot."

"That's the beauty of adulthood. All the fun without any of the inconvenience. I don't understand people who say high school years are the best of your life."

"Let's hope they aren't," he said.

"What do you think the best years will be?"

"Too much late night philosophy."

"I'm serious." I thought a moment. "This year is a contender for me."

Silence followed my declaration. James pulled into the parking lot of the hotel and turned the engine off. I sat nervously beside him, trying to gauge his reaction. Me and my mouth. But we'd both said the big L – and I'd thought we meant it.

After what seemed an eternity, he said, "I've never been happier than I am with you right now."

I took his face in my hands and brought his lips to mine. Forget the hotel. I wanted him this minute.

After a brief indulgence, he gently pulled away. "We're adults, remember?"

It took me a second or two to catch my breath. "Damn."

He was still chuckling as we walked hand-in-hand through the lobby doors, oblivious to the icy look of the hotel clerk.

CHAPTER 24

The picture show was less painful than anticipated. James seemed to think even the most bizarre photographs were charming. I left it to him to figure out who was who. Except for the surgery photographs. The child with the shaved head had to be me. James didn't say a word, until we got to a photograph that made him smile. "Who's that?"

"That's Cattail." The photograph showed a stuffed cat with its head wrapped in gauze and a plastic identity bracelet around its foot.

"What's the story?"

"Dad bought him for me right before the surgery. When I got out, one of the nurses had bandaged him just like me." I flipped a couple of pages ahead. "See. There I am with him, showing off our matching bracelets. The nurses treated me like their own child. I was, sort of. Many of them worked with my mom."

"You were a brave girl."

"At that age, you don't think anything will go wrong. I had confidence that I'd survive. I guess I still do."

"You weren't frightened?"

"Only the night before. I asked the nurse to give me something to sleep. I wasn't afraid of the surgery, just that I'd wake up a different person."

"What do you mean?"

"It was brain surgery. If it altered my brain in a fundamental way, I wouldn't know. I didn't want to become someone else."

"So I assume —"

"Mom tells me I'm the same. I would have liked to skip the prosopagnosia, but that wasn't in the cards."

Ashley arrived to prevent us from pulling out the bad photographs of her. Too late. As a peace offering, James suggested he take us both to the Brew Pub for lunch. He wanted to try the beer anyway, and Ashley's volunteer shift at the hospital didn't begin until 4:00.

The lunch started out fine. James ordered a porter to die for and even agreed to try a fried pickle. We talked and laughed until our sandwiches arrived. I was just about to flag the waitress down to order a refill on my Diet Pepsi when a voice behind me said, "Liz and Ashley Howe. What a surprise."

I froze. I could never forget that voice. It was seared into my brain. My fingers gripped the table. "Lori," I whispered. She'd come up behind me, so I turned slowly in my chair. Jake was right. Lori looked more trollish than ever.

"So Liz, what have you been up to? Are you back for good?"

I took a deep breath, but my heart was racing. "No. I live in St. Louis now. I just graduated from law school."

"Oh." That seemed to have deflated her a little. Then she looked at James. I didn't like the gleam in her small hard eyes. "And who is your friend?" She placed herself between us.

"James, this is Lori Knauf. Lori, this is James Paperelli, my boyfriend."

She stuck out her plump hand. "Liz and I went to high school together."

"So Liz told me," James said evenly. The conversation stalled. I hoped that she would go away. Instead her eyes lit up with the malice I'd seen many times before. My hand started to shake.

"I thought you and Nick were back together."

"No," I said.

"Really? Someone told me that they saw Nick and some girl getting cozy in his car on Christmas Eve. I could have sworn they were talking about you."

I looked at Ashley. She was gray. I felt sick to my stomach. This couldn't be happening.

"I think you're mistaken. Very nice to meet you." James' authoritative tone indicated that the conversation was over.

Lori smiled. "See you around, Liz. Ashley." Then she turned and walked away. I looked back at the two people in front of me. James' eyes were steely. Ashley had gone from gray to beet red.

Ashley spoke first. "I'm so sorry, Liz. I didn't think Haley would tell." Haley was a good friend of Ashley's who was going to community college while she helped out on her parents' dairy farm.

"Haley saw us?"

"No. I did. But I told her. I didn't think she'd tell anyone, but she must have."

"Would someone mind explaining what exactly you were doing with Nick in his car?" James' voice was soft and deadly.

I took a deep breath. This was going to be good. "Nick and I met up over Christmas. I hadn't seen him in a long time, so we went to lunch. After lunch he was going to drive me home. He kissed me while we were sitting in the car. I'll admit to kissing him back, but nothing else happened."

"I can vouch for that," Ashley said.

"You're not helping," I said.

"Right." She hopped off her seat and practically ran to the ladies room.

James still regarded me. "Nothing happened," I repeated. "And it wasn't as if you and I were dating. You hadn't gotten permission to ask me out."

James took my hand. He ran his fingers lightly over my knuckles. "The kiss didn't lead to more because you were in public?"

"No." I watched his long fingers. "I couldn't do it. I knew I'd be thinking of you the whole time. Nick didn't deserve that."

He didn't say anything. I couldn't stand the silence anymore, so I looked at his face. He smiled. "That's the answer I wanted to hear. I could kick myself for not asking you out when I had the chance."

I let out my breath. "I forget I'm back in a small town."

"I'm glad I stopped us from getting carried away last night. Imagine. Twice in one year with two different guys."

"I'm visiting the honeymoon suite. I can't have much of a reputation left."

"I'll see what I can do to fix that."

Ashley reappeared. "All better?"

"That was quick," I said.

"I knew you two couldn't stay mad for long."

"James is very understanding," I said.

"I'm sure you give him a lot of practice."

"I give her as much as she gives me," James said.

The waitress reappeared and I got my refill. I took a sip and the bubbles hit my tongue. Poor Ash, always the victim of unintended consequences. Then, I thought of Lori's beady, cunning eyes. Lori intended to inflict pain. Suddenly, all of the threads that I'd been playing with wound themselves together. The unintended just might be the intended. I had an investigation to do when I got home.

"So what are you guys going to do this afternoon?" Ashley asked between bites of Rueben sandwich.

"I'm happy doing nothing at all," James said.

Ashley wrinkled her nose. "Then Marshfield is for you."

"I like it here," he said.

She dropped her fork. I laughed.

"It's only because you don't live here," she said. "We're all trying to get out."

"Some do come back. It's a good place to raise children," I said.

Ashley smirked. "Yeah. When I'm old and stodgy it'll be great."

"In twenty years you'll be Mom."

"Just shoot me if I ever become Mom," she said.

"I'll remember that."

James paid the bill. We'd dawdled over lunch so long that Ashley asked us to drop her off at the hospital. I gave James a short tour of the adjacent Marshfield Clinic.

"It's like a city," he said.

"The City on the Hill."

"So everyone in town works here?"

"Everyone knows someone who works here."

"That must skew the school system."

I nodded. "I knew a lot of doctors' kids."

"Jake?"

"No. His dad's a radiology tech and his mom is a medical assistant in Cardiology. But Nick is the son of my neurologist, Dr. Lee."

"That explains that."

"What?"

"I'd wondered how you'd broached the subject of your prosopagnosia at fifteen. You had a hard enough time with me."

"My classmates knew about the tumor, but I didn't talk about anything else. My surgery was more than enough."

"Nick already knew?"

"He moved here after the surgery, but I assume so. He did not seem surprised when easy things were difficult for me. The subject never came up."

"Would you have told me if I hadn't forced it out of you?"

"Eventually," I said.

"I told you to trust me."

"Look, most men want you to be able to recognize them. It's kind of a minimum requirement. And I haven't told many people."

"Who have you told?"

"My family. Holly. Janice. You," I said.

"A very select group."

"Now considerably expanded."

He looked me in the eye. "I'm so sorry." For the first time I felt that he really understood what he had done. "But maybe you give your fellow human beings too little credit."

"If you lived through my adolescence, you might think differently."

"We're not adolescents anymore."

"Thank goodness. Despite what you said last night, I wouldn't go back to fifteen."

"I meant what I said last night."

"Which part?" I said.

"Every part, but especially the part about happiness."

"You shouldn't say such things to me in public."

"Your reputation?"

"I might do something that would sink it forever."

He grabbed my hand. "Let's go."

"So I can show you how wonderful you are?"

"Exactly."

I smiled up at him. Who cared about my reputation? Wait. Reputation. Of course. I was an idiot.

CHAPTER 25

Although we wandered around Marshfield every day after that, I managed to avoid Lori. We did run into Jake and had a quick beer after his shift ended. Otherwise, the people we met were all my parents' age. We even saw Dr. Lee when we went to Mills Fleet Farm to buy a gardening tool for my dad. Dr. Lee was looking through a new shipment of camouflage gear. "I want to be ready for the season," he said. Deer hunting is a religion in Marshfield. I asked politely after Nick. Dr. Lee couldn't help but brag. Nick was doing very well in New York.

James loved Fleet. Even though he did not hunt, fish or garden, we still spent two hours in the store. He offered to buy me a camouflage negligee. I politely declined.

"I think you'd look good in olive drab."

"To shoot or to —"

"Definitely the second. I don't want anyone else trying to shoot you."

I had a momentary twinge of conscience. I should probably tell James where my thoughts led me. Then again, I could be wrong. I ignored the twinge.

"Good. It's hard to know with that," I said.

"There's one in orange."

"Blaze orange makes my skin look yellow."

"Some men like the jaundiced look," he said.

"I hope you're not one of them."

"No. Maybe the camo then. As a souvenir of our vacation in Marshfield."

"You're not serious," I said.

"The idea is growing on me."

"Please. I'll wear whatever you want me to. Just not that."

He hung the hanger back on the rack. "Deal."

"Is this your grand plan to make me over?'

"I know what looks good on you."

"Do you do this with all of your girlfriends?" I didn't hide my irritation.

"You're the only one who's put up with it."

"So I should get a backbone and tell you off?"

"If you like."

"The problem is you're right. But I must have the final veto."

"Seems reasonable."

I picked up the hanger with the negligee. "This is my first veto right here."

"I have lots of other ideas."

"I'm sure you do," I said warily.

But, as a sign of good faith, I took him over to Marshfield's only mall and let him select a sundress for the department party. Undaunted by the general lack of selection, he made me try on several until we agreed to a short dress – his idea – in black and white with straps thick enough – my idea – to wear a bra.

Indecision gnawed at me as I stood in my room pulling the sundress over my head. Not about the dress. About my theories on the bombing. The problem was that I had no proof. Some theories hit too close to home for mistake. I stood in my childhood bedroom, the dress half on, staring at those faded stars.

The door opened suddenly. "You're hopeless," Ashley said.

I hastily pulled the dress down. "Don't you ever knock?"

"Not usually. It's more interesting that way."

"For whom?"

"Here, let me zip you up. Mom sent me. James is sitting in the living room waiting. You're done with makeup, right?" She looked at me critically. "Passable. And hair?"

I fluffed it with my hand. "I thought I'd leave it natural."

"As natural as you're going to get."

"What does that mean?"

"You haven't been this blonde since you were two."

"It's called highlights. And how would you know? You weren't around when I was two."

"I've seen enough pictures."

"Do you think it's too much?"

"You can't be blonde enough around here." She was right. Between the natural and the bottle-made, raven-haired women were a minority in Marshfield.

James was much more enthusiastic. "You look great," he said, giving me a chaste kiss on the cheek.

"Is that a compliment to me or to your stylist abilities?"

"A good stylist enhances what is already there."

Dr. Bergstrom's house was only a short distance away on a street that was considered a doctors' row. The houses were large by Marshfield standards, with nice lots, not the postage stamps you often saw in St. Louis. Dr. Bergstrom's house had a particularly large one that extended back almost an acre. It had been landscaped in a manner that seemed both English and Japanese, with sculptural rocks and plantings. There were winding paths through flowering fruit trees and the grape arbor where we'd gotten our Concord grapes.

I'd been particularly close to their daughter Mariah. We hadn't seen much of each other since she'd gone to medical school at Stanford, but she matched at Washington University, so I hoped that would change when she entered her residency training in St. Louis.

We pulled up behind a line of cars. "Looks like some party," James said as we got out.

"They do it a couple of times a year. It helps with morale."

He raised an eyebrow.

"Oncology. Not the happiest area of medicine."

"Of course."

"They were really good to me. Especially the neurooncologist. If he comes, I'll introduce you."

"Is it strange to see your doctors socially?"

"Not for me. I'm his best patient."

"You didn't feel like giving him trouble?"

"I give him trouble every time I see him. I'm talking outcomes, not annoyance."

"Oh."

"I knew that death was not an option. He believed in me."

James was quiet for a moment, and then he said, "That's it. The rational explanation for why I was so drawn to you. You and I are survivors."

"Not my resemblance to Marilyn Monroe? What a letdown."

"I'm talking initial attraction, not what keeps me hanging around."

Mrs. Bergstrom met us at the front door. She was a tall slender woman with short spiky hair. I recognized her by the bright orange sweater. Her favorite color. She wore a pair of the new chunky glasses. They perfectly matched her quirky personality. I memorized them for future use.

"Good to see you again," she said, hugging me. "And this must be James. I feel like I know you already."

"Mom's been talking?" I said.

"Of course. Mariah said you and she were getting together. It'll be good for her to have a friend in town. Now come in, you two. The party's out back."

The patio was made of several concentric circles of brick. The garden spread out below in all of its magnificence.

"Amazing. You'd never know that this was here from the front," James said.

"Mariah and I called it the 'secret garden.'" We walked down the steps onto the circular lawn below. Groups clustered together, plates of food in hand. Everywhere we went, people seemed to know James. Just what had my mother been telling her co-workers? Between hellos, there was little time for private conversation. I found my neurooncologist and made the introduction. James fell in with our friendly banter. Neurooncologists are people too.

Finally, we arrived at the grape arbor. The dappled light created magical figures on the ground beneath our feet.

"So this is what they look like," James said touching a bunch with his finger. "They're almost black. I thought they'd be purple."

"I think this is the prettiest part of the garden," I said.

"And the tastiest. That sauce was amazing."

"I wonder if you could grow these in Missouri?"

"Can you grow grape vines in the yard at your apartment? Now if you lived in a house —"

"I could grow them in your window boxes?" I smiled at him. "You'd need a yard like this to do it. I'll just get my mom to ask for some when they harvest."

He put an arm around my shoulder. "Practical but disappointing."

"James?" I should at least give him a warning. I screwed up my courage. It was now or never.

"Yes?"

"When we get a moment —"

"There you are." I heard Dad's voice behind me. I turned. He had the camera ready. "Just let me get a couple of photos, eh?"

I sighed. This was my childhood in a nutshell. Was it any wonder that there were so many blackmail-worthy photographs of me? Dad always stopped to take a shot at the worst possible moment.

"Sure," James said, pulling his own camera out of his pocket. "Would you mind taking some with my camera too?" I saw the gleam in Dad's eye as he eagerly fingered it. James pulled me close.

My Dad took so many photographs that colored lights swam in my field of vision. I let my eyes adjust and my mind wander. When had I last been taking photos under this arbor? With Nick at Prom. I chuckled to myself.

After another camera discussion of epic proportions, James offered to let Dad borrow the camera for the rest of the party. Dad went off happily to play with this new toy.

James turned back to me. The evening light filtered through the leaves, bathing his face in a honey colored halo of angelic light. I had to remind my lungs to breathe. I reached up and touched his cheek, smoothing the curl of his hair back behind the ear. He put his hand over mine. "What are you thinking?"

"You can't be real." I turned my face up as if to kiss him.

"Your reputation?"

"Oh. Right." The spell was broken. "Maybe we should get going. I'm stuck at my parents' house tonight." We were leaving early the next morning and Dad insisted on making his famous pancakes. None of my newly-honed skills could get me out of that one.

He took my hand. "Good idea." We walked out of the arbor and back to the lawn.

"Your camera?" I said. I could not see Dad anywhere.

"I'll get it tomorrow."

I kept the number of goodbyes to a bare minimum, and we escaped to the car. As we got in, James said, "What were you laughing at back there?"

I hesitated only a second. "Myself. We took prom pictures in that garden. They were hideous - all of us in rhinestone-studded puffy dresses."

I thought about the light of that perfect moment. James as a guardian angel. Good thing, because it looked like I might need one. I had to tell him, but the words caught in my throat. No, he wouldn't believe me.

"You haven't seen my photos. I went to prom in the 80's. I don't think I need to say more," he said.

"Mullet?"

"The works."

It was only as James was about to drive me back to my parents' house that we remembered the surveillance video. I looked at my watch. It read 11:00. Dad was not going to be happy. Then again, this was important.

"Let me have a look. It won't take long. I'm not going to recognize anyone anyway," I said.

James booted up the laptop and opened the file. He maximized the picture so that it filled the screen. Even then it was dark and grainy. A figure turned towards the camera. It appeared to be a large man from his size in relation to the cars behind him. He wore a bulky coat and a baseball cap down over his eyes. He gripped a bunch of balloons in one hand and held a box in front of him with the other. He held the balloons so that they blocked his face. The figure walked slowly towards the camera and then out of the picture. The second snippet showed the same figure walking away from the camera, balloons bobbing above him. He wasn't carrying the box. Hmm. There was something vaguely familiar about the man, but I couldn't place it.

"Run it again," I said.

"Think you might have something?"

"I don't know."

"Here, I'll put them both on a continuous loop." James fiddled with the computer and then turned it back towards me. I watched the images flicker back and forth. There was some light of recognition, like chasing a firefly on a dark night. I let my mind go blank, waiting for the answer that I knew was there. The posture. The arm holding the box. The slouch of the shoulders. I held the firefly in my cupped hands. Of course. Connections.

"Andrew Stimpkin," I said slowly.

CHAPTER 26

"What?" James said. "How?"

"The set of his shoulders. They slope down in a weird way. I noticed it when they brought him into court in handcuffs." I put my hands in front of me to demonstrate. "He has his hands in the same position in the video."

"You're sure?"

"Yes."

"And he's still on the lam." James grabbed his BlackBerry. Fortunately there was cell coverage in this part of town. He punched in one number for a speed dial. I heard a voice pick up on the other end.

"Mrs. Fisher. I'm so sorry to wake you, but is Bill there? It's James Paperelli. I have something important to tell him." A pause. "Okay, thanks." And then, "Yes Bill. Liz took a look at the tape. She thinks she recognized the guy. You're never going to believe this. Remember the prisoner who escaped in Jefferson County?" There was a silence, while James listened. Finally he said, "I know, but she seems certain. She saw the guy in court a couple of times. It's a long story, but she recognized the slope of his shoulders." He smiled ruefully at me. "Yes, I know. That makes sense. We're driving back tomorrow. I'll check in from the road. Sorry to get you up. Okay. Good night."

He hit the off button. "He's going to follow up and release the tape to the public on Monday as scheduled. We'll see if we can flush out any more information."

"I don't think I'm wrong."

"I don't think you are either, but procedures must be followed. Oh, and Bill said to thank you. If this turns out, he owes you dinner."

"I'll remember that. Now take me home before you get too tired. You need to conserve your strength for the drive."

"And the pancakes," he said with a smile.

That night I lay awake, trying to fit this new piece into the puzzle. Assuming my theories were correct, there was just one question that remained to be answered. Where was Andrew Stimpkin? I was exhausted by the time I fell asleep. Ashley knocked on my door way too early. I dressed, brushed my teeth and dragged a comb through my hair. Then I staggered to the kitchen table and poured myself a cup of coffee. I heard the front door open. James looked well rested. My parents stuffed us with pancakes. Then we were saying farewell. Part of me was relieved to be on the road. I had to think.

"That was fun," James said as we drove out of town.

"It wasn't as bad as I'd feared."

"Your family is great."

"You really liked Marshfield? You can be honest."

"I'm not lying. This vacation has been one of the most relaxing ever. And you look better. Zombie Liz is gone."

"I'm glad you liked it. We country folk don't know how you city folk will take to doing nothing."

"I thought you were from town?"

"My town is a lot more country than yours."

"Yet again, you've opened my eyes."

"You're a converted Wisconsinite?"

"Hand me a beer and a brat."

"You have to swear undying devotion to the Green Bay Packers. That's part of the deal."

"I look good in green and gold. And I'm already thinking cottage. On a lake. With a boat."

"It comes with log furniture and a stuffed deer head over the fireplace."

"I'd even put up with bear wallpaper to sit in front of a roaring fire with you."

"When you put it like that —"

"See. The country mouse and the city mouse aren't so far apart."

"If we can agree to bear wallpaper, no chasm is too wide."

But as the drive wore on, I was not so sure. James and I were both thinking about Andrew Stimpkin, but in very different ways. James focused on him as an individual. I felt sure the solution lay elsewhere, but I kept silent. Until I had the answer to the final question, I could not say a word. Maybe if I went back to the beginning. I watched the plains of Illinois roll by as I tried to outline all of the connections. It was like a plate of spaghetti – or a bar exam.

We pulled off on a country exit. The air was warmer and noticeably more humid, but there was a sharp wind cutting the heat radiating up from the pavement. We ate at a McDonalds and then stopped for gasoline. I got out of the car. I stretched my arms over my head. James was right. Zombie Liz had disappeared. I looked over the cornfields. There was a farmhouse in the distance. It reminded me of my painting. Zombie Liz. *Night of the Living Dead*. That house was the perfect location to barricade oneself against the zombie invasion. But there didn't seem to be a graveyard nearby.

Then the pieces clicked together, like the gears of a well-oiled machine. Forget the zombies, it was the living I had to fear. I wrapped my arms around me and shivered. I should tell James. But he would try to stop me, and I needed evidence. No one would believe me without evidence. It was too fantastic. No. I would braid the threads myself and then go to the police.

"You're very quiet," James said as we got into the car.

"Just tired." I smiled at him, and felt the stab of a knife in my heart. Deception was not going to be easy.

But the next three weeks were a blur. I started my job with Janice and was overcome with a tsunami of projects. The publication of the surveillance tape had breathed new life into the investigation. James could not stop working. I prayed that the police would find the answers before I did, but that did not seem likely. He and I managed dinner a couple of days a week. The distance was strange. I missed him. If we lived in the same house, I'd see him for half an hour before I collapsed from exhaustion and fell asleep. The idea now seemed tempting.

Then again, I needed to work alone. I focused on my new project as often as I could slip away from my other responsibilities. I got very adept at following the cars without being seen. I made meticulous notes in a special notebook I kept with me at all times. Date. Time. Location. I also wrote out a complete description of everything I knew or deduced and diagramed the relationships of all of the principal players. I had two copies, just in case, but I was not going to dwell on that.

I took a welcome break to meet Amelia for dinner in Clayton one evening. She'd been ever so guarded on the phone. I had a million questions. She arrived looking perfect in a sundress and strappy sandals.

We ordered and then I said, "What happened with Vince?"

She stirred the ice in her Diet Coke with the straw. "The seduction was a bust."

"Oh."

"But that may be a good thing. I mean, it may not be the end."

"I want the play by play."

"We went to the movie and about halfway through I leaned over and kissed him."

"He pushed you away?"

"No. He kissed me back. He's a good kisser, by the way. You forgot to mention that."

"So things went well?"

"We made out for most of the movie."

"And the problem is?"

"We had a long talk at dinner." She paused. "He's a virgin, Liz."

"What?" I said too loudly. Amelia shushed me.

"He doesn't believe in sex before marriage."

I sat back in my chair, stunned. I thought back to our one and only date. "That's not the impression he gave me."

Amelia smiled. "He's good at what he does. He just doesn't want to do anything beyond it."

"I'm a complete and total idiot. The good Catholic boy. That's what he was trying to tell me with all the talk of disciplines."

Amelia took a sip of soda. "And that's why, once he found out I was Catholic, he asked me so many questions about my family. He wants to find 'the one.' He'd like to see me again, but —"

I nodded. "The very long dry spell."

She smiled ruefully. "Too long. He told me at dinner that he knew he might not be what I was looking for. I'm not the good Catholic girl anymore."

"What now?"

"That's the problem. I'd like to give it a chance. But how long am I going to be able to resist?"

"Hard to know." I thought about my first date with James. Not long.

"We're going to dinner next Friday and see what happens."

"Seems reasonable." A virgin. Wow. That explained so much of Vince's hesitation with me. At least Amelia shared the faith. I was both heathen and harlot. Poor Vince. I smiled to myself.

"What are you smiling at?"

"Love always has to be complicated, doesn't it?"

She sighed. "It wouldn't be love if it weren't."

I told Sister Rita that I could not help with the campaign now that work had started. I was too busy. I told Holly the same thing. This was mostly true. But I still needed confirmation of a few points, so I waited for an inconspicuous opportunity to snoop.

The first week of September, I got an invitation I couldn't resist. Sister Rita had done it again. The spreadsheet was a disaster. She begged me to come by to help her fix it. I told her I would get out of work early. 6:00 for me. She could not make it until 6:45, but urged me to start without her. Wonderful. I had forty-five minutes.

There were still people in the offices when I arrived. This limited what I could do. I wasn't sure where they might have stored what I was looking for, so I sat down at a computer. I would fix Rita's problems as cover and then start the search as discretely as possible. A couple of key strokes were enough to right Sister Rita's mess. The hunt was on.

I looked for any folder that seemed out of place. Donor lists, telephone bank information, canvassing schedules. Nothing strange. Speeches. Someone had saved a copy of every speech Kevin Mason had ever given, including his oft-repeated "Normal Day in America" speech. I had now seen enough of that one to last a lifetime. I looked at my watch. Not much time left.

Then I noticed another folder, not in Speeches, called "A Normal Day." Why would he keep a second file with the same information? Unless it was a mistake. Or maybe not. I double clicked on the icon. A window popped up showing me that the file was password protected. Better and better. The hairs on the back of my neck stood on end.

I stared at the screen for a long time, watching the cursor blink. Then divine inspiration. *Un Día Normal.* I typed "Juanes" into the text box and hit enter. The computer pinged and I was in. I looked at the time on the screen. 6:40. The first folder was called "Creep." Strange name. Wait. Of course. I clicked on one document after another, scanning each for the information I knew must be there. It was. Laid out in black and white. Kevin Mason had no imagination whatsoever. This had all been done before.

I heard Sister Rita talking to someone in the outer offices, so I quickly closed the folder and got out. Who knew what kind of surveillance they had? I pulled the spreadsheet up again and sat waiting.

"So chickie, did you fix it?"

"Good to go." I stood up. "But now I'm leaving."

"So soon?"

"I have to grocery shop. I've been working so late every night, I don't have a thing to eat." How quickly would they figure out I'd accessed the file? Or would they think it was Sister Rita bumbling around? But she would not know the password. I had to warn her without tipping them off. However, the less she knew the better. The time had come to talk to James. Now.

"Don't go killing yourself working, chickie. No job's worth that."

"I won't and you shouldn't either. You're whittling yourself to the bone in these offices."

"Naw. When you're my age you'll understand. Better to be working here than sitting in front of the boob tube."

Another strategy. I searched my brain. And then I had it. "Whistle While You Work." *Deep Throat*. She was the right age to know. I closed the door behind me. Without a word, I grabbed a piece of paper and wrote, "Stay away from the office. *All the President's Men*."

She looked at me. "What?" she said quietly. "Here?"

"Trust me," I replied. She hesitated, and then fixed me with an eagle eye. I stared back at her.

Finally, she nodded. "I trust you."

I crumpled the paper and put it in my purse. "Okay," I said loudly, "that does it. Now you know it's all formatting." I opened the door to the office. "You should really take a rest, Rita. I don't want you injuring your health."

"Good advice, chickie. I'll just do a few things here and then go home."

I walked out of the campaign offices, but I ran to my car. I pulled over a couple of blocks later and called James. Voicemail. I left him a message. As soon as I got to my apartment, I paced the floor, waiting for him to call. After half an hour, I gave up pacing and sat down to write out everything I had just seen while it was still fresh in my mind. Holly arrived and asked me how the day had been. I had to warn her, too. Good thing I knew the chink in her armor.

"Fine. Say Holly, I met Sister Rita at headquarters today and she said that she sees you all the time. I hate to ask, but you're not falling behind on the dissertation, are you?"

"Well, maybe a little. But it's all hands on deck. We're so close."

"The place was wall to wall people tonight. I don't think missing a couple of days will hurt. And you know the work has to come first. What are you going to tell your advisor?"

"Wall to wall people? Really?"

"A giant groundswell of support. Work on your dissertation. Kevin Mason's doing fine without your help."

"Okay, a couple of days. I still have to grade all the stuff from that class I'm TA'ing."

"Good idea." I smiled at her with relief. Now if only James would call me back. When I spoke to him earlier that afternoon, he said he was traveling around, following up on some leads. I hoped that there wasn't something wrong.

When I got in bed at 1:00 a.m., James still had not called. Some guardian angel he turned out to be. I heard Holly come in and drifted off about 2:00 a.m. I didn't sleep well, but dragged myself out of bed early and went to work. I parked down the street, away from the office. At work, I left another more frantic message for James. I also left one on his home answering machine. Belt and suspenders.

I waited all morning and then drove over to his house at lunch. His car wasn't there, so I let myself in. The house was silent. I found a piece of paper and wrote him a note, begging him to call me. I placed it on the kitchen island where he was sure to find it. Then I drummed my fingers on the granite. What to do next? Call the station? I could talk to Detective Fischer. Not that he would believe me. No, I needed to speak to James first. But maybe Fischer knew where he was.

I called and spoke to someone who said he would let Fischer know that I was on the line. I wondered if he would even take my call. I leaned against the counter and drummed my fingers some more. One minute went by and then another. Finally a low voice said, "Hello, Fischer here."

"Detective Fischer, it's Liz Howe, James Paperelli's girlfriend."

"Liz, hello. Sorry, they didn't tell me it was you."

"I'm sorry to bother you, but I've been trying to contact James – it's something urgent."

"He called me this morning from a pay phone. I guess he dropped his cell and broke it or something. He's downstate interviewing some witnesses, so I'm sure he'll be back soon."

"Oh." What to do now? To wait or not to wait? If I told Detective Fischer and he did not believe me, I would be back to square one.

Worse, I would have lost any credibility I might have had. And then there was James. Part of the story should be communicated in private. Better to wait.

"Okay. Thank you. If he calls again, please tell him to call me, would you?"

"Will do. And thanks for the tip about Stimpkin. You could be the first lucky break this case has had."

And maybe the last. "You're welcome. Anything else I can do, let me know. I'm more than happy to help."

He chuckled. "I've got some mighty cold cases that could use a second look. Maybe if you have a free afternoon sometime."

"Just let me know."

"You'll be sorry."

He hung up and I started to pace the kitchen. I would give James until tomorrow afternoon, and then I would go downtown and see Detective Fischer. I had an appointment in the morning that I couldn't miss.

Matt Crandall had been selected for the Saint Louis Art Fair after all. We'd agreed that I would come by his booth in the morning. He said he had something special he wanted to give me. I got another piece of paper and wrote down my proposed schedule for the next twenty-four hours. I even included the number and location of Matt's booth, just in case. I dug in my purse and found the guide Matt had given me with the map on the back. I left it on the counter as well, with a note at the bottom:

Come find me as soon as you read this. We have to talk.

And then, so he wouldn't think I was trying to break up with him, and because, if I had to have the last word, I wanted it to be the truth, I wrote:

I love you more than I can say.

Liz

I let myself out of the house and went back to work. I was running out of time.

CHAPTER 27

Saturday morning dawned bright and clear. The oppressive heat had dissipated, but I was not fooled. Clayton would be an oven by noon. I dressed in a pair of shorts, a tee shirt and tennis shoes. I slopped on as much sunblock as my skin would absorb and pulled my hair back in a ponytail. A pair of dark sunglasses, and I was in business.

I searched in the back of my closet and found an old denim purse shaped like a mail bag with a long strap. I loaded it up with all of my usual junk and threw in the notebook. If James did not call, I would have to do things my own way. Damn the consequences. I slung the purse across my body and opened my bedroom door.

Holly was still half asleep on the couch. "Where are you going?" she said.

"Art fair. If James calls, tell him to come find me at booth 125, okay?"

"Will do," she responded drowsily.

I shut the door behind me and locked it with a key. Joe Henderson was just coming in with bags of groceries.

"Hey Liz," he said brightly.

"Good morning. Can I give you a hand?"

He nodded. I knocked on his parents' door and said, "It's Joe," in a loud voice. I heard the usual shuffling and rasp of the latch. I moved out of the way to let Joe through and to make my escape.

"Have a good day," I said, opening the outside door.

"Bye Liz. Take care."

I would try my best.

Parking in Clayton is an everyday trial. On art fair days, it is a disaster. The streets in the center of town are completely blocked off for the artist stalls and the pedestrian traffic. It was already crowded when I arrived, and it had not been open for more than half an hour. I looked at the map they handed me at the entrance. Shoot. I came in on the wrong side. I would have to walk the whole length of the fair to get to Matt's booth.

The Saint Louis Art Fair is a wonderful experience. If I had not been so worried about my own predicament, I would have thoroughly enjoyed it. Artists come from all over the country to show their work. There is a center stage with music and an entire block of food. And not the fried cheese curds I was used to from the Central Wisconsin State Fair either, but gourmet food of every description. The booths were three-sided boxes with a canvas cover and an overhang to protect the work and the artist from the sun.

Unfortunately, I got lost a couple of times and so saw quite a number of booths as I made my way to booth 125. If I'd had any extra money, I would have been in real trouble. But I had just received a statement with the shocking final total for my student loans. Any desire to do something frivolous was nipped in the bud by an extra set of zeroes.

My watch read five minutes to noon when I finally got to Matt's booth. It was tucked in a quieter section of booths, away from the food and the music. The crowd had thinned considerably, presumably because most people were now in search of lunch. Matt stood behind a table set up in the front of the booth. The table was littered with small paintings on black easels. He'd draped it with a rust red velvet cloth that touched the ground, the perfect complement to his work. Behind him hung some of his larger paintings on metal latticework. It had an edgy, industrial feel, which contrasted nicely with the soft velvet.

"The booth looks great," I said, giving Matt a hug over the table.

"Blair helped. He found the metal panels and the table cloth at the antique mall."

"Has he thought about interior design?"

"You'll just end up with uncomfortable furniture and theater up lights."

"Sounds like the voice of experience."

"Our apartment has been made over many times. He's in a white phase now."

I set my purse down on the pavement beside the table. "Where is Blair?"

"Had to work. He'll be here this afternoon."

"I'm your moral support?"

"Other people said they'd stop by, but you're it for now."

"Have things been moving?"

"I sold more pieces yesterday than I've ever sold before. It's amazing."

"People come here ready to buy."

"They do. And look, I've even got the set up for credit cards." He showed me the machine. It was sitting at the back of the table. I leaned over to suitably admire it.

"You are in business."

"Hey, and I've got something for you." He ducked and dug around under the table. My cell phone rang. I was just about to reach down and grab my purse when I heard a voice behind me.

"Hello, Liz Howe." I froze. The smell was unforgettable. I wrinkled my nose. Damn. I was out of time.

"Sean Thomas," I said without turning around. I felt something very cold and very hard between my shoulder blades. The barrel of a small gun, I guessed. Despite the heat, a shiver ran down my spine. Death was not an option. I had to think this through. First order of business, warn Matt. He was still down behind the table.

"You don't have to do this," I said as loudly as I could without attracting attention. "I'm perfectly willing to talk to you without the gun." I moved my foot ever so slightly so that the toe of my shoe was under the fabric of the tablecloth. I felt a finger press down on it. Good. He'd heard and understood me.

"You'll talk all right, but not here. You're a nosy bitch. Snooping around the office. Following my people. Getting into the Stimpkin mess. Did you think I wouldn't notice? People who get in my business regret it."

"What do you want me to do?" I said, pushing my purse with my foot even farther under the table. Let's hope Matt was good at reading my mind. "Someone's going to notice you have a gun on me."

He laughed and it made my blood curdle. "I don't think so. After wandering all over this place, you finally found me a nice quiet spot to talk business." I took a deep breath and turned around.

He was dressed in a tee shirt and shorts with a windbreaker that hung open, presumably to hide the gun. He wore a baseball cap and dark sunglasses. His idea of blending in, I supposed. We were just far enough in the booth that no one would notice his small pistol unless they walked right up to us. "My car's over there," he gestured with it. "If you come now, I just might let you live."

I didn't believe that for a minute. I had to come up with a plan and fast. If only I could stall him. I heard the faint tinkle of my cell under the table.

"If that's the case, I only have one question. Does Kevin Mason know what you're doing?" I said.

"Fuck Kevin Mason." His voice sounded angry and bitter. "That's all you bitches think about is fucking Kevin Mason." Hmm. Marisol's affair must be out of the bag. I wasn't Marisol or Holly, but if what James said was true about my resemblance to Marilyn Monroe, Sean might believe that Kevin had taken an interest in me. I licked my lower lip seductively. "He has what you don't have."

"And what's that?"

"Me."

Sean reached out and grabbed my breast with one meaty paw. "Fucking cunt," he said softly. He squeezed down hard. I had to bite my lip to keep from screaming.

"Maybe I'll make you forget about Kevin." I could hear the growing excitement in his voice. He squeezed again.

I had a sudden flash of insight. He was just like Angie, thinking he could frighten me. I'd chased her away. Maybe I could do the same with him. I glared at him. "Get your fat hand off me or I'll make you regret it."

That was clearly not what Sean was expecting, but he loosened his grip anyway. I batted his hand down and then soldiered on, making it up as I went. "See, you hurt me and Kevin'll kill you."

Sean looked skeptical. Kevin didn't scare him. Think Liz. Think. What could a man like Sean be afraid of? Not the police – if his interaction with James was any guide. No. But what about the big guns? The ones he couldn't hope to control. "And he'll have to go to the Feds," I said. "He'll roll over on you so fast it'll make your head spin."

"Feds?" Sean said mockingly.

My thoughts moved a mile a minute. I had to make the lie stick. "Of course the Feds! Why do you think I'm sleeping with a goddamned detective? He's the in. It was all part of Kevin's secret plan. We've been stringing them along for months, promising this and promising that, just in case you decided to turn nasty."

"You're lying."

"You didn't think someone as smart as Kevin would forget a plan B, did you?"

I could see a vague flicker of doubt in his eyes, so I added, "Of course you did. He's fooled you just like everyone else. You put that gun down and I just might tell you what I know. Maybe you could escape the trap. Get to a country without an extradition treaty. Somewhere tropical – like Cuba."

"Why would you do that if you're fucking Kevin?"

"Maybe I feel sorry for a patsy like you. Maybe I'm tired of Kevin screwing other girls. What does it matter? I have the information you need. So put the gun down."

"Come with me somewhere we can talk."

"No. You put the gun down and I tell you about Kevin's arrangement with the Feds. That's the deal."

"And then what?"

"That's your problem, but I walk away from this whole fucking mess and you never come near me again. Got it?"

He wavered a second, and then he slowly moved his hand down. I saw my chance. I pulled my leg back and then kneed him as hard as I could in the groin. He shouted. I jumped away, falling to the ground, catching the rust tablecloth and pulling it with me. The table cantilevered forward and crashed down, knocking into Sean, who fired wildly into the air. All hell broke loose. There were screams and the sound of running feet. Then I heard a voice say, "Police! Drop the gun and put your hands up!"

I untangled myself from the fabric and scrambled up. Sean pointed the gun in every direction, but could see that he was surrounded. He threw the pistol down angrily. It skittered away on the pavement. Officers rushed in from every side. They handcuffed him and roughly hauled him away from the booths. A police officer asked me if I was okay. I nodded dumbly.

Matt emerged from the wreckage with my purse. I hugged him tight. "Thank you so much for calling the police."

"I didn't. When your phone rang I grabbed it to muffle the sound, and then I saw it was your boyfriend. I texted him what was going on. What did you get yourself mixed up with, Liz?"

I let Matt go. "James? Where is he?"

"Here." James stood sternly at the entrance of the booth. I had expected a passionate embrace. Instead, he stood there like an avenging angel. I will never in all my life forget the look on his face. It made my knees tremble. And not in a good way.

He came up to Matt and stuck out his hand, but gave him a hug instead. "I owe you," he said.

"Sure. Anything for Liz." Matt hugged him back and gave me a look that said, "Blair will never believe this."

Then James turned to me. "Come." He started walking. I followed him at a distance, too exhausted to feel anything, even anger. Out of one life-threatening situation and into another. We reached his car, and he opened the door for me to get in. I could feel every muscle in my body as I sat down. I was going to be in bad shape tomorrow. That is, if I lived to see another day.

James pulled out and started driving.

CHAPTER 28

"Are you going to speak to me?" I said after a couple of minutes.

Silence. His knuckles turned white where he gripped the steering wheel. I sighed and looked out the window. It took twenty minutes to get out of Clayton traffic and then we were on the highway.

"God damn it, why didn't you tell me what you were up to?" His voice was low and harsh.

"You didn't get my note?"

"What note? I just got back to town."

"Then how did you know?"

"I stopped in Clayton to get a new BlackBerry. I listened to your voicemail and called you back. Only you didn't answer, so I tried again. That's when I got a text from Matt Crandall informing me that he was under a table while you were being held at gunpoint in the middle of the art fair. My God! If the Clayton police weren't already at the fair – if Matt hadn't been under the table – you'd be dead now!"

"Death was not an option."

"Yes it was. You don't tangle with people like Sean Thomas and come out alive. I mean, he'd already blown up Arthur Thornton, trying to get at Brian Kepple. What did you think he'd do to you?"

"You're only partially right about that."

"What?"

"I'll explain when we get to the police station. That's where you're taking me, correct?"

James didn't answer. He just pressed down on the accelerator.

Detective Fischer was waiting for us. "Good to see you both. Glad you're still in one piece, Liz."

I smiled wanly. He ushered us into a small gray room with a Formica-topped table and several hard metal chairs. I looked around for the surveillance camera or even a mirror, but the room was completely bare.

Detective Fischer smiled. "We use this room for our own meetings. No one is watching or recording us. I thought you'd be more comfortable. I want you to tell me everything you know. No holds barred."

I sat down in the chair and winced. I'd fallen hard on my left hip. That was going to be some bruise. I caught the flash of something tender in James' blue eyes, but then he was back to anger.

"I have some theories," I said, getting the notebook out of my purse. I set it on the table and flipped it open to the first page. "And I have some facts."

"Why don't you start from the beginning?" Bill Fischer sat back and crossed his arms over his stomach.

"I'll start with the bombing, but that's not really the beginning."

"We know that the bomb was meant for Brian Kepple, Sean Thomas' ex-wife's lawyer, but was mistakenly planted on Arthur Thornton's car," Bill said.

"The bomb was meant to look like a mistake, but it wasn't. Arthur Thornton was the intended victim. At least, he was Kevin

Mason's intended victim. But let me back up. As you both know, Arthur Thornton had nothing in his life but work and art. Then he met Marisol Ramirez. Photographer, artist, filmmaker. They may have been lovers or merely friends, but the bottom line is that she got him into trouble."

"Women can do that," Bill said with a grin. "Go on."

"Arthur supported Marisol financially, even selling some of his paintings to do it, and she continued to make her art. She got hired by Kevin Mason to make a short documentary about his Common Man Goes to Washington campaign effort. Marisol roped Arthur in to do the bookkeeping for the campaign and to donate money."

"And that's where she met Sean Thomas. He set her up in an apartment and she had his baby. We know all this," James said impatiently.

"So then you know that Sean got involved with Kevin's campaign as a front for his drug operations. What better cover than the campaign of an earnest young politician? Except that Kevin wasn't as squeaky clean as he seemed. He couldn't fundraise like he needed to do to defeat a well-heeled incumbent like Chris Boggs. Besides, he needed a slush fund to cover the costs of some unorthodox campaign methods. So he turned to Sean with a deal. Sean could run his methamphetamine business out of the campaign if he bankrolled Kevin's political shenanigans."

I turned to Bill Fischer. "When my friend Holly told me about how Kevin Mason had infiltrated Boggs' campaign, I became suspicious. No campaign could be that full of leaks. It wasn't. Chris Boggs' office has so many bugs, they'll need to call an exterminator. But that wasn't the only dirty trick. Mason did everything he could to plant evidence and spread rumors in order to trash Boggs' reputation. It was straight out of the Watergate playbook."

Bill chuckled. "I'm just curious, how does a young woman like yourself know anything about Watergate? You weren't even born."

"My history major is finally paying dividends. Anyway, you'll find all of the information in a file called 'A Normal Day' on the campaign's server. 'Juanes' is the password, in case you're wondering."

"So how does the bomb come in?" James said. I could tell that some of the anger had been replaced with curiosity.

"Sean Thomas used the canvassers as deliverymen for his product. He supplied the well-to-do in Clayton and Ladue. It was perfect. Addicts called their orders in and a canvasser for the campaign showed up at the door with a sealed envelope. I'm not sure that the canvassers ever knew what they were doing. Although they had to wonder about why they were only sent to certain houses or why Kevin Mason would solicit support from people outside of his district. I saw one of them by accident one day and knew that there was something wrong. In my limited experience, canvassers never get invited inside the house."

"And the bomb?" James said again.

"I'm getting to that. Sean Thomas had a problem when his wife found out about Marisol. As you both know, his wife initiated divorce proceedings. Her lawyer, Brian Kepple, started to ask some difficult questions, mostly about Sean's sources of income. Sean's lawyer, Reginald Butler, did what he could, but there is a limit. So Sean hired someone he knew from before to plant a bomb on Kepple's car."

"Andrew Stimpkin," James and Bill said in unison.

"Sean made Andrew part of the production team for the methamphetamine. I think one of the labs was located in an old farm house. I'm not sure where it is, but Marisol would know. She took a picture of it and gave it to an artist friend of mine, Matt Crandall. I have a very realistic painting of the house that I'd be happy to show you sometime."

I continued, "Andrew started off well, but he consumed too much of his own product. Sean wasn't smart enough to know that there are two problems with hiring an addict to do a dirty job. The first is that they are bound to mess it up. The bomb wasn't strong enough to kill Arthur Thornton, just maim and blind him. The second is that addicts can be bought. That's where Kevin Mason comes in."

"Just out of curiosity, how did Andrew Stimpkin and Sean Thomas get together? They don't seem the likeliest people to know each other," James said.

"Through Elsa. It was the Albanian connection."

"Sean Thomas is not an Albanian name," Bill said.

"He wears a ring with the national symbol on it. The double-headed eagle. I assume that he's Albanian on his mother's side. That, or he changed his name at some point. Elsa is from Kosovo. She's ethnically Albanian. I would imagine that she and Andrew got involved with the local Albanian community and met Sean Thomas."

"So how did Kevin Mason find out about Sean's plan?" Bill said.

"I'm assuming Marisol told him. She started sleeping with Kevin, too. Kevin is very smart. He could get rid of his own problem and Sean would take the blame. Arthur Thornton had been asking too many questions about the donations pouring into the campaign offices. The money just didn't add up and Arthur knew it. Brian

Kepple and Arthur Thornton drove the same car and parked in the same garage. Kevin paid Andrew Stimpkin to plant the bomb on the wrong car. Maybe Kevin even convinced Andrew that he could still collect from Sean. Sean would think it was only a mistake."

"How did Kevin know that Brian and Arthur drove the same car?" James said.

I looked him in the eye. "Your mother. Kevin was one of the celebrity car washers at the PAS fundraiser. Take a look at the list of donors. I think you'll find both Brian and Arthur were there. And Kevin made at least one trip to double-check. Vince told me that he'd seen Kevin sneaking around the parking garage. If only Vince had tackled him then."

"But if that's true, why didn't Sean make another attempt on Brian after the first bombing? Last time I talked to my mother, the divorce proceedings were still going," James said.

"Two bombings in a row might have been too much. And Brian was spooked. He parked his car in a different place every day. Brian also told me that he'd had to ask for a lot of continuances. Maybe the heat was off. I don't know all of the answers."

"You're doing just fine so far," Bill said with a grin. "You wouldn't happen to know what happened to Andrew Stimpkin, would you?"

"I think he's buried out by the farmhouse. I imagine that Andrew was under orders to lay low after he planted the bomb. I'm sure both Kevin and Sean were plotting to get rid of him as soon as possible. Then Andrew took it into his head to hold his wife and children hostage. Now he was a real liability. Sean reached out to Reginald Butler, who had some pull with the people at the jail where Andrew was being held. I'm sure bribery was involved. They helped Andrew escape and then Sean promptly killed him so he wouldn't do anything stupid."

I pushed the notebook across the table to Detective Fischer. "Here is a summary of all of my findings. In short, Kevin Mason wanted Arthur Thornton dead so he wouldn't go to the Feds about the illegal contributions that fronted a meth distribution system. Sean Thomas wanted Brian Kepple dead because he was asking too many questions about Sean's businesses. Mason paid off Stimpkin to target Thornton instead of Kepple because, since they both drove the same make and model car and parked in the same garage only one floor apart, Stimpkin could tell Thomas he made a mistake. And in any case, if anyone traced the crime backwards, they would finger Thomas, not Mason. Simple."

I looked at Bill who sat with the satisfied smile of a cat who's swallowed a canary. "Now if you don't mind, I'd like to go home. Would you call me a cab?"

"I'll take you home," James said firmly.

Bill Fischer stood up. "Well, I think I need to go make some arrests. Thank you again, Ms. Howe, for your excellent work. Please stay here until we can come up with some security for you. I don't want anyone else trying to shoot you while we round up our suspects. You're too valuable to lose." He winked at me and then walked out the door, whistling to himself.

I got up and shut the door behind him. "Before you say a word, there is another part of the story that I have to tell you. It's about Angie."

"Angie?"

"I suspect Angie's father is somehow involved in the meth business. It's the Albanian connection again."

"What Albanian connection?"

"Her father's family is from Albania. I realized it when you told me that Angie had a bowl like the one I bought. Correct me if I'm wrong, but I think her style is simple and modern. She would never have bought something that elaborately decorated. So it had to be a family piece. My bowl was made in Tirana, Albania. It says so on the bottom."

He shook his head. "Really Liz, I think you are way off base."

"Fine, I may be wrong about him, but I'm not wrong about Angie."

"What about her?"

I hated to drop the final bomb. But he had to know. "Angie's a meth addict herself. She's got all the signs: irritability, weight loss – you probably know better about the insomnia and the hypersexuality. I think she must snort it in powder form. It would explain why her highs aren't so obviously high and her lows so obviously low."

"But —"

"She smells like an addict, James. Like sulfur and ammonia. It's the process of the chemical working its way out through the pores of the skin. I smelled it on her, and then I smelled it on Andrew Stimpkin. He was definitely an addict, so she must be too. And she has to have noticed, because she wears the most overpowering old lady perfume. White Diamonds."

He looked at me as if he didn't believe it and then his shoulders slumped. He covered his face with his hands. "I was living with a meth addict?"

"I'm sorry. I would have told you sooner, but I didn't know how."

He looked up at me like the bottom had just dropped out of his world. It tore my heart in two. I reached up and ran my fingers through his hair. "It's okay. I'm here."

He closed his arms around me, crushing my already bruised body in a tight embrace. He buried his face in the curve of my neck and mouthed the words, "I can't lose you. I can't ever lose you," against my skin.

CHAPTER 29

Instead of driving me home, James drove me to his house. He said it was safer. Then he called Holly and booked a hotel room for her. Kevin Mason had disappeared. I went straight to bed and didn't wake up until I felt James get in beside me. My bleary eyes focused on the clock. It was 2:00 a.m.

"Don't worry," he whispered in my ear. "They found him in Miami. He was getting on a plane to Bogota. Go back to sleep."

"Umm. I'm tired."

"Then rest. Janice told me that you could have as many days off as you needed."

"Wait. What day is it?"

"It's officially Monday now."

"Then I've been asleep —"

"A day and a half," he said.

"Oh."

He gathered me up in his arms and held me close. "Just rest. You'll feel better in the morning."

"James?"

"Yes?"

"I'm ready if the offer still stands."

"What offer?"

"I want to wake up next to you every morning." Then I followed doctor's orders to the letter. James was very gentle. He did not ask about the bruises I had in strange places, and I did not volunteer any information.

The transition wasn't bad. Holly won over the Hendersons and they agreed to let her stay at the same reduced rent I was paying. I think it helped that Joe Henderson started to stand up straight every time she walked by. I let her keep my furniture. She'd sold most of hers when she split from Ben and mine wasn't worth the move. I came to James' house with my books, my clothes, two red satin pillows, a spider plant and the few kitchen items he did not already own. There was only a brief skirmish about closet space. James was the only man I knew who needed lots of it.

He put up some new bookshelves in the office and bought me a desk. I tried to pay him back, but he wouldn't hear of it. "Call it a 'thank God you forgave me for treating you so badly after you were almost killed' gift," he said. I heard the cheep of the bird in my head, but firmly shushed her. James even hung Matt's painting on the wall, although he couldn't understand how I could still like it. But I did. Sometimes it is nice to be reminded that you are a survivor. And I loved the miniature portrait of me Matt had done and put away under the table. I set it on the desk. Matt made me look better than any photograph I'd ever seen.

Soon James' house felt just as much my home as the apartment. James seemed happy, but his family was not. Even in drug rehabilitation, Angelica remained the favorite. James would never confirm or deny this, but I was sure his mother and sister blamed me for Angie's problems. If only James hadn't called off the engagement, Angie wouldn't have gotten into drugs. I'm not sure if James chose to enlighten them on just when the drug use had started. It was still very painful. I didn't bring the subject up.

My parents were a surprise. I'd expected a "that's nice dear" attitude, but my dad had gotten wind of my activities in Marshfield. It came as a shock that I was making adult-type decisions, and he worried that James and I would fight like we had at graduation. He did not want me suddenly out on the street. I assured him that Holly promised to take me back, and hoped he would get over it.

Ashley was all for the move, not just because she wanted me to be happy, but also because it meant she could visit without having to sleep on the floor. I would see more of Ashley now than ever. James assured me that he loved me enough to put up with her. That is devotion of the highest order.

I actually passed the bar and started working even more hours. James had an equally crazy schedule. The case took on a life of its own. Even my glass-Bedazzled jeans played a role. I'd sat on the charred remnants of a piece of the timing device of the bomb. The forensics lab was able to trace the timer to a piece Andrew Stimpkin had purchased at Radio Shack in February, thus definitively confirming my identification of him on the video.

One Saturday morning in early December, after Chris Boggs was sworn in for another term, James and I were sitting in the kitchen having breakfast. I'd just mentioned that Holly and Sister Rita were now fast friends over their mutual disappointment.

"They've been analyzing the field of potential candidates for the 2008 presidential election. They want to pick a winner this time."

"Good luck. With Cheney out of the picture, 2008 is going to be a free for all on both sides."

I nodded. "It should be very interesting."

"Just don't let Holly drag you into anything you don't want to do."

"I was right to listen to her this time. Think what I might have missed."

"I'm thinking, and they are not good thoughts. Can I change the subject on you?"

"To good thoughts?"

"Maybe. I was wondering about Christmas."

"As in the family expectations?" I had muscled my way through the Paperelli Thanksgiving and tentatively agreed to do their Christmas Eve. However, my parents talked of coming to St. Louis for Christmas festivities as well, and so I secretly hoped that I could plead my own family obligations to get out of some further Paperelli togetherness. "I'm still not sure about the Christmas Eve mass. My lack of communion will be obvious. Do you really want the world to know I'm a heathen?"

"You're my heathen. And I wasn't thinking family, I was thinking presents."

"I'm all ears."

"What about going to the jewelry auction to get your Christmas gift?"

"Is that the same auction where they're selling Arthur Thornton's paintings?"

"Yes. I thought we could go to the viewing and you could pick out a few things to bid on. There was an amethyst bracelet that looked something like Holly's ring in the catalog."

I silently thanked God that I had spent most of a paycheck on a Mont Blanc pen for James. "That's a great idea. But nothing too expensive."

"You've inspired me with your Wisconsin frugality. I won't go overboard."

"Okay, maybe a little overboard."

He laughed.

But James was unexpectedly called in to work on the night we were supposed to go to the pre-auction viewing. He suggested I call Holly.

"This is my friend Holly we are talking about?"

"Yes."

"The one who owns one ring she never wears?"

"She's a woman, isn't she?"

"Watch it."

"Just call her and see."

Surprisingly, Holly seemed enthusiastic. When I arrived, she was already leaning over a case, talking with an auction employee. The lady pulled out a number of beautiful items and Holly made me try them on.

"This is lovely," I said, turning the amethyst bracelet on my wrist. The stones caught the light in a blaze of purple fire.

"For heaven's sake, mark it down in the book." Holly flipped open our copy of the catalog. I looked at the estimated price range. Doable. I put a star beside it. Even after we'd examined practically everything at that end of the case, Holly continued to linger.

"Look at some of those diamonds." She pointed to another section of the case devoted to diamond jewelry of every sort. I'm not sure how you could have worn most of it. The glare would blind you. I found the corresponding pages in the catalog.

"Look at some of these estimates." I shoved the book under Holly's nose.

"Dream big, Liz." She pointed to a yellow gold engagement ring with a large marquise diamond. The diamond was at least three carats. "If things had worked out with Ben, I would have wanted something like that."

I looked at her. "You? That flashy?"

"If I'm going to take the trouble to wear it, it might as well be noticeable."

"I totally agree!" A voice said behind us.

I spun around. "Blair."

He gave me a hug. His pins dug into my chest, so I stepped back and introduced him to Holly.

"Is this a girls' night out?" Blair said.

"James wants to get me something for Christmas. Holly and I are examining the possibilities."

"I like that man."

"And you? Where's Matt?"

"Working." Blair made a face. "But he made enough at the art fair to quit that banquet job at the Chase. There were a lot of gawkers who came to the scene of the crime and stayed to buy something."

"Glad to be of service," I said.

"I'm here to look at Arthur's paintings. Everyone wants to see what they go for since he bought so much local stuff. Hey, are you girls looking at diamonds?"

"I was just saying to Liz, I'd want that one." Holly pointed to the case.

"Oh honey, I thought you wanted a noticeable diamond. When Matt pops the question, I'm expecting that." He pointed to an even larger round diamond surrounded by a halo of baguettes. It glittered like the sun.

The lady behind the counter came back over. "Can I get something out?"

"That." Holly and Blair said at the same time. She chuckled and pulled the rings out and laid them on a black velvet cloth. "And for you?" she said to me.

I hesitated.

"Come on, Liz," Holly said.

I looked down at the diamonds with a queer sense of déjà vu and blinked back the memory. I was a long way from the desperate girl I'd been then. There was one ring that stood out to me, a large emerald-cut diamond set in a smooth platinum setting. "Can I see that one?" I said.

"Very you," Blair said.

"It's my favorite," the lady said, handing it to me. "You can't do better than Tiffany's for diamonds."

"It's a Tiffany ring?" I said.

"From a local estate. We have all of the paperwork, of course."

I slipped the ring on. It fit me perfectly. I held my hand up. The diamond seemed even bigger close up than it had in the case.

"Blair's right," Holly said. "That is you. Here, let me get a picture of all of us." She dug her phone out of her purse. We laid our hands on the black cloth and Holly snapped a couple of grainy images.

"I'll give you my email so you can send it to me. Matt needs guidance."

I laughed. "Poor Matt."

"He just has to sell a few more paintings."

"Gold digger," I said.

"Matt must keep me in the style I've become accustomed to."

"Is there anything else you all would like to see?" The lady returned our small fortunes to the case. Blair had his eye on some brooches, so we happily followed him down to the other end.

On Monday night, James and I came early, so we would be in time for all of the jewelry lots. I heard from Blair that the paintings had sold really well on Saturday and the few pieces of sculpture Arthur owned did even better on Sunday. Bidders had come in from all over the United States.

The amethyst bracelet was up early in the bidding. After a spirited tug of war with two other bidders, James emerged victorious. I had a fabulous Christmas present to look forward to. "Do you want to leave now?" I said. No man I knew would willingly sit through a jewelry auction.

"Let's stay. There are a couple of things I'm thinking about for my mom."

"Good idea." James had told me that she was notoriously hard to buy for. "Then I'll take the opportunity to run to the ladies room. Keep my spot."

"I'll try," he said.

"Unless there is someone else you want to sit with?"

He leaned over and gave me a kiss on the cheek. "There is no one else but you." His voice sent a slow shiver down my spine.

I did a quick mental calculation. If the auction went until 10:00, I would have a good three hours before I absolutely positively had to get to sleep if I wanted to get up for work the next morning. Time enough for all sorts of things. I got up quickly. Better not to let my thoughts go in that direction in a public place. I still had a reputation to maintain in St. Louis.

After using the facilities, I wandered back to the auction floor. There was a table with little noshy, desserty items at the back of the hall, along with some glasses of wine. I only had to recognize James that night. And maybe Blair, if he decided to see what happened to the brooches he wanted that Matt could never afford. I picked up a glass of white wine and took a sip. I decided to hang back a moment. There were some little cakes that looked awfully tempting. I took one, promising myself that I wouldn't eat more, and then turned to the auction.

The diamond lots were next. I watched several as I made my way through cakes numbered two and three. When would our three rings come up? I'd left the catalog at the seat, so I didn't know. I found myself sipping on a second glass of wine when the Tiffany ring appeared on the screen at the front of the room. I scanned the crowd.

I couldn't see James or much of anything, for that matter. Too many people. I thought about heading back to my seat, but wasn't sure I would even make it through.

The ring got a number of bids from all over the room. As the bidding wore on, the bidders dropped away, until there were just two. A person on the telephone up on a platform to my right and someone way down in front. The auction employee was just speaking into the phone, giving that bidder the latest offer from the bidder on the floor. Then he signaled the auctioneer, raising the bid again.

I watched them go back and forth with stunned fascination. What had started with $100 increments, moved to $500 increments and then to $1000. Back and forth. $30,000, $31,000, $32,000. A hush fell over the crowd as they were pulled in to the drama of the auction.

The bid was now at $38,000 with the bidder in the room. All eyes turned to the bank of phones. The employee spoke quickly into the phone, cajoling the phone bidder to make another bid. Then the employee raised his hand. $39,000. The room shifted to the bidder down front. Then a murmur of appreciation and the auctioneer said, "We have $40,000. Do I hear $41,000?" All eyes shifted back to the phones. The employee spoke to the phone bidder and the room held its breath. Reluctantly, the employee shook his head.

The auctioneer tried to get the bidding back on track. "Do I hear $40,500?" The employee relayed the information and then shook his head a final time.

"Okay. Going once. Going twice." He looked up at the phones but the employee shook his head one last time. "Going three times." He banged the gavel. "Sold to the bidder down front. Paddle 325."

I felt like someone had just sucked all of the air out of the room. I dropped my empty wine glass. It hit the carpet with a thunk. I bent down quickly and set it back on the table. My hand shook. How could I have been so stupid? Paddle 325.

Then the microphone squawked and the auctioneer said, "Ladies and gentleman, we are going to take a quick break here. I know that this is unusual, but would Liz Howe please come forward?"

I saw some movement out of the corner of my eye. An auction employee was signaling me to move. I put one foot in front of another as the crowd parted before me like Moses and the Red Sea. Everyone turned to watch my slow progress. I felt as if I wasn't in my own body. This absolutely positively could not be real. I dug my fingernails into my palm. The pain felt real enough.

Then I saw James standing at the front of the room. He had the most incredible smile on his face. My heart skipped a beat. I was overwhelmed by a euphoric happiness too great to describe in words. Maybe this feeling was what Angie had been seeking with drugs. But I wouldn't give him back, no matter what.

James took my hand in his. He got down on one knee and smiled up at me, saying, "Liz. Elizabeth. I love you so much. Will you marry me?"

"Yes. With all my heart. Yes!" I could feel the tears running down my cheeks. My knees would give way at any moment. James stood up and hugged me. The crowd erupted in applause.

"Don't cry," he said.

"Tears of happiness," was all I managed to say before the employee in charge of the jewelry appeared with the Tiffany ring on a black velvet pillow.

James took it from her. "Give me your hand," he said. He held my hand steady as he slipped the ring on my finger. It felt solid, a tangible reminder of his love for me. I looked into his blue eyes. Reputation be damned. I reached up and pulled him into a kiss. The applause and the sound of glasses clinking together was a dull roar in my ears.

James pulled back first. My legs seemed like jelly. He put a strong arm around my shoulder. "Now we can leave," he said, forcing me to walk beside him. "Cards?"

"You couldn't have played a better hand." I held up my left hand. The ring dazzled in the light. "This is officially the best night of my life."

"Mine too."

I heard the auctioneer at the microphone. "Congratulations, Liz and James. Now gentlemen, there are a number of engagement rings left and the night is still young. Who's going to be the next to propose?"

The following later appeared in the *Ladue News*:

Mr. and Mrs. Donald Howe are pleased to announce the engagement of their daughter, Elizabeth Anne, to James Antonio Paperelli, son of Mr. and Mrs. Antonio Paperelli of Ladue. Elizabeth is a 2006 graduate of Washington University School of Law, Order of the Coif. She is currently employed as an Associate Attorney at Harrington and Associates, L.L.C. in Clayton. James is a 1992 graduate of Saint Louis University, *summa cum laude*. He is currently employed by the St. Louis Metropolitan Police Department. James proposed to Elizabeth in the first ever proposal at Harville-Chouteau Auctions, after placing the winning bid for Elizabeth's engagement ring. The auction crowd erupted in applause as James went down on one knee in front of a surprised Elizabeth. She said yes without hesitation. A summer wedding is planned for the happy couple.

ACKNOWLEDGMENTS

I would like to thank my family, and in particular my mother, for unstinting assistance and encouragement. Dara, Cindy and Kajal also deserve special praise for their willingness to read this book and give me constructive feedback. It is a great joy to be part of such a creative and prolific writing group. I also send a heartfelt thanks to my colleagues and friends at Security Health Plan, but especially to Julie, Angie (not to be confused with a character in this book), Sara, Tammy and Roseann for all of the support they have given me with the launch of the **Nerdy Girls** series. Thanks also to Bea for her friendship, her knowledge of Colombian cuisine, and for throwing the parties that inspired certain scenes in this book. Finally, thanks to my great friends in Marshfield, St. Louis, and around the country (you are too numerous to mention by name), who have recommended **Murderers** for their book clubs and generally made me feel like a rock star. Thank you for the privilege of your friendship. I hope that this book justifies your continued support of me.

ABOUT THE AUTHOR

Lisa Boero is a practicing attorney who lived for many years in St. Louis, Missouri, but now resides in Marshfield, Wisconsin with her husband and children. Legal experience combined with a strange neurological condition inspired her to write **Bombers and Nerdy Girls Do Brunch**, the second book in the **Nerdy Girls** series. For more information about Lisa and all things **Nerdy Girls**, please see Lisa's website at www.lisaboero.com and her Facebook page, www.facebook.com/authorlisaboero or follow Liz Howe on Twitter @Liz_NerdyGirl.